From Evelyn
To
Edith

1942

NET
NET

ISADORE BARMASH

NET NET

A NOVEL

The Macmillan Company, New York, New York
Collier-Macmillan Ltd., London

This is fiction, therefore the product of my imagination and fantasies. It may appear to reflect certain events, but its characters have never existed as such and its actions have never taken place.

I. B.

The Macmillan Company
866 Third Avenue, New York, N.Y. 10022
Collier-Macmillan Canada Ltd., Toronto, Ontario

Library of Congress Catalog Card Number:
77-180292

First Printing

Printed in the United States of America

AGAIN, TO MY WIFE, *Sarah,*
WITH LOVE

Preface

". . . Of course, you're in business to make a profit.
Especially a net profit. But some sharp guys want to
know what's your real net profit, the net after the
net, with everything squeezed out but the pure
profit. Personally, gentlemen, I think that's a lot of
s-h-i-t. The real 'net net' is the pleasure, the happiness, the joy and the *naches*, as my pop used to say,
you bring to your employees, your customers and
the whole frigged-up unhappy world. Without it,
you've got to be only an animal in a jungle. So, let
me ask all of you, what's *your* net net? . . ."

—ALBERT C. MILLER
*(From an address at the Waldorf-Astoria Hotel in New York
when he was named by his peers to the Hall of Fame as one
of the six greatest merchants in American history. Three years
later his name was quietly stricken from the list.)*

Contents

PART TWO

PART ONE

1

You've Got to Know Al to Understand Him— or Something

Time danced for Al Miller. Money talked to him. Success pasted itself to him like a fat sucking barnacle. Fame plucked him from the ranks and held him aloft. Customers whispered in his ears, then gently kissed his lobes. Children shyly confided what even their parents wouldn't. Competitors quietly closed down the day he opened so that he could have the action all to himself. Throwing open their vaults, banks said, "Take." Manufacturers told their engineers and designers, "This is the kind of stuff Al likes; don't ever forget it if you like that pay check." Then they geared their production entirely around his needs. Truckers and railroads shunted everyone else's deliveries aside. Buying offices risked losing clients to give his buyers first crack at the newest samples that the trade had feverishly rushed in. His greatest rivals just couldn't do enough to show how warmly they regarded him. They released some of their best employees so that he could quickly hire them. They transshipped their own prized goods to him through fictitious middlemen so that he could get a head start. Lawyers and accountants competed with one another to attract such a client. The Government smiled and winked at Al, allowing him not so much to violate the statutes as not to understand them. Life, in plain words, had just hopped into bed with Al Miller at thirty-four.

All this and more everyone was certain of in those early days, such was the legend that had grown around him after only a few years.

He could even have believed it himself except that he would never have believed it. Naïve he was in the midst of his success, but it wasn't all just a warm, cushy womb for him with everything vital being pumped into his navel. And the way people fawned over him sometimes, it made him want to run. In fact, he did run, in a long, loping rout that became as much of a symbol as his flaming red hair and his flashing instinct to put money down only for what would quickly sell. Sometimes they even ran after him, as if they wanted to touch him and by so doing become rich and successful too. He couldn't stand that soft, glowing yearning in their eyes. What the hell was wrong with them, anyway? The only thing to do was to get out of their way.

The day he was thinking that particular combination of thoughts, a rather warm October day in 1954, he sat in the rear of a rather shabby, mostly empty movie house around the corner from his office and stared thoughtfully at the screen. It was almost 4:00 P.M. and soon he would have to call and see if anything was going on. Up ahead, Jimmy Cagney snarled and threatened half of New York. Al loved any Cagney movie. In fact, he loved almost any movie. He was, in fact again, probably the only businessman anyone knew who usually saw five movies a week or on every weekday afternoon. In rough weeks or when he went on the road, though, it was only two or three movies. Even on the road he sought out the local dinky double-feature house on the nearest main street.

Some of his best ideas popped into his head while he watched the chase on the screen. Other times, while all hell might be breaking loose around the corner at the office, he just sat there and calmly watched Cagney or Wayne or Gable or Roz Russell or Kate Hepburn or Pat O'Brien or Edward G. Robinson. As he often told himself, it was just as well that he did take off for a movie when things got hectic. Someone always came up with the right answer. It gave everyone a chance to perform on their own, without counting on the boss to solve things. Besides, what the hell, he liked going to the movies. What could be so wrong with that?

The proof was that everything was going so well.

Fabulously was more like it, success and riches more than he had ever dreamed of, but there were problems, too. Such as the fantasy that people were building up about him and the ease with which everything good seemed to happen to him and how everybody and everything good seemed to happen to him and everybody and everything was making way for him, like the whole world was just carving a big crease across the top of its head for him to walk across. He had his own fantasies, a whole movieful of them, and they went something wild like this.

First, he would run the world's biggest international chain of big stores at the lowest prices, doing everything himself simultaneously in countries continents apart, buying, selling, warehousing, granting credit, billing, hiring, firing (the simple, irrelevant fact that this would be unnecessary if he would be a one-man establishment didn't matter in this surely paranoidal fantasy), whirling across selling floors from customer to counter to cash register to stockroom and back again, endlessly, without fatigue or loss of friendly smile. The beauty of that *geshmack* taste of doing everything yourself so that you knew it would all come out precisely as you would want it instead of you performing muted and feebly through the minds and hands of people who were tired the moment they came out of the womb. Then there would be no one to bother him with claims or compliments or insults— all the same!—or outsiders with enthusiastic suggestions for the dumb-dumb things that the public hated and would rightfully not put its hard-earned money down for. Then he would pursue this kind of wonderful life. He would open the most beautiful, well-stocked, best laid-out stores, all with the lowest prices (a totally vital, absolute necessity!) in the most out-of-the-way places not only in the United States but in Mexico, Canada, Latin America, Europe and even Asia. The kibitzers of the world would gleefully slap their knees and yell, "Look where that *putz* puts up a store! It'll sink into the mud, the desert or the tundra before enough customers ever get there, even if they wanta come, which no sane person would take their life in hand to do!" But what would seem remote, or not solid enough earth or in a poverty-stricken area, would turn out as he had suspected, perfectly accessible, firm in fiber and mass and eminently able to draw customers. There would be such a turnout because his selections and prices and styles would enable everyone to buy the necessities and pleasures of life, and it would be that even simple country roads could be changed by his success and the success that he would turn back to the underdeveloped countries so that those roads could bear the endless streams of customers. Stores, bargains, customers, so why not the staff of life everywhere if their right proportions, if the right equation, could be found? His own life would swoop in a great international circle so that, unlike its current narrow perimeter, he could be on several continents in the same week, talking to his managers (of course, even in his fantasies, he had to be honest and admit that he would need others to help him—didn't he already have "the boys," those unparalleled *nudniks* whose efforts yet sometimes stunned him with their creative bang?) in New York, Buenos Aires, Johannesburg, Amsterdam, Zurich, Paris, you name it.

The brief fantasy was over, really just a rip, a flash in and through the cerebral convolutions, and he laughed, hating for the moment his own juvenility, but not too much. Maybe it was all only an instinctive effort to escape from the burden of everyone else's fantasies about him that made him dream fantasies of his own.

He only hoped that none of his own people believed that everything was coming that easy. It wasn't that way at all. Life for Al Miller was simply a matter of concentrating on what were the essentials for him and ruling out everything else. That was it. He knew, for example, that people were waiting for him in the office, watching to latch on to him for some purpose of their own, wanting to make demands that would deter him from his goal of running his business in the manner to which he had become accustomed. Some at this very moment were probably sitting there wondering where his office might be (he didn't have one) so they could casually walk in and confront him (which is why he didn't want an office in the first place) or where his desk was (he just picked out any empty one when he came in) or to proselytize his secretary (he hadn't any). And when they learned of these things, they were just flabbergasted, and when they couldn't see him after many repeated attempts, they went away shaking their heads.

That's how the head of a $150-million-a-year business behaves? they would stop and ask his people incredulously. And when they were told, in effect, yes, it was, it was said with an evident pride in the idiosyncrasies of a well-loved member of the family.

It was some family. The "boys" and everyone else that he had started out with or accumulated in the last five years. The greatest bunch of people, talents, drives, neuroses and creative hangups in the world. How lucky they all were, especially him, he with them and they with him. As he often told Molly Bradley or Nat Batt or Irving Waldteufel or Matthew Smiles or any of the rest of them:

"Look, we're all just a bunch of lucky bastards and—" nodding at Molly— "a bitch. We got ideas and we draw people with ideas like flypaper and that's what business has just got to be all about. And if we couldn't bounce ideas off each other and come up with still better ideas, hell, we'd be no different than anyone else, would we? Who would have thought of opening the world's biggest electric-blender department just of blenders? We made Macy's and Gimbels start telling each other their secrets after a hundred years because we underpriced them in departments that we stocked even better than theirs. Who sells more goddam giant tubes of national-brand toothpaste anywhere than we do, even if we don't make any money on them? But it brings the people in, boy, does it bring them in! And once they're in, we got them because you can tell by their eyes and their tongues hanging out that they like our prices and our goods. The world's lowest prices and the world's biggest stocks—what a combination! We got the old-line department stores so shook up that half of our lunch traffic in some departments are their buyers and merchandise men shopping us to see how we're doing it. Sure, we latched on to a new concept that a lot of others have, but we made something different of it by working our brains, our tootsies and our asses off and that's why we made it so big. If you got imagination and guts and you're crazy about what you're doing, it's got to pay off. Matthew here—" acknowledging a very fat, genial young man— "came to us two years ago as a stock boy and gave us one of our best ideas we ever had. Any customer who buys at least ten dollars' worth of merchandise gets a fifty percent discount when she eats in the store's restaurant. Wow! Every store we operate that has a restaurant shot up twenty percent in sales right after we started that. So how do you like being a vice-president at the age of nineteen, Mottel?" And so on and on. It was hard for him to stop talking once he got into that particular groove.

The movie over now, Al Miller came out to the fading sunlight, a lanky redheaded man in his early thirties, freckled but fair-skinned, moving with a very rapid stride. He was dressed in a brown suit and a blue sport shirt with open collar. He never wore a tie or dress shirt. His stores sold millions of each and his 4,000 employees wore them, but personally he had no use for them.

It was four-thirty and time to call. At the booth in the drugstore, he could almost look over his shoulder at the three floors of the corner building which contained his company's offices. Zelda, the switchboard operator, answered. She took all his messages and tried desperately also to be his secretary and bookkeeper except that he didn't need or want any. This meant that all she did was take his messages because he never dictated any letters or made any appointments. He could hear her breath catch as he greeted her. She was a tall, statuesque brunette of about twenty-eight who managed to look tall and statuesque just sitting at the switchboard. She seemed fascinated by him and when she spoke to him her voice turned throaty, as if she didn't care a bit if he knew.

She said: "Oh, Mr. Miller . . . There were a few calls, but I turned them over to the others. And there were about five people waiting for you . . . but we finally told them all that you had been suddenly called out of town. Is that all right?"

She was following procedure and oozing sex at the same time. If anything was really important, the person would come back again or the subject would come up again and then maybe again. The system seemed to work well. At least there had been no disasters since he had mapped it out with Zelda. Then he heard her sultry voice again. "Mr. Miller?"

"Yes?"

"Is that all right?" she repeated anxiously.

"Beautiful."

"Mr. Miller?"

"Yes, Zelda, baby?"

"How was the movie?"

"Fine, just fine, Zelda. Thanks for asking."

He heard her breath catch again. "My very distinct pleasure," she said.

One afternoon a week he would go down to Second Avenue, either before or after a movie. There, he would station himself near a combination newspaper and fruit stand and quietly watch the tall man behind it.

The stooped giant would smilingly welcome customers, slowly weighing fruit as though each was a gem, carefully folding the newspaper or fondling the smooth cover of the magazine as he handed it to the purchaser. Most of the time, except at about five in the afternoon when the avenue was busiest, he just sat or stood waiting, to many a larger-than-life figure out of the past.

He still wore the formalized jacket and the long, rather shaggy hair of the thespian. To some, to a favorite customer, to an old colleague, he would quote from a favorite play for a few moments, broad-panning his expression for effect or singing a few lyrics in a hoarse, time-worn voice from a musical of the past. Then, invariably, at the conclusion of this exercise he would rest for just a second or so with his eyes closed and his big gray head inclined, signaling the end of the performance.

One could picture him bowing after cascades of applause on the stage of the Jewish Art Theater or at the Irving Place Theater or performing at some Second Avenue benefit. Once he had been one of the more famous names in the Yiddish theater: Chaim Peretz Miller, skilled both as a tragedian and musical-comedy baritone. Many an East Side housewife—or, for that matter, Bronx and Brooklyn as well—had yearned for him, as had some Yiddish- speaking soubrettes.

The old man would stare bleakly at Al, then radiantly, then a veil would pass over his eyes. "Ah, Albert. It is good to see you." His hand would come groping out from the stand, seeking his son's touch. Chaim Miller was about three-quarters blind and getting worse in a decline that had begun twenty years before.

"How's Mom?" Al asked.

"She is fine, fine. She asks for you all the time, Albert."

"I know, Pop. I'll try to come over more often."

His father's stare was unnerving. Most of it, intent as it was, was incapable of seeing him, but he knew that the old man could make him out. Was the blur in which he appeared to his father due only to bad vision? Not all, he knew.

"How is your business, Albert?" his father would ask. "Are you enjoying your life?"

In his early teens Al had had a great craving to follow in his father's art. It was a combination of his immense pride in Chaim, the thousand recollections of his father's triumphant appearances with other greats of the theater, and his own, personal response to the applause, the accolade of personal success. There was something else in Chaim Miller that attracted and awed his son. It was a personal magnetism, a subtle combining of internal and external forces in and about the six-foot six-inch thespian with the prominent cheekbones, full, expressive lips, shaggy mane and white, sensitive hands. It was the strange, mystical way in which Chaim's extended arm to heaven and the sheer, serio-comic satanism expressed in the deep lines in his face made him not only truly the epitome of *Yoshe Kalb's* central character but easily the most readily acceptable in all the sixty-two roles that are played in that epic of the Yiddish theater. Or the warm naturalness of Chaim's small and major gestures as the heroic father in *Nathan the Wise*, the lofty grace of his body and the grief and solicitude of his facial expressions. For years, the son saw his father either on the stage or in his mind performing those roles so that it became difficult to separate actor from parent.

One summer when he was fifteen Al waited with his mother in the darkened theater in Philadelphia while his father hashed out some details backstage with the troupe's manager. Filled with the thrill of Chaim's just-completed performance, the make-believe magic that had penetrated that theater, Al found himself slowly walking up to the stage and standing on the forward boards in the pose of the last few moments of his father's role. On the partially dimmed stage he tried to recall the words and the gestures in a moment or two of declamation. He had wanted to do something like this for months, but something in him had warned him of its foolishness.

"I said what I said—now do this that I said!" he shouted. He stared out at the dark, shabby theater, the seats, many of them with torn covers, outlined by the dim reflection of the light on the stage. He felt the blood leaving his face and his heart pounding with terror. The vaguely defined face of his mother peered up at him from a front seat. He could barely make out her half-smile. She came forward to him, already a head shorter than he was, but what was there on her face? Not commiseration, not even empathy, nor real regret, but that smile that had equal parts of all and a part that was—derision?

He stiffened and she sensed what had happened. "I can't do this, Mom," Al said.

"I know, Albert. If you would ask Shakespeare and Jacob Ben Ami, they would agree with you."

"I'd drop dead on the stage. I couldn't make it in front of a real audience."

"They're only people," she said dryly.

That night, as he dozed on the train on the seat opposite them, he heard her tell Chaim of the incident and he could see through half-shut eyes his father's face grow stony and withdrawn.

From that point on, Al knew that the last thing he wanted in life was to stand up before others and attempt to entertain them. But Chaim was never more certain that Al was destined to follow him on the stage. Why, then, had the boy mounted the boards that night if not to follow a deep instinct? Of course, he had bolted off after a few words, but what actor didn't feel the tug of stage fright even after years of professional performance? And a boy?

Chaim the father and Chaim the actor-father first became a superimposed image embedded in his son's consciousness when Al was probably no more than seven years old. It was during a typical Yiddish melodrama in some small theater in Baltimore. Chaim was not much older than the young man who was suddenly introduced to him by his stage daughter as her lover and whom he later learned was the son of the man he most hated in the world, a thief, rapist and glutton. But as it went on the stage Chaim relents after three acts of fighting the hateful relationship during which he (1) loses his wife's love, (2) loses his daughter's love and (3) even alienates his beloved rabbi, who vainly tries to reason with him. Chaim relents in the final scene because he is dying of a heart attack brought on by the combined pressures of all his opponents. Chaim expires as the stage father held jointly by his weeping, sorrowful wife and by his weeping, sorrowful daughter as his soon-to-be son-in-law looks on with streaming eyes.

The curtain that descended quickly on Chaim's concluding words, hissed as his life ran out, that he deserved to die because of the grief that he had caused, yanked the audience to its feet, yelling and stamping. Was it a second or two seconds later that the curtain parted again and Chaim, the deceased, reappeared in all his vibrant being, black beard well brushed and neat *yarmulke* firm on his head, his eyes ablaze, leading the rest of the cast on stage like a group of well-trained children?

Toweringly tall, a Jewish Barrymore, completely charismatic with the largely female audience, Chaim halted the applause with palms modestly extended, saying in Yiddish, "We, our troupe that came to you direct from the New York stage, thank you, dear friends, for your outstanding reception to our little drama. We thank you from *teefen, teefen hartzen.*" The latter, which can be roughly translated "deep, deep in our hearts" and delivered humbly in the rumble of a giant redwood of a man, turned the house upside down. Even Chaim's own wife applauded herself silly. Al was stunned at the crash of new applause that greeted his father's personal message. People remained standing and cheering, the men applauding a man's man and the women waving their handkerchiefs and shawls, throwing kisses at the handsome, virtuous figure. The awe that crept in under Al's skin that day never ended.

The week in 1943 that Al was drafted into the Army, he sat with his mother in a Second Avenue theater and watched Chaim perform in *The Dybbuk*, a play of religious exorcism that never failed to chill Al's blood. Twice he saw his father stumble, the second time causing the audience to titter. In the dark he heard his mother talking to herself. "Even glasses won't help him," she muttered. "They don't come so thick."

During the war, Chaim's sight deteriorated to the degree that he was no longer able to perform. For months he lay around the East Side apartment and brooded. Finally, Pesse, his tiny, resolute wife, went around to the theatrical managers' offices and the Second Avenue buildings and was able to get the use of a portion of a small store front where Chaim could sell newspapers and selected small fruit. It took her weeks to get Chaim to come down and several more to have him run the stand himself. But once he was there, a stooped, august-looking, nearly blind man, he began to like it and even got pleasure out of the little performances he gave to the delight of his customers.

While he was away in the service in the Pacific, Al remained troubled by the decision that he would eventually have to give Chaim. He went through two years of duty in combat and rear-area assignments, carrying not just a duffel bag but a guilty conscience, too. Before he returned home, Al's mother wrote to tell him that Chaim had found a new life at his newsstand and that with it had come a renewed zeal to see Al embark on a stage career. He must humor the old man, she wrote, at least in the early months. She continued on this tack when Al was back in his civilian clothes. It wouldn't be hard to do, she said, since no one, least of all Chaim, expected Al to do anything in particular right away.

But from the moment that the old man kissed him on both cheeks upon his return, it bothered Al that he was deceiving his father. Yet when he finally told Chaim that he was taking a job as a salesman at Gimbels, Chaim commented, "For a while, yes, why not? Once you are able to put your feet more solid on the ground, Albert, we can talk of more serious things."

A year after working in the department store, Al made up his mind to start his own business. He had an idea for a store, maybe even two or three, of modest dimensions. And between his discharge money and what he had earned, he had enough to get started. After mulling over the problem of telling Pop, he decided that there was little point in delaying it any further. Pesse objected to his plan of confronting Chaim then and there with an abrupt announcement.

"Maybe—maybe it is better to start what you have to do," she said, "and let him hear about it. He wouldn't be so shocked that way."

However, Al insisted, and together they went to pick up Chaim one night at the stand so that Al could tell him.

"Pop, I made up my mind on what I want to do," he said. "I'm going to open a little store uptown on the second floor and try to sell some merchandise that I'll have in stock. The rest I'll sell from catalogues."

The old man glared at him from mostly unseeing eyes. "A career in commerce? Why do you do this?" he demanded. He stared hard at Al and the son knew truly that his father was seeing him. "For years I have been planning that you should be an artist, a performer, that you should carry on the family name on the stage. But instead you have greed in your heart. What will you do to help the world, a world that is still torn apart from a terrible war? Instead to have a store that will sell merchandise from books? That, Albert, is plain *meshugge*."

"Maybe, Pop, but that's what I want to do. Maybe it won't help the world, but it will help me."

"Nothing will help you," the old man told him bitterly.

Some days, even some weeks, Al would not go near the Times Square offices. Anxious to see some of his boys whom he had dispatched to the outlying stores, especially the newer ones, and to shake hands with the customers in the boondocks, he would leave his home in Queens and take to the highway. Those mornings he would be restless to get started and he would bolt out of the house before six. Ruthie and the kids were, of course, still in bed, and the verdant, tree-lined block would seem as though it were still trying to shake off its sleep.

He would start running, first in a smooth, easy lope and then build up to a sprint, his long, sinewy legs, without any strain or muscle pull, covering the distance to where he had deliberately left his car. The car Ruthie used remained in the garage, but his own car, the low-slung, powerful Cord, he left some distance away so that he could start and wind up his day with a fast mile.

Usually as he would flash by he would startle a milkman at his rounds or a lone man getting an early start on his lawn. He would wave and yell a friendly "Good morning!" so that the guy wouldn't think he was altogether a kook. And then, from time to time, some neighbor would ask Ruthie why Al would be running in the morning when every other man could hardly drag himself up the street to work. Obviously, he was considered the neighborhood's resident character, but he didn't mind. Pressed for an answer, Ruthie, in her characteristically flushed way whenever she discussed Al with anyone else, would reply rather vaguely, "Well, you've got to know Al to understand him." And then she would add with a smile, "or understand him to know him—or something."

That 6:00-A.M. run was one of the best parts of his day. Maybe it was the combination of good feeling in his gut and in his head, the morning peacefulness of the suburban neighborhood and the fire in his heart. Ideas raced through his mind keeping pace with his pounding feet. More than once he had piled into the car hardly conscious of what he had seen along the way, so wrapped up was he in his thoughts. A cop had stopped him once, suspicious of a runner at that early hour. Laughingly, Al had explained that he just liked to move along fast in the morning and forced a note on the young blue-eyed cop. "Here, have a discount on me at a discount store," Al had told him. In it he had hastily scrawled, "To whatever store manager it is. Give this cop anything he wants at cost. Just this time. Al Miller." And more than once the sprint had spawned an idea, a gimmick or a new technique that came so full-grown that he had immediately put it into operation. Like being the first discount chain to install its own product-testing laboratory. Discount stores with a testing lab? It was absurd, impossible in those early days, like something that couldn't be, shouldn't be but maybe ought to be. But it had built excellent rapport with the customers and even with the suppliers, once they got used to the selling potential implicit in it.

Al had also come up with the idea while mobile one morning of having area or multi-department checkouts instead of just central checkouts to curb the rising shoplifting rate. That one, like the testing lab, had proved so effective that it was quickly copied by other, burgeoning discounters. But, Al reminded himself exultantly, he and his boys had been first. Maybe, he laughed out loud, that was why he ran.

Once in the car, he would head for the stores in Jersey or Philly or New Haven or Baltimore, or their suburbs, pushing the speed limit until he hit the open road, whereupon he would push the speed limit even more. Regardless of weather, he drove with the windows wide open, the sun or the rain on his face, depressing the pedal to 70, quite often to 80, the whip of the wind turning his skin cold-pink and the sun bouncing bright glints off his red hair. Again, he was running, running, like a father racing home to his kids after a long absence. And when he came over the rise and saw the sprawling shopping center below him in the valley or in the meadow, dominated by the big, white single-level store with the red-oval sign, his spirits soared and he shot the big car forward like a rocket, scaring the hell out of other drivers entering or leaving.

In the parking lot he would take a quick approximate count, fully aware that a minimum of 50 percent of the cars would represent his customers but fully sensitive to the shifts in the hourly traffic. He could almost tell by the makes of cars on the lot how he was doing in his store—a better than usual predominance of Chevies, Fords and Plymouths over Buicks, Pontiacs, Chryslers and Cadillacs was a good omen. But a cold sweat would bathe him if he saw too many small cars, such as Ramblers or foreign models. Somehow these, as did the big cars, denoted customers for the non-discount stores. But he knew deep in his viscera that this would change soon. He was working on it.

Then he would stand inside the store, usually near the cash registers, and study the customers as they came through the checkouts. He was hypnotized by their facial expressions, watching especially for those who showed exultation (i.e., the store must have made a mistake in their favor) or happiness (they liked the merchandise and the price) or a semi-reluctant willingness (a good buy, could be). But what bothered him were those with the pinched look of skepticism. Once he yanked a dress out of the hands of a woman with that look on her face, telling her, "You don't want this, missus. It's crap, believe me," and refused to let her buy it. Another time when he saw a similar but slightly different frown on the face of a woman with a threadbare coat, he strode over, took the sweater she was about to buy and scrawled on the price tag. He explained, "I'm sorry, ma'am. You almost got cheated. We reduced that garment twenty percent but somebody forgot to change the ticket."

Mostly, though, the vigils at the cash register were sheer pleasure. Unlike many other merchants whose enthusiasm rose or fell depending upon the size of each transaction, Al watched what everyone purchased, his heart pounding when he saw that it was something that he had personally bought or had worked with a merchandise man or buyer to bring into his stores. It wasn't just that it was a confirmation of his judgment or of his judgment of the judgment of others. It went a lot deeper than that. In a way, it expressed his feeling about people. A warmth, sometimes a flush, ran through him when he saw the crowds streaming through his checkouts with the toasters, the TV sets, the suits and slacks, the fans and clocks that he had first put his faith in. Buying something you needed or wanted or craved made you happy, and through some strange form of transference it made him happy that he had made it possible by the exercise of his own choice or that of the boys. So not infrequently, when the customer selection was particularly of great personal satisfaction to him, he became a source of embarrassment to the store's manager and his staff. He would stand close to the register, a tall, lean, handsome man with his teeth bared in joy, his eyes moist and sometimes leaning over to hold himself in. This habit of his naturally got around in the trade so that someone—probably a jealous competitor, Al reasoned—commented, "Al Miller is so happy when anybody buys something in his store that he'd like to kiss their ass." But customers would wonder who and what he was, puzzled as to why he should be standing there with that expression and that stance. Who's the nut? they seemed to say.

In each of the stores he would seek out the manager, who was either one of "the boys" or had been appointed by them. First, their reaction would be a mingled welcome and awe that he had dropped in to see them. And then as he offered his ideas, as he carried forth with his observations of the store, its housekeeping, its displays, its particular merchandise assortment, even the things he had just seen in the market, their eyes would dart away from his, seeking some relief from the flood of rhetoric. Not that he was unpleasant or unkind, not Al Miller. It was just that he had so much to say. Each subject would lead to another and that one to another and he would hardly pause for breath. One of the more zealous ones, though, had learned a real *kunst*. If he whipped out a pad and pencil and started taking notes, Al stopped short and his monologue quickly petered out.

"You don't have to take it down, fella," Al said with concern. "Just get the feel of what I'm saying. Then you can put it to work later."

But the man with the pad and pencil didn't use them after the first or second time. You don't treat Al Miller that way, he soon realized. Not a guy who started the whole company from scratch and practically built a whole industry by himself. As a matter of fact, from the moment he appeared in the store, everyone who worked there was overawed by him. It was like seeing a legend in the flesh. So mostly you just listened to him and suffered in silence. Not that it was suffering exactly, but the guy's zest and word flow was endless, wearing, even excruciating.

After such visits to the stores, Al would slowly walk out to the Cord, climb in and sit there for a while until he caught his breath again. His own enthusiasm and patter sometimes wore him to a frazzle. But it was not something that he was likely to change. Can a leopard change its spots or an elephant drop its bulk or Al Miller be different from Al Miller, the crazy kook? Not very likely at all, he told himself.

Then on to the next store. Most were in the suburbs, only two of the ten located right in the heart of New York. He was, in fact, one of the first merchants in the East who went suburban in a big way because he had sensed even before the fifties that the cities would empty themselves of their cliff dwellers. Later, as the cities rebuilt themselves, other cliff dwellers would come in. But in the meantime, the suburbs would spread out from the cities in an immense checkerboard as millions of war veterans, blue-collar and white-collar workers sought out their little house with the patch of green.

In a day on the road, he might cover three or four stores or more. But shortly after that warm October day in 1954, he out-did himself. He put in almost 700 miles in one day, visited six stores after leaving before six in the morning and fell half dead into the house after midnight. It was his longest tour yet, and he felt it as he let himself into the quiet house.

It had been a disturbing day, too, because the fantasy had caught up with him again that day. You have to get out of New York occasionally if you want to find out what is going on in the big town, he had learned. And so one or two of the managers had told him what his enemies, the old-line department stores and the national-brand producers who refused to sell to the discount stores, were saying about him. They were explaining his great success in terms of the furtherance of ulterior motives of others, an expression of opinion of truly improbable proportions.

It went two ways, this new phase of the recurrent fantasy. One was that he and his stores were being fed goods on a very advantageous basis by a group of large domestic producers for purposes of their own. Their goal? By fattening him up through the provision of extremely favorable prices and preferred deliveries, they planned at some given point to suddenly withhold all merchandise from him, forcing him into a desperate situation and then compelling him to take them in as controlling "partners." They would then be in the retail business in a sizable way, giving them a big jump on and placing them a rung or two on the ladder above their competitors.

The other phase was even better, even more revolting, a fuller exercise of a corrupt but creative imagination.

Since his stores were handling an increasing proportion of imports because many branded producers refused to sell to him, an international cabal spanning continents had formed with the intent to use his growing chain of stores as its expanding point of entry into the United States. The countries referred to were, of course, Japan and West Germany, both rapidly accelerating their gross national product and also suffering from anxiety over export outlets.

Both countries had reportedly agreed that in all of America his company offered a focal point for their products in their search for a favorable balance of payments and were already shipping him considerable goods. Once finding the right funnel—and Al Miller's reputation had quickly spread overseas—the rest would come easy. His competitors would seek to capture the same sources of low prices, quality output and reliable deliveries. The potential for the vanquished countries in the land of the victor was vast. The scramble by American discounters led by Al Miller's example would open a veritable flood. Not even American import curbs could prevent it because, so the story went, there were ways of getting around them, such as transshipment through Canada, Mexico and the domestic free ports.

Disturbed by the rusty cutting edge to these fantasies, he didn't put much faith in their coming from the old-line stores or producers. They could and maybe did stem from some of the other discounters as much miffed at his tactics as anyone on the other side of the fence.

What the hell was wrong with people, anyway? he wondered just before drifting off to sleep. The only thing was to get out of their way—and do just what he had to do.

He slept but almost immediately he had an uncomfortable and insane dream. He had had variations of it before, an aspect of something pursuing him, but this time it was a black balloon of great size that caught up to him and enveloped him and he forgot who he was and couldn't remember except that he saw a vaguely familiar face that turned out to belong to his father, wearing a fond but slightly deprecatory smile. Then suddenly the dream changed scene and his father was standing inside Macy's at Herald Square and looking around with interest and he said, "Hey, Pop, what the hell are you doing in Macy's? You never went there in your life!" And his father replied, "Why, you dumbhead? Because it's the world's biggest store, that's why!"

That morning, Al got up even earlier than usual and left the house running.

2

The Yo-Yos

IRVING WALDTEUFEL, the thieving purchasing agent, raised the picture on the wall, stared through the peephole and carefully studied Molly Bradley in the adjacent cubicle. A slim but highly endowed blonde with fine flesh tints who was, at thirty-three, a good ten years older than she had been at twenty-three, she paraded in front of a full-length mirror. This in itself would not have meant much to the hot eye at the tiny hole if it weren't for the fact that all she wore was a big hat and bikini panties.

Each month Irving stole thousands of dollars from the company but returned them by the fifteenth of the following month because of his great love for Al Miller. Now, goggling at the peephole, he decided that one of the next things he would steal would be Molly. And Al Miller or not, he decided disloyally, he wouldn't give her back.

Molly Bradley, the narcissistic and nymphomaniac fashion co-ordinator, often did things such as she was now doing. The reason she did this was to undergo the exact experience she was asking customers to when she sold them those particular panties, or whatever else it was. Naturally, when such items were involved, she had the doors closed first, but strangely enough quite a few of the men managed to blunder their way in by simple deliberate inadvertence.

There was quite a mob the day the word went out that she was trying out a new brand of bath salts.

Nat Batt, the omnivorous, lying public-relations man, hung up on the phone to conclude his thirty-sixth attempt of the day to obtain media publicity. Only eleven of his efforts had scored, which gave him a success ratio of 1.1 to 4.6. Better than anyone else in the retail PR end but signifying too much wastage. "I guess I'm just an omnivorous, lying PR man," he told himself fondly. "Lots of ideas that mostly stink and lousy follow-through. But those two idea men who work for me better snap shit!"

A fat tub of a smiling young fellow was Matthew Smiles. Nineteen years old and five feet tall, a glutton and three hundred pounds of gelatinous but great promotional talent, he literally overflowed his tiny cubicle. In fact, part of him extended out into the narrow hallway, or appeared to. Eating a double, vertical-type hamburger with not one but two slices of onion, he burped, erased that on the tape recorder on which he was dictating a number of brilliant ideas that would ultimately sell millions of dollars' worth of goods and asked, "What do I do for a topper?"

He answered himself by sending down for a double-rich milk shake.

Harry J. Abner, the forgetful general merchandise manager, sat in one of the largest cubicles, if any of them could be called that, and scratched his flat bald head as he tried to remember something that he had irretrievably forgotten.

According to his records, he had approved from the company's twenty-five buyers orders for goods sufficient for three months' needs. But invoices of new shipments showed that goods currently arriving would carry all the stores through for at least the next six months. He made grooves in his scalp until he suddenly brightened and called his secretary in.

"Honey," he said excitedly, "we're about to have the sale of a lifetime. I mean there have been plenty of sales one month in advance of a season, but three months? Never in the history of retailing! And all we'll have to do is shave our prices a little bit. And everybody was wondering how I became GMM of this smart-crazy outfit!"

William I. Wallenstein, the highly unreliable real-estate vice-president, was a former realtor who had been cashiered out of that industry because in his great zeal he had sometimes sold the same property to several buyers after taking as many as ten deposits on it. Now, in one of the company's cubicles, he took his telephone off the hook to still the insistent ringing.

He did this because, despite the fact that the company was committed to only two new stores a year for the time being, he had just taken an option on his sixty-second potential shopping-center site. Frenzied calls were coming in from developers anxious to turn options into contracts. But crafty Wallenstein knew that he had more than time on his side. He had the avariciousness of people who were not supposed to be avaricious. Competitors, including many of the traditional department stores who were more careful and deliberate, would soon be buzzing vainly like moths against a hot light bulb trying to option choice sites that were already tied up by William I. Wallenstein.

When the company would be ready, he already had under option some of the best sites in the country at prices that were fixed as of the contract date. Should he decide to relinquish them to the old-liners, they would have to pay higher fees, which would put them at a competitive disadvantage. Besides, he had made sure that if a developer insisted on a release for that purpose, Wallenstein's company would be entitled to a dividend on its option fee based on the site's higher value to the new optionee. That in itself had been a coup. So it was not for nothing that Wallenstein's ouster from the real-estate fraternity had brought an industry-wide sigh of relief.

But perhaps the cubicle where the most pressure gathered belonged, quite naturally, to Ernest von Rossem, the treasurer and controller, who had to make financial order out of all the chaos that emerged from all the other cubicles. The problem was, though, that he was himself very disorganized and inclined to use a slide rule, which he had taught himself to use incorrectly.

He was, for example, unable to remember whether he was supposed to borrow from Peter to pay Paul, or from Paul to pay Peter—or was it Pat?

His redeeming quality, however, was that he was the only one of half a dozen financial men who had tried it who could live with the group and their foibles and *shtik* without falling away from a heart attack or ulcers. In his pressure-cooker world of juggling cash flow, arranging short- and long-term debt, paying for them out of operations and still keeping reserves for this and that, he sought desperately to find a guidepost—no, a stanchion —to hold on to for his dear life, an example that he could closely emulate, and he did find it. Al Miller. From that point on, he had no serious problem, other than his daily exhausting frenzies that probably someday would cause him to fall away from a heart attack or ulcers.

And so it went throughout the rabbit warren that meandered over three floors in the shabby old people- and rodent-infested building not far from Times Square.

Near total disorganization, much questionable talent, occasionally shaky ethics, inadequate personal discipline, loose controls, shotgun expansion, budgeting that was never followed, inventory management that was hardly managed, overabundant promotion and coordination that forgot important operational elements—all these emanated from behind the dirty-green partitions that shakily separated the cubicles.

But, amazingly and even shockingly to almost everyone else, it all worked in some strange, insane, illogical and totally unprecedented manner. It all came together in continuous record gains and in consistent increases in market share, both of which became the astonishment of experienced merchants and financial men the country over.

If disaster lapped at Al Miller's doorstep, as some said even in those formative years, the premonitions must have been given the wrong address. So they moved to someone else's doorstep. For the fact was that the efforts of everyone in those executive cubicles as well as those of everyone who worked for them, however misguided or not, contributed to a corporate success that was immediate, vast and continuous.

How did it all work? Like this:

1. Irving Waldteufel's thievery, expressed in terms of buying considerably more products, fixtures and all manner of operational needs the company would ever need so that anywhere between 10 and 20 percent of it was shunted off to a separate warehouse that he owned, was canceled to the company later when he succumbed to conscience pangs and a feeling of tremendous obligation to and affection for his boss. Thus, during the early years when lumber, hardware, display materials, office and warehouse equipment and a few hundred other things were hard to get, Al Miller's stores always unaccountably had them. What would have happened in the absence of Irving's returning them would have been difficult to assess, except that the firm would surely have gone under the first year. As it was, Irving had to content himself with being a pseudo-thief on a grand scale while the company itself could, if it had wanted to, become a supplier of equipment to other retailers. Later, under the spur of Irving's devious mind, it did.

2. Molly Bradley, whose slowly fading beauty and promiscuousness attracted many to her, was nonetheless an irascible bitch. Her mouth could spit venom and often did. But she was probably at least for a long while one of the best fashion dames in the business, either traditional or discount, and much of it was because she always put herself in the role of the customer and then projected her action outward from that. Thus, the bikini panties both from an aesthetic and utility standpoint (she upbraided the manufacturer for sleazy seaming and for pornographic license in the crotch area) were improved by her first trying them on. So it was with everything else. They then sold in the hundreds of thousands on an exclusive basis in the company's stores. Many a supplier who could withstand her foul mouth tried to seduce her both physically and professionally with lavish offers. But she never gave in—to the job offers anyway—despite a not so easy life in the company, for reasons that only she and perhaps but not certainly Al Miller knew.

3. Nat Batt, whose real name was Nathaniel Batganovich, was the oldest of all the "boys," crowding sixty. But only those who were aware of it also knew that he had been one of the biggest characters in the character-crowded public-relations field for over forty years. His work spectrum began with show business, moved to circuses and carnies, then to Hollywood, back to Madison Avenue, moved west to Seventh Avenue and then came to rest for some years in between with an office on Fifth Avenue.

The reason his reputation as a character was so well established was reflected in the fact that he had held something like twenty-seven jobs before starting his own agencies, and there had been roughly eighteen of those. He was a disgruntled, plump little man who could keep his attention focused on any one subject no longer than ten seconds before ten other subjects cropped up, mostly from his own brain, although he was just as prone to swipe someone else's idea as not. He also had a strange relationship with his own staff of four, an unusually large one for a public-relations unit in a retail company, in which its members never knew exactly what he wanted or if or when he would be in. Actually, it was entirely deliberate on both counts, since he wanted them to be free-wheeling and imaginative and uninhibited. He never gave them instructions other than a yelled oath, a gesture at a date on the office calendar and the name of the buyer of the department or the executive involved. Such a combination might have been, "Hey, prick! The twenty-eighth of the month. See Manny in toys!"

There were many other combinations of similar nondescriptiveness.

As for the other matter that confused his staffers, the mystery of his presence or absence in his office, he had worked this out with care and creativity. He had flatly told the four of them that when they saw the door of his cubicle closed he was in and not to be disturbed. Then, one night when the office was closed, he neatly removed a portion of the partition behind his desk, scooped out as many bricks leading to a fire escape as was necessary, and he was in business. Since he locked the cubicle from the inside when he left and no one in the company ever used the fire escape, he had kept his secret. Until he would be discovered, the ploy kept his staff in the kind of all-work state he wanted.

As far as the company was concerned, it was all plus. The PR staff was easily the best in the business, constantly perking with all kinds of nervous energy and far-out ideas, which was just what the stores needed. But there was a dividend to it all, too. Nat Batt spent much of his absences moonlighting as an agent in a large nearby travel agency, where he gave priority to his own company's travel needs, preferred discounts and advance knowledge of rate changes. Al Miller approved of everything Nat did because he was so downright creative.

4. When the people in the personnel department first saw Matthew Smiles, they couldn't believe it. Not just because of his waddle and his immense size but also because he was the first applicant they had ever had who came in lugging a tape recorder. He had just graduated from high school, he explained breathlessly, having completed a commercial course and been a stock boy in a five-and-ten. While working at the part-time job, he said, he had dreamed up a lot of ideas on how to sell merchandise which he had put on tape.

Thereupon, the butterball of a boy, who seemed almost as wide as he was tall, turned on his tape recorder. ". . . You can sell a lot of things if you make people think they're putting something over on you, especially in a discount store. . . . Like make an occasional boo-boo on the tally and undercharge the customer. She'll keep coming back for months trying to get you to make another boo-boo. Meantime, she's got to keep buying until you do, which you don't. . . . Like have a two-for-one sale on out-of-season goods that you bought real cheap. Like give a free tie with every purchase of three shirts. Like give diners dessert on the house or kids candy or old people a little discount. Like give charge customers a gift on their anniversaries or birthdays. That's how you make customers that last. Or . . ."

The interviewer, a bit dazed, turned off the machine and studied Matthew. For all his ludicrous size, his bright eyes, crew cut and neatly knotted tie added to the alertness that his taped remarks indicated. He was immediately hired as a stock boy. But he tried to hide the flicker of disappointment in his eyes. Evidently he had thought that his ideas would earn him a promotion job right off the bat regardless of his youth. But because the interviewer sensed in him the potential that later erupted in the "free meal for every purchase of $10 or more," she dropped a note to Al Miller.

No one, she knew, liked ideas better than he did, and Al took pains to look in on the stockroom often and speak to the boy. Within a few years Matthew's ideas on the tape and many new ones produced considerable added business for the chain, and the tubby young man seemed headed eventually for even bigger things than being named creative vice-president at nineteen. Chairman of the board at twenty-one? some began to wonder. With Al Miller, anything but anything was possible.

5. The reason Harry J. Abner claimed that he forgot so many things was that he had so many things to remember.

In a department store or a big discount store, there are about 125 different departments selling over 100,000 different items. This was all too much for any GMM but especially for Harry Abner, who could hardly remember what he had done the night before. It wasn't that he was just as happy to forget since he was having trouble with his wife and girl friend, but that numbers confused him—in fact, they stopped him cold, which was, of course, a rather untenable situation for any general merchandise manager.

But there was one thing at which he was exceptionally capable and it was practically everything. Through some instinctive capacity that for all he knew may have gone back to some antecedent either in the water salvage or junk business, Harry knew how to turn disasters into windfalls. Part of this may have been due to the fact that his whole life had been a disaster, what with family and romantic troubles, but somehow he had managed to survive it all for thirty-seven years and occasionally to smile. At any rate, he had risen to the top because he had been able to take many a manufacturer's or wholesaler's disaster and, by dint of knowledgeable timing and buying, turn it into a blockbuster of a sale for Al Miller. With equanimity, he could take any department's overstock or understock, where ordinary remedies were impossible, and get considerable sales mileage out of it.

Ready-to-wear, men's clothing, radios, garden equipment, food
—whatever it was—nothing proved to be his undoing.

So he had sold thousands of chemise dresses when no one else
wanted them as "stylish for the lady-in-waiting" (expectant
mother), unmoving wide-wide-lapel suits, Eisenhower jackets
and surplus GI poncho raincoats to pawnshops and secondhand
stores and thousands upon thousands of unwanted Army cots to
writer's conferences and outdoor youth gatherings for $1 apiece
(they had cost the Army $4 each and him 25 cents).

Sometimes—no, quite often—he committed his own disasters,
as he had with his forgetful countersigning on six months' needs
rather than three. But pulling big goofs of his own out of the fire
was an even greater feat and he could do it every time. It wasn't
so easy, but for him, being so forgetful, it became a way of life
and oddly enough sharpened him even further for his major
efforts. Actually, Al Miller was really the GMM of the operation,
but Harry Abner, who more properly might have been called
"senior vice-president in charge of merchandise disasters," was
an invaluable right arm. With his old friend at his elbow, Al
Miller could make no mistakes. Or so it seemed.

6. Wallenstein's shenanigans were of a great advantage to the
company. You would have thought that Al Miller, a kook himself
associated with a bunch of other kooks, needed someone of
Wallenstein's ilk like he needed two heads. But besides the fact
that Wallenstein was one of his oldest friends, the scourge of the
real-estate industry so aptly juggled shopping-center developers,
architects and store designers, zoning boards and competitors
that the company was able to open stores on practically the best
sites along the Eastern seaboard. And in its own good time.

Of course, this meant that the firm had to give Wallenstein
much latitude and he naturally took advantage of it. He had a
constant source of funds available to him to nail down options,
as well as a "reserve" which he used as he saw fit. How he used
the latter, as well as the former, no one questioned, certainly not
at that stage, nor was he volunteering any information either.

All this led to considerable whispering and allegations about
his personal integrity and there was probably something to it. As
one of his closest and most intimate friends put it privately, "All

you have to do is to look at the shifty eyes of that bastard to see that he's one of the world's biggest *gonifs*. The things he gets away with . . ." It was rumored, for example, that Wallenstein's great corporate and financial freedom, plus his own razor-sharp sense of opportunity, allowed him to put some of it to great personal use to the extent that he had acquired ownership of one prominent shopping center and actually operated it as an absentee owner. Thus it was possible that Al Miller might even have been a tenant of Wallenstein's so that his own subordinate was his landlord. But this strange juxtaposition of roles had never been proven.

But what had been proven was Wallenstein's immense value to the company's expansion. Not only had Al Miller been the first to open big branches in the Eastern suburbs but he had also been first to locate several big freestanding, or non-center, stores on major highways. Later, when the rate of expansion would be doubled and even tripled, the company's stores would dot the whole Eastern seaboard and then spread to the West Coast, becoming one of the discount industry's supergiants. In the meantime, in about five years, it already had ten stores going on twelve, then fourteen, then sixteen and so on.

All because the real-estate industry hadn't been able to digest William I. Wallenstein and had regurgitated him into the open mouths of the waiting discounters.

7. Ernest von Rossem, the disorganized and personally insolvent controller, owed both his value and his saving grace to the same fact as seen from two different viewpoints. The fact was simply Al Miller, whom von Rossem had seized upon as his life preserver in a sea of uncertainty and confusion. As a result, not only was he literally able to hold his head above water by latching onto his boss as an example and as a catalyst or sieve for any decision that he had to make, but, conversely, Al Miller, the merchant's kook, found that Ernest understood him so well that he didn't fight him on literally every count as Ernest's predecessors had done.

To be exact about it, Ernest didn't fight him at all. The controller had evolved a simple concept. Every time a budget was submitted to him, he simply signed it in an indiscriminate scrawl that no one could ever figure out and buck-passed it up to Al Miller. Since Al didn't have either a desk or an office, Ernest simply sent it to Al in care of Zelda, the switchboard operator. And since he never heard anything more about those budgets either from Zelda or Al, he assumed that everything was just fine. Many times he had wanted to ask either of them about the forms, but his instinct had warned him not to. As for Al Miller, he never objected to anything that Ernest did. For that matter, if an objective observer had ever taken the trouble to ask Al what it was that his controller did, the answer would probably have been insufficient to fit on the head of a pin.

For his part, Ernest's dealings were mostly with the banks and the accountants, and because of his delicate situation he spent most of his time interpreting what a genius Al Miller was to both the banks and the accountants, rather than discussing financial matters. And they, by the same token, looked upon the skinny, cadaverous financial man with great respect. He was the only controller Al Miller had ever had who could speak about him to the banks and accountants without having a fit right then and there.

If Ernest's particular situation seemed particularly hard for him to believe, it was not very different for the others, either. But the outsider who was fortunate to see the sum, rather than just the parts, had a much better vantage point to evaluate it all. Perhaps he was better off being on the outside at that. Most of the people on the inside had considerable trouble explaining in a creditable manner to those on the outside just what went on in the inside.

8. Of course, with this type of situation existing on the inside, it was essential that there should be someone to keep the lid on things. A leveler, a sane, ordinary straight man who could sit right smack on the middle of the scale and by adroitly shifting his rear end when necessary insure that the balance didn't tip over too far in the direction of insanity.

That person was hardly Al Miller. It was instead the company's operations vice-president, Solly Patracelli, also one of Al's "boys" and perhaps the only one with whom he felt uncomfortable. Al solved his discomfiture in a simple manner. He just avoided Solly like the plague.

It is hardly worth mentioning that Solly's role in the company was untenable and frustrating, delicate and burdensome, bitter and mind-breaking, nerve-racking and nail-chewing. He ate aspirin by the score daily, drank coffee by the gallon and used up family-size boxes of Kleenex by the hour mopping his dripping face, head and palms. But he held everyone at bay, especially those who wanted to make an issue right then and there over some particular insanity of the moment created by an act of commission or of omission by the kooks singly or collectively.

"Look," he would warn a complainant, "let's not lose our heads around here or we'll all go down the drain." More than once in the midst of some madness, that looked like a pretty good idea. But because Solly was a big, muscular guy, with a handlebar mustache and an authoritative swagger that really had nothing but quivering jelly at its base, and a dark, square, frightening face that had deeply etched worry lines that appeared threatening, he brought some measure of calmness to many a tense confrontation.

He also attacked the real cause of the problem, the individuals who were most prone to send the others climbing up the wall. He would, for example, make it his business to stop in at least once a day at the cubicles of Irving Waldteufel, Molly Bradley, Nat Batt, Matthew Smiles, Harry Abner, Willie Wallenstein and Ernest von Rossem and the others and stand stolidly in their doorways until they would look up at him. "How's things, kid?" he would usually ask, adding uncertainly, "Everybody keeping their heads today?" It was hardly a question or an approach that was destined to make him popular, but it was his own way of forestalling the possibility of any one of them going off the deep end. It was in the same tenor as if he had been a warden who every day would put a damper on any ideas that might be popping in the head of his inmates by greeting them with "No one thinking of breaking out today, is there?" Or a bank vice-president making the rounds of his tellers daily to ask, with an unctuous smile, "Everybody honest here today?"

Perhaps because he always was prattling to them about "losing our heads" or "keeping your heads," he was naturally referred to as "the headmaster," or by some Navy veterans as "the master of the head." But it was either Molly Bradley or Nat Batt, both of whom unquestionably had the foul-mouthed capacity for it, who said, especially in connection with his other pet phrase, the admonition that "we'll all go down the drain," that "you can flush Solly all you want to but he'll never go down the toilet bowl."

So it was evident that Solly Patracelli held an important and unappreciated job. Like everyone else in the place, he had fallen both into his job and into his manner of executing it by simple default, each one of them filling just enough of the big vacuum that existed to achieve some measure of personal satisfaction, not to mention a pay check. Solly, however, was especially saddened by the fact that Al Miller paid not the slightest attention to him. Where would Al be, he wondered, without him?

But, again, all that was on the inside. As far as the objective outsider was concerned, he could not help being impressed with the vast success, the increasing market share and the many firsts that the company had achieved.

If chaos was truly eating away at the company's core, and it was only mostly the bitterest critics who were willing to say it, the fact was that the intoxicating smell of success permeated every filthy nook and cranny, every overflowing and uncatalogued file of sales slips, charge accounts and invoices and every reeking cubicle that was deserted at night full of half-filled coffee cups, half-eaten Danish and sandwich scraps in the three ratty floors. How was a smell of success, however rank, possible amid such foulness?

Benny Acropolis, the executive stock boy, came up with an answer of sorts one night as he strode disgustedly along the hallway holding his nose and looking into the dirty cubicles. He had been told by the warehouse superintendent to drop off a batch of invoices and he had deposited them on a two-foot-high pile of already delivered invoices in Harry Abner's empty office.

"I know what's gonna happen to all those invoices," Benny observed. "When it reaches three feet high, that bald-headed jerk in there—" gesturing toward Abner's cubicle— "is gonna toss them in the trash basket. That's just what he did last time. This goddam outfit is headed for the rocks, the way I see it. The way all those yo-yos around here behave, it's a wonder it lasted five years. But, in the meantime, it's doing so great and everybody is so busy breaking his ass one way or another that they got no time to worry about details. Especially the yo-yos. Maybe the details will creep up to their heads someday and swallow them and the whole goddam company up and I hope I won't be here when it happens. Meanwhile, Christ, they're just about knocking everybody dead." Benny, who had really wanted to be a professional welterweight or a jockey but found his real niche at the company, paused and shook his head ruefully. "Nah, on second thought, I think I'll hang around. I even like working in this crazy nuthouse. I hope it never comes apart."

Since Benny was not speaking to anyone but to himself in a virtually empty building, no one apparently was on hand to hear him or to argue with him. But for better or worse, he was, as you can see, overheard. And those who best knew the dark, tough mite also knew that his words sometimes had the ring of prophecy in them.

After all—you have to ask yourself—in the kind of company that Al Miller ran, who should know the real score better than the executive stock boy?

But, in those days, few in the industry even thought such things about Al and his boys. Most everyone who spent any time watching his competitors—and who didn't?—couldn't help gaping at the antics of that wild crew and wondering where they got their *shtip*, their push, their internal and external mobility.

Actually, the evidence of all that began in the early days of Al's company, in 1947 and 1948, when he decided to go discount in a big way. The three tiny walk-up stores were doing just fine—that, is, once he gave the boys a good, solid kick in the pants—but the opportunities that beckoned in those years were just waiting around to be grabbed.

Al had heard about the new types of stores and the new versions of old ones that were bringing people in by the carloads. So he went on the road to see them, dispatching the boys all over the map to see others and report back to him. Without directly meaning to but sort of stumbling into it, they even found themselves researching the origins of low-margin, mass-selling stores and discovered that they had been around for some time, longer than they were old and even before that.

This should have proved once and for all that Al Miller didn't start the discounting wave that eventually swept the whole country. It just seemed that way when he became the industry's most inarticulate and unwilling spokesman. He tried to tell everyone that it had all predated him by many years but no one would listen. So instead of his astonishing success turning him into an impossible braggart, he remained himself, a hapless and strange cross between a likable extrovert and a highly disconcerting introvert. And with flaming red hair yet. The assault on the credulousness of others caused by his persistent disclaimers inevitably made him appear terribly honest and naïve. As a result, when he was apparently trying his utmost to deprecate his own role, he rose even further in the estimation of those who listened to him but didn't believe a word.

Yet, it was all true, predating him by years, even decades, in Bucks County, Pennsylvania, New Jersey, New York, especially in New England, the West Coast and here and there in the in-between states.

It was born, as many significant things are, not because it wanted to be born of itself but because other things willed it into birth and being. But negatively. If that seems picaresque and rather unlikely, consider a situation in which merchants apparently didn't want to sell goods, banks didn't want to lend money, newspapers threw out advertising, manufacturers slowed down their machines because they couldn't find outlets and shoppers who wanted things and couldn't find enough of them just stashed money away. All this, of course, was doing no one any good.

This was happening right after the last big war when the defense economy was massively stumbling into a civilian economy. But long-established sellers and makers weren't quite ready to make big changes. Money was so easy to make that their ingenuity quotient remained puny, despite the great hunger on the part of millions to enjoy all the conveniences that they had given up during the war years. So the question became one of this degree of simplicity: What had happened to the greatly vaunted American style of entrepreneurism when things should really have been hopping and popping?

Many pondered this question, few could answer it and even fewer acted on its implications.

Later, when it all came into focus, everyone let loose a sigh of understanding. It was clear then, even to those who had smiled vaguely at the sight and sound of the infant industry and had quickly turned their backs on it. Had they known instead that that bit of economic protoplasm would spring up almost overnight into a brawny adolescent that would stand up to them with a sneer and then beat them to the marketplace, they would certainly have mashed it out in infancy. Some did try later, however. But it was too late. The overgrown, seemingly cretinous scrapper had good reflexes. It stood up under the occasional blows, sidestepped others, poised itself and spit squarely into the eye of its opponents.

So now then picture the kind of country whose industrial arsenal is turned toward the manufacture of a hundred thousand items impossible to get during the war years. Millions are added to the work force to man the new production maw. The demands of the consumer body are great as the long-frustrated yearning for new cars, refrigerators, radios, television receivers, all manner of equipment, clothing, hosiery and many other items appears at last to be due for satisfaction. The pipelines open to a trickle of output and then more and more and still more.

But picture this, too. The people have unalterably changed, as has their way of living. It comes as a surprise to many in business and government who should have known better and moreover acted upon it that things postwar would never be the same and the reason is what has happened to the people. They have lived through a veritable age in only four years that ranged from peace to war, from placid existence to daily uncertainty, from hope to despair, from endless waiting to tragedy, from atom bomb to its shattering aftermath, from millions exposed to new shores and new races to a return home with all its unleashed dreams. Who could remain untouched, unstirred?

It becomes a matter of who wants change more—the returned men in uniform or those who waited, each traumatized by the nightmare montage. No more do the returnees want confinement in close quarters, no more the epithet and the heavy hand of personal restriction, no more the mind-chilling fear of the next morning or the day after. No, the hell with all that, they warn their families, who agree. Now is the time to catch up with the dream, the quicker the better.

So homes are put up in the cow pastures, the potato farms, wheat fields and overgrown meadows. Roads are not yet adequate, but the builders wield pressure and soon the long strings of highways begin to crisscross portions of the country. And speeding across them from home to store to job is a growing stream of new autos, the first postwar models as well as the prewar relics.

As the fifties dawn, a hundred cities have satellites, large, irregular sites full of low-priced and not so low-priced homes largely financed by a grateful Government under pressure—fertility plots filled with the gleeful cries of children, the postwar babies soon to surrender their cribs to a tiny brother or sister and that one to another and another.

But now picture this, too. A whole new market of customers has opened up, but it seemed to have nowhere to go. For critics of the big downtown department stores, it was simple to conclude that these had been asleep at the switch when the train came roaring by. But the department-store owners were, if not asleep, overly cautious. They had been lulled into overconfidence because they thought that the massive bulk of their big in-city stores were imposing enough to lure many of the new suburbanites. But they forgot that going into the city was a big chore, driving a hazard, and the whole effort could easily turn into an all-day affair with frazzled edges.

A seller's market, finally ending, had also soothed the big-store owners into a false sense of security. Desirable goods were scarce, demand exceeded supply, long lines in stores demonstrated it, as did sparse stocks during Christmas. In that kind of market, the merchant could sell almost everything that he had plus what he didn't have but could put his hands on.

Difficult to believe as it was, through all this Al Miller and his boys were learning. Whether it was Nat Batt scouring ruritalia and shouldering the natives aside, Irving Waldteufel stirring up the dust, occasionally pocketing an item, glaring his way through the farmers' auctions in Pennsylvania Dutch country, Al Miller turning over merchandise to scrutinize the labels or opening closed bins in New England mill outlets, or Matthew Smiles waddling with his ever-present tape recorder through the reference rooms of the New York Public Library, they found that all kinds of discounters had been moving in for years under various guises, raising their heads in unexpected places.

The department stores were finally opening stores in the suburbs, but they were also making another mistake, all of Al's boys took notice. The branches were often near-exact miniatures of the big downtown stores, catering to the broad, middle-income customers. But the downtown stores' bargain basement was left where it was, in the city, rather than putting one in the branch store.

But suburbanites were watching their money and buying with care. Prices had shot up in the postwar period and inflation continued to dent the average spending income. When the belated department-store branches abandoned the great lower-income market in the suburbs, the vacuum was quickly filled by the discounters. They simply moved in with their ever-larger stores, their shopping carts that they had adapted from the supermarkets, the checkout systems, the long opening hours, the large parking lots and their locations on or near the major traffic arteries.

By the time the big traditional merchants saw what was happening, it had already happened. In about two decades, the upstarts had simply overtaken the retail establishment and exceeded it in the volume of billions transacted. In the dizzily spiraling course of the country's economic history, the feat probably ranked as one of the century's most dazzling. However, for most observers, it was at the time hard to recognize it for what it was. One big reason was that the feat was dimmed, confused, misunderstood, diverted and diluted by the presence at its very core of some strange, unlikely characters.

Who?

Who else?

The success of Al Miller and his boys held another ingredient that even knowledgeable observers such as Benny Acropolis, the executive stock boy, and those competitors who were most jealous either hadn't considered or didn't know about. It might even have been a secret ingredient that no one else had.

It was usually furnished on days when Al Miller returned after not showing up for days or even weeks.

He would come in the back way in order to skirt the reception room, where people had been waiting days to see him, and make his way along the narrow hallway. As he would pass, he would catch glimpses of Molly, Irving, Nat or Abner, or he would run into others crowding by him in the hallway. He would feel a swelling in his chest and an unconscious smile would break behind his freckles. He loved them all, even those he hated, he told himself for the thousandth time. Somehow, everyone who was working for him was in a total sense working with him and he appreciated their time, sweat and effort and especially their indulgence—yes, indulgence—because he knew that he was trying and hard to take and hard to understand and even hard to stomach, and so it meant a good deal that they stayed with him and did their bit and more. It was mainly because of this that in all the years that he had been in business, including the time in the company and even the years before, he had never fired anyone and probably never would. Did people take advantage of him? No question about it. But, he admitted to himself and knew it to be true down to the pit of his gut, he was taking advantage of them, too, being Al Miller, and so maybe after all it was an even swap.

Then, through interoffice phone, he would check in with Zelda, knowing that she wouldn't give him away to the waiting horde, and then he would drop in one by one on the people in the cubicles.

He would plop himself into a chair, wave at Molly and ask,

"Hey, baby, what can we do to sell more goods?" He would be totally oblivious to what she might be doing at the moment but offer his question with such expectation as if certain that it would cause a sharp upturn in business from that moment onward.

He dropped in on Molly once on that very occasion when she had closed her door and stood studying herself appreciatively in front of her mirror clad only in her bikini panties. For the moment, she had been startled at his entrance, but since he seemed to take no notice of her unusual state of near nudity, she saw no reason to call it to his attention, either. After all, she had learned to live with him, too, in more ways than one, and so she replied, calmly but actually rather shakily, over her shoulder, "Just a second, tall, red and absolutely virile, let me fix my hat." And so, while he sat there, studying her back and then her reflection in the long mirror, she adjusted the brim of her hat. Then, she turned and moved toward him, her full, protuberant breasts and smoothly round belly shivering and her swelling hips undulating, almost twinkling. With a hot flash in lovely brown eyes she said, "Since you ask, I've been thinking that maybe what we ought to do is dream up a fictitious feminine name and base a whole bunch of merchandise around it, including toilet goods, cosmetics, jewelry, accessories, hosiery and so on and push it for the career girl or young-married. It wouldn't be exactly just another way of offering a store brand but of creating an image for all these dames that like to think they're fashionable and chic and would go for a whole family of products that they could identify with and that would symbolize them."

Her shoulders, breast, belly, hips and buttocks did some amazing things in keeping company with her enthusiasm. Al stirred. "It's great, terrific," he declared.

"What is?"

He grinned. "Your suggestion how we can sell more goods. And everything else, too. When do you want to start?"

"Just like that?" Molly asked with surprise and feigned disappointment. "It's just an idea."

"Ideas are what please," he said.

She smiled and had the creative presence to push her breasts sharply forward. "Who dreamt up that stupid phrase?" she asked, having that not at all on her mind. "That scatterbrained public-relations man up the hallway or that fat, disgusting little kid, Smiles or Piles or something, that you think is so great?"

Al felt his face getting hot as he watched her. She stood now just a few inches from him, her feet at the provocative professional angle and her erect near-naked frame with the surprising pink flesh tints pitched slightly forward in a pose she still kept from her starting days as a fashion model. He could have touched her, and knew she wanted him to, with just a slight elevation of his fingers. He got up instead and stood a little shakily at the door. "Hey, baby, you do just that. Get started on just what categories we ought to work into a program like that and then talk to Nat and Matthew and Abner and get them lined up on their end. We'll decide on the exact name later."

He started opening the door. "You don't like 'Molly Bradley'?" she asked.

He stared back at her for a few seconds, feeling the heat wave in his face beginning to pulsate. "I like 'Molly Bradley' a lot," he replied with a twisted smile, "but not for that."

She threw him a kiss, putting her entire, startling body into it. And, just before she closed the door, she added lowly, "I love you, you lousy, terrific bastard." But he didn't hear her.

He plopped himself down now in Harry Abner's office. "Hey, Harry, howsa kid? What can we do to sell more goods?"

Abner had been sitting there in the manner of a yoga, trying to remember something that he had forgotten to remember before he had actually remembered that he had forgotten it, so that he was at least thrice removed from being capable of answering Al's question. But Al's freckled smile and earnest, confident question triggered some intricate mental valve in Harry and he said brightly, "You know, Al, I'm glad you asked. We got in every one of our stores like five thousand square feet of reserve stock space that we can't use because we got to keep in October summer clothes that we didn't get rid of during the season. We got no space in the warehouse and it's waste space in the stores. Why don't we use a corner of the warehouse, empty it for a few days and put all the summer stuff on sale at only a couple of percentage points above cost and call it 'Our Buyer-Lost-His-Head Sale'? We won't make any money on it, but it'll give the stores room and that's money, too."

Al nodded. "Why not? Maybe we ought to expand it into a general warehouse sale, using the gimmick you mentioned, and get hard goods involved, too. A buyer can lose his head on that, too, can't he? Harry, your idea is great. Do it!"

He shook hands with the GMM, who hurriedly began writing down what had transpired between them so that he wouldn't forget it in the next three seconds.

In Wallenstein's cubicle, Al removed a bunch of blueprints from the single chair, sat and asked the real-estate man, "Willie, what can we do to sell more goods?"

Wallenstein, whose mind was on sixty-five shopping centers, stared at him in amazement. "Sell more goods, Al, are you nuts? I'm a real-estate man. What the hell do I know about selling more goods?"

Al flushed. As his oldest friend, Wallenstein sometimes took advantage. But as they glared at each other, Al yanking his collar open because he was still feeling the heat in Molly's office, the real-estate man saw that Al Miller was serious. "In your business," Al told him, "you come across things that are sometimes geared for merchandising—a new type of entrance or a new pattern of checkouts or—"

"Wait a minute, Al," Wallenstein broke in. "I just got me a brainstorm. Up in New England I saw something that could work for us. A supermarket set up directly adjacent to a discount store, sharing the same wall—"

"And how about with a common entrance, so that they got a brush-off of our business and we get theirs?" Al asked.

Wallenstein nodded, with growing interest. "Sounds good, Al. How about if I check it out?"

Al rose, patting his old friend on top of the head. "You have to ask yet?" he replied, grinning. They began slapping each other around on the back and then on the jowls.

That, even way back in 1954, was the other, the secret, the unknown ingredient.

3

Customers and Whores

"WHAT THE HELL is it?"

"Some kind of a crappy old mill store, I guess," said Al.

"Looks like they moved out and left it for the rats," Harry said.

"If they did," Al said thoughtfully, "the rats are buying."

They sat in a late afternoon, in the late forties, in Al's prewar Olds in front of a square, rundown five-story building that had once been a factory. "NEW ENGLAND MERCHANDISE OUTLET," read a sign above the door in three-foot-high letters. Underneath it was a blurb in smaller letters: "Bargains—Antiques from Fine New England Homes to All the Best New Goods from Everywhere." They watched with some disbelief the stream of shoppers coming and going, many in family groups emerging with full shopping bags or carrying a table, a lamp, quilts, baked goods or a pair of shoes or clothing. Children came out licking ice-cream cones, the smaller ones holding balloons aloft.

"Everyone looks kinda happy, don't they?" asked Al. "See anybody who looks mad?"

Harry shrugged. Why should they? he asked himself crossly. Did anyone of them drive all day with a madman who didn't know when to stop, let alone for lunch or even to go to the bathroom?

Cars, small trucks, even a few surplus Army jeeps filled the small parking area in front of the building. It was almost five on a Saturday and, the crazy way Al drove, they had traveled almost 500 miles that day from New York through Jersey to central Pennsylvania and all the way back and up to Massachusetts all in one day. But Harry wasn't so tired that he couldn't see that the mill outlet had something, judging by the traffic and the stream of families. What was it? Harry could see that Al was impressed. By what? A dirty old building in a textile ghost town? "Let's go in," Al said. Harry reluctantly followed, amazed that the redhead's energy remained undiminished even though they had started their trip at 6:00 A.M.

Al did an odd thing. Instead of going right in, he parked himself at the foot of the steps and talked to some of the emerging customers. Harry listened with amazement. Were they saving money? Is that what brought them to the outlet? What did they buy? Why that? Could he look inside the shopping bag? How far away did they live? Where else do they shop? For what? Do they come to the outlet only on Saturdays? Oh, it's open Sundays, too. . . . A curious group collected around the zealous young interviewer, most people smiling with friendliness, some more warily. Had he come all the way from New York? someone asked. Harry yanked his arm. "Come on, Al, the owner'll come out and have us put in the local pokey."

Al's face was bemused. But he had enough presence to thank everyone profusely before he went inside. Harry held his nose in exaggerated dismay at the old-old odor of dank interior and damp, moldy wood. Immediately, Al rummaged through merchandise, opening drawers to see the concealed stock, holding goods up to the foul light to see what he could see, prying at the labels. Harry shuddered at Al's intensity and scratched his big, open scalp. He was already mostly bald at twenty-seven. Although it was a hereditary trait, he was certain that his two-year association with Al Miller had more than contributed to it.

A few minutes later, after Harry had paused for a Coke at a

refreshment counter in the building and Al had moved on, he found his companion deeply involved in a conversation with a heavy man in a coarse checked shirt in the rear of the building. This was obviously the owner of the mill outlet and he was responding with pride and assurance to Al's barrage of questions. After ten minutes of conversation, however, the proprietor turned away, but Al followed, talking to him and beginning to hound him. What a talker Al is for a shy guy, Harry thought.

He sighed. It had been like that all day, running, talking, running, talking, in the five other stops they had made. Al hadn't wanted to take any time out except that Harry had flatly warned him he would pass out if he didn't have some food by three-thirty in the afternoon. Al had given him five minutes at a roadside stand. But now Harry had decided that he had had enough. He went out and sat sullenly in the car.

Forty minutes later, Al came out with the heavy man, still conversing heatedly. After fifteen minutes of this, the outlet's owner waved Al away, went inside and Al got slowly into the car and settled under the wheel. He still had a sort of trancelike look about him. Then he drove in silence for a good ten minutes while Harry watched him with concern, especially since Al had that look while pushing seventy miles an hour.

"You okay there?" Harry asked.

Al didn't answer immediately, but when he did he said, "You know, that guy is open seven days a week from ten to ten. Even most holidays. He gets local housewives to come in and work part time." He was silent for a few more moments and then said, "Heshy, we're in business."

"In business?" Harry asked incredulously. "You bet your ass we're in business. We already got three stores."

Al laughed, pushing the gas pedal to seventy-five. "No, you shmuck, I mean we're going into a new business." His voice had a new note to it, a hoarse hint of exultation. Harry could see that Al was very excited now, an abrupt change from his comatose state of a few minutes earlier. His eyes were bright, almost fiery, and he was driving so fast that Harry was certain that Al's mind wasn't on the road, or, for that matter, in this world.

Suddenly, catching his companion completely unaware, Al brought the creaky old car to a lurching stop. He began getting out. "Take the wheel, Heshy," he told him. "I feel like a little run. I've been sitting on my *tuches* for so many hours and I got so much on my mind that I gotta stretch my legs. Just keep her at fifteen or twenty and I'll be right on your tail."

So for the next half hour a worried Harry Abner drove slowly along the darkening country road followed by Al pumping his long legs up and down with his gaze fixed on a level somewhat above the big trees that lined both sides of the road until they reached the highway. Then Al jumped in, not even breathless, and drove back to New York without a stop at seventy practically the whole way.

It was almost the next morning that Harry began losing his memory. It was a mnemonic decline that was to culminate some years later in a reputation for his being the best general merchandise manager in the business to work for because he couldn't remember today what mistakes you made yesterday. This not only endeared him to everyone but Ernest von Rossem, the highly disorganized controller, but also gave Harry an image of uninhibited creativity that attracted numerous idea men with talent. It also made him the perfect associate of Al Miller, who was entirely prepared to forget what he had done yesterday but who, everyone agreed, had more genuine creativity than anyone else around. In Al's case, however, it was a raw, native, gut instinct. In Harry's case, it was due to nothing but a lousy memory.

When, years later, the situation deteriorated to the degree that Harry forgot which shoe went on what foot, he hied himself to a twenty-three-year-old psychiatrist.

The bearded, beret-headed head-shrinker immediately slapped poor old Harry down on a hard couch and had him talk for the next eighteen hours. Every couple of hours the head-shrinker sent out for hot dogs and coffee or coffee and Danish. But he wouldn't give Harry any, saying that he didn't want to over-stimulate him since that would violate the free association. At the end of the session Harry, famished and dehydrated, had drifted off into a coma when the psychiatrist woke him to tell him that he was indeed a fortunate man.

Under the set of circumstances that Harry had just related, he was told, he should really not be losing his memory but his mind. "You have an amazingly strong cerebral endurance to exist amid chaos," the young doctor expounded. "But you are losing your memory because of your reluctance to accept what is going on around you. But that's not so bad. At least you have an escape valve. On the other hand, that's not so good. If that escape valve should pop under pressure, your mind might go, too. But that's good. Then, you see, with the temporary but complex condition of no longer maintaining an escape valve because you could no longer withstand the terrible trauma of your surroundings—in other words and in plain language you have lost all your buttons—then we can start standard recuperative therapy." The analyst took note of Harry's crushed look and said, with commiseration, "Well, there is one alternative, young man, but you'll have to do it quickly. Change jobs. Or, better still, leave the country."

As Harry walked out, a broken man, he was certain that he heard the head-shrinker shout after him, "The one I'd really like to get on my couch is your boss, that psychotic Harvey Mueller! We would make medical history together!"

By that time, either alternative that the analyst had recommended to Harry was way beyond him. As for changing jobs, who would hire a mnemonic cripple? And as for leaving the country, he would first have to remember in what bank he held an account, and conceivably when he did go abroad he would have to remember where he came from. But there was an ever greater overriding consideration. He loved Al Miller, that *meshuggeneh* redheaded sonofabitch who drove everyone off their rocker, or, worse, to losing their memories because of his shenanigans, sincere though they undoubtedly were, and to something else, too. In his own way, for reasons that he simply couldn't recall and would never think of mentioning to the precocious young psychiatrist, he sensed that Al Miller *needed* him. Everyone who became closely connected with Al sooner or later lost his emotional equilibrium, underwent a serious change in personality, experienced difficulty in maintaining his sanity—and then curiously wound up feeling that Al *needed* him. It was absolutely impossible to understand, Harry realized upon leaving the head-shrinker's office, and then he immediately forgot what was impossible for him to understand.

What caused Harry Abner to suffer an accelerating loss of memory began with this set of circumstances:

The morning after they returned from this 500-mile trip, Al sat down with Harry and mapped out a plan. First, they would get the rest of the "boys," the other fourteen or fifteen they didn't already have with them, to come in and get to work. This bunch of reprehensibles, stooges, kibitzers, corner smart-alecks, beer-drinking Dodger fans and postgraduate truant-officer escapees from the old neighborhood in Brooklyn would man the new cut-price chain that Al meant to start.

Then, they would send letters on fancy stationery to every important manufacturer of consumer goods in the United States, every major wholesaler, jobber and transshipper and obtain their catalogues. Many of these producers and others would then receive token orders on the most desirable items in their lines.

The "boys" would fan out across New York, all the five boroughs, Jersey, Long Island, Westchester County and Connecticut and contact the purchasing agent of every large business, institution and organization. Circulars would be left with each, as well as hundreds of discount identification cards, entitling holders of these courtesy cards to "at least one-third off any desirable item made in America." Although a shopper would have to show the courtesy card to get in, he would receive two of them, more if he wanted them, when he left. This, Al reasoned, would spread the courtesy around.

Each of the three small second-story loft stores that Al operated with Harry's help would be transformed into showrooms displaying a spectrum of the goods ordered. Inventory on hand would be small and the bulk of goods that Al ordered would be used for display. Whether it was a purchasing agent with a bulk order or a friend or co-worker to whom he gave an identity card, purchases could be made from stock available or by order.

A token deposit would be requested on an item not on hand, and the customer would be notified when to return to receive his shipment. If a customer wanted an item that could not be ordered through any channel available to them, the boys would buy it at retail in another store and sell it to the purchaser at wholesale, the company absorbing the average 35 percent loss in order to create customer loyalty.

Simultaneously, a large vacant store site would be sought in the center of Manhattan so that if everything went well, the operation could be quickly shifted to a substantial ground-floor location. "We're going to bring the mill outlet, the farmer's market, the cash-and-carry and the factory-to-you store all in one package right to the heart of New York," Al predicted. "We're gonna knock the other merchants dead with our daring and then dare the bastards to knock us dead with lower prices. But they won't be able to for two good reasons. First of all, they won't be able to change their business to a cut-price operation because it would mean changing everything else that they do. Second, they won't have their hearts in it."

All this was supposed to be done within one week. This was preposterous, of course. It mostly took two weeks.

By the end of that period, the former camera, luggage and fountain-pen lofts had a completely new air. Toasters, blenders, refrigerators, television sets, golf sets, toys, clothes and a thousand other items were displayed. Many other goods were shown by supplier's catalogue. But there wasn't much change in the staff, Al's boys, only that there were more of them. Sloppy, slouchy, sway-backed types, some still in "lumber" jackets, guys who talked like bookies and some of whom had been one, retailers who had as much right to be waiting on people as longshoremen, some out of factories and others just off the state unemployment compensation lines. Later, those who would remain would humanize themselves, assume the pose of interested parties and some even become acceptable to the eye at their jobs, but not to the other senses or especially to the mind and taste of the customers.

But as far as Harry Abner was concerned, it was all too much, too fast and too impossible for him to accept. How in hell did Al

Miller have the *chutzpah*, the intestines to undertake such a project from scratch and try to put it all together so fast? he asked himself a hundred times. He himself was totally inadequate for the task of being Al's number-two man. He had always been just a clerk or a helper wherever he had worked, a squat, bald-headed guy with flat feet, bad calluses and a big can, but to be Al's chief of staff of a staff like that? It was not to be considered. Once, when he had admitted his fear of complete personal inadequacy, Al had smiled fondly, patted him on the jowls and then given him a pinch on the ass. Then Al had blithely walked away, whistling. Al, it was quite obvious, would never fire him, no matter what. As a matter of fact, as Harry found out through all the vast success and the vast problems that came later, Al never would fire and never did fire anyone. He just didn't believe in it. If a guy made some mistakes, he was never reminded of them and certainly never reprimanded for them. He would either improve himself and know it or, after a while, he would beg Al to let him go. But, in that case, he would never find Al. He was even more elusive than Nat Batt, the omnivorous, lying public-relations man, whose disappearance was engineered by a cunning evil mind, while Al's absences, lapses and dalliances were absolutely instinctive. He was never more elusive than when someone tried to pin him down on professional and especially on personal matters. He seemed to step through some sort of time barrier into a non-zone of existence. It was almost uncanny and simply another reason why he never took an office, had a desk or commandeered a secretary for his own.

Al, of course, had never really been a boss before. Even working with Harry over the previous two years, it had been more like an enlightened partnership, except that unlike most partnerships one partner didn't steal from the cash register when the other wasn't looking and, also, they weren't partners at all. Only Al had put money into the original business, using his Army discharge pay. He had asked Harry to "help out" at good pay, never really having hired him, so that Harry had soon left his job behind the produce counter at a local supermarket. It was just that Al in his own way treated Harry as a partner. He never told him what to do but left lots for him to do, ranging from picking up the pieces that Al always left in his wake to sweeping up the place. At no point, however, did Al ever ask Harry why he didn't do this or that. Everything that Harry did or didn't do seemed to satisfy him.

For Al, the reverse would have been unthinkable.

It was even more unthinkable when the three stores, which Al Miller had anonymously and variously named "Barney's," "Bruno's" and "Simon's," entered their new era as combinations of every discount house that he had encountered.

All the stores occupied small, second-floor locations within two square blocks of each other in midtown Manhattan and were identical in approach even though they had different names. The idea was that if a customer was unable to find what he wanted in one of the stores, he might try his luck at one or both of the other two on the theory that he would still be looking for the same elusive item at a ridiculously low price in another walk-up store. Al had attempted to stimulate this practice by putting up prominent signs outside each of the stores calling attention to the others. Thus, when the customer dispiritedly left Barney's he ran into a bold sign right over the top step of the stairway advising him to visit Bruno's and Simon's. Outside Bruno's, a similar sign suggested Simon's and Barney's and so on.

The first day of the new era, Al walked excitedly into Barney's and was shocked. Four of the boys stood around about the way they had on the corner—slouching, looking sourly at the customers, picking at their teeth with match sticks and responding to questions with wisecracks and even insults. It was clear that they assumed that this was the way customers like being treated because this was what they themselves were used to and that anything else would have been a sacrifice or a corruption of their own delightful personalities. But, being a non-boss, Al said nothing more than a dry "Hi, *shlubs*," and turned to the bewildered customers. Here, he was delighted. The circulars and the courtesy cards had attracted about fifty people to the store's opening. The traffic was sustained all morning, peaked during the noon hour and continued at the morning pace during the rest of the day. And, while Al happily attended to the trade, the boys looked on in a sort of suspended animation.

Around the corner at Bruno's the situation was no different, except that Harry personally attended to the customers, and the same at Simon's. In each of them and differing only in some slight degree, the dozen or so of the boys simply stood there on their haunches and paid no attention to what was going on around them. How many customers walked out of the three stores in disgust, Al didn't want to think about, but he was so busy himself that he had little opportunity to spend on estimates. The first day was a solid success and by its end his mind was on fire with new and better ideas.

He was locking up Barney's after ten that night when Harry burst in.

"What the hell you gonna do with these bastards?" demanded Harry. "Not one of them did a lick of work all day. Let's can them all and see which ones come crawling back and promise to do a day's work."

Al shook his head. "How can we can them, Heshy? They're our pals. We grew up with them."

"Horse shit. They act like they're doing us a big favor. Who the hell needs them?"

Al thought for a moment. "Maybe we ought to give them a little incentive."

"On the first day? A salary, maybe the first they ever got, that isn't good enough?"

"Wait," Al said, a light in his eyes. "I got an idea. The right kind of incentive has got to be a special kind that can motivate them."

"Come on, Al."

"No, I'll tell you what, Harry. Tomorrow, you tell all of them that we're gonna have a sales contest. The one that sells the most goods the first week gets a season's pass to the Dodgers' games. The second week, the top man gets a season's pass to Aqueduct race track. The third week . . ."

Harry looked closely at Al for the crack in his head. "Al, you're off your wingding."

Al laughed with delight. "But we'll include a gimmick. We'll keep giving prizes like that continuously. The same guys will keep winning, right? And they're the ones that we want. The others will quit sooner or later out of frustration and disgust. Their salaries won't mean a thing to them compared to not getting season passes while the others do to the ball games, the race track, the burlesque or a weekend in Las Vegas."

Harry's stare turned from disbelief to something like unadulterated reverence. "You're not just crazy, Al," he said. "You're a crazy genius."

But Al, as it turned out, wasn't really. The survival of the fittest eliminated everyone but Irving Waldteufel, Nat Batt, Ernest von Rossem, Solly Patracelli and a few others of that ilk.

Later, Harry, scratching his flat, bald scalp as if to inscribe it there, had to admit one thing. Al had done his best by his boys, had caused the staff not to be cut but to cut itself by half and hadn't fired a single one of its members. With his memory already failing him and his mind beginning to totter as he took up the burden of working with the survivors, Harry got a vision of what might lie ahead. A peanut of a company that would grow overnight into a towering tree, its branches shaking desperately right down to its dry roots so that the broad trunk would have to hop around just to stay upright. The company tree would have little sap but plenty of "saps," he warned himself.

Al obtained his new, big store, the second major phase of his plan, practically by accident and in a totally unexpected way.

Al looked up one day to find a man regarding him with great interest, a shifty-eyed guy of medium height with thin lips and a sharp nose that ended in a tip. Al recognized him immediately even though he hadn't seen him for many years, last as the nasty, drippy-nosed son of a widow who ran a tiny pickle store in the old neighborhood.

"You remember me, kid?" the man asked.

"Sure," Al said, "Willie Wallenstein. It's been a good coupla years." Al accepted a card identifying Wallenstein as a salesman for a midtown real-estate broker.

"Let's sit," Wallenstein said. "It might just do you some good."

They talked at a vacant desk in the rear stockroom. Al listened with amazement as the salesman made him a startling proposition. Only a few blocks from Radio City Music Hall there was a commercial block that had been nondescript and ragtag for years but now was getting an inflow of good new stores, businesses with street-floor showrooms and even two bank branches. In the middle of it, however, a shabby hotel lingered, named the Aquatic. It was a name that had no particular meaning except perhaps that it might have described the highly transient, even floating nature of the place. The Aquatic, in short, was a whorehouse. Or, perhaps more aptly, it was a hotel which catered to prostitutes and was run by a hotel keeper who was more of a pimp.

"Thanks for the inside information," Al said, "But what's it got to do with me?"

"Wait, wait," Wallenstein said. "It's got plenty to do with you. Listen."

For over a year the Aquatic's owner had been under pressure by the other local businessmen, including the police, who for years had studiously looked the other way, to vacate the premises and allow a more respectable business to take over the site. But the hotel keeper–pimp had another twenty years to go on his lease and had no intention of giving up a place of business that had been so profitable for years.

"Now, this guy is willing to go a long way for somebody who will take over most of the site, say, about seventy-five percent of it, but allow him to continue to operate in back of the remodeled building." Wallenstein said, "He says he'll split the cost of remodeling the hotel to suit the guy that he'll sublease it to and he'll pay for all the remodeling that he has to do to stay in business. In fact, I don't mind telling you that, if you're agreeable, he'll probably go even further. He should normally ask you for a percentage of your business, or at least a minimum subrental, but he won't. And if you want to push him, he's authorized me to say that he will give you a percentage of his business, a piece of the action, if it will take that to cement the deal."

"Is this some kind of a *meshuggeneh* joke?" Al asked.

The salesman's shifty eyes stopped shifting and he laid it right on the line. "Wait, Al. Here's how it will work. A discount store like yours doesn't need any big display windows, right? All it needs outside is a great big sign, a nice double-door entrance and plenty of open space inside. Well, we can alter the front to suit, but inside you got a big, wide-open lobby. There are three floors—and the walls are all partition. We rip out the partitions and you got two more wide-open floors. All my guy wants is that you don't touch the side entrance and leave him a wing of rooms on the third floor."

Al said, "I oughtta throw you out of here."

"Throw me out and you'll lose the biggest chance to make good that any businessman has ever had that you or I know. You're getting it all for nothing, except fifty percent or maybe less, of the cost of alterations. You get forty-five thousand square feet of free—I said free, goddamit!—space in a choice location for at least twenty years. You know what that kind of location would cost you per square foot if you had to lease it the real way?"

Al studied his hands. There was no way of answering the salesman's question without sounding dumber than he felt. Instead, he asked, "Would he continue his . . . his business for the entire rest of the lease?"

Wallenstein laughed. "Hell, no," he said. "All he wants is to stay in business another three years—three years more of bloated profits that will be enough to let him retire to Florida, where he can start all over again and make some more bloated profits. Three years, Al, behind your new store, your great big fat *free* store, where you can sell anything you want to at any goddam price you want to and still make a profit. Boy, you'll have the world by the nuggets!"

He stared hard at Al, a difficult thing to do because of his shifty eyes, and added, since he had been studying Al for over three weeks, "You and your goddam all-holy customers'll never even see any of the tail that comes and goes. That side entrance will look like just another employee's entrance or whatever you and he decide to make it look innocent. Man, what the hell you waiting for? You got it made!"

As Al studied Wallenstein's strange face, the sharply fixed features and the transient eyes, a weird sense of excitement began boiling up in him. There wasn't a retailer in the world who hadn't many times in his career dreamed of operating at a low fixed cost. It could allow him to clobber his competition in a hundred ways, because he could price his goods from a base of greatly reduced overhead. "You know, Willie, your proposition does open up a lotta great possibilities," he said.

"Al, that's the understatement of the month, maybe the year. You could give half your inventory away and still make a better profit than anybody."

But Al had a sudden suspicion, a doubt that it might be nothing but a put-on. "What made you come to me? Why me?"

Wallenstein didn't believe it. "You're not really that modest, are you, Al?" he asked. "In the last few months what you've done in these dinky little second-story operations of yours has spread all over town. Once I laid eyes on you and watched what was going on here, I knew I had my man. Some people are already calling you some kind of a genius or something, but I don't think there's anything like a genius in business. You put the right man and the right idea together and there's nothing in the world that can stop him. The way I size you up, you're going to the top and I may want to come to you for a job someday. Frankly, there are some guys in my business who don't like the way I operate because I'm a mile ahead of them every minute."

"What are you getting out of this—personally, I mean?" Al asked.

Wallenstein laughed nervously. "Now, that's what I mean. Nothing can stop you. My company will get a fee but I get one too. Maybe you don't want a piece of the action—pardon my pun—of my client's business, but I'm getting a tiny little piece of it for myself."

"I wish you hadn't told me that."

"Don't be a horse's ass," Wallenstein told him. "If I didn't have some private incentive, I might not have worked so hard at this project that I came up with the right man. I did come up with the right man, didn't I?"

Al hesitated only a second. "Those girls can have an employee's discount," he told Wallenstein generously.

So that's how Al got his store. Within the three years before he took over the entire building, he and the boys had already made such an impact from their secret sales-to-expense ratio that they were the talk of the whole New York market. Trade journals wanted to write their story and document their skill in store operations. Competitors were just flabbergasted. During the three years, Al closed the three walk-up stores and concentrated on the big one. One of the things that the trade publications particularly noted and competition particularly envied was the youthful and attractive quality that always seemed to characterize a portion of the store's shoppers. Somehow, everyone agreed, Al Miller had learned just how to latch on to the youth market. This was demonstrated by well-dressed young women who swished through the store, leaving behind an alluring impression of delightful perfume, dazzling legs, undulating hips and bright, very bright smiles.

It was Nat Batt (who else?) who brought it all out succinctly from the lurid depths of a singularly dirty mind. "Sometimes you get to thinking that all the customers are nothing but whores," he told a few of the boys. "Here some of the whores are just customers."

The free ride ended in three years, but it was more like a roller coaster. Al's 45,000-square-foot store achieved the highest sales per square foot in New York next to Bergdorf's, Tiffany's, and Korvette's and drew the greatest density in lunch-hour shoppers for its size. Some days when he advertised most heavily, police had to station barriers in front of the windows and let the wide-eyed shoppers in by twos and threes.

A week before the three-year period closed, the Aquatic's owner ceased operations as promised, moved south with his entourage, and Al Miller's sublease turned into a long-term lease for which he paid normal rentals.

But by then, the store had become perhaps the most exciting in town, offering low-low-low prices which baffled competitors and suppliers and delighted the public. It almost seemed to everyone that Al Miller had little or no expenses, which, of course, was impossible to understand. For a time there were some ugly rumors about how he did it, but these failed to take root, mainly because Al's boys, approached to confirm them, did so with derision and glee by prearrangement with Al. He decided that making a jest of it would effectively kill the rumor. For example:

"Hey, Solly, I hear Al Miller's running a whorehouse on the side?" a friendly enemy would ask.

"That's right, pal. You got great sources."

"What the hell has that got to do with running a retail business?"

"What?" Solly was told to reply. "You know any other business that's got a bigger turnover?"

This type of repartee could only have one reaction on the questioner. He could only turn away in disgust and forget the whole business.

But Al was never proud of the extra, hidden reason for his great success during that period. He brooded over it many times but kept his doubts to himself. It was his only black mark during five years of unqualified success resulting from his own initiative, his brains and his guts, as well as those of his boys, and he felt that in agreeing to the deal he had acted as any other animalistic businessman would have.

Some of his associates, however, wanted to take advantage of the situation. Wallenstein, who made a deal with Al before the sublease ended to serve as a consultant, wondered if they shouldn't investigate other non-retailing uses for a portion of the property after the three years were over. But it was Nat Batt who irritated Al greatly by proposing that there were promotional opportunities in the steady, transient trade that came and went behind the scenes.

"We could give the girls' customers a special discount," he suggested quite seriously. "It would be a great way of building up our out-of-town business—we would come out with a catalogue—a lot of these guys are tourists."

Al playfully aimed a big, bony fist in the direction of Nat's face. But the PR man backed off, hurt and disappointed. "You a saint or something?" Nat demanded bitterly. "What would Pop say if he found out about it? He'd kick your damned teeth in."

Al stared, his heart pounding, at the sneer on his old friend's face. "You rotten sonofabitch," he said. They had been sitting in Nat's office when the conversation took this particular turn. Al lunged at Nat, who ducked behind the desk and tore out of the office. Al chased him down the hall. The two of them knocked down a water cooler, pushed people aside, creating a commotion throughout the place, until Al, who was a pretty good miler by now, caught up with the public-relations man. With most of the people in the office watching, Al pinned Nat against the men's-room door with his fist cocked. Then he dropped his arm disgustedly and walked out, his eyes rooted to the floor.

Down in the nearby movie house, Al sat sullenly, not watching the show but hating Nat and himself more. The sharp little publicist had put his finger right on the hot, tingling nerve. What *would* Pop say?

Pop had plenty to say about it, as Al learned some weeks after the chase with Nat Batt down the hallway. Arriving at his parents' apartment on the East Side one Sunday afternoon, Al found them both sitting in the small, crowded living room. Pesse greeted her son in her usual friendly manner, but Chaim turned his face back to *Der Forwartz*. He usually held the paper in his hands, even though he no longer had the ability to read it.

"What's bothering Pop?" Al asked his mother.

She stared at Chaim, shrugged and left the room. Al waited as the old man's glare fixed itself on him from virtually unseeing eyes and the explosion came. "Albert, is it true about the *curvas*, the whores?" Chaim asked in a low voice. "You have a haven for prostitutes where they conduct their business behind your new store?"

So that was it. Al wondered how the old man had found out. He nodded nervously. "It was an offer I couldn't refuse, Pop," he said. "I get rent free for three years for just allowing the former tenant to use a little of his old space behind the store—"

Chaim arose and stood statuelike before Al. "You gave this gangster, this despoiler of young girls, the opportunity to stay in business because of your greed, isn't it so, Albert? If he couldn't find a spineless lout like you, he would have to go out of business, right? That's how I heard it and that's the way it is, isn't it, Albert?"

Al nodded dumbly. What was there to say?

His father returned slowly to his chair, sat and seemed to shrink into himself. After a few moments he observed to the floor at his feet, "A store with an annex that is a whorehouse. Maybe the first new kind of business in maybe a hundred years. Is that what you gave up everything for? Is that a meaningful life?"

"Wait, Pop. I had to have something that would give me the edge on my competition. We've been doing great there—"

"Edge, smedge!" Then the old man was talking about an old colleague and now an idol of his, Maurice Schwartz, the great Yiddish tragedian. "Where are your principles, Albert?" Chaim asked. "Can a man live without principles? Maurice Schwartz was in a revival of *Yoshe Kalb*, a fine drama, when a producer offered him the lead in *The Merchant of Venice*. Schwartz wanted badly to do this great Shakespearean drama, but he refused. You know why, Albert? He said that it was an anti-Semitic play and that he would never appear in such a play. That's principle, Albert, something that you lack very badly. I'm very disappointed in you."

"Pop, I'm sorry you feel that way. They're going to close down soon. It was just a temporary arrangement."

"That means nothing to me," Chaim said. "The whole business proves to me that my only son is not just a scatterbrain but also a money-hungry merchant with greed in his heart. I'm ashamed of you—you . . . you pimp!"

"Pop! I thought you'd be more tolerant with all your travels and experience."

"Pimp!"

Al went to the door, standing uncertainly there for a moment. Chaim was churning himself up into a rage, Yiddish-drama style. "Pop . . ." Al began once more.

"Pimp! Pimp! Pimp!"

Chaim never referred to the incident again when Al came to visit him several weeks later. In fact, at no time after that in the remaining years of his life did he refer in any way to Al's business. He was unquestionably aware that Al was giving his mother money every month, and being given back most of it, to help provide support for the old couple. Chaim was also surely aware that Al's business had been doing extraordinarily well, but he gave no hint of that knowledge. His conversations with Al were always on a personal note, awkward, halting discussions about his wife, Al, Ruthie and the grandchildren.

In the late fifties, when Al was several times a multimillionaire and respected throughout the retail industry as one of its brightest young businessmen, Chaim had to give up his newsstand and remain home, except for occasional walks downstairs. His health, like his eyesight, was failing rapidly, but he wouldn't allow Al to do any more for him or for his wife than before.

Chaim's death in 1959 was peaceful after an obvious final decline over several weeks in the late winter. He closed his eyes one evening and Al and his mother thought that the end had come. But Chaim took another curtain call. His film-covered eyes opened wide once more to take in his audience. He smiled faintly at Al in a strange, happy, eye-fluttering way and at his wife and then Chaim called it a life.

4

Ruthie, Molly and Me

WHEN AL MILLER first met Ruth Bannerman in 1949 in the office of a small housewares manufacturer near the Grand Concourse in the Bronx, he behaved unlike most young men who encountered her. Usually the reactions included flirting in various ways or flatly asking her for a date or using the ruse "How've you been, May?" or making the blatant and ultimate suggestion, "Hey, baby, you and I could make some great sex together." But since Al rarely did the usual or the normal thing, he simply stood there and stared as though she had just stepped through the screen of a thousand movie houses.

Ruth, intent on her typing, finally became aware of a tall redheaded figure gaping at her, his gray eyes full of amazement. She smiled vaguely at him but he didn't respond. He was not asking for her smile but was pursuing some questions that were important for him to answer. And since he didn't return her friendly smile, she shrugged slightly, put him down as an eccentric and returned to her stack of typing.

The thing that amazed him, coming upon her as he did so unexpectedly, was that she resembled not one movie idol of his but several of them. She seemed to be not a dead but a totally alive ringer for Susan Hayward, the sultry movie queen. Then she had something of the look and verve of Ruth Roman. He saw in her a likeness to Ida Lupino in terms of pertness, and it wasn't too remote to see in her the glow of Olivia de Havilland. All these actresses were familiar to him as he sat in the tiny movie houses and watched their magnified beauty and sundry problems with lovers, villains and assorted lechers and killers.

What kept him inanimate and unsmiling was simply the strange feeling of unreality of coming upon someone in real life who was as beautiful as the images he saw on the screen. As was his nature, questions popped up not singly but in a series, like frames ticking away on a movie strip, each one just a bit different from the other one.

Were there women as beautiful off the screen as those on it? Could it be possible that life for real was actually better, more pleasant than life make-believe? Who was this girl anyway? And why was she sitting there, and so absorbed too, in such a prosaic activity as typing someone's silly letters when she should be out winning beauty contests or playing starring roles in Hollywood? The strangest thing of all was that he had just come upon her, this *tsatske*, this delight, but he felt immediately that he had met her before, sometime and somewhere. Was it just on the screen?

Grady, the head of the factory, came out. He saw Al standing there like a statue with his gaze rooted on the girl and asked him what he wanted. Al should have answered because he had come to arrange with the owner for a special line that he could sell in his housewares department, but he didn't. Grady growled at the girl, "Will you please come inside, Miss Bannerman?" and preceded her into his office.

Al, ignoring the grins of the others in the office who saw all this as sex uncoiled, watched with interest as Miss Bannerman moved the few feet into Grady's office. She was rather short, almost perfectly proportioned, slim but on the voluptuous side. She didn't turn to look at him although her back was stiff and her cheeks flushed.

In his office, Grady asked, "Is that guy your boy friend or something?"

"I never saw that man before in my life."

"He's been standing there by your desk staring at you for about ten minutes and you don't know him?"

She shook her head.

"Did he say what he wanted? Like I have to guess?"

She shook her head again.

"Well, tell him to get lost."

She went out determinedly, but he was gone. The rest of the day and all evening, she kept thinking about him with mingled anger and curiosity.

But the next day he was back. He was composed, suave and apologetic. He made a deal with Grady and a date with Miss Bannerman.

Six months later they were married. They lay in bed in a Miami beachfront hotel early the morning after their wedding. They were both very happy, rather drunk and quite tired. He lay without movement but breathing heavily. She raised herself on an elbow and asked, "What's wrong, Al?"

He didn't answer immediately but the sound of his breathing increased. "I think now," he said hoarsely, "that I'd like to get inside you, Miss Bannerman."

She laughed. "Do you think you'll be able to?" she asked.

"I don't know. But I'd like to try."

Three minutes later, there was no longer any doubt about it. He was indeed inside Miss Bannerman.

After, as they held on to each other and sang songs into the darkness, she stopped to remind him that she was no longer Miss Bannerman but Mrs. Miller and she couldn't help wondering about something when they had had their climax. "Were you making love to me or to one of those actresses?" she asked.

Now Al laughed and, before repeating the act, said in her soft ear, "Why didn't you tell me to get lost like Grady told you to?"

"Here's why," she said.

As they learned later, they conceived their first child that night, a good start from any standpoint, and it brought them both considerable pleasure to know that their marriage night, or rather morning after, had been so fruitful. Ruth was particularly happy because she came from a large family and wanted one, too. "So what's the point of waiting?" she asked with a Hayworth toss of her brown hair and a radiant de Havilland smile.

That morning they arose at noon. Al opened his eyes to a flood of sunlight streaming in from the big window and as he turned to look at Ruth he found her eyes on him, studying him, searching his face. As she saw him awaken, she smiled, her blue eyes lighting up with pleasure. "What's the matter, Ruthie," he asked. "You're trying to remember who I am?"

"No, stupid," she replied, her voice creamy, "not who you are but what kind of guy you are." Her hand stole under his cover and ran down his chest and stomach. It paused at his navel, stroking it. "I can't help wondering about all the things your friends told me at the wedding," she said. "Harry said you were one guy in a million but difficult to understand. He said he never knew what to expect from you. That little fat man, Nat something, told me that you were his best friend and his worst enemy. But he loved you because you were loyal no matter what happened. Irving praised you the most. He said you would be the leader no matter what you did, that in any room that you would enter, you would stand out immediately. He said that sometimes he stole things from you but he always gave them back to you or to the firm because he couldn't stand cheating you. Then that strange, skinny man with the funny eyes . . ."

"Wallenstein?"

"Yes. He said that you were the most brilliant businessman he had ever met but the most honest, too. He said something very odd, Al. He said that it was a bad combination and that you were bound to have a lot of trouble because they were self-defeating."

"Why did you have to listen to everybody?"

"I didn't. Everyone wanted to talk about you. It was like they thought I got the biggest bargain in the world. How about me?"

He leaned over quickly and kissed her hard on the lips. "I know who is the big bargain. And it's not me. Didn't Pop tell you that?"

He fell back on his pillow, feeling some pain at what his father had told Ruth at the wedding, repeating things that he had said before to her whenever Al brought her to see his parents.

"Al, you're not the first son to refuse to follow what his father wanted him to do," she said. "You must stop feeling guilty about it. He's an old man and I have a suspicion about why he is so disappointed that you didn't go on the stage, too. I have an impression that he was trying to transfer his own disappointment in his career to you. He would have loved to see you carry on and maybe reach heights in the theatrical profession that he didn't. Maybe he was trying to perpetuate his hopes in you."

The thought had occurred to Al, too, but he had never expressed it. "You're pretty smart, Ruthie, for a dame," he told her. "Beauty, brains and what a bosom! If I could only package it, we'd really have a big item in the store."

She swiped at his head with a pink arm. He reached under and clasped one of her breasts, exposed when the cover fell with her motion. She jumped up, grabbed the cover, and wrapped it around her middle as she stepped away from the adjacent twin bed. But Al was too fast. He yanked at the cover and pulled it away from her.

Ruthie stood fully exposed in the middle of the room. He had not seen her naked before in the daytime. He was for the moment overwhelmed with her startling beauty, its symmetry and wealth. She was only about five feet three inches, but her proportions were perfect. She was a study in soft geometrics, her angles gentle, her curves lush, the circles generously round, the concaves tenderly hollow and the convexes delightfully spherical. She was as pink as a baby, and where she was not, the contrast was arousingly and abundantly feminine.

Al's blood bubbled. He bounced from the bed toward her, but he failed to get to her. Suddenly, she was moving quickly, flip-flopping, somersaulting across the rug in the big bedroom, her front and back rapidly altering position as her limbs catapulted her around the room. She was like a beautiful pink frog. It was ludicrous and beautiful at the same time. He stared first with dismay, then with amusement, laughter rumbling up from his bare chest, recalling that she had told him that she had been quite an athlete in school. In those moments, watching the spectacle that she willingly made of herself in her joy with him, he loved her so much he wanted to cry.

She gave up after a while, somewhat disheveled and breathless. She stood before him, rocking on the balls of her feet, mocking him with her look. "You didn't know that you married a gymnast, did you, lover? I was always one of the stars in our gym classes. And I'm strong, too. What tricks can you do?"

"No tricks. Only this."

His arms reached out for her hungrily. She was delightful, a saucy, athletic, wonderful bitch of a wife and he now obtained a true insight of his good fortune. Then, as he held her close, he realized his own nakedness. Instinctively, his hand reached down to cover himself and he heard with reddening face her laugh of sheer pleasure.

"You're the most beautiful thing I've ever seen, Ruthie," he told her weakly, his face still red.

"So are you, lover," she answered, her grin growing on her round face. "A real Greek god—Jewish style."

They held tightly onto each other. The sunlight flowing in through the open curtains covered them with warmth and they found themselves perspiring together. They moved naturally back to the bed. Breakfast, lunch, dinner, Miami and New York could wait.

Ruthie was strong all right. Not just physically but psychologically. In almost no time at all Al was leaning on her, not so much because he meant to but because he was always so far out on a limb that someone had to hold it firm for him so that he could climb back. The boys, of course, did it in their own fashion, but being the kooks that they were, their attempts to back him up sometimes had the opposite effect. He found himself even farther out on a limb than he had been without their help. This was only sometimes, because as the operation prospered and grew, all of them became proficient, knowledgeable and effective, in a manner of speaking, that is.

Their safety lay in the fact that they happened to work for Al Miller, while their working with one another also helped since they came over the years to understand one another's madnesses and quirks and to combine them into some sort of pragmatic cooperation with one another.

Naturally, Al's new wife, who had worked for several big companies as an executive secretary, had some trouble understanding Al's peculiarities and those of his closest associates. To her, there were definite rules by which executives had to live and which represented their code of behavior. But such was not the case with Al and his boys. There were no rules and certainly no code. Everyone could do what he wanted, broadly, within his category. But what was the category? Harry Abner, who was supposed to be the top merchandiser, often wound up worrying about payroll or, for that matter, toilet paper. Ernest von Rossem, who should have been concerned with the former, often found himself giving the divisional merchandise managers lectures on merchandising because one of the first rules in merchandising was to work according to an order and reorder budget and almost no one was. And Irving Waldteufel, in whose bailiwick the matter of toilet paper fell, was so involved in his own illegal activities that he simply worked according to a foolproof plan. He bought tons of everything and stashed it all away until it was needed either for his personal or corporate purposes, in that order.

After a few weeks Ruthie confronted Al with a big understanding smile and a question.

"It's all a big put-on, Al, isn't it?"

He stared blankly at his little dynamo of a wife of only a month. Sometimes his heart just ached at the sight of her. She had a piquancy composed of practicality, pertness and physical charm that delighted him to his roots. "What do you mean, baby?" he asked.

"I mean that it's all a big joke. The way you seem to run the store and the crazy way everyone works there. How can it all be serious, Al? It's got to be a big front for other things you all do that does make sense. Isn't that so?"

Now he understood. He was a good head taller, but he leaned his head down on her brown bangs so that he looked into her eyes as he said, "Baby, I'm serious as hell. So are the boys, with all their nutty ways. It may look like a great big joke, but it isn't.

The way we operate, crazy as it might seem, is the only way that we could have broken into this business and made it work. This is a brand-new industry, a new way of buying and selling. We're writing the rules for everybody in it even though we don't seem to have any."

She pushed his head back and stared deeply into his eyes. "You mean it, too, don't you, Al?" she asked. "But doesn't it all make you feel unsure of yourself, unsure of what you're doing? How do you know what you're doing is right?"

He cupped her chin in his hand. "The answers to that are that, yes, I'm very unsure of myself and, yes, baby, I am unsure of what I'm doing. Okay?"

Slowly she responded with an uncertain smile. "Okay," she said simply.

From that moment on, she became his protector, his combination wife and mother and his home line of support. She spoiled him and became a willing accessory to every one of his *shtik*. The more dramatically successful he became, the less certain he was of himself. As a result, the more the business thrived, the more he needed her. It was all in an inverse ratio to what it should have been. Without wanting to admit it to herself, Ruthie knew that she had not only married Al Miller but his business, his boys, his monumental insecurities and all the insanity that these entailed.

They learned so many things about each other rather quickly, were dismayed and then delighted with their differences.

She came from a Philadelphia family, her father having had a small pharmacy in a congested area. So she was oriented from childhood along the most practical lines, always concerned with the minutiae of income and outgo. Al, of course, was just the opposite. Chaim had never known to save a dollar and his son had inherited that trait. But Ruthie was determined, especially in the face of her husband's highly unorthodox business practices, to make certain that they saved as much as possible, after setting aside enough to live comfortably. And they did, too.

She wanted five children. Al wanted her to have whatever she wanted. They wound up with three daughters, all replicas of her. None of them, even in maturity, displayed any of the more controversial characteristics of their father. For which he thanked God. And so did Ruthie.

She loved taking care of her home, cooking, raising children, satisfying all of Al's needs. Later, when they were wealthier than either of them had ever dreamed they would be, she developed an expensive taste for antique furniture and antique jewelry. Al, on the other hand, liked to read. He had never gone beyond high school, but he was as well read as most college graduates. He loved to read history of all periods. But he thought buying and collecting first editions was a silly, fruitless and vain practice. When Ruthie suggested that he start, he complained, "What the hell do I care about bindings? It's what's in the book that's important." In a way, it reflected his own selling philosophy.

Ruthie loved gourmet food. Al hated it. His idea of fine food was a good rare steak, fish of all kinds simply prepared and all sorts of delicatessens. When she was able to force him to eat out at a fine restaurant, he was annoyed by all the supercilious service. He was unhappy with all the fancy sauces and sophisticated names for vegetables and soups and was rude to waiters and especially to headwaiters.

He loved good music. She disliked it. She preferred jazz, then swing, then rock, then country rock, progressing from one phase to another with the same sort of consistent enjoyment in the rhythm and in dancing to it. Al loved opera and show music, reflecting his father's tastes, and he never changed.

Their physical enjoyment in each other was another surprise. They had, after all, only known each other for six months before they had gotten married. They had not in that period reached the ultimate in their physical relationship until that early morning in the Miami hotel. So the risk of incompatibility had certainly existed. But the result was amazing to both of them. Almost every night for the first year they had clamped themselves to each other like two sexy barnacles. It cooled down, of course, later, but not much. Their intercourse had a complex pattern, ranging from a maternal reaction to him to participating in various near extremes of erotic enjoyment. The result was that for many years they eagerly looked forward to going to bed together.

One night after a climax he reminded her of her behavior when they had awakened at noon in the hotel in Miami. "Baby, I didn't know what to think when I saw you somersaulting all over the floor, bare-assed, with your gorgeous bosom flying all around."

She began giggling and couldn't stop. "I remember, how I remember," she said. "I guess I was just so happy that I had to show it some way. It was an instinctive reaction. I wanted you to enjoy it, too. I certainly wasn't afraid of what you would think."

"Afraid? I loved it—once I figured out what the hell was going on."

"Want me to try it again?"

"Sure. This time, I'm going to try it with you."

They did, Al not especially successfully, and wound up waking their first child sleeping in the next room. Softly soothing her in her crib, both of them perspiring nakedly, flank to flank, they stared into each other's eyes and made a number of deathless promises.

And so they learned more and more about each other. Over the years Ruthie became the buffer, willingly and often effectively, between Al's naïveté and neuroses and the cruelty and hypocrisy of the world as it was. In his own way, she often thought, he was trying to change the world, a foolish, fruitless endeavor. But by making him happy, by trying to understand him, by catering to his every whim, she could help him in his efforts and hope that she could wipe away some of his pains.

And in the process she remained a very happy woman—that is, until Al got big enough to hire Molly Bradley, the narcissistic fashion coordinator.

The way Molly Bradley came to work for Al Miller was one of the stranger things in what was already a strange corporate record. Her eventual relationship with him was stranger still. No one, except perhaps the big-hatted Molly herself, could have predicted how it would evolve.

After the initial, startling success of the big new Manhattan store, Al began opening branch stores on the order of one every three months with Wallenstein's help and secret, nefarious activities in real estate. After there were already four stores in the chain, with at least that many others charted for imminent opening, Al realized that one thing he lacked was a fashion image—a sort of fashion thrust that would give his stores a certain amount of acceptance with women. He was not foolish enough to think that he could ever compete with Bonwit Teller, Saks or Lord & Taylor, but it was obvious that his stores were entering the big time and they required some fashion authority and guidance in their buying, display and promotion.

He no sooner came to this realization than Zelda began telling him in indignant and puzzled terms about some dame with a big hat who kept coming every day to see him. When she was told as per the routine that Mr. Miller wouldn't be in that day, she hoarsely informed Zelda that she would not be put off by "that kind of crap" but would return every day for a year if that is what it would take to see Al Miller. After hearing about this from Zelda several days running, Al's curiosity overcame his natural instincts and he told Zelda, "Look, you interview her and find out what's bugging her. But don't make any dates for me to see her."

The day after, when he called Zelda, she was waiting for him with the information. Waiting was not quite the word. She literally came through the telephone, her tone harassed, desperate and angry. "She wants a job with you!" she yelled. "She won't take no for an answer, Mr. Miller. She . . ." Then, after a brief sound of tussling, changing of hands, in which the ear and mouth elements reverberated, a new voice came on. It was brassy, breathless, commanding and demanding. "Now just a minute, miss. Hold your water. Mr. Miller? This is Molly Bradley speaking. I must see you. At this very moment. Where are you now?"

It was about three-thirty in the afternoon and Al was not about to tell anyone, least of all a ball-breaking dame like this one, where he was. Actually, he had been sitting in the twelfth-row aisle seat in a shabby movie house rather generously called the Globe, in lower Manhattan, watching a rather bad movie, *City of Conquest,* starring one of his favorites, Jimmy Cagney. He had seen it several times before and liked Cagney's performance while realizing that the movie was a stinker. But he didn't watch movies because he was a critic. He was just an "enjoyer."

He hung up without replying to the pushy Miss Bradley. She had prevented him from asking Zelda what else was going on. The place could be just falling apart for all he knew, and, in a mild way, he resented this Bradley dame for preventing him from obtaining his daily information. But, he decided, it could wait. He left the telephone booth in the Globe's lobby and returned to the movie.

Several days later he came into the office the back way, wandered around talking to the boys, trying to shrug off a strange feeling that he was being followed. This was not an unusual reaction since a good part of his existence was spent with this stone sitting on his back. People *were* after him. Suppliers *were* trying to entice him. Factors eagerly sought his business. His success and its augury for even greater, perhaps fantastic success were like a magnet. Everyone was beginning to want to touch him so that some of the success aura might stick to their fingers.

But this time, it was not just a suspicion. He was being followed. As he sat at a desk to make some phone calls in one office that was temporarily empty, he was startled to look up and see a tall blonde with a big hat come in, look hard at him, smile triumphantly and close the door.

"Aha," she said. "This could be called bearding the lion in his den. But I don't see any beard and I see no lion. But you look like quite a tiger! Whew!" She looked, however, as though she were ready to pounce on him.

She was really tall, about six feet of sinewy, curvy length, her larger parts uncoiling every few seconds in a sort of restless motion. She exuded tremendous sexual and nervous energy even while standing still. "Molly, Molly Bradley," she announced. "Your new fashion coordinator."

"Look, Miss Bradley, you're not my new fashion coordinator or anything else, and who the hell do you think you are barging in on me, harassing me, getting my switchboard operator all shook up—"

"Now you look, Buster," she said threateningly but with a dazzling smile. She sat down on the corner of his desk. "Do you want to be a successful little *shnook* discounter all your life—or do you want to make Macy's, Gimbels and Ohrbach's feel like crawling into a hole? You're just at the stage where you have to decide that. I think you've got everything going for you to hit the top, but you'll never do it unless you make the millions of dames who spend most of the dollars in this country aware that you have something that they want. I hate to tell you this, Buster, but you have an inordinate number of men among your customers, and that's a bad sign and a symptom of your limitations. What are you running, a bunch of hardware stores?"

Besides her sex quotient, she had a brusque charm that was easy to like. She was probably the kind of dame who could work equally well with men and women. And she must be hell's fire with the suppliers, he thought. Al said, "How did you know that we were thinking of adding a fashion coordinator? You got a spy around here?"

"I didn't," she said. "I just decided that you needed one. And that you should have the best in the business. Me, Buster."

She had been with them all, she explained. You name it, she had been there. She could supply a list of references an arm long, but you didn't have to believe the bad ones. You always make enemies if you really do a forthright job. He knew that better than she did, she insisted. But she was fed up with the traditional retailers—"They're so silly old-fashioned and afraid to break the mold that all they do is follow each other like a bunch of sheep, blind ones at that." She was intrigued with the discounters. They were trying something new, she said, or at least different. "I've been shopping your stores," she told him, shifting haunches on his desk, displaying quite an expanse of thigh for him and smiling about it. "You've got something—there's enough different in your stores that I think you're the guy for me. I could do a lot for you that would put you over with the dames—"

She was exciting him. She was obviously both experienced and creative and that, as Pop had said, was what he needed. She was exciting in other ways, too, even though she was no longer a youngster and there were some signs that she was beginning to fade. But that was part of her charm. He could see her value to the company growing because she had been with them all and she had learned a great deal. He would give her great latitude, once she understood that Al Miller's company never did the going thing but started things going.

"You're hired, Miss Bradley. Is twenty-five thousand okay?"

Her delight was fantastic for what it did to her face, her coiling body and the energy of her limbs. She threw herself at him across the desk, but he held her off, pleasantly conscious that he liked the soft-tense feel of her, her perfume and the knowing depths of her eyes. She would be a tough one to handle.

"I gotta warn you of one thing, Molly. You'll be working with a bunch of kooks, executives who seem to do everything wrong but actually make it all come out right. Our lines of command are practically nonexistent. You see, I don't even have an office. I never give any orders. I never have a review of budgets or performances ..."

He was startled at what he read as sheer love, perhaps sudden infatuation, in her eyes. "Why do you think I came to you, Al Miller? You may not know it but you've cut to the heart of what's wrong with retailing. You've thrown out red tape, pomposity, bureaucratic inertia, excessive cost, and a hell of a lot of crappy stuff—"

"Maybe," he told her, "but I have a feeling we make a lot of mistakes."

Now she stared hard at him, wondering if she should say it now or later. But she decided on now. "I've got to warn you of one thing, too, Al. I've got a theory about performance. You have to understand exactly what it is that you're selling to the public. I have to sample everything. How can I do a good job on the public unless I try it first, wear it, taste it, and every other thing that I can do, so that I *am* the consumer, I *am* the ultimate user? That allows me to pretest everything before we put our money into a campaign that shouldn't be ill-conceived. Make sense?"

"Makes sense." He hesitated a moment before underlining it. "How far can you go in something like that?"

"All the way, Buster, all the way."

That should have warned him, because there was more in those words than an attempt at idle prophecy. But it got right by him and he was to recall his naïveté, with no great sense of displeasure, incidentally, a bit later.

Several weeks after Molly was put on the payroll, Zelda, who was one of the few people who refused to accept Molly, told him in one of their phone exchanges that the willowy blonde was anxious to talk to him. He got Molly back on the phone and she asked him to meet her for a drink not far from the office in the late afternoon.

They met, drank a few martinis for about a half hour and then she asked him to come back to her apartment, less than a mile away. "I have something important," she said, "that I want you to see."

Al shrugged but agreed. He suspected that there were some fashion sketches she had been working on at home that she was anxious to show him. Her apartment was in an older Park Avenue building, four large rooms tasteful if *avant-garde*, with abstract paintings, some wildly modern sculptures and harshly Danish furniture. "Sit," she told him, gesturing at a sofa. "I'll be back in a few moments."

Five minutes later, he heard her call him. Her voice seemed to come from a bedroom and the first hints of suspicion began scratching at his innocence. "Al, are you deaf? Come on into the bedroom," he heard her say. Slowly, he went to the door and opened it. At first he didn't see what he should have. It was a lavish room, furnished in completely reverse taste to the living and dining rooms, with heavy draperies, ornate, traditional bureaus, a heavy, multicolored Oriental rug and a vast bed with an intricately scrolled headboard. And on the bed, smiling a remarkable welcome, lay Molly Bradley. She was completely naked.

He stood in the doorway in a pantomime of shock. Her nudity was completely incongruous, totally unexpected, and, he realized wildly, absolutely beautiful. She seemed to occupy the entire bed longitudinally, so extended was she with her six-foot length spread on a silky satin comforter.

"This was the important thing that I wanted to show you," she said as she ran her long arms slowly down each side of her body. He stared at her speechlessly, his heart pounding and trying awfully hard not to think of his wife.

Molly sat up in bed. "Now," she said softly, "take off your clothes."

He came over, staring at her, trying hard not to let his eyes betray him by looking for details, and said, "What the hell is all this about? Is this one of the things that you meant that you could do for me?"

She was gracefully up in an instant, fumbling with his tie and jacket. "Not really," she explained with an absolutely Mona Lisa smile. "It's the other thing. I told you that part of my pitch in merchandising and selling is to sample everything first. Remember? So since I am basically selling Al Miller to the public, I think I really ought to sample him first so that I know what it is that I'm supposed to be pushing. Call it a kind of test marketing. It's all right with you, isn't it?"

By that time she almost had his pants off, since she had been working at him while talking, and he was too far gone to stop. A few moments later as they coupled on the satin comforter, he consoled himself desperately with the unuttered but screamed exhortation: *Forgive me, Ruthie, it's all for the business.*

He was to repeat that exhortation to himself many times afterward because the personal test-marketing program continued for quite a long time. Molly's appetite was insatiable and, as he learned, her enthusiasm in her "work" knew few bounds or inhibitions.

Ruthie, knowing Al quite well by now, found out all about it, of course. Besides all his other hangups, odd activities and exhibitions of withdrawal and reluctance, his sense of guilt was obvious the first evening he returned from Molly. His wife immediately sensed that something had gone over the edge and in a matter of a few days figured out what was going on.

For a week or two she was literally staggered at Al's weakness. But aside from the hangdog look in his eye, he was no different or less considerate than he had ever been, and she began to see it all in a somewhat different light. Soon, while at the same time kicking herself because she was giving in, she decided that it wasn't quite what she had thought. She began to accept it for the great but perhaps understandable extreme that it was— another example of Al's vast naïveté and impossible involvement with his work. It was surely this, she convinced herself, rather than anything that directly pulled away from their own personal relationship. She would never forgive him, of course, but she decided to let it run its course, at least for a while, even though, no matter how she rationalized the foibles of her oddball husband, she was hurt by it all.

For Al, it was a time of immense indecision and insecurity beyond any that he had known before. In addition to his self-doubts about his way of doing business and the uncontrollable ramifications that this caused within his rapidly growing organization, he was bobbing on a sea of sex that was turbulent and threatened to swamp him. The feeling of being followed, not so much literally as by the shadowy presence of dark forces, constantly hovered over him.

When he entwined with Molly and pressed against her possessive sinews, submitting to her monologues and then participated with her in bed interviews on fashion merchandising, he prayed to Ruthie to forgive the exigencies of his career. Liar, liar, he yelled silently to himself as he twisted with Molly on the satin bed. The conflict, sad to say, never left him impotent while it carved its psychic scars.

With Ruthie at night, he lay close to her and smothered a vast self-hate. Would the gathering forces catch up with him? Fast as he was, he couldn't possibly run that fast. And when he told Ruthie at least a thousand times before he gave up Molly as a bed partner that she, Ruthie, was the best thing that had ever happened to him, he was overwhelmed by fear that someday she, too, would catch up with him. She would give him up and he would be shattered. What would then be left for him?

But, during all that time, it appeared that Al's business could only prosper. The sales curve ascended without any dips, his new stores opened at an unprecedented rate and his repute as a great businessman never blinked. Even his net profit grew in spite of him.

So what could be so wrong?

5

The Enigma Makes Good

"SOLLY, SO WHY IS IT SO SLOPPY by the wrapping counters? How can we show we're so neat and clean like Macy's if you don't pay attention? Get a coupla boys over there and make them bend their knees a little it shouldn't be so *schmutzig*. . . . So, Harry, when will we have delivery on those half-price chemises? When the style changes altogether maybe? By then, even S. Klein won't want them for nothing. . . . Mottel, what's with our commercials on CBS? The guy sounds like he's not only got a harelip but he's got asthma, too. All we want is that he should give the people the message, not also humph and pumph and charroo! . . . So, Charley, what happened to that cute sales girl in handbags with the nice smile with the teeth and the pointy little boobs? Our sales in handbags dropped twenty percent since she got moved to costume jewelry. Why did you move her? The customers ate her up. It's hurting, so bring her back with a raise, you hear, kid? . . . Ernie, a big-mouth cutter I ran into yesterday says our payments are two weeks behind. Why? What kinda frigged-up accounts-payable system we got? You know we need every vendor we got—everybody's trying to steal them. Get on it please right away and get all the accounts up to date. . . . So, Natie . . ."

Day after day, night after night, Al Miller stalked his stores in the mid-1950s in an unceasing trek of the fifteen units dispersed across five states. Gently, with a half-rueful, half-apologetic smile, he pursued all the boys, the old ones as well as the new ones who had returned, scolding but not wanting to, his language slipping naturally into a Brooklynese-Jewish patois that everyone understood best.

Other than that, he kept to himself, a relentless, dashing, head-in-the-clouds wraith whose brain was patently so full of ideas that he often failed to say hello to people he knew on the street and walked forgetfully through the dangerous traffic of Fifth, Sixth and Seventh avenues. The great momentum he had launched only six or seven years ago should not be interrupted, God forbid that, because they were really on their way.

Everyone said so and more about the guy, the multimillionaire who walked around day after day in a cheap tweed jacket, rumpled slacks and open sports shirt. Walked was not always the case; more often he ran. For running became tantamount to succeeding, and in Al Miller's case they were both related and independent functions. Running and succeeding, one and of itself and of them together.

Those years he was as likely to come around a corner in a furious sprint as not. People in mid-Manhattan got used to the sight of him—"Here comes that *meshuggener* Al Miller, that crazy discounter; watch yourself, he'll knock you over!"—but were never reconciled to understanding him. One Seventh Avenue salesman put it, "There's that crazy fox again. Look at him run! Where the hell's he going? He knows something nobody else knows—but who can keep up with the bastard?"

Some tried. Once, anxious to make an appointment in the textile–dry-goods district on 40th Street, Al, running, saw two men station their feet flatly in his path to stop him. They were salesmen probably thinking that they could nail him, even if they had to knock him down. But instead he shot out into the street at a ninety-degree angle in front of the oncoming traffic, almost running into an eight-ton truck, then wove in and out among yelling cab drivers until he could manage a wide curve outflanking the two salesmen. The last they saw of him he was shooting down Broadway, laughing and yelling back at them, "Fuck you dummies!"

That was the on-the-run aspect of Al Miller in 1957. But what was the real one?

If anything, he had become even more of an enigma, more of a recluse, more of a creep, as many of the more envious called him, as his success grew. He found his anonymity in the business much to his liking, so that besides having no secretary, no office, no personal files, no business or credit cards, no title, and never dictating a speech or writing a letter or meeting any outsiders in a formal manner, he also stopped making or receiving telephone calls. His only regular contact remained that single daily call to Zelda, the switchboard operator. He never went to cocktail parties or conventions. He refused to have an expense account or salary. All his income came from a pro-rata share of the profits, and while he received most of them, he also shared them with the growing coterie of his boys. Early in the game, when money was tight, he had passed the hat among them and raised several thousand dollars for inventory. He then gave them notes for a generous share of the profits, so that in time every one of them became millionaires.

In the early sixties when bankers and underwriters prevailed on him to go public, the boys became multimillionaires and his own worth rose to many millions.

Yet, despite his anonymity, his fame spread widely. His seventeen-store chain in 1957, or a decade after he went into business with his three tiny walk-up stores, was known as the Red Oval Discount Stores and accounted for more than $200 million in sales and about $5 million in net profits. The name was really devised as a handle for a clear symbol—a red oval stamped on a completely white surface, with all walls in white on one level. Later, when new top executives convinced him that he no longer needed to describe his stores as discount stores, the name of the chain became "Oval Stores" or, more simply, "Oval's." In something more than a decade the public acceptance of the big mass-selling stores was virtually complete, their origin as a compendium of every discount store, farmer's market and cash-and-carry store ever opened virtually forgotten, so that Oval's came to stand as a shopping landmark as much as Macy's, Altman's, Korvette's, Wanamaker's, Famous-Barr, and The Broadway.

And while he shunned industry meetings and conventions, his success and techniques were on everyone's tongue. Strangely, the fact that he was probably the most unorthodox retailer in the business, perhaps the industry's greatest character, helped to cement his prestige within it. Who hates a reluctant hero? Who can really knock a guy who never shows up anywhere? Besides, everyone was learning from him, beginning to copy him. He was as much admired for disdaining the trappings of his success as for his success itself.

And, as everyone reluctantly admitted, he had accomplished it all not so much by coming up with something that was brand new (what is?) as by creatively pursuing a business philosophy that started centuries ago when the first medieval peddler set up a rickety table outside the walls of the manor. It was to ignore the frills that added costs, to push bargains and sell like mad to make up for the small profits.

Of course, this was not all of it by any means and it was this only partial understanding that irked many who studied Red Oval and Al Miller, the boys and all the merchandise for some real inkling as to just what in hell was going on. But the result was that they could only be frustrated. And all was seemingly chaos in the rabbit-warren suites that Al Miller leased as a corporate headquarters in the shabby old building near Times Square. In the stores themselves, whether it was in Manhattan, Long Island, Westchester, New Jersey, Connecticut or Pennsylvania, it was even more impossible to tell. All that seemed to be evident was merchandise, lots and lots of it, low prices, a crush of customers and jingling cash registers. What was behind it all?

If the question ached for an answer, Al Miller, by keeping it to himself, had simply seized the lead in a discount revolution that was cutting a deep swath around the country. In ten years, discounters had carved out sales of $2 billion, mostly out of the hides of traditional stores. About 2,500 discount-store companies were apparently only the vanguard of what was to come. No one those days, except possibly the customers, had anything good to

say about the discounter. But government and private economists and social demographers were intrigued. Since the American economy stands basically on three pedestals—government
spending, capital spending and consumer spending—it struck
these observers that the discounters were doing something important for the economy. They were keeping it from stagnating.
Why? In most cases, the observers found, a customer who
bought an appliance or television set in a discount store for less
than he could buy the same brand elsewhere usually decided
that he had done so well that he could afford to spend the
savings on other merchandise. It was a kind of newfangled
barter system—swapping dollars saved for goods that might not
otherwise have been bought.

A few of the observers on the campuses were heard now revealing their findings. Up to that point, no one but the customers
had spoken out for the discounter, but now he had friends
among the academicians. Even the sleazier among the low-price
sellers took heart and longingly eyed the example of Al Miller,
who, despite his amazing elusiveness, was fast becoming the
industry's most inarticulate spokesman. If he could make it so
big, drawing the admiration not only of the shoppers but also of
the intellectuals, he was worth emulating, following, tracking
down and pinning down. But there was yet another reason why
both the economists and campus observers found new respect
for the discounter, irritating the traditional-store merchants who
helplessly found themselves watching their new competitor
growing up overnight. After the big, new product binge of the
post-World War II period, when producers had spilled out every
conceivable type of item that had been missing during the war
years, their innovative skills appeared to have dried up. No
American producer had come up for almost a decade with any
new product that had any widespread appeal since the television
set. The customer was now sated with everything that he had
been wanting for years, and nothing that the producers had
offered for some time was capable of getting millions of con-
sumers excited.

Except what the discounters were doing. Lacking new products of mass appeal from the factories, the discounter was at-

tempting to bring the millions of customers in any way—and did. And no one did it better than Al Miller, and just on price alone.

It was obvious to the industry-watchers that he could have gone the other way. A careful customer-watcher, he soon realized that he could never keep the shoppers away from the department stores by price alone since eventually other discounters, and even the department stores, would catch up with his prices.

Starting with his first branch store opened in 1950, he told Harry, Nat, Irving, Solly, Matthew, Molly, and half a dozen others who had recently joined him, "Look, we've got to give the public some extras, some schmalz. I don't just mean discounts or values. The customer today is smart and getting smarter. She's sophisticated or thinks she is. Let's doll up the new store and all the rest that we open. We'll pipe in music, cover the floors with wall-to-wall and develop some of our own lines of merchandise that nobody else will have. It'll all pay for itself. We'll romance the lady and make the man feel that he didn't come to shop in a barn. They'll love us right down to our drawers." He turned to Harry, who was scratching his big, flat scalp doubtfully. "What do you say, Heshy?" he asked him.

Abner shrugged helplessly. What else could he do when he was already in the process of forgetting what Al had proposed? He roused himself, but Al had impatiently turned to the others sitting with him for a fast lunch at the Stage. He didn't need to. Molly, Matthew (Mottel) and Nat Batt were grinning at him. Molly had that sex look in her eyes, something that was disconcertingly happening more and more often. "Love it, lover," she breathed. "Boss, it's good—it'll give us an edge because nobody expects carpets, music, exclusive brands in discount stores."

Matthew said. "Listen, it gives me an idea, too."

Nat pushed in several inches of Matthew's fat with his elbow so he could talk. "Quiet, shit. Didn't I always tell you guys that Al was just a fucking genius?" asked the lying little PR man. "Why not—didn't I teach him everything he knows?"

Perhaps the one element in Al's makeup that put Red Oval across from the outset was that he just wasn't greedy so that, in effect, he was one of the few real discounters of his time. Where many enticed the public with a few rock-bottom prices and then laced into them with the rest at standard and even higher mark-ups, Al didn't. He was willing to operate for as little as a 5 percent markup. Then he varied it by category so that the customer never paid more than a 20 percent markup, or less than half that of the traditional stores. And there was another factor here that Al, in his innocence, favored because he knew that customers remembered. "Boy, do they ever remember," he kept telling the boys. It was that by never levying more than half the profit that his competitors did, he knew that he never had to fear for an unhappy customer. Unhappy over quality and service, maybe; on prices, absolutely never.

This, in fact, was one of the things that really stuck in his competitors' craw: the romance that was heating up between Al Miller and his customers. Based on the crowds that waited outside every morning and the warm, homey spirit when they came in, it seemed quite obvious that there was an important rapport. It was a ridiculous love affair, of course, surely worse than that of Romeo and Juliet, or of Edgar Ravenswood and Lucia Lammermoor, for all the ill-favored crosscurrents that lapped around it. Since when does a store owner love his customers and be loved in return and still make a lot of money? Something, everyone predicted, would have to give.

The next bit, of course, was inevitable. What else could it be but that before long his rivals began pressuring suppliers and wholesalers to cut off Red Oval as an outlet? They also threw court suit after court suit at him for allegedly breaking the fair-trade laws on prices.

One Federal court judge got ulcers merely from repeatedly having to face the tall, lean, noncommunicative retailer who listened bleakly to all the civil antitrust charges, confessed to them and paid his fine. He always left the courtroom on a noble note, his face downcast, his stance contrite but his eyes looking back ablaze with new conviction. How much of that can a self-respecting jurist, resigned to the fact that all men are knaves and fools, really take without breaking? The worst of it was that he no sooner happily saw the innocent leave than Miller would be back in his court the next day to repeat the dreary process, and then walk out once again not like a knave or a fool but like some kind of a knight? It was definitely more than the judge, ordinarily a normal, humane man, could bear, and his stomach walls reflected it.

At the very end, the judge could take it no more, his ulcer sending up shafts of fire through his esophagus. He rose in his chair and yelled hoarsely at Al Miller's retreating back, "Get out, you sonofabitch, get out of my goddamned court! If you ever come under my jurisdiction again, I'll throw the book at you!"

How would you like to have the same defendant in your court twenty-two times in one year?

For Al, it was, needless to say, a dedicated battle. The fair-trade laws were loose, probably unconstitutional and obviously doomed to be stricken from the books. So the fight until that point had to be one of principle, and principles, aside from certain immoral failings, were what Al had.

Every time he lost a suit, every time he was denied a line of goods or a brand of merchandise, he simply turned to another item that he could cut in price, legally or otherwise, until he was stomped on. At which point he then repeated the process. The continuing brouhaha in the courts and in the channels of distribution even became a public issue. It was a battle that Nat Batt (as corporate PR man and intermittently as outside PR counsel since he resigned a dozen times to set up his own shop) kept prominently before the public, for it put the Red Oval stores in a favorable light. Customers would write letters to *The New York Times* praising Al Miller's enlightened business statesmanship and courage in the face of the court suits, for offering the lowest prices to the public. And traditional-store executives squirmed when they read them. By inference, since in most cases they had brought the suits, they were being placed in the uncomfortable role of fighting a public champion.

It seemed, in other words, that no matter what he did, Al Miller came out in the guise of a Don Quixote. But unlike the Spanish knight, he had not one Sancho Panza but more than a dozen.

He had the boys.

Soon, too, the suits dwindled, some of the states killed their statutes and many of the suppliers and distributors came back, hats in their hands. Al's Oval stores, with their symbolic gleaming and reclining red eye, had become too big, too important to be discriminated against. Not only did they now seek out Oval business but the suppliers went all the way. They reduced their own prices in order to attract the large orders that Al Miller could give them.

For a while he doubled the number of stores every year—two by 1950, four by 1951, eight by 1952, and then spaced out the newest stores through the late fifties. Practically all the profits were going back into the business in the form of expenditures for new stores, new stock and the hiring of more people.

In the mid-fifties, Al took a long step. Anxious not only to offer the lowest prices but also merchandise that was unquestionably his own exclusives, he instituted an across-the-board private-brand program that only Red Oval could offer. This ran the gamut through all the hard lines under a brand known as TKE. The public, of course, never knew it, but the letters represented the last three letters in the name of a stray dog known as "Mottke" that Al and the boys had found one day years ago in a Brooklyn alley. For several years they had kept it in food and shelter until it had died in happy old age. The Oval private brand also eventually encompassed all soft goods under a brand known as TRU, which was an abbreviated and inverted reference to "Ruthie." She never quite forgave Al for thinking of Mottke first.

One other point must not be ignored. After for many years holding forth on the practical and legal need to enforce fair trade, many American producers of nationally branded goods found that they desperately needed the discounter. They had pushed production to its capacity to meet the pent-up hunger after the war for new goods and then found that supply was outstripping demand. But the energy and initiative of the discounters such as Al Miller offered a new source of consumption to take up the slack in the factories. And so fair-trade and anti-discounter discrimination began to die.

With this, too, the traditional stores stopped their jeering and started competing. They fought it out on the discounter's own grounds—price. Competition stiffened, price wars crackled daily in the country's newspapers, window signs and price tags were whisked away and replaced by lower-priced ones several times a day. Shoppers ran from one store to another, frequently either next door or just across the street, to keep up with the hourly change in prices. And so the public benefitted and retail business enjoyed a brisk revival.

Who had done it all? Who had become the retailing revolution's most inarticulate, most elusive and most unwilling spokesman, even champion? Who, one might say, indeed?

That, in brief, was the real aspect of Al Miller in the waning fifties.

In the late-late fifties, however, the price wars began to take their toll of Oval's profits. As the old-liners matched the discounters penny for penny, Al, for one, decided it was better to lose money by cutting below costs than to lose customers by not. It was a dangerous thing to do, risky and perhaps stupid. The department stores could go right down the line on prices of television sets, refrigerators, transistor radios and branded toys to make loss leaders of them while picking up the markups on high-profit items. Yet, Al went ahead to lower margins on many items, draining any of the water that had remained in his prices and causing his overall profits to slide.

"What the hell," he told Harry, "the customers expect it of us. Didn't we start the whole thing? So, okay, let's take our markdowns with a smile and see what else we can come up with."

Al was, Harry told him, lucky at that. At least Red Oval was still a privately held company with management not accountable to anyone but itself. If it had been publicly owned it would have been obligated to take fast, remedial steps so that the public shareholders wouldn't start yelling.

Then, about that time, there was the famous case of the Hoffman eight-cup electric coffeemaker. This particular price war remained a permanent part of the annals of the electric housewares industry under the rather odd title of "that seven-day perk." Here were the daily price fluctuations:

(List price, $22.95		Wholesale price, $13.95)				
RED OVAL	$17.95	$15.95	$14.95	$13.95	$12.95	$ 9.95	$ 2.98
MACY'S	19.95	17.95	15.95	14.95	13.95	12.95	-----
A&S	19.45	17.45	15.45	14.45	13.45	12.45	-----
GIMBEL'S	19.95	17.95	15.95	14.95	13.95	12.95	-----
KORVETTE'S	19.25	17.25	15.25	14.25	13.25	12.25	-----

Of course, as the table shows, after the fourth day's offensive, no one made any money on the Hoffman percolator, but no one made less money than Al Miller. He was quite proud of that fact. So, at the suggestion of brilliant Matthew Smiles, the obese young man who had apparently come out of the womb holding a file of hot promotion ideas, he took full-page ads in the *Times*, the *Trib*, the *News*, the *World-Telegram* and the *Post* in which he published the table of prices headed by the blurb "SOMETIMES, WE DON'T MIND LOSING OUR SHIRT SO THAT YOU CAN ENJOY A GOOD CUP OF COFFEE!"

But, as Ernest von Rossem, who always looked as though he had just come back from a viewing of the body, observed, "Those ads may do a lot for our joint egos, Al, but right now they represent good money thrown after bad."

Even that didn't bother Al. He regretted the decline in net income that such practices had brought, but he was happy that he hadn't let his customers down. "Call me a *shmuck* if you want to," he told the boys cheerfully, "but what have we got except customer good will?"

"Nothing else that I can remember," said Harry Abner, who forgot that he couldn't remember anything.

"We need better controls," insisted Ernie von Rossem, the controller, who felt ignored.

"I know," popped up Nat Batt, whose face was fiery red and bursting with uncharacteristic truth.

"What?" everyone but Al asked in chorus.

"We need another whorehouse."

Actually, things weren't so bad, considering that this was all happening during the recession, mild as it was, of 1958. Al's net on sales of $300 million had slipped to under $5 million, which was something under 2 percent earned, or just above average for the discount industry. Some of the dip had come from putting a portion of the profits back into new stores in keeping with Red Oval's unprecedented expansion program. Yet, if the decline from the previous year was Al Miller's first setback, it didn't upset those who had come to regard him as an idealistic eccentric whose zeal had to be such that he couldn't always manage a higher net every year.

Others, particularly competitors, and a few bankers, however, used the decline as a vehicle to criticize him. Even though the firm was still in private rather than public hands, they were happy to see that a businessman so unorthodox that he himself didn't even hold a post or have a title in the company he had founded could occasionally fall flat on his face. It restored their confidence in the traditional order of things.

But it was this maligning of Al Miller, and by indirection, of themselves that set the boys to discussing ways of reversing the earnings downtrend and of slapping back at Al's critics.

Strangely enough, while the talk of combined efforts was aimless, it took Solly Patracelli, the operations head who hadn't talked to Al Miller in five years, to take action. He called the top team together late one afternoon for a discussion on the problem. And since everyone had forgotten to include a conference room on the sprawling two floors that housed Red Oval's main offices, it was decided that the only place large enough to hold a meeting of about fifteen people was in the men's john. After a sign was posted on the door, "Meeting in Progress," to keep out those who would enter for natural rather than business reasons, Molly Bradley was also admitted and participated without any self-consciousness.

Standing by the first urinal, Solly, who had probably the toughest job in the company because as operations vice-president he had to be Al Miller's conscience, rapped on the wall. "Let's pay some attention here so we can lay out some strategy," he said, tugging nervously on his handlebar mustache. From a pocket, he popped several aspirins into his mouth and took a swig of coffee from a paper cup, adding, "I suggest that our procedure should be that every man should speak his piece for five minutes and tell all the rest of us what he proposes to do.

Then, if you all agree, we should then have a general discussion."

He looked wildly around at the assorted bunch, not easily seeing them all since Irving, Nat, Matthew and Harry sat half inside the toilet booths, the only place they could sit, with only their feet emerging. Molly leaned against a radiator in back, staring with fascination at Solly's beefy shoulders. Nat Batt, speaking in a muffled voice within his booth, asked, "Somebody die and leave you boss, Solly?"

Repeating an oft-mentioned phrase of his, Solly replied, "Let's keep our heads around here or we'll all go down the drain. You want to take over the meeting, so get off the seat and do it but let's get something done to help out Al."

Since Nat failed to retort, Solly called out each man's name so that everyone could have his turn. The meeting, which was unprecedented, had some far-reaching effects, involving the following proposals, actions and results:

Irving Waldteufel said that the time was ripe for the company to diversify. According to his top-of-the-head estimates, he had variously warehoused around the city something in the nature of $500,000 worth of surplus products, fixtures and operational needs that the company would not require for several years. As a result, he had an inventory worth at a rough estimate of $1.5 million, which could automatically boost company revenue by $1 million if it could enter the industrial products and services market. Of course, this was an entirely different field from the operation of discount stores, but it could be highly profitable since the goods were purchased at volume-buying rates strictly for internal use and thus could be sold at a large profit. Certainly, suppliers of this type of goods would bitch their heads off when they learned how he was using all the extras he had bought over the years, but by the time their beefs would mean anything, the company's net income could be handsomely increased. Operation of the industrial supply business would be simple and inexpensive: No salesmen, extra warehousemen, trucks or accounting systems would be needed. Customers would be asked to pay cash immediately and pick up the stuff in their own trucks from the company's warehouses. It would all be quick, convenient and effective. A bit reluctantly, the group agreed to Irving's plan. He put it into effect immediately. Its expected profits materialized and were listed on the company's balance sheet as "$1 million in extra, non-recurring income." But, canny Irving that he was, as soon as he started the new venture he also ordered a correspondingly large amount of new twine, stationery, toilet tissue, detergent, wrappings, etc., from the regular suppliers so that his ordinarily high surplus would continue undiminished. The two-way traffic functioned smoothly; the profitable outgoing shipments flowed into one line of trucks while another line of trucks arrived with new, lower-priced replacements. By the time Al Miller learned about it, the anticipated profits were in and Irving Waldteufel was happy to accede to Al's order to cease and desist from the practice. He then resigned himself to his normal pastime as company purchasing agent and robbed the company blind.

Matthew Smiles, the then twenty-five-year old vice-president for promotions who had a fixation about food, proposed ·a plan whereby all restaurants in the twenty stores be closed for food-serving purposes one night a week. On that particular night, their space could be allotted to selling merchandise which normal markdowns had failed to move into customers' hands for longer than six months. Since the dispensation of such dogs was always a problem, he said, they could be sold in the restaurants at 10 percent above cost regardless of markdown structure. All revenue from food-serving facilities need not be lost since automatic food-dispensing machines could be moved into the restaurants and stationed along the walls to service any customers who got hungry while they bought the bargains. Not only would the total effort produce more revenue, Matthew insisted, but restaurant space could thus be used to maximum advantage, particularly by selecting nights for the change in services that weren't the restaurants' busiest. If any charities complained that they were being deprived of their usual share of marked-down merchandise, the company could simply send them a cash contribution. It was agreed to let the obese young thinker carry out his plan. It, too, proved successful, if highly controversial, mainly because of the complex housekeeping problems that resulted. Al learned of it late in its progress when he went up one evening to one of the store's restaurants for a roast beef sandwich. Instead, he wound up staring in amazement at the bargain basement elevated to the main floor. Here, too, he asked for the project's discontinuance, but by then it had contributed all that Matthew Smiles had predicted it would. The only problem was that many customers got so used to the change that they expected it to continue and protested when it didn't. They seemed to like the idea of eating and buying bargains at one and the same time. So Matthew Smiles' project left an unexpected residue of customer frustration. And, while his plan succeeded in swelling the company's coffers, the backlash effect on customers was attributed by the group to Matthew's constant attention to his fat stomach. Otherwise, how would he have thought of the plan in the first place?

Nat Batt, it may be remembered, took advantage of his frequent absences from the firm by moonlighting in a travel agency. Those absences were undetected by his frightened staff because he made his daily escapes from his office by removing a partition of the brick wall behind his desk, after which he skipped out down a fire escape. Now, he proposed to take further advantage of the situation by offering his clients in the large travel agency sizable additional discounts if they purchased all their travel needs in the Red Oval stores. He did this purely on his own without informing the large travel agency and thus avoiding what would surely have been a request for a commission from its owners. The result was a sizable lift in such Oval's departments as luggage, cameras, tobacco, sportswear and cosmetics. After several months of resounding success, this project, too, was shelved by Al Miller, who felt that it discriminated against regular Oval's customers. But the project, like the other one, resulted in unhappiness among those new customers who had participated in the special discounts. They assumed, as customers will, that they should continue to receive the same reductions permanently.

However, the greatest fiasco of turnabout involved a plan offered by Harry Abner and resulted, as might be expected, from his horrible loss of memory, which usually came at the worst possible times. The bald, fear-ridden general merchandise manager, sitting in his booth in the men's john that day, came up with a suggestion that so intrigued the whole group that they immediately approved it, forgetting that it was Harry Abner who had suggested it. It was a simple but devastating proposition that would quickly hike corporate profits by underselling Oval's own prices but in the immediate vicinity of Oval's biggest competitors. The plan involved the purchasing of vast lots of seconds, irregulars and slightly marred merchandise of all types. These would be sold in tentlike stores, named rather appropriately "The Low-Rent Tent," which would be put up near such suburban stores as were operated by Macy's, Gimbels, Abraham & Straus and Bloomingdale's. Since most shopping-center leases gave the major store tenants the option to decide what new types of stores could come into the center, Harry quite cleverly suggested that the chain of tent outlets be opened as free-standing, or isolated, stores, near the center, to avoid interference from the big in-center stores. The tent stores were quickly opened, following a barrage of local high publicity such as banners, posters on telephone poles and clandestine scatterings of notices all over the nearby centers at night. In no case was a tent store located near an Oval's unit, but for months the traditional stores never knew what hit them. Harry's lousy memory eventually caused Oval's considerable headaches. Since the arrangement with many of the largest manufacturers on Seventh Avenue, in the men's-wear market and among the big housewares manufacturers, called for shipments to be made on specific days to Oval's regular warehouses, where they were to be separately grouped and transshipped to the tent stores, Harry forgot to notify the warehouse people on the days when the irregulars and production accidents were to arrive. As a result, the faulty merchandise, which was to be priced considerably lower than Oval's normal, first-quality goods, became mixed in with that merchandise and the upshot was a messy confusion between perfects and irregulars. By the time Harry learned of the mishap, hundreds of customers either had called to complain or had stormed down to the Better Business Bureau and demanded an investigation. This happened not once but several times, Harry's memory having the unfortunate failing of failing often. After some months, the twenty "Low-Rent Tents" were folded and were made to disappear into the night. But, again, while the venture helped the profit situation, it may well have caused as many customers to go to Macy's, Gimbels and A&S and to stay there as not.

Somewhat later, when Al Miller realized what had happened— six or seven independent projects unloosed to help him out of his temporary profit dilemma—he was more than touched. It came to him that there was no friend like a friend, a buddy, a "real *chaver*." And no one had even told him of the meeting in the men's john. Not that he would have come, of course. He never went to meetings of any kind.

The first thing he did, after suffering severe conscience pangs about Solly Patracelli, was to drop into his office, almost giving the big, strapping operations boss a heart attack. Solly had, in Al's prolonged absence, almost come to think of him as a ghost. "Hi, goombah," Al said.

"Hi, shmuckstein," Solly said.

Then, after having greeted each other with the nicknames that they had had in the old days, they relaxed. "Thanks a million for what you did," Al said. "I appreciate it. You're doing a hell of a job, goombah."

"Thanks, Al."

"I hope to see you a lot more often, Solly."

"Great."

They shook hands. But it was another five years before Al and Solly came face to face again.

All that notwithstanding, after thinking it over for some days, Al made it a point to explain to all of the fifteen boys (and Molly) why he felt that such profit-stimulators like those they had generated were wrong in principle.

"Look, remember what I told you about all that we got is customer good will?" he told them. "Well, in each of these things, while they boosted our net, it worked to hurt our customers. We gave our own loyal trade a stiff kick in the ass by offering special discounts, by flooding the market with imperfects, by shutting down our restaurants so they couldn't have our usual cheap hot meal one night a week. Even that crazy Irving's idea of starting an industrial-products business out of our own warehouses caused a temporary shortage of toilet paper, hand soap and paper towels in our stores' washrooms.

"Now, maybe all this is just a lot of minor stuff, but I'll tell you something, boobie, spoiling the customer is what has made us in just about ten years the third largest retailer in the whole metropolitan New York area. And in another five or six years we're gonna be the biggest, with even that great big Macy's at Herald Square standing in our shadow. And we're gonna do it by continuing to spoil the customer."

But it took Nat Batt, the official corporate needler, to really give it to Al. "You know, kid," he told his tall, redheaded boss, "sometimes—in fact most of the times—you give me a pain in the ass with those saintly ideas of yours. So help me, that's why I keep leaving the company every few months and set myself up in my own business. But why I keep coming back, I'll never know, because you never change. Don't you ever feel like puking at yourself?"

Al stared down into the hot eyes of the disgruntled plump little PR man and thought, This guy could well be the best friend I got. Aloud, he said, "Natie, I sure do. Every time I shave in the morning, it's all I can do not to throw up. The only trouble is instead I keep kissing myself in the mirror."

Nat Batt tried to kick Al in the groin, but Molly, coming up the hall at just that very moment, grabbed Nat by the back of his belt and deflected his aim. She had acted instinctively, possibly because she had a vested interest in that portion of Al's anatomy under attack.

Yet, despite all this and the warmth that ran through him over what they had done to help him out of his earnings decline, Al came to an uncomfortable conclusion. In a time that they had considered to be a minor crisis, they had acted both in concert and independently. But no one had held them together and filtered their ideas and proposals through a sieve of mature judgment, in terms of merchandising and especially customer satisfaction. The company was getting so big, and it had such a great potential that the time was coming when it would need a top man in residence. It couldn't be him, of course. He had to be on the run, free, loose and easy, to carry out many new plans he had, but he needed someone to take over while he was away. Someone who had the combination of talents and experience that none of the boys either had naturally or had been able to develop.

But who? And how and when and where?

6

Going Public

It was almost the dawn of the Golden Sixties. On Wall Street, the name of Al Miller inevitably rose again that fine September morning as did the occasional weird sun that threw a pregnant shadow over the New York Stock Exchange, Merrill, Lynch, Pierce, Fenner & Smith and over the bird-spattered statue in front of the Old Sub-Treasury Building.

Both the man and the celestial body had the same uncertain quality that morning. But for the three men huddled in a conference room in one of the Street's most prestigious investment-banking houses, it was not the vagaries of the weather but of the man that crinkled their eyes and mouths. To them, he smelled of money, stock appreciation and growth potential, if they could only figure him out.

"He's quite obviously a kind of genius," said Walter Solomon, the youthful-looking head of the investment-banking house, adding ruefully, "but I can't quite feel the guy or touch him."

The short, burly old man who faced him directly across the oval table cleared his throat impatiently. "We don't have to feel him or touch him or do anything else to him," said General Horace Boatwright, Ret. "Let's just get him the hell down here and find out if he's worth investing twenty-five million dollars in."

"You can't do that," put in the third man calmly. "You'll just scare him off. We don't know that he wants to go public. I've done some legal work for him and his company and I have accumulated a good deal of respect for both of them. But he is personally a very shy man and he doesn't know how to play games. We'll have to make a decision before we get him down here and then either confirm it or drop it depending on how he reacts."

Having said that, Gordon Leon Jones, a lanky, slightly grizzled attorney, leaned back in his chair to regard the others, thinking, These two bankers don't know what they're in for. He'll tie them all up in knots if they think they can predict his behavior.

The stocky, heavy old man, who was head of an insurance company that among other things provided funds to investment bankers, nodded reluctantly. "All right, Gordon, you're the only one who personally knows him, so we'll play it your way. Now, let's see what we already know about him and maybe we can all come to a joint decision."

The trio bent to the piles of records and papers before each of them and for perhaps fifteen minutes all was silent in the room except for Boatwright's heavy breathing and the rustling of sheets, as they tried to absorb all that their offices had accumulated on Red Oval Stores. Gordon Jones had a particularly big pile in front of them, a group of thick legal briefs, but his eyes merely skimmed them, since he knew the Miller situation well. What occupied his mind, however, was a question bigger than whether the investing public would buy the issue of Red Oval Stores. It was whether Al Miller could survive—thrive?—as head of a public company or would he simply die in captivity?

Walter Solomon looked up and stared at the others with a slight smile. "I think I'm beginning to get a glimmer of the whole thing," he said. "It's really a matter of some guys maturing later than others. In Miller's case, I think going public will turn out to be the final step in his process of maturity, so that he'll respond well to the responsibility and the challenges."

Boatwright shifted his bulk resentfully in his chair. But Gordon Jones tried not to reflect the admiration he felt for Solomon's mental process. It was definitely a thinking concept and might well contain the answer to the entire matter. The attorney studied the investment banker, wondering when it was that he had matured. Handsome, well turned out, his dark hair neatly brushed around rather high temples, Solomon in his early forties had a look of a man who had arrived at the top of his profession either despite nepotism or because of it, but, having arrived, he would stay there because he belonged at its pinnacle. Actually, after having graduated from Harvard Business School, he had joined Dickster, Hoppman & Co., the large brokerage and investment bankers, had engaged the attention of its principals, then married one of their daughters and was now a general partner in Dickster, Hoppman, Solomon & Co. His success hadn't all come from his favorable marriage. He had brought considerable new business to the firm and had led its diversification into underwriting and venture-capital placement. He was smooth, intense and usually right on target in his judgments.

Only Horace Boatwright didn't think so at the moment. "Maturity?" he asked. "What in God's name does that have to do with our decision to invest our money in a company that's obviously a one-man business? Either he's already a man—or he isn't. My firm isn't about to take a big stock position in a company that isn't ready to accept the responsibility that goes with public ownership. Are they ready—or do we have to hope they are? It's not actually any different from a military battle. Either you are ready to mount an offensive with men, material and strategy equal to the task, or you're not. If not, you sit tight and hope to God the enemy won't take the offensive. It's just that blamed simple."

His red, choleric face reflected the strain of his self-assurance. Referring to a military campaign came naturally to him. A former career major general in the United States Army, he had accepted retirement to become chairman of the board of one of the largest insurance companies in the country. As a disciplinarian and strategist, he had risen high in the Army hierarchy but had been relegated mostly to high administrative posts in the Pentagon rather than to field commands where he could turn his principles from theory into practice. He had left the armed services with a fine record on paper but with deep frustration, which, unfortunately for him, he could not publicly express because he remained loyal to the military establishment.

This knowledge of his inner feelings by another would have surprised and irritated General Boatwright. But the attorney had taken pains to learn as much about the other two men as he could in order to decide if he wanted to be associated with them either in the discussions or in the proposed first public issue for Red Oval. There was more than a minimum degree of risk in it for him, too. His reputation and his time. And, he told himself, somewhat brutally, more than enough money to try it too. Off the top of his head it could amount to almost $1 million in fees over five years or less for his firm, which meant that one third of it would be his.

"Gentlemen," Jones said, rousing himself, "I suggest that we could accomplish much more if we accept each other's viewpoints as questions to be raised, perhaps of Al Miller himself, rather than as hard positions that each of us lays down, and as points that are posed for discussion, too. After all, we all have the same objective, haven't we? We want to do the right and proper thing by everyone, don't we?"

He leaned back, pleased with the judiciousness of what he had said. His personal style of persuasion was always soft, equally quasi-legalistic and quasi-humanistic, and it went well with his manner and personality. He had a lean-cropped head, with white at the ends of his moderate sideburns and a gaunt, serious look to his thin face, but a casual undergraduate stance to his body and in his walk that he had developed over the years. It was a likely combination that had made him a popular corporation lawyer, easy to take for a wide spectrum of entrepreneurs from the man-eating dynamo to the whimsical, elusive type such as they were now discussing.

As Gordon Jones had expected, both Solomon and the general agreed and the discussion settled down to a trading of ideas and viewpoints that began to prove more fruitful.

Solomon read aloud from a set of balance sheets that his firm and Gordon's had prepared. "There are a few discrepancies between the two of these," he said, "but in the absence of an official breakdown which we can't get until we directly approach the company, I find that the differences are minor. What we have here is an eleven-year old company with sales of about three hundred and forty million and net income of about six point seven million. There are twenty-four stores in seven states, selling a broad base of general merchandise at so-called low-margin prices in direct competition with the leading department stores in the same area. Growth rate on an annual basis has averaged twenty percent, about the best in the entire retail business. Total current assets are about thirty-eight million, consisting mostly of inventory, and current liabilities are about twenty-three million, mostly consisting of accounts payable. Ratio of these is about three and one half to two, which is good for the retail business."

"What are their fixtures, equipment and leaseholds worth?" asked the general. "And what are their expansion plans?"

"Fixtures, equipment and so on have a value of about sixteen point two million," read Solomon. He looked up at Gordon Jones as if for confirmation. "Their expansion program is just about the most aggressive in their field. For a while, they were opening new stores every two months, doubling the number every year. Then, when Miller hit about twenty stores, he slowed down the new-store pace, which was good because his earnings two years ago hit a slump. But last year, when it resumed its climb, he decided that they ought not only to return to the former pace but to exceed it. Over the next five years, they've set plans to double their number of stores to just under fifty."

This was news to the insurance-company executive, his "Hmmph" emerging unconsciously from somewhere in his abdominal area. He glared at the stockbroker and asked, "How in hell can he do that? That's almost six stores a year. How can he locate the right sites and where was he planning to get the funds to open that many stores?"

"Suppose you take those two, Gordon," Solomon said.

"Certainly, Walter. General, you've got to understand first of all that this is an unusual company. By flaunting many of the traditional rules of retailing, Miller and his team—he calls them his 'boys'—have been able to come into the same neighborhoods and markets in which stores such as Macy's and Abraham and Straus have been the dominant retailers for decades and carve out big sales volumes right under their noses. I won't go into much detail on that, except that on store sites Miller has a real-estate man on his staff who has been going around the country for years tying up some of the best potential sites. You see, what he does is to take options on any of them that look promising long before anyone else even hears of them and then he keeps renewing the options. He's got more shopping-center developers running around in circles than any ten likely lessees you ever heard of—but when Red Oval is ready, he's got the best sites for them, having kept them out of circulation until the right moment."

"I see," Boatwright said, not quite assured.

"Now, on the matter of the funds, he has been working with a large number of banks on an individual basis for his long-term debt, while plowing back practically the company's entire profits into the business for working capital and for capital expansion. You see, one of the really admirable things about what Miller has done is that he has developed a core of top executives who have a great *esprit de corps*. In the beginning, when he needed some money for inventory, his 'boys' pitched in and he responded by giving them notes equivalent to profit-sharing. These people, General, are a bunch of old friends from his days as a boy whom he has brought into the company. No one even today is drawing much out of the business, but naturally, when and if the firm goes public, they have a substantial equity that will give them big blocks of stock."

The general leaned forward as if they had reached an important point in their talk. "You didn't quite answer my question about how they would get the funds, Counselor, to open all those stores. Operating profits will hardly be enough, will they, and wouldn't bank credit come hard for such a big appetite for expansion?" he asked.

Gordon sat back, gesturing at Walter Solomon. "General," said the stockbroker, "that's why Jones and I came to you with the idea of helping Red Oval Stores and Mr. Miller to go public. We think the time is right now for him to take this step. A public issue of about twenty-seven million dollars will give him all the funds he needs for new stores for at least the first phase of his new program. In a couple of years or so, if things go well, it would be natural for him to offer another issue to finance the final phase of that expansion program."

Boatwright sat quietly digesting it. After a few minutes he asked Solomon, "Do you think the investors will buy the issue? After all, this kind of man and the fact, as the counselor here points out, that his entire team consists of old neighborhood cronies of his—do you think the public will have the respect for them that it should to buy one million shares of their stock? What I mean to say, gentlemen, isn't this crew kind of slim pickings for the public?"

Solomon nodded in a careful and respectful way. He arose slowly and went to the window overlooking Wall Street and gazed down on it, his back to the general and Jones. There was no question at all in their minds that Boatwright had touched on one of the paramount issues. With his back to them, Solomon's answer, delivered in a rather hoarse, intense tone, surprised them, especially the attorney, who had come to like, even admire, the neat, self-contained stockbroker.

"Will they buy the issue, General? Yes, they'll snap it up," Solomon said. "But, if they had any brains, they wouldn't touch it with a ten-foot pole! You know why, General? It's not because this 'crew is slim pickings,' as you put it. If they've come this far in eleven years as a private company and reached that level of business and income, they're definitely worth investing in. No, what I'm referring to is the plain, unvarnished truth, General Boatwright, that the bulk of the twenty-five million investors in this country are not only stupid and lazy but worse, they're romantics. They don't do their homework and they sit on their hands and allow management to walk away with the company treasury. That's bad enough. But what's worse is that the average family man, the average widow, the average housewife who puts money into stock in this country falls in love with a company, with the guy who runs it, with the company's television commercials and with its products. The result is that they develop a sense of idiotic loyalty, sticking with management through thick and thin regardless of how erratic the stock is or how far it falls. They completely ignore the fact that the only way to make money in the stock market, the only way to beat it is to buy and sell. Selling actually is more important than buying. But no, the investors in this country have an idyllic dream about stocks—that if they hold on to them long enough, they are bound to cash in. General, I'll tell you something, but if you repeat it I'll be drummed out of Wall Street: People who invest long-term in stocks and stay with them would be better off putting their money into a savings bank. They'll do at least as well that way as they will by buying a stock and staying with it permanently. Yes, I know there are examples that show just the reverse, but they are exceptions, few-and-far-between exceptions. Has anyone ever made a study and compared them? I have."

He turned to face them now, his handsome, dark face silhouetted against the skyline of lower Manhattan and the Hudson River. "Now, what's most likely going to happen to Red Oval's stock—that is, if we decide we want to sponsor Mr. Miller and, of course, if he decides to go along so that he can have the funds to become the biggest retailer in America? It will do very well for quite a while and then—" Solomon's arms swept down like twin guillotine blades—"plop. The price-earnings multiple will reach twenty, even thirty, and then a few years later it will be something like five. Why? Because retail stocks, unlike what some people think, are volatile. One dip in the economy and every economist in the country starts publicly decrying the health of consumer buying, because it's such a basic barometer of economic stability. Next thing you know, consumer buying is down and it keeps going down. And there's one thing more about it: Consumer buying declines quickly but it recovers very, very slowly."

He sat down, his face clearly worked up now, but he wasn't quite finished. "But all that is, of course, nothing for us to worry about. We will do very, very well with the issue. General, your company will have a year to two to maybe three years to sit with the millions of dollars you put into Al Miller's stock before its appreciation starts approaching a plateau. Don't ignore the man's highly aggressive expansion plan. The stock ought to be good for a ten- to fifteen-point rise every year, at least one point for each new store. And then, a while before he hits that near-fifty stores, you sell. And we advise our good, big, institutional customers to sell. And Gordon here, he sells. And I, in my anonymous street name, I sell. . . . Have I made myself clear?"

The general replied, "Admirably, Mr. Solomon." He glanced rather strangely at Gordon Jones and then directed his question apparently at the two of them. "Haven't we failed to resolve perhaps the most vital question of all—whether this Al Miller is capable of managing a public company with more than one million shares in the hands of the public?"

"I thought we had covered that point," Gordon said.

Solomon nodded. "You didn't care for my analysis, my thought about the man's finally reaching maturity. But what more do you think we can do to examine that matter? Surely his reaction when we present the proposition of a major issue—"

"Bullshit, sir, bullshit!"

The three words leaped out of the general's mouth with the force of bullets. They stared at him in dismay, not understanding what had stirred him up so suddenly. He was furious, his semi-bald head rigid, his black eyes distended, his mouth tightened to a slit. His short, pudgy fingers gripped the tabletop hard and it seemed for a moment as though he would jump on top of its rich, dark-red surface.

Glaring at Solomon, Boatwright said, "You haven't told me everything about the man by any means, have you?" Then, turning to Jones, he added, "Nor have you, sir. Why, this man Miller is an absolute weirdo—he's a threat to the American free-enterprise system—an oddball that I wouldn't have in a company of mine, either in the military or private sector, if I wanted to value my very life. The fact is, gentlemen, that you two have been holding out on me about this man's strangeness, perhaps even irrationality haven't you? Well, I expected it, you see. I took precautions." He paused for effect and added: "I've had a private detective on him for the past two weeks." Then, after another pause, he said bitterly, "And what we've uncovered, gentlemen, if I may still call you that, is extremely disturbing. I am not sure that this man shouldn't be in a mental hospital."

The general rose now, a stern, pudgy figure on fire with the depth of his convictions and the true nature of his discoveries. He strode around the table and it was his turn to stand before the window, his back to them, staring down into Wall Street. He was plainly outraged, offended and hurt as it had become increasingly clear to him that they would not unveil the secrecies of Al Miller to him.

He turned back to them and there was an odd light in his eyes, a brightness deep in them that held triumph and even vindication. Gordon wondered if the general wasn't finally spitting out his frustration over years and years as a desk-bound brass hat in his behavior as the head of the giant insurer. What punishment, what stern commands, what military discipline was he meting out in the vast glass tower a few blocks away where he held forth? Had he finally been successful in obtaining his field command? Gordon wondered.

"Are you gentlemen aware of the personal habits and the immoralities of this man?" asked Boatwright. He smiled, his thin lips parting reluctantly. "Are you aware that he never comes into his company's office, that he never attends any meetings, that he has a widespread reputation for avoiding decisions and personal confrontations? And these men on his team that you speak of so favorably—are you aware of their backgrounds, their odd, even dishonest behavior, the corruption and skulduggery that permeates the entire top organization that this man has put together? It is unquestionably without a parallel anywhere in American business, gentlemen. What is your reaction to that?"

He withdrew a folded sheet of paper from an inside pocket, glanced at it briefly and then returned it to his pocket. Angrily, he said, "This man has been involved in at least two incidents of immoral behavior, one that is still in process. For almost two years he has been shacking up—yes, shacking up—with a woman who works for him. Yes, this man who has a family, a fine wife and three children. And the liaisons are not clandestine, mind you, because a number of people who work with him know of it. They even laugh and joke of it, as if it were an inside company joke and to be condoned as such."

He glared at them as if daring them to consider it a joke, too.

Then he said, "And the other immoral incident, which I am certain you both know of. The fact that for some years in his first big store he allowed a house of prostitution to function behind the store. Oh, he finally had it closed, but not before he shared in its profits and unquestionably participated in its activities."

The general walked slowly back to his seat, sat down and said, "This is the man that you are proposing we put our money on? Gentlemen, I can only say that I am shocked at your behavior."

Gordon was tempted for a brief, irresponsible moment to laugh. The burly little general, sitting there like a symbol of outraged self-righteousness, was just too much to accept at face value. What had ever happened to barracks-house bawdiness? Were they all such paragons of strictly puritanical behavior in the Pentagon? And then Gordon, who had found that probing personal motivation was vital in his own activity, got the flash again of Boatwright's years of despair in Washington while other, younger, flashier men reaped the medals and the glory. So Boatwright now was acting out a role, a role he had vainly sought for years, but its timing for them was simply terrible.

He heard a stir across the table and glanced over at Walter Solomon. The smooth, dapper stockbroker whose personal steadiness was widely admired was neither smooth nor steady now. He frowned and his well-manicured hand shook as he pointed at the general.

"All right, General, so this guy Miller is an oddball," Solomon said. "So he avoids decisions and skips out on crises. He even cheats on his wife and once he made a deal with a pimp. But let me ask you a question, General. How much do you know about the American businessman? You fellows in the Pentagon really lead a cloistered life. You meet plenty of industrialists, contractors, and so on, as they and you come face to face in the so-called military-industrial complex, but how much do you know of them? I've been meeting them under all sorts of circumstances for over fifteen years and I can tell you that there are few saints among them but plenty of rascals, profligates, thieves, whoremasters, you name it. What makes you think that a successful businessman is any better or any different in his personal behavior than anyone else? Disabuse yourself of the idea. He isn't."

Boatwright's rigidity had eased. The angry color in his face was fading, turning pale, and his eyes were fixed almost hypnotically on Walter Solomon.

"Shall I tell you, General, of some of the big businesmen I know? You would recognize their names immediately. There's one who ditched his first wife for his mistress, then ditched his mistress for another one. There's another who stole his oldest son's sweetheart because he was lonely since his wife died. I don't want to mention the number who have had some racketeering connection or influence some time in their careers. Shall I mention the businessmen who prefer homosexual relationships to normal ones? What about the number of big corporate executives who are put away for fraud, for dipping into the company treasury? I could go on and on, not that I want you to think that all businessmen are typical of what I have described, but many I have mentioned were or are heads of public companies. Most of these people didn't want to be like they are or maybe they did. They're human beings, General, just like you or me, but that doesn't necessarily make them ineffective as businessmen. Most businessmen have a flair for business that creates economic growth and accumulates money, but few of them are saints, General. And I have a suspicion that when you compare Al Miller's qualities with his faults, he's more of a saint than most of them."

Gordon glanced at the general. His eyes had fallen from Walter Solomon's face to a spot on the table where two lines of grain bisected and then wandered away from each other. His pudgy fingers came up to slowly trace the two granular meanderings as if seeing the two disparate viewpoints in them. Solomon kept staring at the general, his frown deepening. In that moment Gordon's admiration for the natty stockbroker had never been greater. The man had simply gone way beyond nepotism into some higher realm of personal fulfillment. If the general was fighting the Pentagon's system of political assignments, what was Solomon fighting—his father-in-law, his wife or the thousand sneers of those who had never made it?

With an audible sliding in his chair, the general lowered his bulk so that it appeared to recede from the fray. He had finally met his enemy in the field, thought Gordon, and had gotten his head pushed in. What could be more devastating to a military type who had been aching for a big battle for years?

"General?" asked Walter Solomon softly.

Boatwright looked up at him with a dull hate.

"Shall we call the man and set a date?"

"Yes, damn you."

Solomon showed no reaction except that his eyes flickered. He glanced at the attorney. "Gordon?"

"Walter?"

"Call him."

They met with Al Miller a week later for lunch in the dining room of the New York Stock Exchange. At 12:45, Solomon, Boatwright and Gordon Jones sat silently at a table facing the door. The discounter was already fifteen minutes late and there was no word on how late he would be. Seeking to dispel the feeling of tension that existed at the table, Gordon said, "He should be here soon. He doesn't know the neighborhood too well. Wall Street is sort of out of his usual orbit."

Boatwright cleared his throat without much comfort. "Did you tell him what the purpose of our meeting was?"

"Yes, General. I spoke to him about it in detail."

"What was his reaction?" asked Walter Solomon.

"He didn't have any."

The three saw him simultaneously. A tall, thin man with closely cropped red hair came to the dining-room entrance, looked in briefly and walked away. A few moments later he was back. He spoke hesitantly to the headwaiter, who nodded deferentially toward their table and ushered him over. As they threaded their way through the close, crowded room, the three at the table stared at one another with some surprise. Miller wore a dark-brown corduroy jacket, tan slacks and a black sport shirt with open collar. He also wore white sneakers.

All three rose a bit shaken to meet him. Gordon did the introductions and the headwaiter, who was trying hard not to sniff audibly at Al's attire, seated him. There was an awkward interval as they sat and contemplated Al Miller. Once again Gordon rose to the occasion. "I dropped in on your new store in Westchester this past weekend, Al," he said. "It's a beauty. Is that the first of your Red Oval Villages? The store was very crowded."

Al smiled with obvious pleasure. "Yeah, it is the first of our new Village concept. I must have been there the same day you were. Was it last Saturday? Right. I never saw a better turnout for any new store that we opened. The customers seemed to act like they belonged there."

Solomon grinned. "That's an unusual way to look at it. I know a few merchants personally. All they seem to be doing is listening—listening to the sound of the cash registers. How do you mean that the customers acted like they belonged there?"

Al relaxed, popping a small roll into his mouth while they waited for their drinks. He was on home ground now and there was no stopping him. "What I mean is that it's really easy to tell if the crowds act like strangers or friends," he said. "If the people walk around or stand in the aisles and look, it means you got troubles. There's a barrier—a feeling that they're in a strange place or out of place. But it's not when they move from the main aisles into the departments, when you see them opening up the garments to see the linings, the labels, if they stick their hands in the pockets, or if they go over to a small TV portable and turn it up or flick over the stations. If you see a woman holding a dress up in the mirror against herself and then call her husband over and there's a kind of excited, happy thing in her voice. You watch their faces, too. Stores are supposed to be exciting, in a way, like the theater or movies. What the hell are you really doing by asking people to shop except to take some of their time away from things that they'd rather be doing and spend it in your store? And how the hell do you do this? You make the merchandise exciting in fashion, price, color, feel, workmanship and in utility. You make the store have a warm feeling by using warm or bright colors, occasionally using pastels so it won't jar on them. You work your backside off getting the sales people to act at least friendly and anxious to serve them. You give them plenty of free space to park, give them the little amenities, which, in my book, means a few food vendors outside, soft-drink and coffee machines, so the kids don't *nooge* them too much. You—"

Boatwright broke in. "Tell me, young man, what do you mean by Red Oval Villages?"

Al took in the burly little man with the gray hairbrush mustache and felt his instincts jangle. He thought, I bet sooner or later this prick is gonna tell me he personally hates shopping and doesn't know why everybody doesn't. Aloud, Al explained, "It's like an integrated, one-stop shopping center, where the public can buy everything it needs all in one place. It includes a department store, a supermarket, a carpet and furniture center, an auto service and accessory center and a bunch of service units. All of them carry the Red Oval name, but some of the smaller stores and departments are leased out."

Al accepted his drink from the waiter, raised it slightly in a silent toast, and glanced over the rim of the glass at the others as he drank. Solomon's eyes were shining and his face had that rounded look of pleasure, even enthusiasm. Gordon's gaunt face was composed and happy. They understood him, he thought, but the short old man frowned and looked angrily into the contents of his glass.

"You know, young man," Boatwright began, "I personally hate shopping and I don't know what it is that brings millions of people out every day to crowd into all the stores. Far as I'm concerned, you can do it all out of a catalogue."

The others laughed, but Al replied, "General Boatwright, we've never gone into the catalogue or direct-mail business because that's not really the retail business. I like to see my customers in action because then I know what they want and what I should do. Even Sears, Roebuck and Ward's don't do all their business from the catalogue. The stuff they sell in those books just reflects what they sell in their stores."

They ate silently for a while. Gordon studied Al, realizing that they had better get down to the serious point of the meeting because he had a feeling that Al had a low patience point. But he was surprised again at Miller's loquaciousness. Hell, he thought, the guy's not really all shy, despite his reputation. He's probably just shy about everything but the retail business.

"Walter," Gordon said, "I wonder if we shouldn't really be getting down to business here?"

Solomon nodded. "Right as hell, Gordon. Al, Gordon's already told you about our proposition. We think that your company is just about ready to go public and that there ought to be a good market for your stock. The revenue will come to a gross of about twenty-seven million dollars, which should be sufficient to provide funds for the first phase of your new expansion program. It would also establish an equity for your own ownership and the share in the business that you've given your colleagues. I don't have to go into all the benefits of public ownership, I think. Of course, you would have certain responsibilities, too. For the first time, you would have to answer to a board of directors, who in turn would have to answer to the shareholders. But being a public company would open up doors to you that you don't have now. . . . What do you think?"

Al popped another small roll into his mouth, nodding his head as he chewed. He then speared a large chunk of filet mignon into his mouth and kept nodding with full, distended cheeks. Boatwright stared at him in disgust. Then Al finally cleared his mouth enough to answer audibly, "Yeah, Walter, I think the time is ripe for it. It would certainly make life easier for us and help us build for the future." Boatwright stirred with resentment, causing all of them to regard him with surprise.

"I'm glad to hear that you are interested, young man," the general said, "but I would like to ask you a few questions, if I may."

Al was in a good mood now. He threw a mock salute at Boatwright and said, "Fire away, *mon général*." The drink and the good food warmed him and he felt in good company, at least in regard to Solomon and Jones.

"First, I want to say that ordinarily as chairman of the board I don't personally get involved in investments our company is considering, even if they are as large as the big block that we would contemplate in the case of your issue," Boatwright said. "However, because of the unusualness of the situation on top of the large size of our contemplated investment, I have personally involved myself."

Al continued to nod and masticate but not as perceptibly as the general resumed. "The big question, or questions, on my mind frankly involves the matter of the management of your company. First, your top executives. Now, I think you will admit that they are mostly an unusual group, given to full rein in expressing their idiosyncrasies. In fact, I might say that most of their habits personally disturb me and make me wonder how they would function under a public ownership."

Staring at the searching glare coming from Boatwright, Al stopped eating and said slowly, "They're unusual all right, General, but I think they're goddam good. Maybe not by everyone's standards, but everyone's standards aren't running our business. We can't run our business by the way someone else thinks, can we? Of course not. So let's take Heshy—that's Harry Abner, our general merchandise manager. He's been with me from the beginning, a guy who knows more about buying and selling goods than anyone I ever met, outside of myself. He's got a lousy memory which sometimes gets in the way, but in his own way he's very effective. Take Irving, Irving Waldteufel, the greediest, most dishonest purchasing agent in the country, but he can get more supplies and equipment than any two other guys I know. And, despite a game he plays, he has yet to steal a cent from the company. Take Willie, our real-estate man. A prize, an absolute prize. A *momzer*, too. I won't even go into details on him. He's just a plain fucking genius, General. I pay him more money than anyone else in the place because, frankly, without good real estate, without the right sites, the best store in the world is nothing. Sometimes I think real estate is more important than retailing, but if you got to be a retailer, baby, get yourself a good real-estate man. So now let's take Nat Batt, the most lying, most undependable public-relations man in New York—but the best there is. Again, let's not waste time on details. He's gotten us a better press in the consumer and trade books, on the air and on television than any other company in the business. I hate his goddam guts sometimes, General, because in his business he knows how to stick a knife in. We have fights. Every couple of months he quits and starts his own shop and then five months later he's back. The sonofabitch loves me, he's like a brother. So, all right, let's take Mottel—that's Matthew Smiles, a fat slob of a kid with the brightest promotion mind I ever met. Take Molly Bradley, our fashion coordinator, who can run rings around any store you name. Sure, once in a while I have to give her a feel, a *kvetch*, just to let her know I love her. She's a dame, after all, General, a different kind of being that's ninety-eight point two percent emotion. Then there's Solly Patracelli, a natural-born Mafia type who keeps things moving around the place. Then there's Charley Binns, our hard-goods merchandiser, who got bounced after he spent twenty years with Macy's and can tell us all their secrets, our biggest competitor, because a guy who wants to get even does more than his job. There's Izzy Baum, who handles our soft-goods merchandising. He's quite a guy, General. He used to be a manufacturer on Seventh Avenue, got into trouble with the Internal Revenue, went bankrupt and now helps us tremendously because he knows all the ins and outs of the rag business. We also got—"

He stopped short. The general seemed to be gasping for breath. After a few moments he recovered. "This is the bunch of executives who will manage a company that we want to bring public? They all sound like thieves, demagogues and hoodlums. Walter, I—" Boatwright turned indignantly to the stockbroker, who now sat tensely and with growing concern.

Calmly, Solomon said, "Al, you must explain to the general how you get all these people to work constructively together."

Knowing he shouldn't but doing it anyway, Al said, "I don't do anything to get them all to work together, Walter. I just let each one of them do whatever the hell he wants. And they do it in such a way that it all comes out right in the end. Lemme put it this way—Red Oval is the most successful and most dramatic growth company in the discount and the entire retail business because we made our own rules. You can't judge a phenomenon like ours by usual or routine standards. Every one of my people —and I've named only a few of them—are outstanding in their fields whether their personal habits are bad or not. You just can't take a hard position with people who are temperamental but great talents."

Walter Solomon and Gordon Jones were satisfied, but General Boatwright remained distressed. He said hoarsely, "I won't argue the point with you, Mr. Miller. But I will ask you one thing more. Are you yourself capable of running a public company?"

For the first time Al lost his composure. He had been toying with a dish of peach Melba and suddenly much of it was on his lap. He mopped himself clean and said rather shakily, "General, I can't answer that because I just haven't had the experience of doing it. I think I can—but I also recognize the fact that I need someone else to help me. As a matter of fact, I'm on the lookout for a president who can help me to run things. But so far I haven't found one, although I have an idea about how to get one."

This disclosure appeared to surprise all of them. But of the three, Boatwright most quickly recovered his original, relative poise. Or rather he returned to his characteristic yearning to reach for the jugular. He said, "Mr. Miller, I have been disturbed by certain things I have heard about your personal habits. And in an effort to understand them better, I did a bit of research. Since I still have some friends at the Pentagon, I was able to get hold of your Army service record. And, I might say, I was appalled."

The others were shocked. Gordon half rose in his chair, saying angrily, "Now, damn it, General—"

"Quiet, sir!" the little general barked at Gordon. As he did the other day when he had revealed that he had assigned a private detective to check up on Al Miller, he withdrew a folded sheet from his pocket. Glaring at Al, he said, "You have a most checkered war record, Mr. Miller. You saw combat in the Marshalls and in Bougainville. And you were wounded. You were awarded a Purple Heart medal and you received a Bronze Star. For bravery, wasn't it, but in the rear area rather than in combat? That's strange, isn't it? But what disturbs me is that there were two occasions when you went AWOL. That means you were in the guard house twice, doesn't it, Mr. Miller?"

Hungrily, Al stared at the exit. He hadn't counted on this,

although he had been reluctant to come in the first place. Gordon Jones had made it sound worthwhile, as had the stockbroker. But he didn't dig the general. "I'll tell you, General," Al said hesitantly, "I went AWOL because I hated Army life. When we finally got back to the rear areas after combat, I took off twice for a week at a time. I just wanted to get the Army out of my system. But each time I came back on my own. That's why I got short sentences in the stockade both times."

Boatwright took him in with eyes that were beginning to soften a little. "You haven't really changed, Mr. Miller, have you?" the little general asked.

"No, General," Al replied. "And I never will."

There was a strange expression on the general's face. "How did you win the Bronze Star, young man?"

Al grinned. "I don't really know why the hell you're going back so many years, but I'll tell you. A guy was caught in a truck that crashed. It caught on fire and I pulled him out of the cab. The next day, I went AWOL. They gave me the medal when I was in the stockade."

"I see," said the general. "Yes, I see."

Al laughed. He could see that Boatwright did see—something —but what? "I'll tell you, General, and you won't like it. I hate war and the Army routine like you hate shopping," Al said.

Boatwright glanced at the others and now he was smiling. "I see what you mean, young man. I see indeed." To Walter Solomon, he added, "Walter, I am agreeable—if this young man is. Let us put our money on him—and pray."

A few minutes later, Al got up abruptly and shook hands all around. "I gotta go," he said awkwardly. "I got a date with a store."

He started walking out in a room that was much less crowded. And suddenly he wasn't walking any more. He was running. He padded out of the large imposing room in an easy lope, then in a sprint and disappeared out into the hallway. The three men stared after him in amazement. It was now plain to them that he was only too happy to be rid of them, their questions and their lack of understanding. It was also clear to them why he wore sneakers. He could run faster.

Downstairs, Al dialed a number in a public telephone. "Hello," he said. "Lemme talk to Sam Schulte. Tell him it's Al Miller."

A strong, resonant voice came on. "Al, how are you?"

"Sam, I gotta see you. I want you to help me find someone."

The voice hardly paused. "Sure. Come out to the house any night you want. I live out in Kings Point."

They agreed on a night the following week. Then Al put in a call to Zelda.

7

"Ready, Lover?"

A COUPLE OF DAYS before he met with Sam Schulte, Al was compelled to take stock of himself in one of those periodic, compulsive appraisals that seemed to follow some episode in which he was even more disappointed in himself than usual. More of a lout than a laser beam, or words to that effect, was what he would conclude at such times, shedding at least a single fat teardrop of self-pity to moisten his self-hate.

In the past, the appraisal had come, for example, after an incident with the boys when he had decided that he had made some serious misjudgment. They were totally inadequate for the big task that he had set up for them, the incident convinced him, and his choice of them merely gave them the chance of riding his coattails. Another time it had been just the other way around. He had despaired of the true value of what he was doing and was convinced that in a totally selfish way he had set the course of their lives on a hopeless mission that could only bring them frustration, grief, even ridicule.

At that point, in either case, he would experience a sinking feeling and a simultaneous flash of recognition that he was a natural misfit with some sort of thyroid or brain-cell deficiency. A guy with so many idiosyncrasies and hangups that one would think that he considered them all forgiveable because of his undeniably great qualities. His mood would descend from that in a deadweight fall and it would last sometimes an entire day and throughout a sleepless night.

The new, rather shocking self-appraisal fell upon him, at least in its starting stage, at about eight o'clock that evening as he sat in the lurid living room of a flashy motel on a Maryland highway. He was waiting for Molly Bradley to put the final touches on her face. He had taken the room next door. They were on an overnight trip to one of the Baltimore stores where some new fashion departments were being traded up, and they had decided to see the completion of the changes through the next day.

Molly emerged. He was taking her to dinner and she was obviously looking forward to it. They had spent some time at the store before settling in the motel nearby, but she wasn't tired. Instead, she came at him with a big smile, an exaggerated hip swivel, radiant in a green beaded, tightly fitted, Hong Kong pants suit that Oval's sold in its best departments at prices lower than anyone else. He watched her slow undulating approach, an erect, almost six-foot blonde with fine flesh tints and a stance that was naturally and rather astonishingly provocative. He had never seen a woman quite as lithe and quite as full-bodied in one slim person.

"Ready, lover?" With her pearly smile, bright orange lips, heaving, green-beaded bosom, flaring hips, silver shoes, she was a devastating animal.

He didn't reply, breathing heavily. She returned his stare for a long moment, her smile quickly expanding so that her tongue slid out briefly over perfect white teeth. Suddenly, in an instinctive movement, she began undressing, removing all her clothes. A little pile grew at her feet. On top of it she neatly placed the last item, her silver-buckle shoes. She rose with her big smile as he reached for her and together they glided into the bedroom. It was, however, during those next brief, four steps that he found himself once again in that recurring process of agonizing self-appraisal.

What kind of person—no, all-American heel—is this Al Miller? This tall philandering bastard, sinewy but strapping, red-headed and as handsome as a young rangy tree at almost forty, he was, he knew, a neurotic mess. Inwardly a mass of insecurity, outwardly the idol of perhaps a whole generation or two of both young and middle-aged executives. A success among successes, already a millionaire many times over and the founder of a company about to go public with running annual sales by the proposed new fiscal year of about $500 million. But the sharp ones, those with the finely honed instincts, the heads of insurance companies, some jealous competitors among the discounters and the heads of traditional stores, they all knew: He is headed for disaster. But no one knows it better than he. Who else is as conscious that his immense success is a happy accident? Who knows that so many ideas dart through that lean, red-topped head that most are hardly ideas but only half formed, no more than electronic tentacles of restlessness and nervousness rather than a creative formation of conscious gropings and subconscious phenomena? Who knows him, in other words, as he does? Who would want to?

On the stiff, strange bed, he twisted with the rangy blonde (in his mild form of schizophrenia he can appraise himself cruelly in the midst of ongoing activities) and wrestles with her to see who will wrap one's legs around whom. She wins and then, flip-flop, he wins, and then, flop-flip, she wins. Pleased with her success, she prepares herself, the fine, clearly drawn features of her face softening with the complete easing of the inhibition that she wears like an easily discardable mask. She lowers herself on him, her lips parting with anticipation, and suddenly she has him, big and bursting and prideful, his appraisal of self forgotten, totally forgotten.

He moves painfully, loving, hating her. She moves with him, demanding, not asking, insatiable. A pain envelops them both before it explodes into a non-pain, into a concert of pleasure in which they submerge into each other endlessly, unceasingly, into the jabbing, the pulling, the easing, the slipping, the returning, the welcoming, the inning, the outing, the repeating, the roughing, the smoothing, the paining, the again easing, the reaching, the straining, the bursting, the uncontrolling. The end into a beginning and the beginning into nothingness. The death-life, the heaven-hell, the un-paradise, the wide, unbelieving eyes and the shock of the thunder of truth through the terrible trip-hammer pounding.

Afterward, the agonizing appraisal (not reappraisal because it is a continuance rather than a second look at an original self-opinion), lying there, staring into her eyes. Lovely brown, they smile at him, unashamed, unapologetic, but pleased, pleased. Within him, it is just the reverse. Hate and recrimination, scorn, himself as the big target. Soon, he hopes they will fade out of him, but they grow instead. When will his real worth reach to the heights in which others hold him? The answer is, quite clearly, unclear but nonetheless conclusive.

They sat naked now on opposite edges of the tangled bed, Molly staring boldly with concern at the self-torture that hung out of his eyes.

"Whatsa matter, lover-baby, surprised?" she asked, grinning. He shook his head.

"Don't be," she said. "It's not the first time for me."

His head swung toward her. "Why tell me that?"

"I don't want you to think that you're the only guy I went for all the way."

What could he say? "All right," he said. "So I'm not. What're you trying to prove? That you're an A number-one tramp?"

Her face grew serious. "That's not what I wanted you to think, you dumb bastard," she told him. "I thought if I told you you weren't the first one, you'd get rid of some of that guilt. It's written all across your silly face."

She was right, of course, but he felt more guilty than ever. She was, however, wrong about why. He had decided during that fragmented self-appraisal that he had to break it off with her.

He had been wanting to almost from the minute it had all started with her more than several years before. Like every other man who had ever come across her, he was attracted, even though, at the first meeting, he had behaved as though he wasn't. That soon changed, of course. Molly was complex. He had never been able to figure out how sincere she had been in her excited claim that she had to know him personally to his depths, that in order to sell him she had to sample him first to the fullest. It was obvious to him, of course, that it had been part come-on, but he couldn't discount the fact that in many subtle ways she did express him, his personality, his peculiar drives in her fashion merchandising operations. It was never overt but implicit. Often, he would hear her in passing insist to an associate, "Will it sell? Will the customers enjoy it? Can't we try to think how we could make them happy and cream with high fashions at low prices?" Once, he had barged in on her while she was explaining to a woman copywriter, "Baby, try to understand that Oval's wants to do more than sell a woman a dress or a coat. The Al Miller Collection means that her way of life is what we understand best. Can't you get that concept in your copy? Orgasms are fine, tell her, we approve of it, but don't use those words." She had looked up in that moment and flushed under her fine flesh tint. "Right, Al, isn't that it?" His heart had pounded with gratitude at her sensitivity. The next night they were together, though, he had made love to her in a way that had little to do with corporate *esprit*.

Their liaisons were not frequent but always impromptu. They came, however, fairly regularly, about once in every two or three weeks. When he was with her, Ruthie's face never came between them. But when he was home, he was always dogged by Molly's presence and he hated himself for it. Ruthie knew, of course, not that he had ever said anything. But she had found out for herself, and although she never said anything about it, her patience with him and her love for him were worse than spoken accusations. And so it had been all those months, he realized, the indecisive, elusive Al Miller caught between two very decisive, two very loving women. What it all meant was that he just had to break it off with Molly, having pushed their relationship far beyond any reasonable level of risk and sanity. Something had to give and it could be his home. And maybe his life.

What was she thinking in her corner of the bed, he wondered, her nudity beckoning him and yet repelling him because clasping her at the moment would be a bottomless pit for him.

Aloud, he said, "I wish for God's sake that you'd put some clothes on."

"No, I will not put any clothes on, you sonofabitch," she said. "You can get dressed if you want to, if it softens those little-boy pangs that are just oozing out of your face. I'll tell you what I'm thinking of—why don't you just drop dead?"

He understood, of course. She suspected that he was so troubled that he couldn't respond to her in the way he usually did. He moved over to her side of the bed and ran his hand down her smooth back. The flesh contact did, as might be suspected, have an effect on him. He withdrew a little. "Come on, Molly, you're cold. Let's go out to dinner."

In his car, they sat silently. If she really had suspected what he had in mind, she wouldn't just have been irritated and angry. She would have become hysterical. He had no idea of how he would break the news to her, but somehow that night had to be their last together.

They hit the highway and she relaxed against his shoulder. Something is going on, she thought, but he won't tell me. If she would take things easy, not forcing anything, she realized, he would soon tell her. In the meantime, he seemed to be returning to a closer semblance of himself. He drove very quickly, outdistancing all the other cars but somehow sensing the proximity of a trooper's car. On the way, they passed one of the newest Oval Villages, the massive white building with the reclining red eye gleaming in the moon-wash, the smaller units and service shops in varied pastels lined on either side of it so that it all resembled a new, waiting city. He pulled over into the center's road and drove slowly through it. The stores were just about closing and the crowded parking lot was emptying. Oval's had just completed another successful day, it seemed.

She sensed his satisfaction but could not quite keep the bitterness out of her voice.

"That's it," she said. "That's the real sex in your life, isn't it, baby?"

He stiffened, throwing her a startled glance. "What the hell are you talking about?" he asked.

"Just that, lover. I mean that's what gives you your biggest hard-on, isn't it?"

Now they were out on the highway again. "What's happening to you now?" he asked. Before he had been low, and now it seemed to be her turn.

"You're what's happening to me," she said.

They ate in an attractive roadside restaurant with a three-piece rock group that was just so-so, but the trio's blast and pounding helped to drain away some of the evening's surprising rancor. They lingered over an after-dinner brandy and then another. Molly forgot her vague troubles of the last few hours and told him how happy she had been working with him. Her hand closed over his. "Sure, I hate your guts a lot of the time, but that's personal bitchiness on my part," Molly told him. "I can't have you except when the job brings us together—and then sometimes like tonight you get so distant, so far away from me, that I get scared stiff."

But professionally, it had all been smooth and gratifying to her since she had come with him. Like with the rest of them, he let her have her head and actually, as she told him, he wasn't taking much of a chance because there was still some pretty great stuff in that head. It hadn't been like that everywhere. Not by a long shot. In many companies, especially retailing, there was a constraint among the executives. Things were done by the book generally, while in the fashion end, where she had come up from a model, the creativity quotient that should have been the main criterion of performance was held to be of minor consideration. Not rocking the boat, being a handmaiden to the male executives, or, more precisely, not making them seem dumber than they were, was the primary requirement. And demanded.

But Molly Bradley could never live like that, she assured him. She locked horns, butted heads, made ripples, staged incidents, made confrontations, or, by any other cliché, she fought to break the mold. But instead she had broken herself not once but half a dozen times. At roughly thirty-nine, she had been a store fashion coordinator for about twelve years and she could give you chapter and verse on what it was all about after the ladies' auxiliary, the consumer advisory boards, and the Scarsdale women's luncheon club all went home. The frightened executives, the unknowledgeable, pompous brass that forgot that what the public wanted was more attention, not less, certainly not to be treated like peasants, like clods. But a fashion dame's role, hers at least, exposed her to more because she had to live or die every day on whether she knew what the public wanted. And so her frustration against stupid mid-executives and arrogant, snobbish top executives was greater than most. "The real hell of the problem is that stores have gotten so fat and sassy the last ten years that they really don't give a damn whether the public likes them or not," she said. "The fact is that they're there—on the site—and so the public flocks to them like flies to sticky paper. That's wrong, of course. The discounters like you—especially you—showed them how wrong that was."

Not to be able to buy what you see in the market, not to be able to advertise what you know is right, not to be able to make that bridge with your customers because you know them, they're like you—who the hell needs it? Of course, if you wanted to get involved in a few affairs with the men who countersigned the orders or who shipped the goods, things could be a little different. They could ease up and your frustration would be lessened. Oh, she had done it. Make no mistake about the tussles in the office that wound up as tussles in bed. There had been plenty of them and some had helped. But not enough, not enough to make up for everything else that you lost. You were, in fact, better off to deal at arm's length with the homos, the fairies in the business, of which there were more than a few. They were for the most part some of the more talented ones, they had the color, the feel and the creative guts to do things, and doing things with them was one-dimensional because as far as the man-woman relationship was concerned that was what it was. Maybe in some ways, she said wistfully, it was the best way.

They were getting back into the Cord now and suddenly, impulsively, she grasped his arm and kissed him on the cheek. "Al, I've never been so happy anywhere as I've been with Oval and with you. I've enjoyed my work from the first minute—and I think I've been able to pull my own weight, haven't I, lover?"

Turning to her, he was surprised to see that her cheeks were wet and that fat tears hung in her eyes. "What the hell," he told her roughly, "you've been great. You know that. I've told you so, so what is all this?"

She sat quietly beside him in the car as he got back on the highway. He was shaken by her emotion and the insight that this gave him about her work in the company. Her relationship with him was something else again, and his throat tightened as he realized that breaking away would now be even harder.

Back at the motel, they sat for a few moments in her room chatting or just sitting there when he glanced at his watch and saw it was a few minutes past midnight. He yawned. "I think we ought to hit the sack, Molly. Tomorrow looks like a busy day."

She nodded brightly. "Warm my bed tonight, lover?" It was a routine question that was to have a routine, affirmative answer. But Al, knowing what he did, couldn't bring himself to take advantage of her. "No—no," he said, "I'm kind of bushed, baby. I'll see you in the morning."

She stared at him with surprise and he knew she could see right through him. "What is it, Al?" she asked. He could see her pulse visibly pounding in her throat.

He started moving toward the door that separated their two rooms, not trusting himself to answer her. But he didn't get very far before she was at his back, her arms clasping him around the chest, and he could feel her body trembling against him. She almost knew, or sensed, but the not really knowing had sent a storm of fear through her.

"Al, goddamit, answer me! What is it?"

Her breath was rough in his ear and he could feel her heart pounding in her breast. He had let it suddenly go too far in the last few moments not to tell her. He turned and faced her. "Listen, baby, you've got to understand. I have to break it off between us. I just can't live this double life any more. I can't do it to Ruthie or to you and I got the world on my back all the time—"

"Al, you can't!" she cried. "No, not now, give me a chance to get used to the idea—"

He shook his head. "No, that would be even more painful for both of us. This is it, Molly, don't you see? Where the hell were we both heading, did you ever ask yourself?"

"I don't give a damn about that. Please, not tonight!"

He shook his head once more, avoided her desperate reach and opened the connecting door and closed it on her.

In the other room, she tried to open the door. He locked it from his side. Then he leaned close to it and said, "Go to sleep, Molly, and stop acting so hysterical. Cutting it off clean is the only way."

He started getting undressed, but she kept scrabbling at the door from the other side while maintaining a running diatribe against him: "You rotten bastard. Why are you suddenly doing this? Is it because you're going public and some fucking banker told you to drop your whore? That's what it is, isn't it, you bastard? Is there some other dame—I'll kick her ass in. Open the door, Al—tell me you'll wait—"

"No!" he yelled back at her. "Now, shut up. If you want, we can talk it over in the morning."

"I don't ever want to talk to you—about that or anything, you sonofabitch!" she shouted back. "Who the hell do you think you are—the biggest cock in the world? You can't throw me over like that—I won't stand for it, not even from you."

He went into the bathroom and washed up, the water drowning out her shouting. When he came out, she was still in good voice but her comments were less frequent. They seemed to be coming from a low point on the other side of the door. She had evidently slipped to the floor and lay there against the door, yelling imprecations and entreaties at him.

"Big-headed bastard, I hate you!"

"You think you're so hot—you're not so hot."

"Prick, that's all you are."

"You kook, everybody says it."

"I'll never let you go—you rotten, no-good bastard."

After a while, she was quiet, but he could hear her hoarse breathing near the floor. He waited a few more minutes and then opened the door. She lay beside it, half conscious, stupefied, drained. He lifted her and placed her in the bed. He gently undressed her, washed her face and put a damp cloth on her forehead. She opened her eyes once, took him in and tried to spit at him but couldn't quite manage it.

He left the door slightly open, just in case she might call for him, and went to his own bed. But it was a long time before his conscience would let him off its hook.

That night, he got it again in a totally unexpected way. Ruthie greeted him with a kiss. He had come home late and the girls were already in their beds. He looked in on them and then came down again. She stood at the foot of the steps, watching him descend. He tried not to show the effect of the day's emotions, but he could see that she sensed something. Throughout the brief late meal she studied his face. When he finished, she asked, "It's all over, Al, isn't it?"

He nodded, gently, wearily. She came at him like a mad witch. Her fingers raked his face and tore at his hair. Her knee went for his groin. She was a wild woman who had been waiting impatiently for him to take action. Once he did, she was ready to wreak her own vengeance. He fought her off for a full five minutes, tasting the blood that her scratching raised on his cheeks before she gave up and ran upstairs. His testicles ached dully where she had kicked him.

A few minutes later, she came down. She helped him wash and clean the scratches with cold water and then she went to bed by herself. He collapsed in a chair and wished that the last two days had never been born.

8

Talking It Over with Sam

SAM SCHULTE SAT in the kitchen of his home in Kings Point, Long Island, and waited patiently for his visitor. In the vast, gleaming kitchen of a vast, gleaming house strung across 175 feet of one of the highest promontories in Nassau County, he slowly sipped a glass of sherry and pondered with mingled pleasure and bewilderment the phenomenon of Al Miller.

The hungry, gaunt discounter stimulated him and caused him to marvel once again at the ability of the American business strain periodically to renew and refresh itself. Miller had his faults, plenty of them, he realized, but in little more than a decade he had burst like a screaming rocket over the heads of the nation's retail community. First, it had been Manhattan, then the city's other boroughs, then the suburbs, then the Eastern states, the Midwest, the South and soon it would be the West Coast. Everywhere, it seemed, the Red Oval stores sprouted and where they did the appearance of the sprawling white structures with their gleaming, reclining red ovals had a surprising, inexplicable attraction for local residents. Was it his imagination or had Miller taken pains in his newest stores to have his artists shade the twenty-foot ovals so that they appeared to be eyes watching, summoning, even winking at all who passed?

Shaking his head in a pleasant sort of confusion, Schulte got up and went to a sideboard to refill his glass of sherry. In a far corner of the great, California-style ranch house, the largest in the affluent Kings Point area, his wife, Barbara, secreted herself in her studio, painting the endless abstracts that she favored. Their two children were away in school. In other parts of the house, the three sleep-in servants were busy or idling. T-shaped, the showplace of the entire area, its bright yellow visible down in the bay and valley for miles on a good, clear day, a symbol of ultra-affluence that irked some but aroused envy among many others, the five-year old Schultes' residence lay there in the streaming moonlight like a shiny new ocean liner with all its awesome power. But its seventeen lavish rooms were mostly silent, except for the many appliances and electronic devices of all sorts that Sam loved emitting polite, disinterested, humming, perking or buzzing sounds.

Schulte was one of the wealthiest men on Long Island. It was a fact that he never denied but fostered by building a home that he admitted had cost him over $400,000 and by stationing a Rolls-Royce on his double driveway. A new Cadillac stood at curbside as if a secondary accessory, but it was an accessory that was changed every new-model year.

His wealth was rumored to be and actually was of such an immensity that he himself was not certain of it. Estimates ranged from $75 million to $300 million, but it was probably somewhere in between, a figure which even his detractors agreed was not to be sneezed at. The vagueness about his holdings was explained in the fact that as a developer and financier of total-home communities—"Communities, Unlimited—We Finance, Develop and Permanently Improve Your Home, Your Town, Your Life"—he held vast amounts of mortgages as well as the land and properties under his domain until their payments could be satisfied by thousands of hopeful homeowners. Besides, it was impossible to accurately state the full extent of Sam's private investments. All he would ever say about them to any idle queries was that he had years ago ceased checking the daily stock fluctuations "because it doesn't matter any more." In any case, it was obvious that the trappings of his wealth represented only the tip of the iceberg. There may even have been an iceberg underneath that iceberg.

Feeling the call of nature, Schulte, a stocky, well-set-up man in his early fifties with a dark, dour face and haunting black pupils in limpid irises, took his bottle of sherry with him into the nearest bathroom. Situated between the kitchen and a large den, this particular room was his favorite among the house's ten bathrooms. At considerable expense, he had had it mounted and decorated in Gold Age Renaissance, even to the extent of having not only wall but ceiling frescoes. The gold inlays were, it must be said to his credit, only gilt. But this particular submission to humility was offset by the commode. It was an authentic replica of a famous Medici throne with the exception that it had a drop seat. He sat there now with a smile, one hand resting on the carved arm and the other holding the bottle of sherry to his lips, comparing his career with Al Miller's.

Perhaps the difference between the two lay in the calling that had summoned both from the first days of their business lives and which had continued throughout their careers. Both had come from poor or modest New York backgrounds. Sam's compulsion had always been to "make a dollar," while Al Miller's was to "sell the kind of goods that people want." Although Sam thought that the younger man had a strongly idealistic turn of mind, he conceded to himself that there needn't be any difference between the two callings. Except that as followed by them in particular, however, there was. It was a not so subtle difference that was reflected both in their businesses and in their life styles.

A former salesman who had sold real estate on weekday nights and weekends while studying law in his twenties, Sam Schulte had decided to drop his studies when he saw how much profit could be earned in selling houses. This was especially so in the case of building a house and then selling it yourself. He did this, financing it all the way by a series of loans from relatives so that he would have to pay no interest. He then had a group of houses built for him, obtaining from standard lending sources the smallest interest rates he could find. After several years of increasingly large profits and increasingly large projects, he decided that the real money could be made in broadening out to include financing and selling of all the interior needs that a home or apartment development would need. Then it became major high-rise buildings, office structures, industrial parks and large institutional buildings. He also became a large developer of stationary mobile homes and modular housing, one of the first in the industry to operate as a vertical developer.

But although both his business and his life style were both branches of the same tree, they were entirely different. Every phase of his diverse business, which had sixteen separate corporations, was tightly budgeted. Deviations from the norm expenses were charged to the last penny against the next fiscal period's costs for the identical activity. Each corporation was accounted as a separate profit center and Schulte rode herd on these sixteen profit-making entities like a gun-slinging ranch foreman.

His private and home life was directly the reverse—lavish, ornate, completely indulgent on behalf of himself and his family. It all demonstrated an ostentatiousness of a patently deliberate nature intended to dramatize his immense success, which had been attained by the sweat of his own brain from humble beginnings.

It was strange indeed, he thought, sitting there on his commode-throne, how Al Miller's business and private life represented double reverses from his own. Not only were the differences between business and home style different from his own, but the differences between the two phases were reversed. Miller's administrative philosophy was about as completely freewheeling as seemed possible, with costs and profit controls loose and easy, in marked contrast with his. And, as far as Al's home life was concerned, it was entirely different from his. Al lived in a medium-income section of New York in a ten-year-old, $50,000 Colonial house he had bought with some trepidation from an original owner who had made a nice profit in selling it to him. The decor was tasteful but modest. Even Ruthie's penchant for antiques was hardly extravagant, while Al's personal indulgence centered on his Cord car and an overflowing library of books, mostly history. The total way the Millers lived was in Schulte's view completely out of harmony with Al's vast stake in his highly successful business.

Sam took a final, small swig from the bottle. He adjusted himself and paused before a mirror that took up an entire ten-foot wall of the bathroom. The reflection, tinted flatteringly by hidden luminescence behind the glass, pleased him. He pressed a glass-topped button on the side of the mirror and he was immediately bathed in a soft spotlight. He often used this when he was preparing to welcome guests. He could see himself more or less in the most ideal circumstances, his dark, saturnine countenance, carefully combed shock of thick hair and probing set of his long, dour jaw all transformed somehow into an aspect of beneficence and warmth. It put him, in other words, in a mood in which he liked best to be presented to important guests.

He flipped off the spotlight and faced his true self in the mirror. His big jaw hardened, his soft jowls froze, and his eyes snapped. He snarled and pointed harshly. "Basta! You!" he rasped fiercely. A hoarse laugh, a deep gurgle of self-appreciation, worked up through his heavy chest. This aspect of himself was the one that frightened men and turned them into quivering boys. But now he smiled, his broad nose wrinkling, his lips curving high, he sighed and the haunted look stole back into his eyes. One could virtually admit a man with that expression into one's heart or pocketbook. It was the one with which he ruled annual stockholders' meetings or industry meetings or charity-pledging events where his harsh strength seemed to lay waiting at the ready just beneath a warm, smiling, paternal mien.

He had met Al Miller several years ago at one such charity dinner and had since run into him several times. Al's telephone call a week ago had pleased him, as he was always pleased when people came to him for advice. Over the years, many had come to the wealthy businessman for help, mostly in the form of counsel on business or personal problems, and it was probably to his great credit that he never refused and never failed to help. Much of his response to the requests was egotistical, he knew, perhaps megalomaniacal (he was that, of course, he admitted to himself with some odd pride), but he enjoyed the intellectual challenge that each problem presented. The fact that many people of any importance in the New York business community eventually came to him to be a sounding board for their problems was as much a basis for the great respect in which he was held as was his wealth, his business success and his philanthropies.

But, studying himself, he could hardly steal away from the pleasure it gave him. He struck a pose, then several. Olivier as Hamlet soliloquizing. Lee J. Cobb as Willy Loman. Leonard Bernstein as Leonard Bernstein. Schulte as Al Miller?

He should, he told himself with a laugh and a sigh once again, have been an actor. He could perhaps have been a far greater performer than Chaim Peretz, Al's father, whom he had once seen on the Yiddish stage. But "could you make a dollar in it?" he asked himself. Of course not. But it gave him a vicarious pleasure to know that some of his oldest employees referred to him privately as "Olivier."

As he heard the front-door chime sound, he snapped off the mirror light, standing in the darkness for a moment. The latest chime sounded quite well. It was a bell-like version of the opening three chords of Beethoven's overture *Coriolanus*. Previously, for periods of several months until he tired of them, the front-door chime had variously played the four-note fate theme from Beethoven's Fifth, the final notes of Sibelius' Fifth and three triphammer chords from Stravinsky's *The Rite of Spring*. Somehow, he felt, they seemed appropriate for his home.

Quickly, he left the bathroom. His visitor had arrived.

Ito, the Japanese butler, hovered uncertainly at the front door. His natural Japanese trait of correctness was offended by Al Miller's open sport shirt, baggy slacks and the fact that he was carrying his tweed jacket over his arm. The butler sniffed, bristling like a terrier about to bark. Al stared at him in surprise, hot and perspiring after having parked a mile away so he could unlimber before arriving.

Sam waved Ito away. "Al, it does me good to see you," he said.

"Same here, Sam."

Schulte took him into the kitchen, where he always sat with those who needed help. He did this because it eliminated any feeling of formality and put his visitors at ease. Ito appeared at the doorway, his eyebrows raised as if to ask if he could be of help. "No, no," Sam told him with a smile. "We won't need you, Ito. You can go play with yourself." Sam laughed at his own coarseness and the Japanese joined in as if he understood it to be humor of a high Occidental order.

Sam raised a new bottle of sherry to pour for Al, who shook his head. "No sherry?" Sam asked.

"No. I'll take some milk."

"Milk?" Sam got some from the refrigerator and poured a glass for Al.

"I like milk," Al said, sipping, "when I got things on my mind. It soothes my stomach and it gives my brain a chance to work."

Sam, into his second bottle of sherry in as many days, nodded. Long ago, in past experiences with Al Miller, he had found that it wasn't practical to pin down everything that Al said or to ferret out the discrepancies in his philosophy. Al, on the other hand, found Sam Schulte too literal, too naturally prone to hone in on things that you meant but hadn't quite said the way you wanted to. Nonetheless, for over a week, he had had the conviction that Schulte would help him solve his problem.

"What," Sam asked, "do you have on your mind?"

"Well, it's kinda complicated."

"Wait, Al," Schulte broke in. "Before you get into that, I'd like to ask you a question that's been on my mind."

Al paused. "Shoot," he said.

"Am I crazy or do I see right? Are you changing the ovals in your stores' signs to look like—like eyes? I'll tell you, Al, I get that feeling when I pass your new stores that they're watching me. What are you trying to do—make the customers feel guilty about something like not coming in to shop?"

Al laughed. "Hell, no, Sam, not guilty. Just observed, like we're aware of them and friendly. All I did was ask our painters to shade the ovals in slightly different colors, deepening them toward the center so that the middle of the oval looks like the pupil of an eye."

"But why? Why?" Schulte felt that he was in the presence of an odd, striking, perhaps disconcerting principle.

"It's just a gimmick to make people more conscious of us and for us to seem more conscious of them. That's all, period. We've had some interesting comment about it, not all favorable but most of it was. People expect us to be a little different. They never know quite what to expect from us and that's good. That makes us exciting."

"I see," Sam said doubtfully.

"Do you, Sam? You've got to be in the retail business to know what I mean by exciting."

"I think I do, Al, I think I do."

Al was on his launching pad. "In my business, you have to be a showman. But even more important than that, you have to show that you care. That you want to serve the public, not just sell them goods. You know what would be the most ideal name for a department store? 'Your Friend.' Honest. That's all the name you would need. But you'd have to do a hell of a lot to back it up so that the name would mean something."

"That's a hell of an idea, Al," Sam said, but he really didn't think so.

"I'll tell you something else. You know why 'Your Friend' is a good name? Because for some reason that is hard as hell to pin down, Sam, the American consumer is suspicious of the merchant. He sees him as a *gonif* who always charges exorbitant prices and makes excessive profits. Then he equates with that the lousy service he gets in a lot of stores and he wonders why it is that he pays such high prices. Somebody must be taking it off the top, and so it has got to be the storeowner. But if you can convince him from the name all the way through to your sales lady and your truckman that you are his friend, you oughta have it made."

Sam nodded. He was beginning to regret his question.

"One thing more I gotta tell you, Sam," said Al. "If, on top of that, you can add a dimension of excitement, you oughta be able to beat the pants off your competition. Like I said before, you've got to be a showman. It's got to be excitement all the way through—in your merchandise, your presentation, your prices—especially your prices—your advertising, your windows, your catalogues, everything."

"By the way," Sam insisted, deliberately changing the subject, "what the hell is this problem anyway?"

Al took a refill on the milk and then plunged in. "Sam, it's like this. The business has gotten to be pretty big. I need some help in management, some experienced, talented guy who can be president and chief operating officer. A responsible man, a good administrator, a merchant, too, if possible, a guy who can get a lot of temperamental horses to run together. A guy who can take an awful lot of shit and dish it out right back. But he shouldn't be a dictator. That would mean disaster for my team."

Schulte listened and nodded. He also was listening for some sounds up in that faraway corner of the big house where his wife's studio was, some reassuring sounds, but he heard none. She could be difficult. He hoped there would be no scene while Al was still there.

Al continued. "The way I see it, Sam, you know everybody and you can put your finger on everybody. I personally happen to know that you've helped a lot of people, people who needed people and people who needed better jobs."

"That's true, my boy, very true."

"So, lemme put it very simple, Sam," Al said. "Who you got?"

Sam got up, holding the bottle of sherry aloft, and began pacing the gleaming tiles of the immense kitchen.

"All right, Al," he said, taking a neat swig from the bottle and wiping his lips with the back of a hand. "First, you've got to answer a few questions so that I can zero in better on the best candidate. Now, let's start with why you need this man at this particular time. You've been doing fine up till now running the business yourself, with your old bunch of cronies helping out. What in particular is pushing this now?"

"That's easy," Al said. "A Wall Street underwriter and a few other financial guys have come up with a proposition to make us go public. This isn't the first time but now I think we're right for it. It'll give us all the capital to carry out the bulk of our new big expansion program. But at least one of these guys has an idea that we're a one-man business. I told them on my own hook that I felt I needed a number-two man from the outside. They grabbed the idea like it was theirs and the upshot is that I've gotta find the guy before they'll put us public."

"Fine. How do you feel about taking on this man? Will you make place for him and what about the boys—will they resent him?"

"I'm all for it, Sam. I would want him even if we didn't go public. I need some guy with the skills of administration and coordination that I don't have and don't have time for. Sure, I'll make place for him. I don't want a guy with a great big stick, but I recognize that I need a man who can coordinate things while I'm running around looking over the organization and working in the market. The trick, Sam, is to find the right man. If he is, I don't think the boys will try to kill him. If they know I want him, that should almost be enough for them. Frankly, I hoped that one of them would develop into that particular guy, but it hasn't happened. Not yet, anyway. Maybe the trouble is that they're all pretty good in their jobs by now so that I got a pretty talented, maybe even sophisticated bunch of specialists but I got no in-house general."

Sam Schulte made no comment on this. Instead, he stopped short in his pacing, peered at the label on his bottle of sherry and grimaced. "Crap, pure crap," he said. "Too much body, not enough finesse." He corked it hard with the palm of a hand and suddenly pitched the bottle through a screened window. It tore through the wire mesh and broke shrilly on the patio below. "That's one thing you'll never be accused of selling, Al," Sam said. "A spurious product. I can't say that for all the discounters. Now, may I say something else?"

"Sure," Al said.

"My friend, I'm going to tell you something that I've never told you before—how much I admire what you've done in the last ten or eleven years," Sam told him. "Your creativeness and your drive, the courage that you showed, you've taught all of us, especially the older ones, something that we didn't know. Having bright new ideas and the guts to carry them out—how many do? But one thing I like most about what you did was the way you rubbed their noses in it. I'm talking about all the frozen faces in the New York establishment, the traditional snobs, the oligarchs who thought that they and only they could dominate this market. Not to mention all the haters, the anti-Semites, the anti-youth crowd and the anti-everything crowd. Do you know that you are anathema to them?"

"No," Al said, "I didn't."

"And you don't much care about it, either, do you?"

"No," Al said. "Not much. I always try to figure out what's behind the opposition. If you can put your finger on the motive, I figure, then you can soon tell whether you should worry about it. I guess most of it comes from jealousy, insecurity, fear of strangers and strange ideas."

"Well, maybe, but they'll never forgive you for what you did. Every time they see a new Oval's go up, it's like a kick in the *pupick* to them. But there's something else they'll never forgive you for. They'll hold it against you longer than anything else."

"What's that, Sam?"

Sam leaned over the table, his face close to Al's. "You mean to sit there and tell me you don't know what it is? All right, my friend, I'll tell you. You knocked down one of the big pillars of the Establishment, Al. You made a pearl out of a sow's ear. You took a bunch of plain, ordinary guys, just plain corner bums, school dropouts, and you made men out of them. By giving them responsibility that no traditional kind of business has ever given to unqualified people, you made those characters of yours, those kooks, into top corporate executives. You destroyed the myth that to become a seventy-five or eighty-thousand-dollar-a-year man, you had to go to Harvard grad school or Dartmouth or the Wharton School first. You even spiked the myth that such a man even had to go to college. Do you ever think they'll forgive you for that?"

"I guess not," Al told him, "but who cares?"

"You've been lucky, Al," Sam said.

"Maybe."

"I'm not even sure that you need a second man," said Sam.

"Maybe you ought to wait a little while and see how some of your boys develop."

"No, I think now is the time."

"All right," Schulte said, "all right, if that's what you want."

"So," Al said impatiently, "tell me already. Who you got?"

Sam Schulte straightened up from the table, but before he could answer, the attention of both men was diverted by a shrill sound at the kitchen doorway. A handsome woman in her mid-forties, clad in a painter's smock, stood looking at them with derision and even contempt in her eyes. The sound came from a chirping noise she was making with her lips, aimed particularly in Sam's direction. Slim, artificially grayed in an attractive bouffant, she kept chirping away at Sam while holding a two-foot by three-foot canvas behind her. There was a strange set to her fine blue eyes. Al, who hadn't seen her in about two years, was surprised at the wayward look that they held.

She came in slowly, her smile straying from one to the other, the oddness in her eyes disturbing them both. Gesturing with her head toward Al, she asked Sam, "Another one of the supplicants? Help me, help me. I beseech you. Otherwise, I think I will layeth me down and dieth at your great big hairy feet."

Then, to Al, she said, "Mr. Miller, how are you? Tell me, have you ever considered how it would be if you were married to God? I have been for over twenty-five years. And it hasn't made me feel very big. In fact, I might say that the close proximity to the human divine has made me feel very small indeed. It's not very difficult to understand, you see. If you have to keep looking up day and night, way, way up, to see that godlike face, it makes you feel very small. And you get a hell of a crick in the neck for your trouble, too. The distance, you see, is just too great. God should never marry a mortal, a poor, weak, soon-to-die mortal. Sam knows it by now, of course. I've been dying for almost twenty-five years. Wouldn't you if you were a woman legally living with a man that's ten times bigger than life and is so involved with himself, what he wants and doesn't want, what I should do and shouldn't do, the children, too, what everyone should and shouldn't do, even the whole world, that he can only be God? Wouldn't you say?"

Al didn't say and so she repeated, "Well, wouldn't you say?"

"Barbara, perhaps you ought to go to your bedroom and lie down," suggested Sam.

She chirped angrily at him again. Then, bringing the canvas forward from behind her, she held it up for Al to see, a wild abstract full of indiscriminate lines fighting indeterminate colors.

"Some painters in the not so recent past were intrigued by the Deity," she told Al, "and painted endless variations. I'm doing the same thing in the modern idiom. Except—it's such a strange thing!—all my paintings in the last two years have been of my husband. Don't you see him here? He's that fluttering, jagged line that goes from one corner to the opposite one. That's my Sam. You see how he dominates the world? No wonder everyone comes to him! He's so full of electricity—see that!—and sparks fly from him to everyone who needs him. Of course, they're the other lines. And everyone does need him. And everyone receives his help. And everyone loves him. Everyone except his family, of course. Especially except his wife. Personally, I can't stand him. I never, never could. You know what I call this new painting? 'The Bastard God'!"

Schulte strode to the door. "Helen, damn it, where are you? Help Mrs. Schulte to her room!"

In a minute, his wife was gone with a faint echo of her chirping lingering on. The two men sat at the kitchen table, avoiding each other's eyes. Sitting there with his hands covering his eyes, Sam said, "She's not really as bad as she sounds, Al. She's been under a doctor's treatment the last two years and every once in a while she gets this way. I thought it was a bad reaction to change of life but her doctor says it's a mild form of schizo. She goes days on end like a normal person, and then bang!—she's off again."

"I'm sorry, Sam."

"Don't be. She has the best care money can buy. Two years ago she had a nervous breakdown and I guess she never quite recovered. This woman, Helen, who was just in here, is not an ordinary servant. She's an attendant and therapist that I hired to be with Barbara all the time. She really takes good care of her. I'm sorry that this happened, Al. Where were we?"

Al began moving his chair back. "Sam, maybe we ought to let it go."

"No!" Sam was emphatic. "No. That wouldn't help you—and it certainly wouldn't help her, would it? Now, where were we?"

Al sighed. "All right. I was asking you—so who you got?"

Sam returned in a few minutes with several thin sheaves of computer stationery. They were the type of large sheets used in computer print-outs that had come to be described by anti-computer wags as "elephant toilet paper."

He dropped several sheaves on the floor but spread one out across the table. It had six leaves. Al could see its title, "Chief Operating Officers," with each man's categorized description listed across the six pages. These included such vital statistics as age, religion, education, family formation, its ages, income history, and so on. The very last category was listed simply and mysteriously as "f.q.," and against each man's name in this column was inserted an index number, apparently using 100 as a base.

As he pored over it, using a hairy-tufted finger as a rule across the six leaves, Sam smiled at Al's stare and said, "Over the years I've gotten so many requests just like yours that I decided to systematize all the records that my secretaries keep on such things. We put everything on the company computer, a sophisticated piece of equipment, mind you. We've been keeping up to date, and we've got everything down pat and concise."

"How many names you got on that list, Sam?"

Schulte riffled through the sheaf on the table and glanced down at those on the floor. "Oh, I'd estimate about possibly three thousand. Of course, you understand that these represent a culling of at least fifteen times that many, Al. What we've got here are three thousand of the most effective executives who might just be available in three major categories—chief executive officer, chief operating officer and executive vice-president or general manager. Frankly, I don't want to get involved in anything below that in rank or more specialized. Anyone looking for that doesn't need me or my girls. They can go to a professional head-hunter."

"I'm just amazed, Sam."

"Amazed? If you knew how many times I've been asked to supply names for candidates in any one of these three top posts, or how many times my advice has been sought out on merger proposals, new stock issues, new financing, stock-option plans, restructurings, you name it. Hell, I've even been asked to give advice to the lovelorn—on a high, social and corporate stratum, of course. But all this helps on a couple of levels. If I can help someone, why not? They're grateful and the men I place are grateful. But there's something else, too, Al. There are darned few businessmen in the entire country who are as much on the in because of this little private service that I supply as I am. And, candidly, being on the in in my business—is there a better way of making a dollar?"

"The entire country, Sam?" Al asked.

Schulte's hairy finger paused before a name. "The world is a better way of putting it. You want a top man in France, West Germany, England, Japan, India, Mexico, South Africa, I got one."

Al's vision of Sam Schulte was changing rapidly, virtually minute by minute. The man's sheer overview of things was beginning to dazzle him. Godlike? Perhaps Barbara Schulte's view of her husband was not so schizo. Al said, "What the hell does that 'f.q.' stand for at the end of all the categories?"

"You're observant, my friend," said Sam, looking up from the sheets. " 'F.q.' is a sort of additional dimension I included to pinpoint our evaluation. It stands for flexibility quotient. In my opinion, it's the one key characteristic that every corporate management should consider in hiring one of its three top men. How far will he bend—how far should he bend? Each situation calls for a different tolerance, but in any case the failure to consider it could be disastrous. That's why I include it." He smiled now with a shade of self-deprecation. "I've had two computer assistants who were critical of 'f.q.' One called it the 'flagellation quota.' The other had a cruder turn of mind. He said it meant the 'fucking queer' characteristic of the man. Needless to say, both these computer technicians are no longer with the firm. Now, are you ready for some candidates?"

Al nodded, a bit rocky. "Okay, but you can forget the 'f.q.' bit as far as I'm concerned. I'm much more interested in a man's other qualities."

Sam seemed slightly offended but he pushed ahead.

"Here's one. Montgomery Wilson, forty-four, used to be a big man with Sears, Roebuck, mainly in the catalogue end of the business. He's been a consultant for five years, would like to get back in harness. He's—"

"No consultants, Sam. If he was so anxious to get back in operating a business, five years is a long time to think about it and do nothing."

"Fargo Downey, thirty-nine. A brilliant retailing tactician out of Broadway-Hale Stores. Parents named him, a sentimental gesture, after Wells Fargo. Became operating head of one of their big divisions at Broadway at the age of thirty-two. He's still there but wants some bigger horizons."

"Maybe. Who else you got?"

"Marcus Simmons, forty-eight. A banker, not a retailer, but he's considered one of the top administrators in his industry. He helped reorganize the Merchants' National in Kansas City, then teetering on failure because of big outstanding loans that were frozen in the drought years. He would like to apply his ideas in a broader spectrum than banking."

"No bankers. I got enough of them snapping at my heels outside."

"Here's another. Dewey Levinson. He's thirty-three, one of the real bright ones out of the Wharton School. Combination of retailing and manufacturing experience. Right now, he's number-two man in his father's carpet manufacturing business, but he did wonderfully at Macy's after starting out in the executive training squad—"

"Maybe, but probably not. I find that Macy training leaves guys too rigid. Give me his 'f.q.,' by the way, not that I care a hell of a lot."

Sam disdained giving an answer. He knew that Al was riding him a bit. Testily, he said, "All right, tough guy, let's go through a bunch of others quickly. Paul Struthers, thirty-seven, lawyer and—"

"No."

"Emil Ginzberg, forty-nine, tops in chain stores, now at Federated."

"No."

"Richard Chambers, forty-one, a brilliant tactician in centralized operations. Allied Stores has been after him. It would be a coup for you—"

"They can have him. With my compliments."

They went through ten more candidates that Sam liked but Al didn't. Then ten more. And ten more. Hours had passed and they were no nearer a solution to Al's problem than when he had arrived hours earlier. It was almost 2:00 A.M., both of them rather groggy despite the new bottle of sherry before Sam and the bottle of milk at Al's elbow, when they hit pay dirt. It had come after a brief, rather heated repartee on why Al was rejecting so many good men without expressing a desire to see them.

"I don't know, Sam. Call it instinct. I hear the combination of the guy's name, the age, a little of his background, I get a smell of him and I don't like it. But give me the right one and I'll know it right away."

Schulte shrugged. How can you argue with a man whose instinct always seemed to be one hundred percent right? The older man's finger running slowly down the page stopped quite suddenly as if stuck there. "I believe I've got the man for you, Al," he said excitedly. "Ben Baron. They call him 'Bright Ben.'"

"That's a good beginning. Let's hear."

"He's thirty-six, University of Chicago, business major, a bachelor. He's president of one of the Midwest's top fashion-store chains, does over one hundred million dollars in sales with a high net profit. The owner, who was getting on in years, took a shine to him and brought him in to revamp the business because it was losing ground. He took it over and within two years brought it to the top share in its area. Trouble is, though, that he changed it so much that the old man brought suit against him. Ben wouldn't let him break the contract and refused to vacate, so the owner had no other recourse. It's an unusual story—the changes were too much for the old man to accept even though they proved to be so successful—Al, I think this is the man for you."

Al, too, was excited.

"Al," Sam repeated, "I tell you, this is the man for you. You want to meet him?"

"I do, I sure do."

"Good," Sam told him exultantly. "I'll get him on the phone. He can be here by six A.M."

"What?"

Sam grinned, Jovelike but human and happy. "Why not, Mr. Big Instinct?" Sam said, with a grin. "You said when I gave you the right one, you would know it right away. So here he is! Why wait?"

Al nodded slowly. "Fine, good, great," he said wearily. Sam was already at the telephone on the sideboard. "You can grab a couple of hours' sleep in the den, Al, until he gets here. Maybe by seven A.M., you can have your man."

He busied himself at the phone, fully recast now in his barking, snarling role. Al arose to go into the den.

A figure stood in the kitchen doorway. It was Barbara Schulte in an elaborate robe, long dark hair brushed, lips carefully rouged and cheeks carefully made up, eyes clear and poised. Behind her loomed the heavy-set figure of Helen, her attendant. With a happy, loving smile, Barbara told Al, "I couldn't help overhearing some of it. I'm delighted that Sam has been able to help you. He thinks the world of you and it's good to know that he can do something for you."

Schulte continued to give careful instructions on the telephone without expressing any surprise at the appearance of his wife or at the amazing change in her behavior. But Al was stunned. She was completely rational at 2:30 in the morning, probably more rational than he was. He watched her in amazement as she went to Sam at the sideboard, leaned her handsome head against his and said, "Sam is really the most unselfish person in the world. Do you have any idea of how many people he has helped over the years to solve some of their deepest problems? The number would stagger you. No person I know has such a big heart or the great capacity to express it as my Sam."

She kissed him with a moistly audible smack on his dark cheek. "And he's really just about the most wonderful husband in the world, too. Sam, say you agree."

But Sam waved his arm in protest. He was talking to Ben Baron, trying to explain at 2:30 in the morning from 800 miles away that he was about to be given a once-in-a-lifetime opportunity. Barbara, however, insisted in a firm, appealing manner. And so Sam cupped the earpiece in his hand and recited, "Yes, honey, I do agree. I am simply wonderful."

She exited with a pleased flush on her face, blowing them both a kiss.

Groggy, exhausted, drained, Al stumbled into the den for some place where he could dump his weary bones. He probably should have asked for the guy's "f.q." index, after all, he thought. But it didn't matter. In just a few hours he would be meeting Bright Ben.

PART TWO

9

Bright Ben

SOMEHOW, about the time that Oval's went public, a tremor of legitimacy ran through the top executive ranks.

The snapping up of more than one million shares by the investing public in less than a week pounded the message home to Al's boys. The sheer responsibility of their new franchise and the recognition that their collective efforts constituted a company that was now listed on the American Stock Exchange made them all straighten up, gulp a few times and decide, if it were at all possible, to become normal, unkooked, untraumatized types.

But if there were any who actually appeared to succeed in this, it was William I. Wallenstein. The former scourge of the real-estate industry became seemingly overnight the most traditional member of Red Oval's management. He wore black pinstripe suits with vest, fine English broadcloth shirts, striped ties with Princeton colors and expensive black wing-tip shoes. Although he had never had a mouth quite as foul as that of, for example, Nat Batt, Willie now spoke softly, with deliberation, and with, befitting his new manner of dress, a slight British accent. The problem here was that his new clipped tones had more than a trace of Brooklynese but it was the only flaw in an otherwise perfect rendering of the big-time corporate executive.

Wallenstein even had an executive secretary who had a secretary. And every pending or completed action, every deal, all correspondence, unlike the recent past when Wallenstein's egglike head served as his filing cabinet, was completely recorded, filed and even cross-filed.

All that, however, was only the surface aspect. Underneath his banker's exterior and his calm, devoted demeanor, the *gonif* thrived. His new guise was actually a cover-up for what was to come. In a locked drawer lay the blueprints, already put in motion, for what would be the zenith of Willie's career—the most ambitious and fraudulent scheme in the history of both the retail and real-estate industries. This project called for the establishment of a complete city of about one million persons in the Pennsylvania hills with a Red Oval Village as its focal point. The city hall would occupy a building which would back onto the main Oval store so that traffic would flow from the municipal complex directly into the store and vice versa. All other municipal buildings would be interconnected with the city hall, and thus with Oval's, so that the store would be heir to all its traffic. But more than that—who could ever accuse Wallenstein of being just another company man?—all the city's buildings, schools, institutions and services would be leased. So who, you might well ask, would be the city's landlord? Wallenstein, of course.

But, to be fair about it all, if Wallenstein even in his new guise remained one of the country's most unsung thieves, his new project would not hurt but materially help his employer. Its sales and profits would be greater in that proposed store than in any other. It gave him a nice, warm, unselfish feeling as he contemplated this likelihood and wondered how the name Wallenstein, Pennsylvania, might go.

One morning he was in the midst of a telephone call which would have carried the plan one step further to fruition when the door of his cubicle banged open and Al Miller and a short, smiling man entered. Before Wallenstein could hurriedly hang up, Al said, "Willie, meet Ben Baron. I guess you've heard those rumors that I let leak out. Well, they're right. When our board meets tomorrow, Ben will be our new president."

Wallenstein shakily leaned over and shook hands with the small, neat man. "Congratulations, Ben," he said. Then, turning to Al, he said, "I got to talk to you, Al. I got a deal cooking in Pennsylvania that's—"

Al waved it aside. "Not now, Willie. Not now."

This was generally the manner in which Ben Baron met all the others. There was no announcement. Al's policy of dealing with all his key men on an individual basis was pursued quickly that morning. His conviction that important announcements are better prepared for through the advance planting of rumors so that everybody can get used to the idea before it happens satisfied him in achieving its primary goal. One reason for this was that there was an inverse ratio to the speed in which the dissemination of the rumor was guided and the timing of its actual materialization. In other words, the rumors were slowly planted, carefully fertilized and neatly fed with blank stares, raised eyebrows, or sudden losses of memory when someone cornered him to ask if the rumors were true.

But after some weeks in which everyone seemed to writhe under the uncertainty of it all, Al quickly and stunningly nailed down the rumor by presenting the fact. For all intents and purposes, it was by that time a *fait accompli*, even though no one had really known it all along. It was Al's way of avoiding painful confrontations, although in actuality it turned out to be a painful process for everyone.

Finally, after meeting some two dozen people in something less than fifteen minutes, Ben found himself being guided, escorted, even pushed into a vacant cubicle at the end of a long hall. It seemed still to smell of a warm body, as if one, someone, had just been ousted from it while still living and breathing. "This is your office, Ben, at least till we find something better," Al told him with a self-conscious twist of the lips. Then, as if to explain the situation, if that were at all possible, Al added, "Hell, I don't even have an office for myself. I always figured I'd leave that for the guys who work."

He laughed feebly, but Ben Baron nodded brightly and agreeably. He sat down behind the scarred, shabby desk, tried to make himself comfortable but caught a splinter on the warped chair, grinned, removed it and then smacked his neat head with a hollow thunk against the dirty, green partition behind him. Al took a chair, put his feet up on Ben's desk and regarded him happily, if a trifle anxiously.

"So what do you think, Ben?" he asked. "Don't spare the gripes. Give it to me straight."

Ben nodded again, wisely, even affectionately. "That's the only way I know how to, Al," he said simply.

He hesitated now in order to think it over. Al studied him again, telling himself once more that Ben Baron was both one of the smallest and neatest men he had ever met. Not that the Chicagoan was so diminutive or so neat that from the standpoint of either trait he was so unusual. It was rather that from the standpoint of the combination of the two traits and their effect on each other that he was a rare specimen. In other words, he was about five feet three inches, short, of course, but not tiny, not fat but well formed if a trifle fleshy. But the fine worsted suit, dark-blue shirt, white striped tie and Italian shoes, all uncreased, unmarred—and the way he seemed to be poured just right into everything—perfectly matched his concise form both in essence and in manner. It was difficult for Al, who certainly couldn't care less about what he wore, to imagine Ben Baron getting up in the morning to face the problem of deciding what he should wear that day. It was entirely, at least in Al's vision, as though the right, the proper, the immaculate clothes just leaped up at Ben. Choice would be so natural that it would not be a choice. It would be an instinct.

The perfection-sans-effort extended not just to clothes but to the small man's physical characteristics, too. He had bronzed skin, just the right dark tones at the temples and under the eyes to confirm fully an outdoor masculinity. Bold strands of hair extended just enough from his dark-blue French cuffs. His hands were square, just a trifle large for his size, well veined but not too well veined. But it was his head, round, shaped significantly by a thick, closely shaped coiffure, and his face, also rather round, with small but definite features, that virtually perfected the image.

Virtually, that is, but for one more not insignificant item. His eyes. He had almost black pupils in limpid white irises, sparkling with light and brimming over with intelligence. His eyes were at once childlike in their purity but age-old in their recesses. If a man's true depths can be measured in his cranium, his heart or his genitals, Al thought, in Ben's case it was his eyes.

"Why do they call you 'Bright Ben?'" Al asked, breaking into the man's meditation.

Ben's eyes, which had been gently directed at the opposite wall, now focused back on Al. "I really can't say for sure, Al, but it goes way back when I started school. Some old biddy of a teacher pinned the name on me because I was an exceptionally good student and it stuck with me all those years. It's kind of silly, I guess. I wish people would stop referring to me that way. It really doesn't mean a thing."

"So," Al pursued, "what do you think? I don't usually ask anybody to sound off on Red Oval. But, in your case, I want you to. In the past three days, you've seen more than half of all the stores, you spent three to four hours in each, and today you met practically the entire top staff. So tell me, already, what do you think?"

"What do I think?" Ben's beady eyes took in Al's sweaty suspense, his overanxious stance, and glued themselves onto them. Al had noticed before that quality of concentration that beamed out of Ben's eyes. To Al, the tiny, dirty cubicle appeared to expand around the neat little figure.

"Assuming you won't hold me to all this months from now, I do have some preliminary thoughts," Ben admitted. "What you probably don't know is that yesterday I had a preliminary session with your controller, Von Rossem, and with Harry Abner, your merchandise man. That means that I had occasion to study the balance sheet and the merchandise budget within the same short period of time. As a result, I must tell you this: Al, as the head of a public company, you're in serious trouble."

"I am?" Al's voice held more than a slight tremor. But it came from surprise rather than fear. When, he asked himself, wasn't he in trouble every day of his life? "Tell me," he said out loud. "Don't keep it a secret from me."

"All right. Let's examine what you have and analyze it. After roughly ten or eleven years of existence, you've got a company that just went public, doing about five hundred million dollars in sales with a net profit of about two percent. That's a phenomenal accomplishment, Al, no question about it. But you didn't bring me in here to pat you on the back but to help you. I've seen enough of the Oval stores and studied the merchandise mix to be certain of one thing: As a public company which should aim at improving its profit margins, your chances of doing that are small unless you change your concept."

"How do you mean change my concept?"

"You've got to improve your productivity. You're getting about a range of between ninety and one hundred ten dollars a square foot in sales, with something like sixty percent of your floor area devoted to hard goods and about forty percent to soft goods. As I see it, Al, you've got to reverse the ratio in favor of clothing and related items, making the change gradually into a roughly fifty-fifty arrangement, and use the extra ten percent of space for soft goods as a high-profit, high-yield area. If that works out well, then you go another ten percent to accomplish the second step of this profit-improvement plan."

Al nodded under the bright light-beam of Ben's gaze. The little man stared at him full of inner knowledge that suffused all the way through to a total outer confidence. How the hell did this guy, this Bright Ben, come to such confident convictions so goddam soon? Al wondered. Maybe it was true that a stranger could look at the business with really fresh eyes. "What," Al asked, "do you think we oughta do?"

"There's only one thing to do," Ben said. "Go high-fashion."

"High-fashion . . ." Al exhaled the two words hard from an unprepared gut. "High-fashion?" he asked, inhaling now.

Ben nodded. "You can get fifty to sixty percent markup in both classifications and items, Al. Not only will that hike your general profit margin, but it will give you an additional dimension with your customers. The smartest department stores know that. They know that big, diversified stores like theirs ought to have big, diversified clienteles. Why should that be so different for a two hundred-thousand-square-foot discount store? And if you sell high fashion at a discount—who can say for sure that you won't get the affluent market, too?"

"Well, it's not our field, Ben," said Al, "but why not? It's worth a try."

But Ben, it seemed, was not yet done. As he started again, raising a well-manicured hand to say, "There's a little more, Al," Al had the distinct impression that Ben Baron had merely unfurled one of his many layers. Obviously what lay behind the bright eyes was a hell of a lot more than "a little more" and that out of the depths of Sam Schulte's "elephant toilet paper" he had gotten for himself an amazing little man.

"What I'm alluding to involves another aspect of the profit picture," Ben proceeded. "I'm referring now to expenses. As I wandered around the offices here with you, meeting everyone, and seeing the headquarters operation, it seems quite clear to me that there is considerable duplication and wastage, lack of co-ordination and lack of communication because of the cluttered, inefficient offices you have here. Also, I was dismayed to find that some of your service departments, such as store planning and layout, display, and so on are located a mile away in another office building. I think there is only one solution to this problem, which can accomplish two apparently conflicting goals—reduce costs by coordinating all administrative and service functions in one area and so make everything more efficient and at the same time add to nonoperating revenue by contributing lease income—"

"You mean . . ." Al began, his pulse trip-hammering.

Ben nodded sagely, but without any sort of blatant triumph. His dark pupils glowed in their lakes of limpid, white self-appreciation. "Yes, Al, I mean just that. An office tower to house all of the company's executive and service operations and lease out all the other floors to other commercial tenants. It will be located right in the heart of the city, a proud monument to what you created."

"I see what you mean."

"The basement and first five or six floors would, of course, be a new Oval's downtown store—"

"Of course!"

"And on top of it would be everything else. Over the executive penthouse, where the whole world could see it, we might put a one hundred-foot Red Oval that would be lit up all night—"

"We could make the goddam thing revolve!"

"And maybe change colors or have alternating messages on it, like the time, the weather, the humidity, that would provide both a service and a blurb for us—"

"Like 'Oval's for the World's Smartest Shoppers!' "

"The new store in the building would have our first high-fashion operation, giving us our new face to the world, while we would install high fashion in all the stores. But the new one, that would be our flagship!"

In his enthusiasm, Al had risen and leaned over Ben's desk, pounding him on the shoulders. "Bright Ben, Bright Eyes, or whatever the hell they call you, you're a bright bastard!"

Then Al paused, searching Ben's face for reassurance. "You think we can do it? And once we do it, you think we can make it work?"

Ben smiled back at him. His eyes glistened, pure, ingenuous but totally certain, like a baby's, a thirty-six-year-old baby's, that the world as he envisioned was as it all seemed. "I see no problems," he informed Al flatly. "I see no problems at all."

True to his nature, Al made no formal announcements to the staff of what he and Ben had decided to do. He leaked enough information in the showrooms of Seventh Avenue and Broadway to make sure that it would filter back to the Oval staff. It did, the rumors feeding on themselves and growing fat and overblown. He himself became more elusive than ever to avoid direct confrontations with the boys or the other executives. Someone would see him in the office, holler, "Al, wait, I've got to ask you something." Then some other person would pass between them, or the coffee cart would come by, and the Al who was supposed to be there was no longer.

Ben said nothing either. He already knew that Al's reluctance to spill anything was a manifestation of a peculiar belief that things will take care of themselves if you leave them alone. It was one way of easing a difficult announcement, in this case, a double one, into the stream of public consciousness by permitting part of it to become known outside the main circle. Taken to its extreme—and it often was—the principle, if it could be called that, could even more effectively have been carried out by leaking a wilder rumor, patently erroneous but with a kernel of truth, and then, after it had collected enough exaggeration, suddenly introducing the simple truth, to the relief of everyone who had expected much, much worse. To Ben, it was Al's way of pre-softening the opposition.

Of course, the first time that Ben accidentally met Al coming out of the movie house around the corner one late afternoon he realized that Al's rumor-announcement technique was in all probability something else entirely. An escape from the realities of executive life. Yet on that particular accidental meeting outside the movie-house lobby, Al had reacted with considerably more equanimity than Ben did.

Clamping his arm on Ben's shoulder, Al had said, "Boy, he's some pisser, that John Wayne. What he did to that banzai attack shouldn't happen to Macy's and Gimbel's!"

Even when Al decided that the time was ripe to spring his dual announcement about going high-fashion and building an office tower in Manhattan, his first inclination was to have a statement issued to the staff and to the press under the joint imprimatur of Ben and himself. But the little man convinced him that the boys would resent it and so they decided to hold a meeting with them at a nearby hotel and announce it. Ben read the actual statement while Al looked out the window, finding much that interested him down on the street. When Ben finished his smooth recitation, there was complete silence. Al was on the way out before anyone, except that he found his path blocked by Nat Batt. The fat, bald PR man seemed irate, but instead he told Al, "At least it's not another whorehouse, you sonofabitch. We oughta make the front page of *The New York Times* with this. Are you sure you're in your right mind about putting a one hundred-foot oval on top of the building?"

Nat was right on both counts. The story made the *Times*'s front page, and Al had not been in his right mind on the big oval to straddle the penthouse. The zoning rules wouldn't allow it. The reaction to the double announcement was mixed. Everyone among the boys and the rest of the company's top level liked the idea of the new national headquarters building. The only apparent exception was Wallenstein, who felt that as the real-estate expert he had been ignored, particularly in his new role as the company's most traditional and correct officer. He was, of course, justified in feeling slighted. But once both Al and Ben promptly apologized to him, he pitched right in. It turned out, in fact, which should not have been surprising to anyone who really knew him, that Wallenstein had on his own put binders on two midtown buildings as potential store sites. But that, in itself, should not have been surprising to even those who didn't know him. He had binders on so many buildings and options on so many sites that he probably even had the Mayor of New York worried as to whether he, the Mayor, was landlord or tenant in City Hall. If that was to be the case in the proposed Wallenstein, Pennsylvania, after all, why should New York City be any different?

But a predominantly negative reaction centered on the other announcement. What was Oval's doing going high-fashion? All the boys seemed upset by that, frightened probably being a more accurate description of their state of mind. It was fear of the unknown, fear of invading an entirely new area of merchandising, of developing new price lines and new sources. Everyone responded in his own inimitable way. Harry Abner put it succinctly: "How the hell can I remember all this high-fashion shit when I can't remember the regular stuff I'm supposed to sell?" Irving Waldteufel: "This'll mean an upgrading not just in merchandise but in all our ladies' rooms, too. What am I gonna do with all the mountains of cheap supplies I got stashed away?" Ernest von Rossem: "It will surely add to our already immense inventory woes." Of course, there was the "just when" contingent, too. Smiles: "Just when I had a dozen new ideas on other projects that I wanted to present." Solly Patracelli: "Just when I was beginning to get everyone in line they have to bring in this new guy with new ideas." Benny Acropolis, the executive stock boy: "Just when I was starting to think that these nuts were getting straightened out. How the hell can such a low-class bunch of guys know anything about high fashion?"

But the one who was most upset, who was, in fact, livid about it, was, understandably, Molly Bradley. As fashion coordinator for Oval's none had been more ignored in the decision to venture into couture-type clothes. She was so angry about the snub that for weeks she seriously contemplated confronting Al and Ben Baron and knocking their soft heads together.

There were other reasons why she was angry. She was still nursing a grudge against Al on personal grounds. She was convinced that their breakup was temporary but for quite a while now his reaction toward her had been purely and wholly business. Then, as did most of the others, she resented his hiring of Ben Baron. He was an outsider, a so-called proven merchant of ready-to-wear. According to her interpretation, this indicated a lack of confidence in her, even though, in actuality, he had been hired more for his administrative ability than for his knowledge of merchandising per se. And, as a sexy but quite tall woman, she was also annoyed that her new boss was so short.

Stopping in Nat Batt's office one morning the day after she met Ben Baron, she said acidly, "I've never known a short man who didn't have a short pecker. And I mean you too, itsy-bitsy."

She brooded about it all to the extent that she decided to confront Al Miller and find out what it was all about. It was naturally impossible to contact him in the office, so she waited until the next time there was a Jimmy Cagney movie in the theater around the corner. When she saw Al go into the movie house in mid-afternoon, she followed discreetly after a few moments. The next thing Al knew, involved as he was in the guns and the snarls on the screen, was a familiar perfume wafting around his nostrils and then a soft hand slipping into his and the greeting, "Hello, lover, you bastard."

Surprised, he turned toward her and saw, in the reflected light, the lovely profile of the bitch he had loved and then spurned. Instead of the dazzling smile that should have accompanied her warm greeting, however, she gave him an icy stare.

"Yeah, Molly, what is it?" he asked, staring at the screen.

"What is it?" she asked indignantly. "I want to know what the hell is going on. And look at me when I'm talking to you, you bastard!"

He looked at her. His heart skipped a few beats. She was still a dazzling animal, more so when angry. It seemed to fit her personality. "All right, baby," he said. "Let's have it. What's burning you?"

"Where do I stand with this new little guy in the picture? That's what I want to know."

"Stand? Just like you did before. He's gonna run the shop under me. But that's got nothing to do with you. You're still our top fashion *mavin*. What you say goes in that area."

"Oh, yeah? Why didn't you and he consult me on that high-fashion business?"

He watched the movie intently for about three minutes. Then he turned back to her and said, "Look, Molly, that was a stupid oversight on my part. I personally should have talked to you about it. I'm making no excuses for myself. But if it means anything at all, I was so sure that you would agree that I didn't think of asking you about it. But I should've and you're right as hell to be burned up. I'm asking you to forgive the unpardonable. Okay?"

She stared hotly at him and then immediately began cooling off. "Okay," she said. "Okay. What do you want me to do about the high-fashion thing?"

"Work with Ben. He doesn't know the New York market. Introduce him around. And be nice to him, Molly. It'll be a long time before he feels comfortable with a wild, crazy bunch like ours."

"Be nice to him?" she asked. "How can I be nice to a guy you put over all of us? Who the hell is he? What the hell is he?"

"We need him, baby," Al said seriously. "The company is big enough for newcomers, especially when they got talent and credentials like his."

She rose abruptly and slowly walked up the aisle. Just before she went out, he got up in his seat and said out loud over the annoyed audience, "Thanks, baby. I won't forget it."

She returned to the office and strode past Ben Baron's secretary and opened his door. Baron, on the phone, glanced up at her with surprise. He continued talking for a minute and then hung up.

"I just had a talk with Al," Molly told him, "and he said I was to give you all the help you needed. I'm completely at your disposal. Where do we begin?"

He studied her. He had undertaken a study of all of Al's key executives and she had come off with top grades. Once he accepted the fact that Al's boys were an unorthodox crew and ruled out their idiosyncrasies, most of them came off surprisingly well. He had heard, in the process of making his study, of Molly's relationship with Al but he had also ascertained that it had ended.

"I'm delighted, Molly, that you feel that way," he said, "One of my initial problems is to break the ice with everyone around here. You know, it's that same old thing with a lot of successful companies. If you weren't in on the start, you don't belong. But I want to belong. So it's good to know that you're behind me."

He got up from behind the desk and went to her and shook hands, Continental style, with a decorous kiss. She was stirred in spite of herself. He was quite something, she thought. A small, almost perfectly proportioned man, with the softest yet brightest eyes she had ever seen. When he had first met her, those eyes had been guarded, self-protective. Now they were warm, appealing, even inviting. Their little-boy quality intrigued her.

"You know," she said softly, "I couldn't be more with you on this high-fashion idea. We've sampled and tested it on items and it's clicked with us. Matter of fact, I've anticipated this. Could you drop around my place for cocktails tonight? There's something I would very much like to show you."

He nodded with genuine interest. "My pleasure," he said.

That evening she let Ben into her Park Avenue apartment. "Sit. Make yourself a drink. I'll be back in a jiff," she said. After taking in the *avant-garde* decor, he looked forward with anticipation to her return. He assumed that she had some fashion sketches that she wanted him to see. He assumed this even as he heard her sultry voice summoning him from the bedroom. He walked briskly in, confident, dapper, contained, and not at all prepared for what she wanted to show him.

As she gathered the hot little man to her cool, flowing loins, Molly said rather cruelly, "Want to know what Al said to me about you? 'Be nice to him. It'll be a long time before he feels comfortable.' Are you beginning to feel comfortable, Ben?" In the next few minutes Molly found herself with two widely disparate thoughts. One was: This I do for you, Al Miller, you cruel, rotten, wife-loving bastard. The other was simply that it was wrong to make generalities about short men.

Ben Baron let himself out of Molly's apartment just before midnight. He took a cab the few blocks over to the Waldorf, where he was staying for the time being. Al had insisted that he take a suite there until he found an apartment to his liking. A smile played on Ben's lips all the way to the hotel, up the elevator and even when he came into his room. In only a week at Oval's, much had happened and all of it wonderful.

Al had been wrong, Ben told himself, at least about one thing. It would not be a long time before he felt comfortable. He was already comfortable. Nothing that he had ever done in his life, no experience that he had ever had, no professional challenges that he had ever met had been as gratifying as what he had experienced in the last few days. As he undressed and stepped into the shower, it seemed incredible to him that he had made so much progress and that his fortunes had taken such an upturn since the 2:00 A.M. call from Sam Schulte in Kings Point only a few weeks before. All his life, he realized with a chill of humility, good things had always seemed to happen to him. As a child in the Chicago public schools, teachers had immediately taken to him and remained steadfastly loyal. In college, the faculty seemed to seek him out for special attention. As a business major, top corporate executives heard about him while he was still an undergraduate and had invited him to their clubs or homes in an early effort to lure him into their businesses. And when he had entered the fine specialty-store field because the childless widower who owned the company had shown such a paternal interest in him that Ben sensed a golden future for himself, his resignation from the large mail-order house where he had gone after graduation was cheerfully accepted. It was as if that company's management realized that some special role in life and in business awaited him and there was no point in reminding him that he owed them something. Did he really owe them anything because they had quickly plucked him from the trainee ranks, savored him and promoted him at least every year in the eight he had spent there? And he a Jew at that in an overwhelmingly Gentile company? But, as he had consoled himself in the occasional moments of guilt that he had felt in those days, he had more than earned his way through his accomplishments and contribution to their profits.

His father, a wholesaler in the stationery business in a Chicago suburb, had always been his greatest fan, predicting for years that Ben would reach to high places—"anything he wants will come to him." But his late mother, a heavy woman who had spent most of her life alternately worrying about her weight and worrying about her son, had not been so sanguine. "The trouble with you, Ben, is that everything comes to you so easy that you never have any doubts about yourself," she had told him many times. "A person should have to ask himself once in a while, Am I right, did I do what I should do, what did I forget? But not you, son. God gave you looks, brains, personality, the eyes of an angel, everything you would want for yourself. But no qualms— about anything. Maybe He even gave you the quality to always be right. I hope so for your own sake." But those expressions had merely infuriated his father. "Leave the boy alone!" he had railed at her. "Do you want to mix him up? What kind of an unnatural mother does the boy have?"

In his ultimate impasse and dispute with the elderly owner of the specialty-store chain, Ben had had occasion to recall his mother's comments and wonder if they contained the roots of his problem with the old man. Ben had found that old John Dewar's paternalistic feeling toward him had vanished once the differences between them turned sharp and acrid. As he pushed ahead with projects that boosted the old established company to record profits, it became clear to him that the old man's disconcerting unhappiness stemmed from a desperate desire to retain some identity with the company that he had founded. Whereas on one hand he was compelled to applaud the successful moves of his protégé, he was on the other hand driven to a lesser and lesser role in his own business. Why the hell would a man in his late sixties want to keep an iron hold? Ben would wonder. And then he realized that as a widower without children or outside interests, the old man was drowning in loneliness and a lack of usefulness.

Unquestionably, Dewar's suit against Ben, seeking to break his contract, was a sign of senility. The more Ben refused to vacate—leave after turning the company around and before he could really cash in?—the more adamant and the less logical the old man's will became. And so the call in the early hours from Kings Point had again demonstrated how it seemed that good things always happened to him. But never before had it been when his own situation was rapidly approaching a crisis.

Out of the shower, dried, standing warm and refreshed at his window looking down on Park Avenue, Ben recalled with a smile his mixed emotions when he arrived at Schulte's home at 7:30 in the morning New York time. Sam had seemed fresh and eager to him, a dominant, compelling figure in a velvet bathrobe. But, routed out by Schulte after only a few hours' sleep, Al's sallow face and big thumbs yanking at his eyes had diluted Ben's enthusiasm. Was this gawky figure the famous, precedent-setting, ingenious discounter whose exploits were a topic of hot and envious conversation even in Chicago? But during an immense breakfast in which an unexpected guest was Barbara Schulte, surprisingly both luscious and demure at what—forty-five?—Al Miller's astute questions and his sensitive reactions had revitalized Ben's interest.

Below him the Park Avenue scene, the occasional lights, the aura that the huge hotels and apartment buildings imparted, the feeling in his head that he had arrived not only in the affluent heart of New York but at a pinnacle of personal attainment toward which he had been inexorably moving all his life—all this raised Ben into a state of emotional euphoria and excitement.

He left a single light on at his bedside as he slid under the covers. He didn't particularly like the dark and, besides, he wanted the light because it would help him think a bit more clearly and perhaps in some way slow down the boom-boom of his rapid pulse rate.

Imagine coming up with two major action moves, together to cost many millions, in less than a week on the job! And recalling Al Miller's unrestrained enthusiasm for both the new fashion approach and the building of the new tower, Ben for a moment, but only a moment, wondered if it all wasn't too easy. Why hadn't Al or his long-time colleagues, supposedly geniuses all or so they gave the impression, come up with those ideas themselves?

There was only one answer, he told himself proudly, and that's why the name sticks.

Six months after Ben Baron's arrival, Al and Ruthie stood on a Seventh Avenue corner one warm spring evening, staring with interest, amazement and some confusion at a big hole in the ground. They gaped through a window in the wooden fence that surrounded the corner excavation. On each side of the fence large signs read:

ON THIS SITE

WILL RISE

THE NEW 42-STORY NATIONAL

OVAL'S BUILDING

WITH THE WORLD'S FINEST

HIGH-FASHION

DISCOUNT STORE

ON THE PREMISES

⁓

BEN BARON, *President*	W. I. WALLENSTEIN, *Vice-Pres., Real Estate*

"Everyone's name but yours," Ruthie observed.

Al shrugged. "Who needs it? Ben's name and Willie's name are on the sign in case somebody's interested in leasing space. Not that there's that much left. With a year to go, we're already seventy percent leased."

"Still," Ruthie insisted, "it would be nice to have your name there. I'm going to call Ben tomorrow and tell him—"

"If you do," Al told her with a grin, "I'll call him afterward and tell him to forget it."

She linked her arm through his and they walked up the avenue. Ruthie was happy. Molly Bradley's preoccupation with Ben had lifted the threat which Ruthie felt constantly hovered over her, despite the break-off at least a year before between Al and "that slinky blond bitch," as she called Molly. And Al's satisfaction with the things that Ben had done appeared to have removed a burden from her husband's mind. Al, she thought, had less to run away from these days, fewer shadows that fell on his shoulders. Suddenly she looked behind her and gripped Al's arm. "I think we're being followed," she said.

As he turned around, Al noticed a figure about a block away dart into a store doorway. He laughed, pulling his wife along. "It's nothing," Al said. "Probably some eager-beaver insurance salesman or Seventh Avenue guy shadowing me. It happens all the time."

They walked for another block. Ruthie stopped at the corner and looked back, trying to visualize how the forty-two-story rise of the Oval's building would appear from two blocks away. It would be one of the area's tallest buildings and imposing in its combination of glass, concrete block and gleaming aluminum shafts. "Do you really think you know what you're doing, Al?" she asked with concern. "It seems that you are placing a lot of confidence in Ben Baron's ideas. How do you know he's right?"

"I don't," Al replied, "except I know it here." He punched himself in the gut.

Ruthie smiled to herself. At least she felt that she was smiling to herself. Try pinning Al down to a logical explanation, a rationale, she told herself, on things that he knew were right by instinct, if not exactly by common sense. After almost thirteen years of marriage to him, she still couldn't get over the fear that much of what he and his boys did was a "put-on," so deeply ingrained was the conservative, pragmatic environment in which she had grown up. But everything that he and they had done up to that point had succeeded, even though their methods had clearly augured for a disaster. And now that the neat little Ben Baron had joined them and had almost immediately come up with two of the most startling ideas in all their history, she was more baffled—and perhaps even more concerned than ever. What kind of a weird spell did Al cast over people who came into close proximity to him?

They started walking again, but both of them were startled by a move just behind them. They whirled, seeing themselves virtually face to face with the man who had ducked into a doorway a block or two before. It was Wallenstein. His lanky, cadaverous body was taut and his shifty eyes were agonized. The fine, sedate English clothes seemed at odds with the desperate look on his face.

"Al," he said, "I gotta talk to you. I got a deal cooking in Pennsylvania that's the biggest, goddam thing that—"

"Now now, Willie," Al said gently. "Not now."

Wallenstein moved around to block Al's way. "But I gotta have a decision. It's urgent. If I do it now, the company'll cash in and I—"

"You think it's that good, huh?" Al asked, surprised.

"Yeah, I sure do. Lemme tell you—"

"I don't want to hear about it, Willie. You just go ahead and do it."

Wallenstein's long jaw dropped. It was *the* deal of his dealing career and Al didn't even want to hear what it was all about. "Look, lemme tell you what—"

But Al had moved off with Ruthie, leaving Willie to stand there talking to himself. Prompted by some vestige of honesty, decency and conscience that he hadn't felt in his adult years, Wallenstein shouted after Al, "Hey, I hope you won't be sorry. I mean I hope you won't blame me if—"

Walking a block away at a rapid pace, literally dragging a bemused Ruthie, Al may or may not have answered. Wallenstein saw his arm jut up toward the sky in a derisive gesture and a few words floated back to the real-estate *gonif*. He wasn't sure, although his hearing was perfect, but he could have sworn it was something like "Only one worry at a time." He couldn't tell and he never did find out.

10

"You Are Very Cordially Invited..."

THEY CAME IN A TIDE that filled the eighteenth-floor Penn Top of the Statler-Hilton to overflowing and spilled out into the hallway. In their eyes danced curiosity, hero worship, a yearning to clutch the golden bodies that was in part love and in part the bright-green flame of greed. Who worried about distance? Some lived practically around the corner. But so deep was the need to come, see, touch the human embodiment of one of the country's newest and most exciting businesses that many traveled hundreds, even in some cases thousands, of miles to get there. They were old. Many still were bright-eyed retired and hoping that they had found Nirvana in fifty, one hundred, two hundred or three hundred shares of Oval's common; others were doddering and semi-dead except that their eyes, jowls and tongues flickered spastically with some still faint tentacles of hope; and others who had come in their forties and fifties to Oval's and had grown old in its service but nonetheless retained a feeling of proprietorship, *esprit* and, of course, hope. They were middle-aged. Professionals and working people whose relation to and investments in Oval's were a double source of pride. One, because they bought goods at savings there and sometimes reminded the sales girls with a nudge in the ribs that they were shareholders, you better be careful, boobie, and, two, because they sensed (or wanted to believe) that they had wisely latched onto a good thing by also becoming part owners in their favorite store. They were young. Newly married couples who congratulated themselves in having socked a portion of their wedding presents into Oval's stock; young families in which the father or mother had either a relative or a friend at the store who advised, "Buy a few shares—get in on the ground floor—this company's going right through the roof!" or who simply wanted to identify with the kind of young, virile, dynamic business that epitomized their own life style, which was, not so coincidentally, young, virile, dynamic. There was even an eleven-year-old boy with thick glasses from Queens who came in proudly holding aloft his stock certificate in one hand and in the other hand a long list of questions he intended to ask no matter what.

Many were attracted not merely by the president's letter attached to the proxy statement, reading, "You are very cordially invited to attend our first annual meeting of shareholders" but by rumors that the management would serve lunch.

But for the far vaster group, there was a common thread of hope. It tingled. It warmed. It snapped. It grew hot. Especially when a file of a half-dozen men came out of a side door at the front and began taking seats on the platform. Its last member was a lean, bemused, redheaded man. At his appearance, a spatter of applause broke out and it grew in volume until for a few moments the large room rang with it.

Through it all he sat frozen, his eyes rooted to the floor but occasionally they darted toward the side door. Would he stay? Would he bolt? Would he just sit there and writhe? A few of the kibitzers started placing bets in the audience.

As photographers darted among them snapping pictures, the six sat tensely. It was eighteen months since they had gone public, the first annual meeting having been postponed successively until legally it could not be held off any longer. They were all surprised at the turnout, double what they had expected. They were also surprised at the emotional wave that welled forth from the tiers of faces.

For some moments, the six and the 1,237 confronted one another silently, taking measure. Few in the audience had ever seen any of Oval's officers, except for Al Miller, who had been widely publicized in spite of himself. So they studied each man and his placard, trying to relate him and his function. But the effort was at first fruitless.

In that brief interval they tried again. The names were known to them but the bodies seemed independent from the names, not particularly reflective of the tag or the function. They read them again. Irving Waldteufel, secretary; Harry Abner, vice-president; Salvatore Patracelli, executive vice-president; Gordon Leon Jones, counsel; Ben Baron, president and treasurer; Albert C. Miller, chairman of the board. No, there was no use. They would have to wait until the men, the names and the voices merged.

Gordon Jones, lanky, cool, relaxed, leaned over toward Ben Baron, whispering, and the tiny, immaculate man rose and stood before the rostrum. He rapped sharply on its surface with a gavel. "Ladies and gentlemen," he said in a firm, youthful voice. "Welcome to the first annual stockholders' meeting of Red Oval Stores Corporation. We are all delighted to finally meet you face to face. My name is Ben Baron. I am president of your company."

Briefly, he introduced everyone at the head table, each one but Al Miller rising and acknowledging the polite applause. "Now I want to list the agenda of our meeting," Ben said, and he did. It was to elect a board of directors of twelve members, to consider and vote upon a proposal for a new company employee stock-purchase plan, to ratify the selection of auditors, and, he said with a smile of invitation, to "transact such other business as may properly come before the meeting."

At this, seven people rose simultaneously, three of them quickly grabbing hold of the microphones that had been placed around the room. But it was the eleven-year-old boy whose voice flooded the public-address system and thundered into everyone's ear.

"Sir! Sir! May I have the floor? My name is Wilfred Mason. I am a sixth-grade student at P.S. 111 in Queens. I own three shares of Oval's and I want—"

Immediately a heavyset woman in the rear seized a microphone and shouted, "Mr. Chairman, he shouldn't be allowed to talk—he's only a minor!"

Factions on behalf or against Wilfred Mason were instantly heard, but Ben rapped hard on the rostrum. "Please, let's have some decorum," he said. Then, pointing with his gavel at Wilfred, he added, "You're out of order, young man. But since presumably you will be a big stockholder someday, I'll allow you to talk briefly now. By the way, how did you become a stockholder anyway?"

The boy's voice pounding away in the overenergized public-address system was considerably bigger than he was. "Sir, I began reading the financial pages when I was nine years old. I saved up all my money from mowing lawns and delivering newspapers. My father helped me to pick out the stocks that I wanted to buy. My principal in school advised me, too, and he let me use his phone to call my broker—"

"Fine, young man," Ben broke in, impressed. "Now, what is it that you wanted to ask?"

Without hesitation, the boy's vast voice boomed out over the room: "Sir, sir, why does the price of Oval's common stock keep going down?"

Around the room, a chorus of murmured approvals arose. A man wearing an old straw hat got up and yelled, "That's just what I wanted to know!"

Ben nodded. "All right, all right. We'll answer that, but all in good time, all in good time."

He read the list of the directional nominees. There was some scattered booing now, especially when the names of Walter Solomon and General Horace Boatwright were read as nominees to succeed themselves.

"Mr. Chairman!" Before Ben could shut him up, a stout white-haired man in a loud sports jacket sputtered into a microphone, "I want to know—what the hell good does it do us if we got Wall Street and Inter-Continental Insurance on our board of directors if their advice on investments ain't paying off for us."

Before Ben could answer—actually he didn't want to answer but simply to tell the man to shut up until it was time for "other business"—a worn, unhappy woman strode up the main aisle and stood irately just a few feet under Ben. Pointing an accusing finger up at him, she demanded, "Tell me something, Mr. Chairman. If you guys get such big salaries, why don't you make sure that the stockholder doesn't lose money? I put all my life savings into your stock. I bought five hundred shares for thirty dollars and now after eighteen months it's only worth twenty-eight dollars a share! I'm a poor widow—do I deserve that? All you guys do is to take care of yourselves. I think we ought to throw all of you bums out!" She gave Ben her back and marched up the aisle to an outpouring of applause.

Three others tried to be heard at the same time. But Ben, red-faced and frustrated, gestured to a man who sat at a table in front of the amplifier for the P.A. system and all microphones to be shut off. The three would-be speakers babbled on, competing with one another but knowing that no one else heard them. Finally they sat down.

Ben felt himself trembling. Only fifteen or twenty minutes and already the meeting was out of control. The stock market was in one of its cyclical slumps, perhaps in more of one than usual. Oval's stock was down with all the rest, perhaps, Ben admitted ruefully to himself, also more than the usual. But why all the excitement? Why couldn't the shareholders take the long-term view, the one that he felt counted, because there was so much going for the company that its future appeared wonderful?

Everyone waited, knowing and resenting the fact that the chairman had taken a disciplinary action by ordering the auditory power to be shut off. He looked back at the audience while it simmered. Finally a tall, solemn-looking man in a pin-stripe suit arose and stood quietly. Most people knew him. He was John H. Hurlburt, a professional shareholders' representative who for years had first vainly and later successfully sought to arouse the corporate conscience for shareholders. He had, after years of yelling himself hoarse at annual meetings, arrived at the role of stockholders' statesman.

"Mr. Hurlburt?" Ben began after gesturing for the P.A. system to start again.

"Mr. Baron, in the interests of getting to the heart of the meeting," said Hurlburt, "perhaps it might be well to dispense here and there with parliamentary procedure and answer some of the questions as they arise. Perhaps we can ask Mr. Solomon, whose knowledge of Wall Street is paramount on the board, what he thinks of the prospects for a revitalization of our stock."

Ben Baron had no serious objection and, in the audience, Walter Solomon got up ready to answer. But, visibly disturbed, the attorney, Gordon Leon Jones, leaned over toward Ben and said, "Don't get trapped in that, Ben. It will mean total havoc during the meeting and we'll have to stay here seven or eight hours. Make everyone follow the rules." Ben nodded in agreement.

The audience would ordinarily have resented such restrictions, but, unfortunately, the attorney's words had been clearly heard around the great room since he had uttered them only a few inches from Ben's microphone. There was a restless stirring across the many rows of seats. Hurlburt slowly sat down, his face flaming. He had tried to be a peacemaker and, for his pains, he had been slapped. He promised himself to extract his revenge.

Walter Solomon also sank back into his chair. He was just as happy that the questioning had been curbed. The particular question he had been asked was out of line, anyway. No board of directors should ever predict when its stock would change in value. That was never due to any action that a company took but to a reaction by investors, often of an unpredictable nature. But next to him, as Ben Baron rapped for order, the burly little General Boatwright rumbled, "Some military discipline, that's what they need, dammit. Order is everything—and everything is order."

For the next forty minutes Ben carried on with only minor interruptions, naming the rest of the twelve directors, then taking a ballot and outlining the proposal for a new employee stock-purchase plan and taking a ballot.

"Mr. Chairman!" A new shrill voice broke out over the P.A. system and sent shivers of concern and anticipation throughout the audience. A voluptuous redhead with heavily made-up eyes and rather large red lips breathed hoarsely into a microphone, standing parallel to Hurlburt who quickly got up with her. "My name is Harriet P. Brown," she said, "I am a stockholder representing myself and other stockholders. I want to ask the handsome Mr. Baron and that incredibly sexy Mr. Miller when we can please hope to get a dividend. A company so successful with such a profit record should return some of its gains to the shareholders. Now, I am wearing a jump suit I bought in the new Oval's store in Manhattan—all I paid for it was nineteen ninety-five and I had to fight my way through a bunch of other girls to get it, and I mean I had to claw and I had to fight. It's an import and that means a high profit—so why can't we start getting a dividend, Mr. Baron and Mr. Miller?"

Hurlburt had stood about as much as he could. The audience was torn between agreeing with Miss Brown's dividend philosophy and disliking her brassy manner. Hurlburt demanded, "Mr. Chairman, this lady—I say lady advisedly—is out of order. What does all that have to do with voting on the auditors?"

"You shut up, you sonofabitch!" Harriet P. Brown yelled. "It's right when you get up and interrupt but wrong when I do, isn't it?" Near her, two older women advised her to sit down and be quiet, one of them adding, "A lady doesn't use that kind of language." She whirled on them and shouted, "You shut up, too, you old hag! You're just jealous because of my looks. That's why women hate me but men love me—right, Mr. Baron and Mr. Miller?"

Ben rapped for order and glanced warningly over at the P.A. control man. The two corporate gadflies sat down after leveling looks of hate at each other. Ben proceeded with the vote on the auditors, who were duly elected. Then, taking a deep breath, he said, "Now, for any other business—"

"Sir!" It was Wilfred Mason, the eleven-year-old stockholder. "Sir, about my question—"

"Mr. Baron, as a former merchant, I rise to inquire into certain policies" from a burly, elderly man holding a sheaf of papers.

"My name is Sadie Levinthal, Mr. Chairman. Last week I had a very unpleasant experience in your store in Chicago" began a woman in a mink.

Ben waved them all away. "Please, some order if you don't mind. One at a time as I recognize you. But please, let me admonish you. Any question of a personal nature, such as an experience with a sales girl, has no place at this meeting. If you

have such a complaint, please remain after the meeting and see
Mr. Nat Batt, our public-relations director—"

Standing in the wings just near enough for Ben to hear, Nat
muttered, "Fuck 'em all."

"—and now, you, Mr.—"

He recognized a young man who had been waving frantically.
"My name is Harold Whitcomb, Mr. Chairman, and I represent
the Pyramid Fund," the young man said. "We too have been
disturbed by the decline in the value of the stock and we are
wondering, sir, if the move into higher-priced fashion was a wise
one. We understand that profit margins have been disappointing
in those new departments, and, of course, we are anxious to hear
your report on the first quarter's results. But can you enlighten
us as to why the move into high fashion was made and if it is
true that it has been disappointing during the entire year?"

Hurlburt was on his feet again. "Mr. Chairman, that young
man anticipated my next question. I think we would all like to
hear why it is that the company took such a radical departure
and why it is not working out according to expectations."

"Ben, you lovely little man, I think the move was wonderful—
look how sexy I am in this wonderful little jump suit?" Harriet P.
Brown paraded up the aisle wiggling and shaking provocatively.
Cries of "Sit down, you hussy!" or "Just a show-off, aren't you?"
and similar ones were directed at her. She and another woman,
older but as indomitable as she was, faced each other and
traded insults. Hurlburt's exasperation was audibly heard on the
microphone: "Shit!" At least five others who wanted to speak
stood helplessly, trapped into silence by the intensifying exchange between the women.

On the rostrum, Ben banged and banged, glancing over once
at Al Miller, seated at the end of the table. He seemed cool and
withdrawn.

Ben had the P.A. system turned off again and waited a few
moments until everyone, conscious that they had been silenced
electronically, quietly sat down.

Motioning to the man at the amplifier and nodding at Whitcomb, the representative of the mutual fund, Ben said, "Mr.
Whitcomb, let me see if I can answer your questions. Now, we

decided to venture into the couture field because of the higher profit opportunities. However, in retailing, as you must know, it is axiomatic that it takes anywhere from one to three years to make an impact in a new field. Millions of Oval customers didn't exactly come to us overnight, either, although it is safe to say— the figures prove it without any question—that they stayed. So, we are certain, it will be with our new venture. We estimate that within six months our margin on couture goods will be between twenty and forty percent above those in similar but lower-priced departments."

"Well, that's fine, Mr. Chairman," Whitcomb said, now back on his feet. "You're asking the stockholders to wait at least another six months for an experiment that has drained I'd estimate between thirty and fifty cents a share from earnings in the hope that it might pay off later. Can you comment on the earnings drain and how much the company has spent so far to get into the high-fashion business?"

Ben swallowed. He didn't care for the questions but saw no way out of it. He conferred briefly with Gordon Leon Jones, who shrugged and whispered a few words. Ben straightened up. "I'd say that your estimate was a bit low. It was more like fifty cents to seventy-five cents a share on an annual basis. As far as our expenditures for entry into the high-fashion field, I can't give you precise figures because that would help our competition. But I will tell that in round numbers it is well over twenty-five million dollars."

Many in the audience gasped. Both figures were considerably above what had been reported in the press.

The burly, elderly man who had been a merchant seized a microphone and yelled, "You guys ought to have your heads examined! You're taking a wonderful company and you're letting it go down the drain! Let's hear from Al Miller. He's the guy we ought to hear from—we invested all our money into this company because of him and yet he sits there and he don't say a word. And what the hell's wrong with your board of directors? Are they a bunch of dummies—did they just sit on their hands when management proposed that move?"

In the audience, Walter Solomon forcibly restrained General

Boatwright, who had started up after the last speaker, brandishing his swagger stick. At the rostrum, Ben glanced at Al Miller, whose averted eyes and continuing preoccupation spoke louder than any response. He had no intention of answering.

But Hurlburt was up again. "Perhaps Mr. Miller has no desire to respond to that question. Obviously he was party to the decision—he is chairman of the board, after all. But I would like to ask him this. Last February Mr. Miller and Oval's were the subject of a cover article in *Time* magazine—a fine tribute it was, too, I might say, under the title of 'Prophet of the New American Consumer,' but there were some things in that article of a disturbing nature. I refer to his statement 'I'm not in favor of dividends. I think that earnings should always be put back into the business.' I also refer—" Hurlburg paused and held up a copy of *Time*, apparently the exact issue—"to the statement 'I believe in giving every executive a lot of leeway. In fact, once I give him a job and charge him with the responsibility of it, I never even see him any more.' Now, Mr. Chairman, I think that Mr. Miller has an obligation to explain to the shareholders if he indeed made those statements and, if so, if that kind of philosophy isn't directly responsible for the recent lower earnings trend?"

Ben glanced once again at Al Miller. Al's face was almost beet color. Ben conferred again with Gordon Jones, discreetly covering the microphone with his fist. Then Ben said softly into the microphone, "Our counsel says that Mr. Miller isn't legally required to, but it is entirely up to him if he wishes to reply."

Everyone's gaze was on Al as the microphone was taken off its stand and passed to him. He looked up, his eyes agonized, and he stared back at the stockholders as though paralyzed. In a crushed voice that carried all over the hushed room he replied, "I . . . I . . . I . . . I was misquoted."

After a few moments of stunned silence, the room erupted into a cacophony.

Hurlburt: "All I can say is under cumulative voting, this sort of nonsense wouldn't happen."

Unidentified: "Any guy that lets that happen I think we ought to boot his ass out—right now!"

Sadie Levinthal: "It's those snippy sales girls. A good sales girl can make customers happy!"

Wilfred Mason: "Can I have a note excusing my absence for my teacher?"

Whitcomb: "I urge management to reexamine its merchandising policies."

The former merchant: "I will be glad to advise you—for a very reasonable fee, of course."

Harriet P. Brown: "Three cheers for Al Miller, America's smartest and handsomest merchant!"

Harry Abner: "Motion we adjourn the meeting. And I second the motion."

Tension, uncertainty and confusion lapped around the toes of the board of directors as it convened shortly after the stockholders' meeting ended. The twelve directors met on the same floor where the stockholders now ate their boxed lunches, courtesy of Oval's. But the two doors were bolted and Pinkerton guards had been posted outside each one. General Boatwright had insisted on it and Gordon Jones, who had handled the arrangements, had complied.

After the stormy stockholders' meeting, the board had silently gathered and for several minutes the seven inside and the four outside directors had avoided one another's eyes. But occasionally they looked over at the doors with hope. Al Miller, the chairman of the board, had disappeared in the melee that followed the abrupt end of the earlier meeting. His departure had been so sudden and undetected that everyone was certain he wouldn't be back, perhaps permanently.

Walter Solomon, the board's vice-chairman, cleared his throat and said brightly, "Well, gentlemen, we might as well get started. We've got a lot of business to attend to and lots of problems to discuss. I would like to say a word or two about the meeting that just ended, particularly for those here who aren't as familiar with stockholders' meetings as I am."

He glanced for a moment around the table. Ben Baron seemed crushed. Harry Abner, Solly Patracelli, Irving Waldteufel, Nat Batt, Willie Wallenstein and Matthew Smiles all had the same look—a mixture of resentment, self-defensiveness and defiance. General Boatwright's tiny, porcine eyes were hot and angry. Gordon Jones' expression was amused and cool. The fourth outside director, Professor Harrison Winters of New York University, appeared deep in thought.

Solomon resumed, assuming a jauntiness he didn't quite feel but expressing a deeply ingrained philosophy. "I wouldn't let the storminess of the meeting affect you too much. Annual meetings are about the only time a stockholder has a chance to be heard. All year long he feels like a tiny cog in a great big money wheel and he wears an inferiority complex that weighs him down. So, one morning a year he comes into town and he gets the psychic pleasure of throwing darts at management. Then he goes home, relieved and refreshed for a couple of days until he starts feeling again like the nobody and the ignoramus that he does all year long. . . . All right now, so we had a rough meeting. The *Times* and the *Wall Street Journal* will rip into us tomorrow and all our competitors will enjoy our discomfiture. A week later, it will be forgotten. But I want to remind you fellows that the stockholders love the company as much as ever, believe me, despite the noise and the brickbats. Out of twelve hundred or so who were present at the meeting, how many spoke out in complaining terms? Twenty, twenty-five? That's what, two percent? The rest sat there and enjoyed the show. And that's what annual stockholders' meetings are—a show, an entertainment, a concession to the democratic corporate process, and you know, as I do, what bunk that is."

He glanced again around the table and silently congratulated himself on the effectiveness of his message. The expression of the inside directors, Oval's seven officers, had eased and the tension had slid away. A silly grin had replaced the defiance on the faces of Harry Abner, Irving Waldteufel, Patracelli and one or two others. But Ben Baron's face still wore its harried edge and the little general continued to sit there boiling.

"That was very well put," Gordon Jones said gratefully. "I suggest that we're all a bit ruffled because this was our first annual meeting and we were all hypersensitive because of it. Now, Mr. Chairman, may I suggest that we follow the agenda for this meeting that the executive committee prepared. You will all find copies of it in front of you and—"

But he wasn't able to continue because directly across the table General Boatwright banged his fist down with a heavy thud that suddenly shocked all of them.

"Bull, bull, bull!" Boatwright bellowed. "Let's forget the frigging agenda and get right to the heart of our problem. Just what the hell is wrong with this company? Walter, every reservation I had eighteen months ago when we were trying to decide if this company should go public has come home to roost! What can we do to knock out a better profit? That's what demands top priority right now!"

Walter Solomon regarded him with surprise. The fat little ex-general was always surprising him with his outbursts. But he did represent Oval's largest source of private financing and his insurance company's portfolio held the biggest block of stock next to that of Al Miller himself. "Perhaps you're right, General," Solomon said softly. "We can get back to our agenda afterward."

"You're fucking well right I'm right!" Boatwright shouted. "I'd like to go around the table and hear an excuse—no, let's call it an opinion—from everyone. What's happened to our profit picture? What's happened to our stock? Let's start with you, Mr. Baron."

Ben paused, glancing around at the ten other faces. He saw little sympathy on any of them and it suddenly hit him, as if it were a blow under the heart, how alone and exposed he was. Where are you, Al Miller, you cowardly bastard, when Bright Ben needs you?

"Well, General, let me put it this way. I still believe strongly in our trading-up program and I'm just as much convinced that it will catch on," Ben said. "It takes time—sometimes more time than we would think it does—for a change to make impact. I would recommend a bit more patience."

The general's eyes bulged. His fist tightened around the small swagger stick that lay on the table before him. "Patience," he told Ben, "is a commodity that I have damned little of right now. We have seventeen million dollars in stock in this company that we could have in computers or education systems or frozen food, any one of which could give us a better return. Patience my foot, sir!"

Harry Abner was next clockwise and he quailed under Boatwright's burning stare. "To tell you the truth, General, I wasn't consulted on the shift to high fashion. Frankly, I think we priced ourselves out of the market when we went that route," he said. "But I think we can recoup the situation. Let's cancel all outstanding orders of the better-priced stuff, take our markdowns and hold a gigantic sale . . ."

Patracelli was next and he immediately demurred. "I'm an operations man, not a merchandiser," he said. "But I'm convinced that one of our big problems is that we never have enough meetings. One of the big reasons is that until the new building is finished we don't have a room big enough to meet. So . . ."

Irving Waldteufel was next. "I don't want to cop out on the question, gentlemen, but I'm afraid that I'm going to cop out. I think it was all a mistake. We're a store for the mass audience—where the hell do we get the *chutzpah* to go into the high brackets? But this isn't my bailiwick. If it's supplies you need, I'm the best man in the business and how I get them doesn't matter to me. Supplies, fine; skirts, no."

Nat Batt had been against the move from the onset, but "then, shit, they never asked me. Al Miller doesn't give a crap for my opinion on anything but publicity—and you know how much use he's got for publicity." Wallenstein shifted in his seat. "I haven't paid much attention to it, to be honest about it, gentlemen," he said. "I've been busy in my own area and that area keeps growing every single minute."

Matthew Smiles, unlike the others, was willing to fight on. But along entirely new lines. "The way I look at it," he said, "all we need is a socko idea. Who buys high fashion, anyway? People who live a faster life, who've got an ego that's got to be exercised all the time. Exhibitionists, right? Now, all we have to do is to appeal to their life pace, their ego and their exhibitionism. Why not build a special entrance for them? With maybe a plush red carpet rolling right up to the high-fashion departments? Or a real jazzed-up shop fully enclosed but with its own windows right within the regular store. Or . . ."

The general had been quietly listening to the seven Oval's executives but he had been exploding inside. He was appalled at what he interpreted as a complete lack of insight, talent and professionalism. Why, he wondered desperately, feeling the hysterical frustration that had overwhelmed him often as a deskside general in the Pentagon, had he allowed himself to become involved with such absolute dummies and yardbirds? What had happened to his ability to make command decisions and sound value judgments?

Controlling himself with difficulty, he turned toward Professor Harrison Winters, who sat next to him. "Professor," he said hoarsely, "you haven't given out with one goddam word, but I have a strong conviction that you've been doing considerable thinking. What's your opinion?"

The retailing scholar stirred uncomfortably. He was a quiet but alert man in his early sixties who had written fourteen books on the merchandising and economics of storekeeping over a thirty-year span. While he had never worked in a store, he was widely respected for his knowledge of retailing. But he had labored during his career under a self-imposed handicap. He knew, or suspected, that much of what he said on his chosen subject would be scoffed at on the basis that he was a theoretician, pontificating about a field that was as difficult, as intricate, as hard-nosed as any in the entire business world.

And so he said, somewhat self-deprecatingly, "Of course, I speak only as an academician. But I've been studying the retail scene for a considerable period, as you know, and some of my ideas may have become a bit hardened. I agree with Ben Baron on the practical side of his argument but not on the concept. I agree, in other words, that it takes several years for a retailing change to make impact, but I disagree that a company that has had a vast success should shift price lines in such a way that you are bidding for virtually a complete new market. You see, gentlemen, my studies of over thirty years as a dispassionate observer of the retail scene has convinced me of the absolute truth of one axiom: You decide what you want to be and then you must do everything necessary to achieve that image. Anything else is simply diversionary. Every big success in retailing history has proven that. And every failure has proven it in a negative fashion. I may be risking some ridicule when I say that frequenting a store on a consistent basis is for many people the same thing as going to a doctor or dentist or even pharmacist. Trust, faith, confidence, but above all obtaining the right results. If any of those are lacking, the public will drop you so quickly your head will spin—but, by the same token, the public has confidence only in specialists and even department stores, discount or otherwise, have to specialize whether it is in price brackets, merchandise mix, or degree of service and probably in all three. So I think, gentlemen, that Oval's move into high fashion or couture was a violation of the rules."

Around the table there was no immediate comment. Ben felt the heavy pain under his heart spreading and he wondered again, Where the hell are you, Al Miller? They're tearing me apart joint by joint. Boatwright's squarish, determined face wore a grim grin of gratification. He glanced over at Walter Solomon and said, "Only you and Gordon Jones to be heard from. Let's have your opinion next on the table, Walter. You two got me into this."

The smooth-faced, suave Wall Street broker was upset for a variety of reasons, not the least of which was resentment at the abrupt manner in which the little general had taken over the meeting. In Al Miller's absence it was Solomon's prerogative to conduct board meetings. But what bothered him as much was the certainty that Boatwright would blame him for the bad judgment in devoting and investing so many millions in a concern that had made such a wrong turn. His own enemies would rejoice. There were many who labeled each of his successes as due to nothing but the nepotism that had catapulted him to the top and likewise hailed his failures as evidence of the indiscriminate choice allowed by that nepotism. All this would take detailed, dexterous explaining in more than a few quarters, he realized, and there was no longer any point in delaying the inevitable. So he said, "Well, the facts are that after an expenditure of twenty-five million dollars, earnings had dropped thirty percent in three consecutive quarters and our stock has gone down about thirty-five percent. We could, I suppose, keep dropping in good money after bad, but that would be another mistake. I think that unquestionably remedial action is called for and as soon as possible."

The general nodded. At least, he told himself, Solomon was willing to take his lumps. He glanced now at Gordon Jones across the table. The attorney had been the most relaxed in the room. His friendly, wise, shaggy-dog personality had been the only leveling influence in the room, not that it had changed much. Feelings were too high. "What do you say, Counsel?" Boatwright asked him.

Strange, Jones was thinking as he felt everyone's curious attention on him, how everyone in the room was on the griddle because Al Miller had given Ben Baron his head. But they, he realized with satisfaction, had made the decision, even if by default. The decision-makers, he told himself, swallowing his own callousness, have to bear the brunt of their bad judgments, just as they would reap the credit for the wise ones. And so without emotion he said simply: "Ditto."

Boatwright expelled a whoosh of breath. So it was all decided. Raising his swagger stick, he turned and pointed it directly at Ben Baron. "It's quite clear, isn't it, Mr. Baron, that you have led us down the wrong road? I don't quite know what you can say in your own behalf, but I do know what you should do. And so does everyone at this table, I venture. Is there anything you would like to say . . ." Boatwright paused, his head feeling oddly light. He had been about to say, ". . . before we pass sentence on you?" but he caught himself and substituted "before we proceed?"

Ben nodded understandingly. "Yes, I appreciate the opportunity. Nothing quite like this has ever happened to me. Usually when I have made important changes in policy I've been allowed the time to carry them out and they have always succeeded, without exception. Of course, I know that this is a public company, but I still insist that eighteen months is not enough. Nonetheless, I'm in no position to insist on it."

There was a scuffle outside one of the doors, the one not near the still lingering stockholders. The door opened and Al Miller came lurching in, brushing off an irate Pinkerton guard. It was instantly easy to see why the security officer had been reluctant to let him in. Al, perspiring and hot, had somehow and somewhere managed to change from the business suit he wore at the meeting. Instead, he had on a sport jacket, an open-collared sport shirt, baggy slacks and white sneakers. It was, both Solomon and the general recalled, the exact outfit he had worn when they had first met him that day almost two years before for lunch.

But as he sank into the single empty seat around the table, they saw that he had an addition. He held an ice-cream cone in one hand. He was licking it with pleasure, rolling the dabs around on his tongue. Everyone was appalled, surprised, intrigued or delighted, depending upon his own disposition. At the end of the table, Nat Batt whispered but loud enough for everyone to hear, "That sonofabitch. He doesn't give a shit. They haven't got him yet and you can bet your ass they never will."

But the general, having dropped his stick in dismay when Al had burst in, rallied. "Well, Mr. Miller," he said, "your timing is good. It may be considerably better at making personal appearances than at offering fashion goods to the public. I was about to ask where in hell the chief yo-yo in this asylum was."

Al ignored him. He continued for a few moments enjoying his ice-cream cone and gazing around at everyone. Unlike his normal behavior, he appeared calm and well poised. Suddenly, with a defiant gesture, he took his half-finished cone and dumped it, tip up, in the center of an ashtray sitting in the middle of the table. Everyone sat with open mouths looking at it. Al turned to Ben, a forlorn little man sitting hunched in his chair, and asked, "So, you're still alive? Good for you."

He gave Ben a reassuring smile. Then he turned to all of them. "Gents, I'm sorry that I ran out on you. I just had to get away from that damn meeting. You know where I've been? I've just come from three of our stores, our nearest ones, and I've brought good news for you. People are still buying, our cash registers are banging away, lines are waiting at our checkouts and the day's receipts, I found out, are the best we've had in weeks. The world, I'm happy to tell you, hasn't gone to hell . . . I think we ought to cash in our high-fashion operation. But I think we don't have to take a real licking on it. I'm sure that Harry, Nat, Mottel, Molly and the others can come up with a big sale that will not only sell out much of our stock but make it so good that everything else in the stores will cash in too. We can even spread it out for not one but several sales, over maybe a couple of months. Then, I figure, it might make sense to see if we can't use the best elements in it to open one or a chain of swinging specialty shops. If it goes, terrific, we've added a plus to our business. If it doesn't, we can pull out of it fast without getting into any extra expense. Maybe our mistake was to include the high-priced, high-fashion stuff right within our regular stores. Who can tell how we can make out if we sell it under its own identity—not related to Oval's directly? We've got the merchandise, with some newer stuff still on order, so I think it's worth a gamble. Anybody want to knock it down?"

No one did, at least not immediately. And not even afterward, especially when Al added, carefully studying his fingers, "I'm personally willing to take a gamble on it. After all, I'm still the biggest stockholder in the company, so I'm shooting the biggest craps of all."

After summary, negative action on such matters as dividends and having postponed making any changes among the officers, the board meeting ended. Everyone quietly departed, leaving Al sitting at one end of the table and Ben Baron at the other end. They didn't say anything for a while in the empty room and then they found that they were smiling at each other.

"Al," Ben began, "I am resigning."

"I'm not asking you to."

"I know," Ben said earnestly. "But I was way off and my value to Oval's is over. The board and the staff have lost confidence in me."

"I haven't."

"I fouled you up."

"You carried the ball—but I let you. No, you're gonna stay."

Ben covered his face with his hands. "I can't, Al. I can't stay on as a failure."

"What about Schulte's 'f.q.' measurement? You got a real high grade on flexibility. You gonna run out on that?"

" 'F.q.'?"

"Yeah, 'flexibility quotient.' That's what it means, doesn't it?"

Ben nodded miserably. "Yes, it does."

Again, they sat silently for some minutes. Finally, Ben said, "I've made up my mind. I've got to quit. You see, there are other things going on at Oval's that concern me. I'm worried about this crazy new project of Wallenstein's. Did you know about Wallenstein, Pennsylvania, Al? He's building a town and a shopping center in western Pennsylvania that will include the town's city hall, police and fire departments. That means that Oval's or Wallenstein—I don't really know which—will own and operate a whole town, with the mayor, the police chief, the fire chief and everyone working for him—or us."

"I know, Ben," Al said vaguely.

"Can you imagine what will happen if the general gets wind of it? He'll skin us alive."

Al shrugged. "Not if we make a good profit at it," he said. "Isn't that what everybody wants?"

"Al, I just can't take the chance. I'm pulling out."

Al took him in carefully. Ben's handsome face was drawn, white and his eyes were full of a distant fear.

"All right, Ben, if you want."

"There's no other way for me, Al."

"You'll always be Bright Ben to me."

"You're not . . . disappointed in me?"

"Me, disappointed? Not me."

"Thanks, Al, very much."

"I'll give you a great reference."

"Al . . ."

The neat little man bawled.

11

Sam Comes Through Again

IN THE HANDSOME SITTING ROOM of a condominium just off a golden beach in St. Thomas, Sam Schulte sat at the table and swore at himself. Then, in a flickering of facial features so rapid that it resembled the sequential opening and shutting of a camera lens, he laughed raucously, scowled, leered, smiled, pouted, and damned himself again, activating the range of his present, imminent and potential moods.

As the bright sun generated a black fire in the heavy mat of hair on his bare chest, he wished that the solemn figure of Al Miller at the window wasn't there to witness the well of emotion and power that he felt in himself when those chainlike moods of self-expression fell upon him. Always, he was embarrassed by the feeling of omnipotence that swept him during such emotional storms.

But since Al merely stared out the window, Sam calmed. With one hand he tilted the bottle of sherry to his lips and with the other he leafed through the sheaf of computer printouts on the table before him. Now and then his secretary, Priscilla Terry, young, dignified but piquant and voluptuous in a tiny halter and perhaps the tightest pair of short-shorts that Al Miller had ever seen, came in from the other room. Primly, she handed Sam several more sheets, eluded his instinctive and absent-minded pinch and withdrew.

At the window, Al Miller occasionally studied the scene in the room but mostly he stared out at the sweeping expanse of white-yellow beach and multicolored sea.

He was still a bit dazed. Less than twenty-four hours ago he had phoned Sam and found that he was on a brief vacation in the Caribbean. But Ben Baron's departure had generated such an urgency in him that he had telephoned Sam in St. Thomas and explained his problem. A few hours later Al arrived at the tiny St. Thomas airport and was greeted by a chauffeur and car that Sam had sent for him. And within a few hours Miss Terry had arrived from New York with a big box of sheets from Sam's executive-search file.

Since that morning, Schulte's twenty-two-foot sitting room in the year-round apartment he maintained in St. Thomas had been turned into a makeshift office. Almost every hour Sam would turn from his studies to phone New York and ask an associate to check on the performance and status of a name on his lists.

As he scrutinized his sheets, Sam asked again, "Where did Ben fail? Or did we make a bad value judgment, Al?"

He seemed genuinely puzzled by what had happened and none of Al's previous answers to the questions had satisfied him. Al said, "Sam, let's just say that I put him in an untenable spot. I let him go too far in a situation that wasn't loose. I got a bad habit of letting guys that work for me get in over their heads."

Schulte said, "Now, don't you go having self-recriminations. You gave him an opportunity and I guess that the only thing that happened was that he turned out to be a boy in a man's job."

He tilted the bottle of sherry again, a trickle of wine dribbling down his chest. "Hell," said Sam, "it's a risk we all take when we put a guy in a position of responsibility. What we've got to do now, *boychik*, is find you a man instead of a boy."

Al's attention went back to the window. Out on the beach, about one hundred yards away, her legs submerged in water up to the knees, a woman in a bikini painted at an easel. It was Barbara Schulte, whose pleasure at seeing Al last night had surprised and dismayed him. Lucid, attractive and poised, she had kissed him warmly.

"How nice to see you, Al," she had said. "Your coming down here may just turn out to be the nicest thing that will happen at St. Thomas."

She had kissed him again and Al had moved away from her, concerned that Sam might be offended. But there was only an amused look in Sam's eyes as he had ushered Al into the apartment.

As he walked back now to sit down with Schulte, Al tried to clear his head so that he could be of some help to Sam. But he could not push aside the biting memory of two incidents that had happened only a few days ago and which had sent him flying 1,800 miles to solicit Sam's help.

Ben Baron's announcement that he had resigned the morning after the stockholders' meeting had had a curious effect on the boys. It wasn't so much that they hadn't expected Ben to move out sometime soon. Obviously, he was not one of them and didn't understand the way in which they worked together. But they had gotten used to the handsome, neat little man, his personality hadn't created many ripples and even his ill-fated drive to shift to high fashion had been done in a way that stressed the profit objectives rather than their error in not having made that move before.

As a result, after some hasty arrangements following the directors' meeting, they had reserved a room above a prominent Italian restaurant in Manhattan and thrown a dinner for him. Ben Baron sat among them all, his face soft and beginning to work a little, gazing around at them with an expression of having suddenly made friends among a bunch of strangers. Off to a side, an accordionist played Italian melodies.

Each one rose to toast Ben in his own fashion.

"Wherever you go, Ben," said Harry Abner, raising his glass, "it'll be hard to forget you, even for a guy with a lousy memory like me. *Salud!*"

Irving Waldteufel laid it right on the line. "If you ever need any supplies, Ben—if you ever need a guy to teach you how to steal for yourself and the company—ask me. Your health!"

Wallenstein was generous. "Should you in your next endeavors ever need a site for a store or for anything, Ben, come to me. Believe me, I got 'em to spare. *Zu Gesund!*"

Molly, however, didn't toast Ben with wine. She stalked over, a dazzling grin on her face, and stood beside him. She took his hands and placed them on her buttocks. "Take yourself a good feel to remember me by," she told him. Then she leaned close and whispered, "The best lay you ever had, Buster." She straightened up, looked hard at Al Miller sitting at the end of the table and added, "Give me a good little man any old time, you know what I mean?"

But it took Nat Batt—who else?—to capitalize on the mood of the event.

Short, fat, bald, baggy-panted and hot-eyed, Nat jumped up and instructed the accordionist to follow him with the right melody. He raised his glass and sang or rather croaked, struggling with the lyrics and gesturing at the rest to join in after a couple of choruses:

> "For he's a fucking jolly good fellow,
> For he's a fucking jolly good fellow,
> Which no one can ever deny,
> Unless he just plain wants ta lie.
>
> "Ben don't know much about sell-o,
> But he's just such a fucking nice fellow.
> It makes me cry to hear his goodbye,
> So, why, Ben, why?
>
> "We always thought he was just a little shit.
> But he really turned out to be quite a hit.
> He taught us a lot, but he ain't so hot.
> If he was, he'd hang aroun' and watch us go down.
>
> "Cause everyone says we'll fall
> Specially that little gen-er-al.
>
> "But if you gotta go, Ben, well, oh then,
> Go head and leave us, sure it'll grieve us.

But we'll have that forty-story building to
   remember you, you bum!
Just in case we ever need a forty-story building
   to jump down from!

"But we're not mad, we're just glad
You helped us beat down Macy, Gimbel and Sloane
We sure never could have done it all alone.

"So we're gonna change your name—on our walls
It won't be Bright Ben, it will be Big Balls!"

"Now, everybody—'For he's a fucking jolly good fellow, For he's—' "

Nat sat down suddenly. Tears eased down Ben's cheeks. Everyone's face was a bit twisted. Molly sobbed audibly. Al said, "Besides all his other faults, like being the world's biggest liar, Nat is the world's lousiest poet. But what he said, Ben—that's just how we feel. You'll always be one of us."

Now Al turned and gestured at Solly, who went out and brought in a large square box.

"Just a small token from us to you," Al told Ben. "We feel you demonstrated them to a high degree in the short time you were with us. And we want you should have this as an expression of how we feel about you."

Solly and Harry opened the box and cleared away the tissue paper. Ben reached in and extracted a heavy object mounted on a plaque. It was a giant pair of bronze-plated testicles.

The other incident occurred a few days after the stockholders' meeting when Walter Solomon asked Al to come down to his office. In the conference room of Dickster, Hoppman, Solomon & Co., Al also met General Boatwright and a tall, keen-eyed, whiplash thin stranger who wore modified Western clothes.

"Meet Bill Stringer from Houston. He's head of the Great Panhandle Fund," Solomon told Al. "Great Panhandle is vitally interested in Oval's. They've been accumulating Oval's stock and now they own about 575,000 shares of common."

"How y'all, Al?" the Texan said.

Al nodded warily.

They sat around the table. Walter said affably, "We thought that we should have a private session, Al, after what happened at the annual meeting and afterwards. With Ben Baron's resignation, you need a new president and we'd like to talk to you about that and we also wondered what you planned to do about improving the profit picture."

The general cleared his throat like a phlegmy frog. "Chm, chm. I must say that I was dissatisfied with what we were told at the board meeting. What precisely are your plans, Mr. Chairman?"

Al stared bleakly at the three expectant faces. There was a hard shell to them that he didn't like at all. It hit him hard in the stomach at that moment that while he frequently had a warm feeling about having offered Oval's shares to the general public, the real beneficiaries had been what these three represented. Wall Street, the bankers, the insurance companies and the mutual funds had not only gotten their feet inside Oval's front door but they were also sitting in his lap and on top of his head, too.

"I thought that we had covered all that stuff the other day, didn't we?" he asked weakly.

"Not really, Al," Walter Solomon said. "But, in any case, Stringer's fund represents the owner of a very big block of stock now. He's entitled to know what you're planning to do to hike your earnings."

The general's short fuse was already sputtering. "Chm, chm," he said again. Then, having accomplished that, he demanded, "What the hell is your current, running net, anyway, Mr. Miller?"

Al glanced out the window for a moment. If he were only out on the road burning it up with his Cord, he could breathe freely and think clearly. Then, turning back to the hard curiosity around the table, bitterly sensing the wind of a great flow of new problems, he replied, "Why don't you better ask me what's my net net?"

Stringer's keen eyes glinted. "What all—what's that, sir?"

"Well, I'll tell you, pardner," Al said tightly. "Some guys call it the net after the net income, with everything taken out but the pure profit. But I call the net net the real value of what we're doing, the joy we bring to our employees, our customers and the whole goddam unhappy world. That's the net net."

There was a stunned silence around the table. What did I do, Al thought, drop a stink bomb into the room? The first to rally, probably because of his military background, was the general. He exploded. "What the hell does that have to do with running a business?"

Walter Solomon stirred uncomfortably. "Really, Al," he said.

Stringer's voice was almost toneless. It had a slight nasal quality but no discernible quality on the sound scale. He said, "Down home, we call that bull-stalking when there just ain't any bull in the vicinity."

But Al stood pat. "The way I've been operating the last fourteen years, gents, I found that if I concentrated on keeping everyone who either works or comes into the store happy, the profits just rolled in by themselves. And, even though we went public almost two years ago, I still don't see that the principle has to be thrown out the window."

"Then I would say, Al," Walter Solomon said, "that you've got to open your eyes wide and realize that the picture has changed. You're responsible to your stockholders now, especially your big ones but the small ones too, and a haphazard approach to achieving profit goals just won't work any longer."

Al took them all in again, seeing their shell hardening even more. It was obvious that they were all in firm agreement and that the stockbroker had just enunciated in the most definite way the big change that had descended upon Oval's since it had started in business. He arose. "We'll see, gents," he said. "We'll see."

He was walking out on them and they didn't like it. Hurriedly, Stringer put in, "What about finding your new president? How is that coming along? He could be the key to the whole problem, if he turns out to be a good, solid, gun-slinging administrator."

"I'm working on it," Al said stiffly, halfway through the door.

As he moved out, Boatwright added, "Make sure you get a

tough, hard-nosed man. You need him badly. You might even consider a military man."

But Al was already out the door and gone.

He watched carefully as Sam's hairy finger ran down the six leaves of the printout sheets entitled "Chief Operating Officers." The finger stopped now and then but then kept on going. "You know, Al, I think this time you've got to give all the frozen faces a guy that they can't possibly use their prejudices against," Sam observed. "Ben Baron tried a few daring things—but the profits didn't go along. So they cut off his head and tried to throw a harpoon at you."

Al nodded. "I know it now—but where do we go from here?"

Sam didn't reply. He flipped a page. "If I can be candid," he resumed, "I agree with you that you let him have too much leeway. But, on the other side of the ledger, Ben lacked self-discipline. Discipline's the true mark of an executive. Don't you agree?"

It was, of course, the worst kind of question to ask Al. He felt uncomfortable and he must have shown it because Sam smiled and placed a reassuring arm on Al's. "Don't worry, *boychik*. We'll find you a good man and your troubles will be over."

But Al's reaction was doubtful. "The worst part of it, Sam," he said, "is that I don't know exactly what I'm looking for. I thought Ben was just right. I bought myself a merchant-administrator and he turned out to have ideas, too. So what do I need now? A guy without ideas who can just administrate? That's not enough. I need someone, too, who everyone can funnel ideas through so that he can stand in for me when I'm away. What the hell do I need, anyway?"

"What do you need? What does anyone need?" Sam said, shrugging. "Somebody to stand off the wolves—that's about all and that's plenty. Let's face it squarely, Al. No matter who you get, the company's still going to be you—your drive, your brains, and you making all the final decisions. That's the way it's got to be, regardless of what they teach the young men in the graduate schools. Committee decisions, team management, presidential offices—they're nothing but crap. That's the kind of stuff that's put out on the PR wires to keep the stupid stockholders happy, just in case they get scared that the founder, the top guy, is suddenly going to keel over someday and the business is going to be left like a ship without a rudder."

Sam added, "That's what it's all about, *boychik*. Pure panic. They're scared shitless, the stockholders both big and little, that you might pass out. So all they want is a stand-in. But it doesn't mean a thing, not one goddam thing. All right, let's get down to business. There is one difference, however, Al, that you should take into consideration. In one big way, Ben Baron's appointment left you worse off than you were before. Your profits dipped and your stock reflected it. Now, you've got the wolves howling and snapping at your heels. That means that you've got to produce someone good, with at least the aura of authority and strength. We can't have another Ben Baron."

He bent to the sheets and rattled off a series of names and qualifications. Some were men whom Al had heard about, most were not. But none seemed to be right, probably because he didn't know what he was looking for.

Al went over to the window again, looking out as Sam continued to suggest other names, other qualifications. Barbara Schulte was no longer out there painting, although he hadn't heard her come in. Al idly heard Sam telephoning and asking someone in his New York office to check on the current status of an Alexander Smythe and a Sidney Holland. Then he joined Al at the window. "Let's quit now," Sam said. "We can resume tonight and pick it up again tomorrow."

Dinner was a quiet one out on the patio, off to a side of the apartment and facing the sea. After dinner, Sam invited Al to fly over to San Juan for gambling in the casino, but Al declined, saying that he preferred to take a swim. Barbara said she would join him on the beach after a while.

An hour later he sat in the sand under the bright stars, missing Ruthie and wishing he were home. He had asked her to come to the Caribbean with him, pointing out that she could use the few days in the sun, but she was reluctant to leave the girls. The beach was almost white, reflecting the bright moon, and the sky was dark blue, almost purple. It was a night of contrasts. Even the breeze was warm, fanning him with a caress so that he began to feel an ache in his loins.

The ocean was warm, too. He swam slowly along the shore line, enjoying the pull against his muscles. He treaded water awhile and then swam farther. In a few minutes he swam back to the slight rise on the beach where he had been before.

As he lay there letting the wetness dry on him, he heard a voice behind him. It was Barbara Schulte. She had put her hair up in a bun and looked young and winsome in a translucent beach robe. "Hello, Al," she said. "You look lonely."

He sat up. "I am," he told her, "but not any more. I'm glad to see you, Barbara. Sit here next to me."

She did, removing her robe. Her bathing suit was of the briefest type, which made the maturity of her ample curves obvious and yet somehow appealing. She smiled with amusement at his frank stare. "*Zaftig*, huh?" she asked. "I'm not apologetic. A woman should look like a woman, not like a boy. But then, I'm not a youngster any more. Sam and I have been married more than twenty years."

"He's quite a guy, your Sam," Al said. "He's doing a lot for me."

She studied him. "Think so? I think he enjoys playing the role of God."

"Maybe, but there are times that I think I need some help at that level."

She laughed. "The modesty of some men and the arrogance of others. I have to laugh. Businessmen are so like little boys, each one fighting to pick up the biggest bunch of marbles. Do you know who Sam admires most in the whole world of business?"

"Who?"

"You."

"I don't know why. I got all kinds of problems—"

"I don't know why, I don't know why," she mimicked. "Look, Al, I don't want to talk about Sam and I don't want to talk about business. I just want to relax with you and maybe try to understand what makes you tick. I've always been intrigued by the great paradox of Al Miller. How can you be such a *shlemiel* and yet such a big success?"

He shrugged. "That could be the question of the century," he told her.

She laughed again, this time with mirth, and he stared at her. He felt the stirring in his loins again. She sensed his reaction and he saw that she had sensed it by the sudden visible throbbing of the pulse in her throat. She arose abruptly and said, "How about a swim, Al?"

"Sure."

She pulled him to his feet. "In the nude?"

Before he could reply, she had removed her wispy top and bottom. As he stood there uncertainly, she pulled at his trunks. "Off you go, man. Don't be bashful."

They stood now facing each other, revealed in their nakedness. He was surprised and embarrassed at his quick reaction. She stared at him and smiled happily. "I think . . . I think that I could almost love you, Al," she said with a broad smile. She was, in the wash of the bright moonlight, quite lovely to him. He grasped her and she came to him, hard and hungrily. She was amazingly soft, amazingly full-bodied, amazingly scented, amazingly . . .

But she pulled away and grabbed his hand. "Let's take a swim," she said and pulled him toward the water.

They swam together, alongside each other and then holding each other. The water slid by and through them with warm sluices, but such was their excitement that it felt cold to them. Their hands groped for each other and they smiled at each other, at the things that they did to each other. The night seemed to stretch away forever for them, but they knew that they had been in the ocean only a short time. As they floated in each other's arms, Al's guilt, of course, lay close to the surface, as it always did, but in the midst of its gnaw he told himself that what he was doing had no relationship either to Ruthie or to Sam. It was something totally unrelated to anything else that existed in the world that lay beyond the water. But he knew deep in himself that this was a self-deceiving lie. Nonetheless, floating with Barbara, languidly locked into the softness of her body, it didn't seem to matter.

They left the water finally and tumbled together on the beach, just at the point where the ocean lapped at the sand. Breathing hard, she pulled him toward her, completely vulnerable. But his guilt surged up anew and he held himself back. Glistening, wet, nude, she smiled at him with a matter-of-fact bitterness. "And they tell me I'm crazy," she said.

"I can't do this to Sam," Al said, feeling foolish as he took in her nakedness, reacting in spite of himself.

"Sam?" she asked. "I never heard the name."

He got into his shorts and threw the robe over her. "Let's call it a night, Barbara," he said. She nodded, closely searching his eyes, and not very gently slapped his face.

In the morning, Sam announced at breakfast that the climate and general environment of St. Thomas were not conducive to a successful completion of their project. That, he told them all, they could best accomplish back in his apartment in New York.

On the plane, everyone was preoccupied with himself or herself. It was a small private plane that Schulte frequently leased, along with pilot and copilot, for trips back and forth to the Caribbean. He sat by himself in a front seat, poring over his personnel sheets. Barbara sat in the seat behind him, perturbed and rather grim-faced, occasionally shooting an angry glance at Al, who sat in the rear. Behind Barbara sat Priscilla Terry, and she too, it seemed to Al, bore a resentful expression as she glanced at him. What did she know? Had she by any chance observed the scene on the beach last night? He shrugged inwardly. What the hell difference did it make? He had done enough and he couldn't do more to hurt Sam. Look what Sam was doing for him.

Schulte's Park Avenue apartment was sumptuous, twelve rooms all lush, but one room was more impressively lavish than all the others. It was a thirty-five-foot living room, with two nine-foot sofas in a strange gray suede flanking a ten-foot desk, the highlight of the penthouse in one of Park Avenue's most luxurious apartment houses. Barbara had retired somewhere into the recesses of the triplex and Miss Terry had deposited the papers on Sam's desk and left.

Sam came back to the living room bearing a tray with his inevitable bottle of sherry and a tall glass of milk for Al. "Well," he said, "all the choices boil down to only two, Al. I've had my office check out the current status of two men and I'm satisfied that in present terms either of them measures up to your needs. I'm talking about Alexander Smythe and Sidney Holland. Now, tell me something, *boychik*, what do you want to find most in your new president?"

"I don't really know, Sam. As I said back there in St. Thomas, what I need most is a guy who ideas can funnel through and who can stand in for me."

"All right, let's try Alexander Smythe on for size. He's fifty, president of a major consumer finance company in the South. He started as a bookkeeper, studied accounting and law at night, and quickly moved up the ladder. He expanded and diversified his company from what was essentially first only a loan-shark outfit into a finance company that has one of the largest accounts receivables in small loans, auto loans and commercial financing in the entire South. He's an unusual combination of drive and humaneness—he won't carry deadwood, but last year he received a top regional award for his community and humane activities."

"How's his 'f.q.'?"

Sam cocked a quizzical eye at Al. "Do you really care about that?"

Al shrugged. "Maybe if I had worried more about Ben Baron's 'f.q.' I wouldn't have gone for him. By the way, what the hell does 'f.q.' really mean?"

"I told you, Al. It stands for flexibility quotient. How far will the guy bend? How far should he bend? Naturally, each appointment calls for a different tolerance, but it should be considered."

"How is Smythe's flexibility quotient?"

Sam consulted his sheets. "Better than Ben Baron's," he said, looking up. "But in this particular case, I'm not sure that it is very important. Smythe's is rated at sixty-five percent. That means that six and a half times out of every ten, he will demonstrate the inclination to adjust his attitude and behavior to the pressures of the situation. I'm wondering, frankly, if you don't need a guy whose quotient is in the thirty to thirty-five percent area."

"You mean a disciplinarian?"

"Right. And that's why I chose Sidney Holland as a prime example of that."

"Sidney Holland?" Al tasted the name for a second or two and shrugged. "So who and what is he?" he asked.

"He's forty-nine, the son of a tough, old sonofabitch who founded a coal yard up in New England after emigrating from Poland. The old man added almost a whole town to it, including a couple of textile mills, a tannery, a shoe factory, and a whole string of movie houses. But he died suddenly when Sidney, his only son, was still in college and the boy had to leave Harvard and take over the empire. He turned out to be twice as tough as his father ever was and maybe twice the businessman. He spun off most of the undesirable companies they owned and expanded the good ones. A few years ago he went public but he still retained about twelve percent of the stock. He may just be interested in finding a new horizon and in investing a good chunk of money into a business in which he gets a vested interest. Wall Street, incidentally, rates him very highly."

"What's his 'f.q.'?"

"You really want to know?"

"Sure."

"Twenty-eight percent."

Al whistled. "Tough guy, huh?"

Sam nodded slowly. "I think maybe that's what you need."

Al didn't respond. He still didn't know what he needed.

A light flickered in Sam's eyes. "I got a thought," he said, reaching for the bottle of sherry and taking a good swig. "Let's test him. What do you think of calling him on the telephone and saying that this is *Fortune* magazine and we're doing a cross-country survey. Our objective is to determine management attitudes and behavior based on Wall Street pressures. We pose a dilemma to him. A major financial institution has decided to invest fifteen million dollars in a company if it will grant some favoritism gestures such as a deal on warrants to buy additional stock at a discount or a very favorable conversion rate on debentures that will become common stock. Now, all this, we'll point out, will benefit the company and the average stockholder in the long run, despite the private privilege he grants the new investor. All we want is Holland's reaction for an attitude survey. Let's see how tough he is or isn't. Are you game, Al?"

Al agreed reluctantly. It seemed an unreasonable thing to do to anyone. And he was not at all sure what it would reveal. But Sam was already on the phone, and in a few minutes he had his man. Sam's histrionic skills amazed Al. Sam was first a competent secretary, then a male interviewer. "Now, Mr. Holland, we're conducting a national survey of top management. The results will be published shortly in *Fortune* and copies of the complete findings will be sent to everyone who participated. Now, what is your reaction to this situation."

When it was time, Sam shared the earpiece with Al. The answer came across very clearly and explicitly, in clipped and disciplined tones: "My reaction to any such crooked proposition would be to hang up and immediately call the Securities and Exchange Commission. I would also make a press announcement so that I could impale the bastards with their own dishonest proposition."

Sam's elbow kept banging delightedly into Al's ribs. "Watch this, *boychik*," Sam told him, shielding the mouthpiece. Then he said into it, switching to the full authority of his own voice, "Mr. Holland. Mr. Holland. A confession, sir. That was all just a put-on. A test. Actually, this is a call from Exemplar Executive Recruiters. Your name has been suggested to us as one who might be interested in changing positions. But we always like to test our candidates first in an informal way and that's why—"

The invective and expression of spleen that sputtered out of the earpiece was rare in its vehemence and articulateness. The contact ended with an abrupt click from Holland's end.

Sam hung up happily. "His 'f.q.' is twenty-eight percent?" Al asked in pure wonderment. Sam nodded triumphantly and Al found himself also nodding, nodding.

12

Order Is Everything— and Everything Is Order

SIDNEY HOLLAND'S ADVENT as the new president of Oval's missed coinciding by only one day with the opening of the forty-two-story headquarters building in Manhattan. To many people, Al not excepted, this was not so much a coincidence as a symbol of accumulating strength in the midst of vast change. There was something towering about the man and the building. Both were, of course, tall and new, but also impressive, austere, pulsing with strength and defiant in their hauteur and the strangely abrupt way in which they confronted the viewer. Although Al Miller was hardly to be counted as a typical or average observer, he was one of the many who reacted with curiosity and surprise the first one hundred times or so that they saw either the man or the structure.

Holland was erect to the point of ridiculousness, taut as a steel cable and as self-contained as a perpetual clock. His eyes had a blazing quality which immediately put everyone on the defensive even before he spoke. He was formed in the shape of a towering "T," broad in the beam, narrow in the heft, lean in the descent. And except for a trace of worldliness, almost of *weltschmerz*, which tended to strike some uncertainty in his beholders, everything else in him screamed out at them—efficiency, dispatch, a grinding demand on all, including himself. Or so it all seemed to those who were prepared to be easily impressed, of which there were many.

The building, too, was tall, erect and taut, in much greater proportions than the man, of course. But all these traits were magnified by its "skin," a shiny aluminum alloy, interspersed with millions of steel links, which allowed the structure to "breathe" and thus provided it with many technical benefits of an unnamed nature. Nonetheless, the sunshine catching on the combination of aluminum sheen and glare of the yellow links seemed to ignite that "skin," and the effect, seen at the right moments, was dazzling. At one point not long after the Oval's tower opened, the Civil Aeronautics Board complained about the disturbing effect on approaching aircraft of the sun's reflection on the building, but nothing came of it.

Somehow, in the month between his decision to join Oval's, buy several million dollars of its stock and his actual appearance on the scene, Holland's reputation as a tough man preceded him into every corner of the musty old offices that were being vacated for the new ones. As a result, there was much in the way of preparation, reevaluation of personal idiosyncrasies and the display of *shtik*, the discarding of old invoices, some of which had never been paid, and even the transformation of personalities at least on a superficial level. In effect, a sweeping-out process began before the new broom even arrived.

As a result, a number of things happened. Wallenstein packed in his Wallenstein, Pennsylvania project, turning back both the leaseholds and the deeds to the town authorities. He also closed out eleven related or subsidiary corporations of Oval's, which were at least quasi-personal in nature. This still left quite a real-estate development and venture empire, but its most conspicuous features had been carefully obscured from public view.

Irving Waldteufel removed mountains of supplies from one warehouse to another, strategically confusing the records so that even an eagle-eye would become bloodshot from attempting to fathom them. But he, too, continued to operate a number of fringe businesses, all made possible by his overbuying, for the benefit of the company, and not very incidentally for himself.

Harry Abner decided to take a memory-improving course. He sensed that any hard-nosed chief operating officer would find great difficulty in understanding how a general merchandise manager could effectively function with a woefully bad memory. So Harry paid a considerable sum for a crash course. Unfortunately, in the midst of it, he apparently forgot the name and address of the school and so could not complete the course. At least this was the excuse he gave himself when he found that he was making absolutely no progress at all.

Matthew Smiles went on a diet. Only twenty-three and drawing a salary of $75,000 a year, he had gradually become conscious of the incongruity of a three-hundred-pound youth making that kind of money in a public company trying to tighten its belt. The boys admired his talents but they could not resist making jibes. Nat Batt's superficial poetic bent had gone to his head since the farewell dinner to Ben Baron, and lately he had taken to greeting Matthew with such remarks as "Here's Tub, the *Shlub*," or "There's Smiles, he fills aisles with piles and piles." Wallenstein went so far as to present the young man with a counterfeit deed to "Obese Acres—Where You Can Open Your Belt and Cover the Landscape." Thus reinforced in his fears, Matthew went on a diet, dropping about sixty pounds in a few weeks. But like so many fat people who eat to relieve their nervous frustration, he decided at the end of that period that he had proved his point and then gained back sixty-one pounds in an orgy of eating.

Molly Bradley met the problem head-on by resigning her post. However, because she felt that as a consultant her immorality and untraditional behavior would be more acceptable, she had Al Miller reappoint her as a full-time adviser. Then she proceeded to carry on as never before.

Ernest von Rossem engaged a nineteen-year old genius at City College to teach him at last how to use a slide rule properly. Solly Patracelli, who as operations chief was convinced that he would be the first to feel the weight of the new lash, showed uncommon initiative. He hired a researcher to prepare a complete dossier on Sidney Holland and convinced himself that in objectives, if not in performance, he was the new president's alter ego. What differences there existed between them Solly hastened to rectify. As a result, by the time Holland came on the scene there was an Italian version of himself waiting breathlessly in the wings. It was, as it turned out, the last thing in the world he either craved or wanted.

Nat Batt did nothing. So certain was he that the new man, in his efforts to turn the company around would need a crack public-relations man more than ever that Nat decided to sit tight and be the same lying, omnivorous PR man that he had always been. "PR-wise," he informed his four cowed underlings, "this guy has got to be an improvement on that *meshuggener* Al Miller. He never knew what the hell we did in this department, much less would he ever demean himself to say anything nice about the truly great job we do." But in making this assumption about Sidney Holland's potential attitude and behavior, Nat Batt made a serious misjudgment.

And what of Al Miller himself? What did he do to prepare for the appearance of his new choice to fill the president's office? Truly, need there be any question? He absented himself weeks before Sidney Holland arrived and didn't show up until weeks after Holland arrived.

And so the new man materialized. He did so with such a display of logistics, aplomb, authority and purpose that he struck mingled fear and respect into the hearts of everyone. His arrival was due on the second day after the new building opened. His suite of three rooms—a sitting room, his own private office and an office for his secretary—had been set up weeks in advance by the boys in cheerful browns and beiges, colors that they had decided were suitable to their new chief. Next to his, a large single room had been allocated to be Al Miller's first office. But despite the awesome new building and the symbol of having arrived that it connoted, Al never did occupy it. As the months wore on, that room became the scene of late blackjack and pinochle games—after Sidney Holland had left for the day, of course.

Nat Batt was the first of the boys to see him in the flesh. The PR man did this by the simple expedient of leaving his own office door ajar by two inches and by stationing his fat, disgusting, oily body in the gap. When Holland arrived, an imperious figure of a man striding through the offices unerringly and instinctively into the one he sensed to be his own, Nat hysterically shut the door and ran to his phone. He consecutively called about a dozen of the boys and gave them all the same desperate information. "What a long, fuckin' drink of water this guy is! I give you guys one week." Then he turned on his shaking staff and yelled characteristically, "You better snap shit, you sonsofbitches! This time I mean it!"

Despite the fact that Holland did not ask to meet any of the company's top executives for a full week but stayed closeted in his office on the forty-second floor, instructing his secretary to request all departmental budgets and plans so he could study them, a number of Oval's employees and executives caught various glimpses of him. From these, enough bits and pieces could be put together to give them some sort of an outline to the new man but not much substance.

Zelda, the switchboard operator who had been pained in recent months by Al Miller's absence and lack of comment (he had even stopped phoning in), saw Sidney Holland even before Nat Batt spied him from the partly open doorway. As she glanced up from her sleek new board, she saw a lean, lanky, distinguished-looking man in a Homburg and Chesterfield coat. He had a big-boned head, a wide, lined face, long, aquiline nose, piercing gray eyes, king-size ears and a jutting, dogmatic chin. He passed without in any way acknowledging her, but the prim, dumpy, middle-aged woman who followed in his wake, painfully lugging a heavy briefcase, nodded to her in a moderately friendly manner. Zelda, who now had an assistant, blinked meaningfully at her. So that was *him*. He could have been a banker, a diplomat, a high United Nations official, an important politician or statesman, but to her he seemed just right as president of a $750-million-a-year corporation. "Class," Zelda declared out loud, "deserves class."

Proud of his genuine skill with a slide rule at last, Ernest von

Rossem decided to save his secretary a trip and personally brought out to Holland's secretary two departmental budgets which he had adjusted. "Miss . . . ?" he asked uncertainly.

"Mrs. Elizabeth May," she said with a touch of a smile. "Mr. . . . ?"

"I'm Mr. von Rossem, the company controller," he said. "I have the budgets and plans for the two hard-goods divisions for you."

As he handed them to her, he indulged his real purpose and deliberately glanced into Holland's office and saw him standing thoughtfully at the window, his back to the door. Based upon the angle from which his massive head was poised, it appeared that Holland was studying the bulk of Macy's Herald Square only a few blocks away. Was he already fixing a bead on "The World's Largest Store"? Much impressed, von Rossem turned away, his heart pounding with sudden exhilaration, hope and fear in his cadaverous rib cage.

Matthew Smiles was in the new executive john a few days later when Sidney Holland came in. As they stood at adjacent urinals, Matthew said brightly, "How are you, sir? I am Matthew Smiles."

Holland—at least the obese young man assumed it was Holland—finished, adjusted himself, washed, carefully studied his reflection in the mirror, made some corrections, and as he went out looked Matthew over and asked, "You are?"

Disturbed, Smiles waddled into the offices of the nearest boys. "He's a cool customer," he told them. "I just met him in the john. He really gave me the freeze. Brr!"

Of such similar small and diverse parts was the first week's outline of the new president drawn. At the week's end, Mrs. May called twenty-four staff and divisional executives to tell them that Mr. Holland wanted them to meet him in his office at nine the next morning. That, they uncomfortably realized, would be Saturday. But at least some of their suspense would be ended.

As he took them all in through veiled eyes Saturday morning, Sidney Holland was filled with cold, unreasonable fury. They all sat there shaved, brushed, smelling smugly of after-shave lotion and reeking of hair tonic, with a soft, doglike look of anticipation in their eyes as though they all expected to be patted on the head. Yet his examination of their operating statements, plans and budgets in the last five days had revealed to him the most confused, fouled-up, loose, extravagant thinking and strategy that he had run across in twenty-five years of business experience. The sheer effrontery and irresponsibility that this showed, combined with their obvious complacency, filled him with disgust and a deep instinct to throw them all the hell out of his office.

They stared at him and he stared at them. Most began to stir uncomfortably as though they sensed his true mood. As he tried to decide whether to take the batch of papers on the desk and throw them at their vapid, openmouthed faces—a patina of idiocy seemed to have settled over them as it dawned on them that they were not about to be patted but probably batted on the head—he realized that his anger was of such a degree that he just could not think clearly.

Such moments of anger, even of hate, were not exactly unknown to him. As he sat there, wondering what to do to express the distaste that he felt for them, he recalled another time when he had been confronted by such a dilemma—how to behave in face of an unreasonable affront and how he had resolved it.

It had happened many years ago, when he was still a Harvard undergraduate. He had come home from Cambridge for a weekend and found the big, empty Colonial house full of the reek of whisky and the tired body odor of old men and he realized that another long poker session, which would last several days, was already under way. His father would frequently invite in half a dozen cronies, all successful or retired businessmen or elderly near-indigents of the neighborhood who fawned on him, with whom he had grown up in the Polish section of Boston, to play cards with him, drink, foul up the place. After a long session well into the morning, they would all fall onto the nearest sofa, chair or bed, or just on the floor, and sleep sodden and dirty until noon. Then they would awake, hustle the man and wife who served his widowed father to provide food, whereupon they would start their game again.

Sidney let himself in quietly that weekend, tiptoeing past the noisy brawl in the living room, and went quietly up the steps. Except for the illuminated parlor, the house was kept dark by his father, Isaac, reflecting the old man's own dourness and bitterness. Ever since his wife had sickened and died all in one day when Sidney had been only sixteen, Isaac had seemed to lose what little interest he had ever had in his only son. The death of that quiet, proud woman, who by the force of a gentle but determined personality maintained a semblance of decorum between father and son, had abruptly removed the one common thread that existed between them. A wall then fell between Isaac and his son and each had receded further from the other.

For weeks at a time, Isaac would never even inquire about him. As the old man sought desperately to forget his wife's untimely death, he had turned to drinking, gambling and promiscuity. The son's direction had been loneliness, frustration, masturbation and tears, all supplanted when Sidney had graduated from high school by a harsh independence and self-discipline. The old house in Newton, outside Boston, once made pleasant by a calm woman's devotion to her family, had become a trap for an isolated father who often ran away from it and an isolated, bitter son who found that he had nowhere else to go.

That weekend, Sidney kept to himself, avoiding the presence and the noise of the roisterers in the house. But as he was leaving Sunday evening to return to Cambridge, trying to walk quietly by the reeking parlor, his father heard him and called to him. "Hey, boy, come here!"

Sidney hesitated. It was ironic that in the last few moments that he would be home he would be unable to avoid another confrontation with his father. He edged toward the front door, but Isaac's voice pursued him. "Come in here, Mr. Harvard."

Uncertainly, Sidney came back to the living room. His father, a heavyset, glowering man with white shaggy hair, arose from the group and strode toward him. "All weekend you been home and you didn't come in once to say hello. What's wrong with you, boy?" he asked.

Sidney shrugged. "I didn't think you would miss me. You're so busy with your friends."

Isaac turned to them. "What do you think of that, hey? He doesn't even want to say hello to his old man." His heavy hand moved to Sidney's lapel, his collar. "Fancy-shmancy," Isaac said. "Clothes and money he'll take from me, but hello he won't give me. This he learned in Harvard?"

The others laughed, the game proceeding without Isaac for the moment. But the father's hand remained on Sidney's collar. "No, that's not right, boy, not right at all. I spent my whole life trying to raise and support you. Where's the little bit of respect I should get, hey?"

Isaac was drunk, but the fire in his eyes didn't come from liquor. "All right," Sidney told him, tight-lipped. "Hello."

He made a move toward the door, but Isaac's hand tightened on his collar. "Not so fast, Mr. Harvard. Don't they teach you in that expensive college to honor your father?"

Isaac's cronies howled. Sidney felt his face getting hot and he stared with trepidation at Isaac. His father asked, "Don't you hear me, boy? You shaming me in front of my friends?"

"Are you trying to shame me in front of your friends?" Sidney asked hotly. "Since when do you give a damn whether I live or die? Hello you want. Okay, hello."

Isaac's hand darted quickly from Sidney's collar to his face, giving him a stinging slap. "Respect, goddamit!" Isaac yelled.

"You sonofabitch!" Sidney shouted back.

Isaac yanked hard on his son's collar, pulling Sidney's face close to him. "Don't you—you call me that," he warned. "Everything you got in the world I gave you. Did you ever work an honest day in your life, hey? Where is your gratitude, boy?"

Everyone had stopped playing cards. The battle was more exciting and they looked up at father and son with drunk, tired eyes full of amusement. "I'll tell you what you gave me, Isaac," said Sidney, his heart pounding as he tried to ignore them. "Heartache and shame. That's what you gave me—with your carousing, your drunkenness, your dames and your curses. You're not the only one who had to face up to Mom's death. It's been like my father died, too, the way you've been behaving."

Isaac flinched. Glancing self-consciously at the coterie of old friends, he asked archly, "What were you doing all weekend?

Were you in the bathroom all weekend? I know what you do in the bathroom, don't I?"

The others laughed. His cheeks flaming, Sidney said, "Whatever I do, what does it matter to you? You're just a weak old man who can't stand up to life. I had to do it all on my own, without your help."

"I'll fix you," warned Isaac. "I'll take care of you. Just wait. Now get duh hell out of here—or I'll throw you out, you—you masturbator!"

Sidney took in his father, his tortured but hateful old man's face, and a trickle of fear began to flicker through him. Isaac was his only living tie to his mother. To break up with him now, that old Polish truckman who had made good, that crude, cursing, wenching, craven old man, would probably be permanent. Anger swept through him as he realized that Isaac had only meant to demonstrate his authority over his son in front of his fellow poker players. The humiliation, the display of distaste that he showed for his son, that didn't matter one little bit to Isaac.

A few moments went by as everyone stared expectantly at him. Then quietly but decisively he removed Isaac's hand from his collar, said "Good-bye," and walked out.

A month later, Sidney came home again. A month after that his father was dead of a stroke.

But Isaac kept his promise. In his will he left half of his estate to a skinny waitress with whom he had been having an affair for several years.

Clearing his head of these memories, Sidney Holland asked each of the twenty-four men to rise, identify himself and his function and relate what he actually did in the company. This involved a sheepish, self-conscious process that lasted an agonizing fifteen minutes for all of them but Holland. When this was completed, he got up, holding aloft the batch of plans and budgets and said, "I have read and studied all of these carefully. As a result, I have only one thing to say to all of you, after which this meeting is terminated. Each one of you is on probation for the next sixty days."

Then he stepped to the window, opened it and hurled all the papers down to Times Square forty-two stories below.

They all went looking for Al right away, naturally, but of course he was not to be found. He hadn't even waited to depart until Monday, the first weekday after the announcement that everyone would be on probation. Sidney Holland hadn't cleared his decision with Al, but in their initial meeting in Sam Schulte's Manhattan penthouse he had insisted on a free hand and Al had been only too willing to give it. "I know it will take time for you to show results, Sidney," Al had said. "So let's say that for the first six months you got the whole ball game. If you need me, just holler."

As they stood around in the carpeted, green hallways of the new executive offices, worried and tense over the announcement, the boys decided that they ought to obtain clarification from Al. And then, later, when they found that he was incommunicado— in fact, they couldn't even learn where he had gone—their tension mounted. Obviously, Al had been party to the decision that they were all on trial, otherwise why had he suddenly disappeared? "He's some sonofabitch, some pal," moaned Nat Batt, always one to snipe at Al Miller. But the others, the most loyal ones, such as Irving Waldteufel, Harry Abner and Willie Wallenstein, demurred from any such comments. Privately, they were worried as hell, seeing a big threat hovering over the empires-within-the-empire that they had created, but they were certain that Al wouldn't let them down. It was inconceivable.

Within a short time—a matter of days, actually—Sidney Holland and General Horace Boatwright met and found themselves in deep and total accord.

The general took the initiative. As usual that morning he was being driven to his office deep in the caverns of Wall Street by his chauffeur, a former Pentagon military-police sergeant whose bulldog manner appealed to Boatwright. As the gleaming black limousine slid by the Times Square area, the squat little ex-soldier rapped on his chauffeur's shoulder with his swagger stick and said, "About face, Danny. I am going to make a stop."

He strode through Oval's offices with military precision, stoically ignoring the expressions of curiosity and surprise. Like a guided missile, he honed in on the right suite, then pushed open the door marked "President" and finally stood at an unquivering parade rest before the taut length of Sidney Holland. They confronted each other, the five-foot four-inch retired general and the six-foot three-inch chief operating officer, studying each other solemnly, silently, unblinkingly. Twenty-one and a half feet separated them across the room, but both sensed immediately without uttering a single word that there was no gulf at all in their temperament, philosophy, life style.

"Sir?"

"Boatwright here. Brigadier General, U. S. Army, Retired."

"And one of our outside directors," Holland acknowledged.

"We were to meet next week at the regular board meeting," said Boatwright. "But I decided instead to appear in advance and extend my greetings."

They approached each other, nodded curtly and shook hands. Each was startled by the hard similarity of the other's handshake. The tall man gestured to a chair and the short man sat down. Holland seated himself facing Boatwright. It was 8:45 A.M., and he thought coffee might be in order. "Would you care for something, General?" Holland asked. "We have a small but well-equipped pantry."

Boatwright was pleased. There was nothing as indicative of good planning, he had always believed, as preparing adequately for one's basic needs. "Yes," he said. "Bourbon and soda with crushed ice."

Surprised, Holland tried not to show it. At 8:45? He went to his desk and rang for Mrs. May. When she came in, he ordered bourbon for Boatwright and black coffee for himself.

Waiting until she had closed the door behind her, Boatwright leaned forward and confided, his tiny eyes ashine, "I heard about your first major order, Mr. Holland. Putting the entire staff on probation. Ah, that's a well thought-out move. I can't tell you how much I concur in that decision. Both in its principle and even more in its practice—tossing their plans out the window. That was command behavior, I tell you!"

"Thank you."

"You have my utmost support and backing, sir," Boatwright said gratefully.

"Thank you."

Mrs. May came in with the refreshments and then discreetly withdrew.

Boatwright took a long swig while Holland sipped. Putting his glass down, the general said, "I also want you to know that I heartily concurred when your name was presented to the board as candidate for president of this company. Ordinarily, I would have insisted on meeting you in person and in questioning you in detail, but in this case none of that was necessary."

Holland nodded in appreciation.

"Perhaps you'd like to know why? Your dossier spoke for itself in words loud and clear, sir."

"Thank you—again."

Boatwright drained his glass with a second long swig. Placing the empty glass on the floor, he said, "One thing more, Mr. President, so that you know the kind of person I am. I took the precaution of checking you out in some detail. I won't go into how much detail or the manner or the trouble I went to except to say that even before your candidacy was formally presented I was already certain that you were the right man. Your dossier only confirmed what I already had learned. And I might say further that I impressed the other directors with my conviction about you."

"That's very gratifying to me, General, coming from you," Holland said. "Another drink?"

Boatwright reluctantly shook his head. He added, "I noticed right away that your record is marked by a strict attention to discipline and by calling every executive who has ever worked for you to strict account for his decisions and judgments. That, sir, impresses me not a little."

"I believe in it wholeheartedly, General."

Boatwright arose, short, bulky, jowly but uplifted. "Order is everything," he announced, "and everything is order."

"I couldn't express that better myself," said Holland.

The general moved to the door, gently swinging his swagger

stick. For the first time in quite a while he felt that the big burden on his back was getting lighter. His tremendous position in Oval's stock seemed safer and even well guarded, finally. With his hand on the doorknob, he said, "This is a great company, Mr. Holland, a great company. With fifty-six handsome, well-stocked retail establishments in one hundred percent locations and annual sales of seven hundred fifty million dollars, we should be earning more than just two point two percent on our business. With the right sort of supervision—with the proper command— it can earn considerably more. It can be an even greater company, offering much greater leverage for its stockholders and much benefit to our national economy. I leave it all in your good hands."

They shook hands with fervor. Boatwright gave Sidney Holland a miniature salute and left. As the door closed, Holland could not curb the smile of satisfaction that wreathed his face.

About three weeks later, when Al Miller returned, he found many things changed. Most of them he did not care for. Some of them distressed him quite deeply. And a few of them, just a few, sent an icy chill down his spine. Learning of them the first day he was back, he brooded about them all the way down to the afternoon movie.

13

"You Don't Have to Be Jewish to Have <u>Chutzpah</u>"

HE WAS ELECTED into the Retailing Hall of Fame just about that time. In perpetuity, although it didn't quite work out that way, his bust was to reside in a small, hallowed alcove of the trustees' room of a leading trade association. He would share the distinction and the alcove along with such illustrious late greats as Frank W. Woolworth, James Cash Penney, John Wanamaker, General Robert E. Wood of Sears, Roebuck and Michael Cullen, otherwise known as "King Kullen," the founder of the first contemporary supermarket. The symbol was modest but the recognition was vast, monumental, in fact, considering that he was a discounter and that he was nominated and elected by a combination of both conventional merchants and discounters.

He had, of course, tried at first to run away from it. He didn't believe in awards or formal recognition or honors. They were for people who savored public acclaim. But once the word began getting around that a petition was being circulated—there was nothing formal about nominations to the Hall: only when, every decade or so, there seemed to be a ground swell for a particular nominee—everyone took pains to urge him that he should not spurn the award should he get it. The exhorters included his closest associates in the company, the boys, as well as Sam

Schulte, Gordon Leon Jones, Walter Solomon, Ruthie and, eventually, Sidney Holland.

The gist of most of their arguments was that "If you don't want to take it for yourself, at least accept it for the company." But it was Ruthie who made a telling point with "If you don't want to accept it for the company, at least accept it for yourself. And if you don't want it for yourself, accept it for me."

But the argument which Al used against it, without articulating it—that is, except to himself—was that it was "goddam strange that this is all happening at a time when I feel a fight coming on." However, he knew that the ways of fame are strange indeed, timing being not one of the reliable elements in public recognition. Or, maybe, he told himself irritably, it was. The fact that Sidney Holland, a well-known and respected businessman had sold his own business in order to come in and take the president's role in Al's company added another mantle to the growing repute of Oval's founder. He was, he became convinced by others and then convinced himself, in short, nothing less than chairman of the board of one of the major American retailing companies at the age of forty-four, a statesman of commerce and a nationally known figure whose pioneering business concept had resulted in the creation of a multibillion dollar industry.

The upshot of all this was that on a July night in the midsixties he sat on a stage in the grand ballroom of the Waldorf-Astoria and saw himself inducted into the Retailing Hall of Fame, a mythical institution housed in a mythical structure to be visited by a mythical audience. But the participants in the induction ceremony and banquet were flesh and blood. Fifteen hundred persons paid one hundred dollars each to attend, the proceeds to be contributed toward the support of three local schools of retailing and merchandising. A Hall of Fame journal, containing institutional advertisements by both retailers and especially suppliers, raised another $100,000. The proceeds would go to completely remodel the sagging, peeling interior of the trade-association building where the new bust would join the five others.

And, unbeknownst to Al Miller, a prestigious-looking, cloth-bound biography of the new Hall of Fame laureate was prepared. Nat Batt had served as editor and all of Al's boys had contributed recollections of their association with him. Loyal Oval's suppliers contributed ads, these proceeds going into the company's employee pension fund and scholarship foundation.

Al sat on the Waldorf stage with about forty others who surrounded him as a council of honor. Ruthie, next to him, seemed uplifted, full of pride and love. All the Oval's officers sat scattered among the group, with Sidney Holland, at Al's instigation, sitting as far away from him as possible.

After a Metropolitan Opera soprano opened the ceremony with an inspirational rendition the accolades began.

"Albert Miller is one of the greatest merchandisers of our time," said Arthur Huggins, dean of the School of Economics and Business of Arizona State University. But he was soon outdone by Professor Horace Albrand of Harvard, who stated flatly, "Albert Miller is quite clearly one of the six greatest merchants in American history. . . . He unloosed the imagination and talents of a whole new breed of retailers, who, following his leadership, provided a new dimension of service to the American consumer and made major, continuing contributions to the country's economic life."

The next speaker was a grizzled trade-journal editor who emotionally traced Al's difficulties over the years, first with his own burgeoning and sometimes conflicting instincts, then with competitors, suppliers, the courts and politicking legislators spouting "fair trade" for all it was worth at the polls. "But he took them all on," he said, "and one by one he defeated them all. He was a Joshua who swallowed the whale!"

Both the mayor and the governor spoke in turn. Strangely enough, neither fumbled by hailing the wrong honoree or by mispronouncing his name or that of his company. Both were eloquent, genuinely rising to the occasion. This, as the handsome, boyish mayor put it, "was one of those momentous times when we note the phenomenon of a humble and simple man who rose to a pinnacle of personal achievement that covers all of us with glory."

The governor, suave, at home with any audience and confident with the back-up of many millions in his family coffers, held forth for fifteen minutes. After finishing, he raised his hand in a familiar gesture and read a congratulatory telegram from the President. Concluding that, he personally handed it to the honoree, adding, "I think, Al, that I can also add an invitation from the President—'Come on down 'n' see us, y' hear!' "

However, it was another speaker, William Picon, a major figure on Seventh Avenue, who posed the question that added a proper perspective on the whole situation. "What, one is tempted to wonder, would have happened if there had been no Albert Miller?" the fat, genial manufacturer asked. "It is difficult —no, impossible—to imagine. The thought, especially tonight, is an awesome one. But, thank God, it is academic, and we owe that, it seems, to one person, whom I would now like to introduce."

He gestured grandly toward the stage, and Pesse, Al's mother, arose and came forth to join Picon. A wave of applause rolled up toward her. Tiny, a bitter, dry widow, her face wavered and tears began flowing down her cheeks. She turned toward Al and blew him an old mother's kiss. Encouraged by Picon and everyone around him, he came forward and joined Pesse, both of them arousing a storm of applause.

After a few minutes, Picon gently urged Pesse back onto her seat on the stage and Al was left alone to face the audience. He then gave his famous speech, unrehearsed and unprepared, which was reported throughout the country, printed verbatim in the Congressional Record and in *The New York Times* and picked up in many newspapers and journals. Its best-remembered excerpt was ". . . Of course, you're in business to make a profit. Especially a net profit. But some sharp guys want to know what's your real net profit, the net after the net, with everything squeezed out but the pure profit. Personally, gentlemen, I think that's all a lot of s-h-i-t. The real 'net net' is the pleasure, the happiness, the joy and the *naches*, as my Pop used to say, that you bring to your employees, your customers and the whole frigged-up, unhappy world. Without it, you've got to be only an animal in a jungle. So, let me ask all of you, what's *your* net net? . . ."

Oval's chairman and its new president didn't meet again face to face until three months after Holland had been in office. He arrived at his usual hour of eight one morning and to his surprise found Al Miller sitting in his office waiting for him. Al said smilingly, "Hi, Sidney. What can we do to get more business?"

Unfazed, Holland sat down at his desk, lit a cigarette and said, "I think a better question is how can we make more money. Oval's has never had any problem getting the business but not so good at making money on it. Right?"

Al shrugged. "No question about it, Sid. But don't forget that the more business we bring in—and keep our fixed expenses low—the more leverage we naturally get on profits."

Holland stared steadily at Al for a few moments, saying nothing. Al began to squirm. Finally Holland asked, "Where have you been for the last three months, Al? We missed you."

Al was startled. "Where've I been? At the end of a telephone if you needed me. I like to get out to the stores and see what's going on. In the last three months I've been to every one of our fifty-six stores—I've talked to the managers and department managers of each one and to plenty of customers everywhere. I got a feel for what's going on like I never had before. That's where I've been."

"It would have been nice—and helpful—if you had been around to share some of the problems," said Holland.

Again Al shrugged. "I told you that for the first six months you got the whole ball game. I thought you'd like it that way."

"If you will recall," Holland said, "that was your idea. I never asked you to do that. The fact is, Al, that a lot has happened while you were away. You weren't here, so I went ahead on my own. And I don't mind telling you that it has made a lot of difference."

"I heard a few things," Al said. He voice was a little tight. It seemed that it didn't take much on Holland's part to set him off, but there was something else. He didn't care for his own refer-

ence to the leverage on profits by drawing more business and
keeping fixed expenses low. It was the sort of hypocrisy, both
inward and outward, that he despised and usually almost always
avoided. What the hell was he trying to prove anyway?

Holland, tall, austere, determined, strode now to the big window behind his desk. Puzzled, Al stared with surprise as Holland drew a thin, opaque curtain across the window which allowed a suffused sunlight to stream in. Then, pushing aside the
heavier drapery, Holland unveiled a roller or cylinder at the top
of the window and from it alternately drew down three large
cloth charts. Each one rolled up within the other. But as each
was unrolled, the opaque curtain let the sunlight through and it
seemed to illuminate each chart.

As he unrolled each, Holland read off their titles: "New Table
of Organization." "Profit Centers by Area." "Cash Flow and Assets to Debt Ratio." He held the last one unrolled and turned
back to Al. "You can see, Al, what my thrust has been. Controls,
controls, controls. Nothing gets by anymore because it was forgotten or undetected." He paused and added, somewhat
vaguely, "You could say that the principle here is order is everything—and everything is order."

Al snorted.

Ignoring him, Holland said in a profound manner, "Let's draw
a quick profile of our company. The way we are going, we will
have sixty stores by the end of next year. We've been opening
stores so fast—are you aware of the fact that for a period of
about two or three years we were opening a new store every six
weeks?—that we were concentrating more on the physical expansion than on building an organization. We've been over-
staffing the headquarters but starving the line. In military terms,
that was like building a massive Pentagon staff but not filling the
table of organization in the field. At the same time, the corporate
office was absorbing considerable extra costs of personnel that
should have been allotted to each store or to a regional group of
stores. So you had a combination of two evils and it was draining
away both your expenses and your service capacity in the stores.
It also meant that you were not compelling the people on the

line to accept sufficient responsibility. Do you understand what I'm saying?"

Al wasn't the type to grit his teeth. Instead, he felt his head beginning to pound and his feet getting that restless feeling. Uncomfortably, he also couldn't help noticing Holland's shift from the plural "we" on the more abstract matters to the singular "you" when he stressed the pragmatic faults of the company's practices.

But Holland was hardly done. He was, in fact, just warming up. He reached up and pulled down from above the roller a blackboard pointer. With it, he traced some of his actions on each chart, deftly drawing each one down for a few moments, releasing it with a snap and then drawing down the next one.

"You see here that with a few firm changes in policy that I have cut down the corporate office staff by about twenty-five percent. Then I regrouped all the stores into regions, transferring the staff overage to line jobs, and will shortly recommend regional directors who will have complete responsibility to operate as many as a dozen stores as separate profit centers. If they do not produce at least a minimum profit or return on investment, they get no bonuses, and if they fail that in three successive fiscal quarters, we will replace them. Then we will reallot expenses from the corporate office to the regions, which means that each one will have to absorb those expenses while still reaching at least the profit norm . . . What do you think?"

Al got up. His head hurt, but his common sense told him that Sidney Holland was probably doing some useful things in his reorganization plan, "It doesn't sound bad at all," Al said, "but, of course, the test is how you will carry it out."

"Not at all," Holland countered. "The real test will be on what results we get. You have got to get rid of the idea, Al, that you're running a household, a family, instead of a big business that has to constantly improve its return on investment. That's the basis on which stockholders invested in this company. You gave up the right to run a private business in the manner that you were accustomed to when you went public three years ago."

"Maybe I did," said Al petulantly, "and maybe I didn't." He

added, "I'm still not convinced that running a business and keeping your employees and your customers happy are two separate things."

Holland's eyes brightened. "Yes, your Hall of Fame speech." But the tart expression on his face was not entirely appreciative. He came over and approached Al. "One way of carrying out everything that I proposed is to make some major changes in our top corporate posts. There are two or three vice-presidents that I think we could easily do without."

"Like who?"

Holland stood his ground. "Like Nat Batt, Harry Abner and Solly Patracelli. You know that Nat, though he hardly looks it, is over seventy years old? And his ideas of public relations are of the old press-agent ilk that went out twenty years ago. He's a nasty little bastard, too. I think we ought to retire him."

"And Harry Abner? And Solly?"

"Well, let's face it, Al. Harry is physically and mentally incapable of performing his job. Anybody with a memory that bad and with his ulcers is more of a threat toward disaster as general merchandise manager than a time bomb in our distribution center. And he's such a liar, a psychopathic liar. In fact, so's Nat Batt and a lot of others around here. As far as Solly is concerned, he's completely incapable and just a buffoon as far as the rest of the staff is concerned. The harder he tries to be effective as chief of operations, the more the rest of them laugh at him."

Al kept nodding and nodding, afraid for the moment to speak because he would have exploded. But his noncommittal manner seemed to encourage Holland. Grinning, the distinguished-looking Bostonian decided to go one step further.

"As a matter of fact," he continued, putting his arm on Al's shoulder, "there is another, perhaps final phase of our reorganization that I would like to suggest to you. I know it is quite early in our relationship to tackle it. But since you seem to prefer to spend most of your time out in the field and it's obvious that you find the headquarters duties irksome, I'd like to suggest that you consider relinquishing your posts as chairman and chief executive officer to me. As the largest shareholder and company statesman, you could be just as valuable as, say, chairman of the executive committee. Oh, I don't mean now—but sometime in the foreseeable future—and it would allow me to facilitate my program by dealing directly with the board."

As Holland had been talking, it had become increasingly more difficult for Al to absorb it all. But something was coming through to him in tones like the pounding on a large Chinese gong.

Trying hard to control himself but finding himself shaking, Al said, "What you just said proves, Sid, that you don't have to be Jewish to have *chutzpah*. You can even be a Polack from Boston. On Nat, it's no. On Harry, it's no. And on Solly, it's especially no. And on me, I didn't hear a word you said!"

Al came running home that night more perspired and more frazzled than he usually was. The mile from car to house seemed longer than it should have been and he felt that he wasn't running with the usual sense of enjoyment.

The girls were chattering away at the table when he arrived and Ruthie was occasionally joining in as she hovered over them. He kissed his hand and patted the twelve-, fourteen- and sixteen-year-old heads with it. Then he gave his wife an absent-minded peck on the forehead and went upstairs to change. When he came down in a sport shirt and slacks, the girls had dispersed to their various haunts and Ruthie quietly waited for him.

She studied him for a moment. At forty-four, he was still lean, handsome in a rangy, restless way, still as redheaded as a beet. But his eyes kept focusing away from her and she immediately sensed that some new troubling element grated on him. As they sat down to eat, Martha, the black cook serving them and fussing over them, Ruthie tried to divert him by talking about the girls and her own day at home.

But it didn't quite work. His eyes kept avoiding Ruthie and he ate sparingly instead of in his usual, wolfish way. The skinny, lanky cook snorted indignantly at him a couple of times as she came and went from kitchen to dining room. "You a sad man tonight," Martha said, snatching away his plate. "Not eatin' my food, not talkin' to your wife. Whyn't you go out and come in all over again? Sourpuss man."

Al grinned at Ruthie as the cook stalked out into the kitchen. He loved that stringy old woman and would have been heart-broken if she ever left him. He spoiled her without shame. She had been with them for over fifteen years and they all felt about her as he did. He had bought her a car so that she could drive back and forth from her home in the Bronx and had financed a technical-school education for her youngest grandson, a boy who had gotten himself in trouble a few times.

Martha returned with dessert for the two of them, including a super-size portion for Al. "Eat, sad man," she commanded, "or I'm gonna tell your little wife 'bout all the bad, bad things you do when you run out of here every day."

Afterward, he tried to relax first by reading from among his large history collection and then by spending a half-hour on his rowing machine in the den. But it didn't quite work, either, and he knew that Ruthie was beginning to worry.

In bed that night he tossed for a while and then just lay staring into the dark. After a while she said, "What's wrong, Al?"

"Not much," he said.

"The new man?"

"Holland, you mean?"

"Yes."

"Yeah."

"What happened?"

"Not a hell of a lot, I guess. He wants to make a lot of changes, like can a few of the old-timers or shift them to lower jobs—like me, for instance."

"You?" She sat up in bed and breathed angrily down at him.

"Well, you know, he feels that we got a lot of deadwood in the place. He wants to can Nat, Harry and Solly and he thinks sooner or later I oughta move over to executive committee chairman in favor of him. All in less than three months that he's been here. And that's not all. He wants to decentralize the oper-ation and divide up the responsibility among different regions.

That's not such a bad idea—but I got a feeling about him that I don't like."

"What is it?"

He paused, not quite sure of his own analysis. "I'm not sure exactly yet," he said after a few moments, "but I got a feeling— there's like a gong banging in my head—telling me that I'm gonna have to watch this guy like a hawk."

"Can he really hurt you?"

He didn't answer. Instead, uncomfortably, he listened to his rather hoarse breathing. He sensed rather than saw Ruthie still sitting up looking at him. Suddenly she was stirring, moving about. Then she said, "Come here, Al." He moved toward her and, with surprise, found her naked. Her body, so familiar and yet so fresh to him, was warm and slightly perfumed. He felt aroused and yet a few moments later lay back frustrated and disgusted.

"I can't even do that any more, baby," he said miserably. "I don't know what the hell is wrong with me. I used to be Mr. Automatic Starter."

She laughed. "You're tired—and a little put out. I diagnose your physical problem as strictly temporary and mental at that. Al, why don't you go to see Dr. Felix? He can help you to relax a little and that's all that you need."

"That head-shrinker again? I told you I don't need him."

"Maybe you don't need his help, but can it hurt? He's supposed to be such a good man."

For months since the fiasco over Ben Baron, she had been urging him to visit a Queens psychiatrist whom she had heard much about, but Al had consistently refused. The next morning she worked on him again and the morning after that. He finally gave in—about three months later.

"I'll never know what really got me here, Doc, to lay here and toss and moan like a pregnant dame about to pop. Ruthie is one of those typical Jewish dames who treats their husbands like one of their kids and so she practically kicked me all the way over here. . . . I really got no problem at all, except that I can't eat much, I don't sleep and lately I can't even get a hard-on. Outside of that, I never felt better and everybody tells me I'm on top of the world. . . . Dr. Felix? Is that your first or second name? Second name? Your first is Fred. Okay, Fred, I'll tell you frankly that I almost took off when your nurse brought me into your office. I don't like talking about myself. But when I saw you at your desk, I saw that you were about my age and you had a kind face. I thought, 'Shit, he looks like a nice Jewish guy. So how, like Ruthie says, can it hurt me?' So here I am, Fred, talking my goddam head off, parked on my ass on your leather couch. I know I'll be sorry, but as long as you're not a reporter—boy, how I hate those lying, goddam, sanctimonious bastards—they tell you all they want is the truth and then they write the truth their way—I know what I'll say in this room won't go any further. Right? You don't have a tape recorder rolling, do you, Fred? . . . To tell the truth, I'm a little worried about not eating, sleeping or screwing so well. I was always great in all those departments. What—you want details? Well, ordinarily I like eating everything, except I hate fancy restaurants. I don't like a lot of dopey-looking waiters hanging over my head asking me every ten seconds if everything is all right but never give me a glass of water. The food is too rich, too saucy and it always gives me the heartburn. I like simple food, Jewish or Italian style, like my wife makes. I like Nathan's hot dogs and fish sandwiches and I'm a sucker for pizza and beer. Usually, I eat like a horse and hate to get up from the table. As far as sleep, I never sleep more than five hours a night. Usually I read until late—history, especially Renaissance history, fascinates me—and then I'd creep into bed next to Ruthie and she always makes me come awake. . . . Now, that brings me to the third subject, intercourse. My wife and I have been married sixteen, seventeen years now and we once figured out that on the basis of two and three quarters times a week—the fraction is because some weeks it was three times and other weeks it was twice and sometimes it was once or nothing—we had intercourse at least nineteen hundred times. Now, even you, Doc, got to admit that's quite a number, but I'm not talking just about quantity. It's quality that counts more, and Ruthie and I have been one hundred percent compatible—quality compatible!—in fact, one thousand percent! So that's why for the past three months it's been bothering me that things haven't worked right in bed. I mean I'm healthy as hell but I just can't get it up any more. . . . What about my childhood and my youth? Well, I was a happy kid and my parents were good to me. I was an only child, but they didn't spoil me. My mother was and is a matter-of-fact woman—but my father was a great actor and performer on the Yiddish stage. I guess I was a great disappointment to him because he wanted me to be a performer, too. But I just didn't have what it takes to get on a stage and amuse people. Can you just imagine me performing in front of people, Doc? It took me three months just to come here and give a private performance! I'm a businessman and even when I was starting to do well, he didn't think it was much. I don't blame Pop. But I'll tell you one thing, Doc, he was one of the finest men who ever lived—he had a personality that could project like a living thing right out to the audience. He made women cry and men cheer—he brought many people happiness and even when he made them sad, he made them happy. And when he made them happy, they loved him. . . . You know, Doc, you got me on this kick about Pop and I can't stop talking. I often used to wonder why it was that Chaim turned into a great actor and, lemme not be modest about it just this once, I turned into a great merchant. You might think I'm kinda nuts, Fred, but I gotta feeling that we were both trying to please people in our own way. Pop did it on the stage with *Yoshe Kalb* and *The Dybbuk.* I think I, too, got this thing with people, only in my way I do it by selling them refrigerators and coats and shoes and wigs and what not. Like Pop, I guess, I got my own audience, too, and I like to play to them my way, not the way most merchants do, maybe, but the way I can do it best. I told you it was crazy, Felix, but lemme ask you a simple question—who can say for sure that retailing ain't a helluva lot like show business? Every day is a new performance and the curtain comes down every night. The guy who said there's no business like show business—did he ever work in a store? One day in Oval's— handling all kinda customers, making them feel like they gotta great deal but making a buck, too, and keeping them happy— and I'll bet he'd change the name of that song. . . . Can I have a glass of water, Fred? My throat's getting dry. . . . Thanks. Now,

what else would you like me to spout off about? Do I get along
with people? Pretty good, I guess. But I hate phonies and hypo-
crites, but that's only a small percentage of the population. A lot
of people, though, think I'm naïve, a soft-head, sort of a *shmuck*,
because I let everyone who works for me do what he wants to
do, but I figure that the guys that are stringing me along will get
tired of fooling me after a while and either improve themselves
or take off. If you want to call me a *shmuck*, too, Doc, go ahead
and be my guest. It doesn't bother me, because I believe that as
long as you make people happy, make their lives beautiful, like
my Pop did, I'm not exactly a nothing, a nobody. I mean, what
are we here for, anyway? . . . Look, I'm not denying that a lot of
people think that I'm being taken for a ride and maybe I am. I'll
take that chance, if it will just help a few people to grab hold of
their opportunities. What does it cost? Some pride, some self-
respect? Nah, it doesn't bother me. . . . Fred, Doc, Felix, am I
boring you by any chance? Boy, that's the last thing that I want
to do—especially at these prices. I know you're a professional
ear because that's how you help people, but I'd feel lousy if I
thought my life, my spilling out my guts to you, was making you
yawn. For God's sake, Doc, tell me, willya? . . . All right, all
right, so you're just a little tired. I thought you were starting to
fall asleep. You do keep lousy hours. Well, I guess every job has
its drawbacks, right? . . . Do I ever feel any pressures? How do
you mean? Opposition, people working at cross-purposes to
mine? Strange you should ask, Fred. Yeah, I guess I do. Lately,
I've been getting a feeling that I'm working against a kind of
power bloc. Four guys. But maybe the word 'bloc' is wrong.
They seem to be pushing hard at me and not together but separately. There's Walter Solomon, a stockbroker who decided I
oughta go public and kept coaxing me and telling me that the
only way a businessman can get big is to go public. He's a
friend, or maybe he *was* a friend, but now that I've been public
a few years, I'm starting to wonder if it wasn't the biggest mistake I ever made. Then there's General Boatwright, a tough
retired Army man, a fascist at heart. Solomon got him to take a
big position in our stock and since then he's been a deluxe, king-
size pain in the ass. What's bugging him? I'm not so sure, but I

don't think it's just the fact that he's got one of our biggest blocks of stock—I kinda think that he looks at business like a military campaign. To him, it's a field problem or something like that. . . . Then there's this new guy, a Texan named Stringer, who runs a mutual fund called the Panhandle Fund. I got a feeling that if I don't deliver a better market price on the big block of stock Panhandle bought, he's gonna plug me or something. He looks like a gunslinger and there's a mean look in his eye. . . . The last man—I left him until last on purpose—is the one that I don't mind telling you worries me more than the rest of them. His name is Sidney Holland. I hired him nine months ago to be president of our company and he's already told me he's after my job. What? Is there any connection between his arriving on the scene and my personal troubles that started three months ago? You're asking me, Doc? I doubt it, but that's why I'm paying you your big, fat fee, isn't it? At least, that's why Ruthie sent me here, right? Anyway, like the rest of them, this guy Holland is fighting something. I checked him out before we hired him and, look, I'll tell you, he's had a tough life, even if his father had a lot of money. His old man was a Polack immigrant who came here and built a big estate with just his bare hands, but he always gave Sid a rough time, like some old-timers do, and the kid grew up hating his guts. Funny, he hated his father and I loved my father, and here we are barking and pushing at each other. Life can get real mixed up, Doc, can't it? . . . I didn't hear that, Fred. You said it kind of low . . . I don't know about the pressure, they're not ganging up on me or anything like that. It's just, I guess, that when you get big, you have to take on the pressures and the responsibilities. I bet I'll be all right tonight or tomorrow—it's all just an adjustment, right, Fred? . . . Only sometimes, sometimes it hits me how everything seems to get in the way of what you want to do. I never meant to build this company up into a great big muscle-bound giant. I just wanted a business that would mean jobs and serve a lot of people. It got big in spite of me and maybe too big for me. No matter what I did the business kept growing and growing. I kept opening more and more stores because Willie and I found good sites that we just couldn't leave for the next guy. But I guess when you're a big baloney in a butcher shop, you can't expect to be treated like you're a hot dog, right, Doc? Sorry about that. . . . But it wasn't what I was figuring on and probably—you made me talk it all out, Doc, didn't you?—that's why all of a sudden I can't eat, sleep or make love to my wife like I used to. . . . I will get cured soon, won't I Doc? Tell me, willya? Hey, Doc, Fred, Felix—Doc, Doc, *Doc!* I'll be goddamned. The sonofabitch fell asleep after all!"

14

Sidney Has a War Plan

"Ask Sidney!"

The phrase was uttered at least a thousand times in the next two years along the gleaming halls and neat offices of Oval's new headquarters perched high over Times Square. There were other variations of it, too, all in the same vein of resigned helplessness, such as "See Sidney," "Contact Sidney," "Clear it with Sidney," "That's what Sidney wants." It was never "Tell Sidney," "Let Sidney find out" or, worst of all, "Ignore Sidney." That was unthinkable.

So pervasive was the impact of Sidney Holland's personality on the company that many of the new people he brought in hardly realized that there was above him a chief executive officer by the unprepossessing name of Albert C. Miller. Even the boys, having receded into a time of twilight and painful austerity, sometimes wondered if Al hadn't been sucked up into the bowels of some ratty, cockroach-ridden movie house somewhere. His big new office, bright, sumptuous, but always empty, offered mute confirmation to his absence and apparent lack of interest in the developing situation. To Nat Batt, whose advancing age did not blunt the shaft that he could deliver, it was nothing less than desertion under fire. "Where's that redheaded sonofabitch," he muttered often, "when we need him most?"

On the surface, however, not much seemed changed, outside of the new physical surroundings and the appearance or infiltration of many new faces. The old executives still maintained their jobs and their fancy titles and pursued them with much apparent enthusiasm and even new formality. In all, there was a briskness, a matter-of-factness and a brightness along the five floors on top of the new Times Square store that was infectious and stimulating, especially for the newcomers and visitors. But the center of power, of decision, the fulcrum of the business, had shifted from nowhere, or from being split twenty different ways among the old cubicles, and had moved into Holland's office.

Harry, Solly, Irving, Nat, Wallenstein, Molly, Matthew and von Rossem were all functioning as before but yet not as before. Many of their prerogatives had been usurped by the new executives hired by Holland and given authority within agreed-upon limits by Holland. To a man—no women were hired by Holland —the newcomers were young, tight-lipped, vest-wearing, non-retail- but computer-oriented, crewcut, well formed, confident but appealingly self-deprecating, lean. All had one common trait. They resembled Sidney Holland, in style, behavior and bearing, although not particularly in appearance. But, unlike him, they didn't ignore the top executive tier that he had inherited. They were all interested in what Harry, Solly, Irving, Willie and the rest said and did, obsequious, in fact, and above all attentive. They were, in a word, learning. But the boys *knew*. Eventually, the learning would become something entirely different, like marching in and assuming command.

For a while, until they learned to live with it, what this did to some of the boys, like Harry Abner and Irving Waldteufel, was not to be believed.

Harry, for example, found himself with two assistants, bright-eyed, thin-lipped MBAs who sat at twin desks outside his office. Abner had not only his usual mnemonic problem, his memory deteriorating at an even faster rate than his hairline, but he just couldn't remember which of his two assistants was which, which was soft goods and which hard, and so he frequently issued orders vis-a-vis soft goods to one when he meant to apply it to the other on hard goods and vice versa. Neither of the reticent young men, knowing nothing whatsoever about retailing, were able to either correct or countermand him. They were just, it must be remembered, learning. And so confusion, which the new executives were supposed to be correcting, was simply being compounded.

Waldteufel's situation was different and worse. He found himself dogged at every turn by a new assistant who had a disturbing habit of cocking his head every time Irving opened his mouth. This was disconcerting to the tricky, lying purchasing agent because the odd tilt of his assistant's head was, to him, at least, more suspicious than it was curious. Thus, even in those infrequent moments when he was being honest or ethical, or just carrying out the most routine aspects of his life, such as phoning his wife, it gave him a feeling of uncertainty as if he were instead calling either his bookie or a friendly pimp. He began to doubt himself and to confuse his activities, so rattled was he by that constant head-cocking.

So it was not so unexpected when he called his wife one day and snarled, "Put down ten dollars on Hot Nuts!" and when he phoned the pimp whom he used from time to time and asked, matter-of-factly, "What's it tonight, sweetie—fish or meat?" Of course, he quickly recovered in both cases, but the experience shook him. The young man's continuous head-cocking threatened to turn him honest—a condition that would so reduce his effectiveness in the company that he knew he could no longer be of service to it. Would Sidney Holland, Irving wondered, see the reverse logic in that?

Few things, even what was apparently logical, it seemed, could be explained to Sidney Holland. He appeared not to want to address anyone directly, but prowled the offices studying all that went on. He rarely asked for explanations. Instead, when he felt that some remedial action was called for, which was often, he summoned the appropriate individual and summarily directed him to change his practice or his behavior, whichever the case might be, to a new one that he, Holland, had already devised. There was no room for discussion, much less argument. Take it, in other words, lump it or leave.

Since all of these involved activities in the corporate offices and since Holland never went out to visit any of the stores—he couldn't have cared less about them—at least half of the summary judgments proved ill-advised. They were simply coldly analytical, the fruit of in-the-office decisions, often totally unrelated to the actual process of moving goods off the shelves into the customers' hands. But Holland learned nothing about the errors of judgment. No one had enough courage to tell him and he would rarely discuss his judgments with anyone. He was, in his own way, even more remote from the business than Al Miller was in his way.

Midway in the first year of his tenure he made one such judgment which almost cost Oval's many millions in sales but for Al Miller's interception and literally chewing up so that it couldn't be carried out. Holland had considered it his masterstroke up to that point. It was to cut down within a forty-eight-hour period Oval's entire inventory by more than $20 million just by informing Harry Abner and his six divisional merchandise managers that each of the latter was to reduce immediately his stocks by $3.33 million. As Holland rightly figured, the number of merchandisers times the pro rata inventory reduction would certainly equal $20 million. This, he reasoned, although somewhat incorrectly, would mean that much more dollars in operating income. But what he didn't take into account and Al did was (1) the fact that much of the merchandise to be deleted from the stock list were high-appeal items that served as traffic-pullers and sold much other goods too; and (2) profits in the store business represent dollars earned from dollars invested. This was not the same thing as refusing to activate the dollars invested. It was a direct violation of the classic axiom of the merchant—"You can't sell goods from an empty wagon—even if you work like hell."

So, while Sidney Holland did not know of any such nuances and did not venture into any of the stores except the new Times Square store, which was right there in the Oval's Building, to buy some personal needs, Al Miller did both. Those nuances were old stuff to him—in fact, he had devised a few of his own—and he was spending all of his time now in all of the stores around the country. As a result, when he heard about Holland's new order, he came in one night, seized the written order out of Harry Abner's hand and chewed it up before Harry's astonished gaze.

"That's the end of that stupid order," said Al, masticating away. "This way I can be one hundred percent sure no one will get it—only the john!"

Months later, when Holland found that his plan hadn't worked, hadn't, in fact, been allowed to work, he wanted to fire Harry on the spot. He knew, of course, that he couldn't fire Al Miller, and, on second thought, as he confronted the quivering Harry in his office, he decided that he couldn't fire Harry, either. It would mean out-and-out war with Al and he wasn't quite ready for it.

"Get the hell out of my office, you incompetent shit!" he told Harry furiously. "One of these days, I promise you, I'll have your head!" As Harry slunk out, Holland waited until the door was closed before he added out loud, "And one of these days I'll cut off that redhead's head, too. And that's a promise!"

Zealously enforcing the principle of "Ask Sidney," "See Sidney," and "Clear it with Sidney," he pushed ahead doggedly toward this goal. He showed unusual skill, even tact, for a while, a highly sensitive ability to nail down the planks of power at all levels and a thoroughness that made even such wide-eyed but hard-nosed observers as General Horace Boatwright gasp with admiration. As for Al, he didn't know a thing about it, except in the most general terms, until he found disaster suddenly staring him in the face.

It wasn't necessary for Holland to formulate any program. One had emerged full-blown in his consciousness the day he had walked in to occupy his office. And later as he contemplated the full outlines of the gigantic foul-up he had inherited, he found that his instincts were sound. All he was required to do was to add flesh and muscle to the bones of his plan, or, perhaps put another way, to apply the plan and superimpose it upon the ridiculous situation that he had found. Then, as he studied the progress of the exercise, he would refine it at leisure, even enjoying and savoring the success of each phase. But to assume that this alone was the Sidney Holland manner was not to fully appreciate him.

So what he did was to put it all on paper first, in all its premeditated detail and in its long-range sweep.

He spent six hours after the normal day dictating it all to the tiny Mrs. May. When he had finished, she went over the many pages of her notes for potential errors. As Holland stared at her with a strange, piercing scrutiny, a corner of her mind sent out a warning signal. She knew from years of having been associated with him that he despised criticism but more than that he craved reassurance from her. But she was frankly appalled at what he was contemplating. It was nothing more or less than a blueprint for a raid on the company that had recently hired him. The Protestant ethic that had been ground into her as a child but which had become diffused over the years whimpered in protest, even if ever so faintly.

But she expressed none of this, despite the vagrant recollection of the simple, trusting face of a thin, redheaded man who had occasionally darted through the offices. The certainty that he was to be sacrificed to the plan committed to paper made her grimace with distaste. Holland didn't seem to notice it but waited for her overt reaction.

She arose to her small height with a polite groan, enough to make it seem natural. Closing her dictation pad, she said admiringly, "That's a very effective program, Mr. Holland. It can't help but succeed."

He studied her. "Perhaps," he said, "but I want to update it every two weeks, incorporating all the errata and exceptions that we run into. That means that every second Monday evening I want you to come in here, shut the door and get ready to take a new version of the plan. I'm leaving nothing, absolutely nothing, to chance."

As she regarded him, the dark straight lines under his eyes and the hard, congealed set of his mouth showed her that he had never been as determined to carry out anything before. He was the most intense man she had ever met, but cold intense. He frightened her and he attracted her, but he frightened her more.

So she said simply, "After twenty years, Mr. Holland, I would like to say that I admire you intensely. Few people have such— such great determination."

"Thank you, Mrs. May."

Holland's plan was simple, tripartite and jugular in its thrust. First, he would set up his own cadre. The teams of young men that he had installed in the offices of most of the top executives, particularly among the boys, were largely a feint, an end run and thoroughly expendable. Out of them, he knew, would emerge a handful of executives who would eventually succeed the boys. But the new management team that he hoped to establish would be based more on others that he would bring in at strategic intervals. Some would be hired from the company he had sold to come to Oval's, men whom he had carefully trained in rebuilding the skeleton of his father's business empire.

Others would come as a result of two ongoing executive searches he had arranged by outside firms. The blueprint was that by the end of two years more than thirty of the key jobs in the corporate offices and in the field would be filled by his own appointees. That would mean virtually a clean sweep.

But how he would accomplish this in the face of Al Miller's certain opposition was, Holland was convinced, one of the prime reasons why he would surely succeed. It was really so simple as to be undeniable. He would keep a dossier on all thirty or more existing executives, the boys' being more detailed than the rest. In it would go records of every mistake they made, regardless of scope or effect on profits. Memos would be circulated to each man, stating the facts of the error, misjudgment or infraction and requesting an endorsement by signature on each. Not signing any such memo would be a breach of discipline subject to any penalty Holland desired. Thus by his own admission, each executive would find himself impaled by his own misdeeds or performance failings. When it came time to replace him, the appropriate dossier would be pulled and he would be confronted with its contents. At that point, Holland reasoned, faced with the proof of their inadequacy, few men could put up any resistance. Downgrading or discharge would be accepted with resignation, if not gracefully, because there was no way of squirming out of it.

Blackmail? Holland shrugged at the thought. Hardly; it was discipline, assignment of responsibility and all in a good cause. He put this phase of his program into operation immediately. And it began to work like a well-oiled machine.

Second, he had learned a long time ago that the man who controlled the cash box ran the business.

In Oval's, however, gaining control of the cash box was actually not so easy because it was too easy. In the pre-Ben Baron days, Al Miller had also filled the post of treasurer in addition to chief executive officer, which meant in reality that there was no treasurer at all. Gordon Leon Jones, a pragmatic as well as a fine legal mind, had looked over the cash flow balance, as well as the debt-to-assets ratio, once a month, just to make sure that Oval's did not stumble too close to the brink of bankruptcy in its headlong rush to expansion. When Ben Baron appeared on the scene, Al Miller and Gordon Jones had quickly and mutually decided to unload the treasurer's function as an additional responsibility on the little Chicagoan. Since then, the treasurer's function had fallen by default on both Solly Patracelli, the operations vice-president, and Ernest von Rossem, the controller. It was a very loose arrangement, not only because of the mentality of the two people involved but because the pure function of treasurer should not have been combined with that of operations, which spends a big chunk of money and is in effect a debtor, or with that of control, which is supposed to be a check on the treasurer, not his instrument. Thus, the practice was in theory as though a debtor had one hand in the till and the inspector had the other. In theory, then, this was the wrong practice. It was probably the wrong theory and the wrong practice.

But if this seems confusing, it was nothing less than appalling to the new president. How the scrutiny and control of money could have deteriorated to this deplorable state was another example, in Holland's opinion, of the zoolike atmosphere in which Oval's operated. Changing this phase of the operation to suit himself was like taking candy from a baby, even easier, but because of this it could have easily been suspect and so he decided to accomplish it in steps.

Step number one was, of course, to take control of buying. So he set up a system of checks and balances that prevented buyers from spending more than $1,000 without obtaining prior approval from the merchandise managers. Merchandise managers, who generally operated fifteen to twenty departments, could not approve more than $15,000 to $20,000 in purchases without obtaining prior approval from their general merchandise managers. These executives, who managed about fifty departments each, could not authorize expenditures of $50,000 or more without obtaining prior approval from their superior. And who was their superior? In this way, Holland controlled the buying.

Step number two was to gain control of all operating expenses. This was somewhat more intricate than controlling the buying. Holland worked it out effectively by adopting the same sort of check-and-balance system on departmental and divisional expenses. But since retail costs are heaviest in labor, merchandise and promotion, he decided to place his greatest emphasis on these. He ordered a 20 percent reduction to be effected instantly in all these costs by making this a direct criterion of performance of all three vice-presidents involved. This order threw Solly Patracelli, Harry Abner and Matthew Smiles, the unhappy recipients of this dictum, into a tizzy, because failing to do this would inevitably mean the cancellation of their annual bonuses. Each was in such a state of hock by year's end that the bonuses represented a lifeline, and so Holland's ploy proved an unqualified success.

Step number three also followed this pattern. Since Holland's goal was an overall 20 percent improvement in earnings, a cost reduction equal to that percentage became the target for every increment in the money flow of the company. The only problem was that this was to be accomplished with no diminution of the performance in all levels of the business. It was as though a twenty-mule team was reduced to sixteen animals but was to haul as much and as quickly as twenty. Or an armored tank column of one hundred tanks that had been cut to eighty vehicles but was required to produce as much firepower and clout as the original one hundred. Could the mules and the tanks hold up under the strain? Not very likely, but the order was issued regardless.

In total, the net effect of all three fiscal steps was to deliver to Holland virtually a complete rout of all initiative and to give him an iron hand on the business. "The only fist in the cash box," he promised himself with satisfaction, "will be mine. And it will be a clenched fist."

Third, his grand plan, secretly spelled out on paper and updated every two weeks, was to obtain chief executive power even before he obtained the title. This was to be done by undercutting Al Miller both within the organization and among the directors. By carrying out the other phases of his plan, he had for all intents and purposes already undercut Al's power within the company. Now, all that was needed was to undercut him on the board. In that effort, Holland already had a willing ally in General Boatwright. It was a role that the insurance company executive cherished, and he set about it with gusto. The deadline was May 7, six months or so hence, when the directors would meet following the next annual meeting to elect Oval's officers for the new fiscal year.

A few months before that scheduled event, a number of Al's boys had a late dinner in the city and invited Molly Bradley to join them. The eight sat glumly in the rear of a Greek restaurant in the fur district, dabbing the heavy bread in the bean paste and avoiding each other's eyes. Irving Waldteufel, squat, saturnine and unhappy, thought that they ought to set up an empty chair for Al. "He's here in spirit, maybe not in body," Irving said. "It's only right."

But such was their mood that everyone else rejected the idea. With practically no conversation through the antipasto, the thick soup and the shish-kebab, they ate stolidly. Molly eyed them all with doubt and suspicion. She didn't trust a single one of them but she loved them all. She didn't understand, though, why they had all decided to meet, and particularly why they had invited her. What the hell were they after? And why? It had to be some kind of a con game.

She said so, out loud, flatly, and with a few choice four-letter words. They all stirred uncomfortably and finally Wallenstein kicked Nat Batt under the table and said, "All right, Nat. You got the big mouth. So talk."

"Okay, dammit, I will," Nat said. Turning to Molly, he said, "Baby, it's no news to you that we're all in hot water. Holland is after our hide, yours, Al's, everybody's, except his own boys. So we got together a few days ago and had a brainstorm."

"Yeah? What?" Molly said.

"Well, it's this way. We figure Holland's got a woman problem. We never met his wife, but from what little checking around we did, we found that she's a cold, frigid-type society broad, New England style. They got no children, they never go anywhere together and they got no compatibility at all, the way we hear it."

"That's very sad," Molly said happily, "and it really breaks my heart. But it couldn't happen to a nicer guy. What's it all got to do with me,"

Nat paused, his heavy chops working and his beady little eyes suddenly over-anxious. His head jerked, he looked hard at the others, and he spat out, "What the hell d'ya think, Molly? You want me to spell it all out for you?"

"Spell it out for me."

"All right, I'll do that. We think that you can do a lot to soften up Holland. Take him up to your goddam apartment and show him your goddam sketches. The worst that can happen is that he'll like you, he'll want to keep seeing you and you can put in some good words for all of us. The best that can happen, of course, is that he'll soften up and act a little bit like a human being. That's gotta be good for all of us—and especially for you."

She was shocked. She stared with hot, accusing eyes around the table, a hard, derisive laugh beginning to crawl up her throat, but no one would meet her eyes.

"In other words," Molly said, stifling the laugh, "you want me to act for real like the company whore?"

They all met her eyes now. It was not Nat Batt but Wallenstein who answered, his shifty eyes dancing all over his wizened face. "If you feel like putting it that way, we can't stop you. But why don't you give it a chance? For yourself, for us, for Al?"

She thought about this preposterous idea for a few moments, her normally clear, bright brown eyes smoky and undecided. Then she straightened up with a smile that was almost but not quite sweet in nature. A light of pleasure, even of anticipation, shone in her eyes.

"All right, you bastards," she said. "Why not?"

Less than a month before the annual stockholders' and directors' meetings, Sidney Holland was working late in his office, dictating into a tiny recorder the speech he would make to the board. He was so engrossed in the project, speaking in the most simple, crisp terms that he could devise, that he did not at first hear the low rapping on his door. Finally, he heard it and ignored it.

After a few moments he shut off the machine. There was definitely someone at the door, someone seeking him, and it annoyed him. It irked his sense of organization and corporate propriety. He was alone, Mrs. May had left hours ago, and he had carefully locked the door before he had settled down to his important task. Earlier, he had had a simple dinner at a nearby restaurant and had quickly returned to the office, eager to get to his work.

Irritated, he got up, strode to the door, unlocked it and flung it open. He was surprised to see that it was Molly Bradley. She wore a simple white dress that clung with ardor to the flowing lines of her figure. She had on bright-orange lipstick and had that night allowed her hair to fall low around her shoulders.

"Miss Bradley," he said tonelessly.

"Mr. Holland," she said. "May I come in?"

"I'm very busy, Miss Bradley. I never see anyone without an appointment and not very often then. Would you call my secretary tomorrow?"

"Please," she said, beginning to push the door ajar. "It will just take a moment."

Reluctantly, he decided to let her in. She came in and sat down on a leather sofa in the center of the room. Holland leaned against his desk, eyeing her warily. Her bright smile, framed by vivid, orange lips, put him off. He was also put off by the simple but evident fact that she wore little under the tight dress. He cleared his throat nervously, asking, "What's on your mind, Miss Bradley, that couldn't wait until the morning?"

She nodded brightly. "It may seem like nothing, Mr. Holland," Molly said, "but I've become quite concerned about my personal role in all the restructuring of the organization. Will I still have a job when it's over? I know I'm just a consultant now, Sidney, but I've had only a little contact with you since you took over almost two years ago. You aren't going to ignore the important role of fashion in any new plans you have for the company, are you, Sid?"

What a hell of a nerve, he thought angrily. The spurious question, the striving for intimacy. What was she really after? As he opened his mouth to tell her what he really thought, she crossed her knees in what was, to him, a devastating manner. Something like hot fear surged painfully up from the pit of his stomach. Many times, his father had drunkenly accused Sidney of being afraid of women, that as a boy and young man he could not and would not face up to a normal relationship with them. "That's why you always go to the bathroom—I know what you do in there," Isaac had said over and over again, winking, winking. Since the recollection was always coupled with the memory that the old man took pains to make such statements in front of his cronies, each such incident held a double source of pain. And each recollection brought with it a black mood that settled over him, lasting for a while after the memory eased, as it did now. Even his marital relationship with his wife had suffered from the constantly recurring memory. Isaac, he thought wildly, still had the capacity to inflict pain from beyond the grave.

Running a big hand across his quivering eyes, Holland murmured, "You needn't worry yourself greatly, Miss Bradley." He stood up straight now, fully himself again. "Now, tell me, what exactly is the real reason you barged in on me?"

She took him in with widening eyes. "Yes," she said, sighing, smiling. "There is something else—something I wanted to show you."

"What?"

She got up slowly, her eyes transfixing his. "This," she said. Her hand moved swiftly to a zipper. She pulled it down, shivered and her white dress slid to the floor. With a smile of pride and a stance that promised, she stood stark naked in front of him.

Forty-two floors above Times Square in an office that he had tried to keep sacrosanct, Sidney Holland stared in disbelief at the nude woman. Six feet tall, no longer a youngster but magnificently formed, she confronted him with a raw challenge that raised a storm in his head and his heart. But not, unfortunately, in his loins. It was his old trouble.

As he goggled at her, she moved slowly toward him, her long pink arms outstretched. "Sid," she said breathlessly, "don't fight it. No one else does. Why not here—in your office? Could it be more convenient? You can have me whenever you want."

She stood now only a few inches from him. His head was full of a blaze of excitement and confusion, hot and cool. The blackness of his mood returned and poured out of his eyes and mouth. "No—no, you bitch!" he cried out. He pushed her away. As he recoiled from her his hand scraped across the top of his desk and touched a letter opener. He seized it and started after her. She whirled away from him in fear and as she did he stabbed her with the sharp object in the center of one of her pink buttocks. She screamed.

Molly ran out screeching, and he came after her. They bolted up the long, empty hallway leading from the top-executive section into the large, open area for middle and junior executives, Molly naked and dripping blood from her bottom and Holland pounding hoarsely after her.

As they reached the three-quarter point of the open area, Nat Batt stepped out from behind a pillar. With a momentary flash from a big camera that he cradled in his arms, he poised before them and snapped a close-up view of the chase. "Got you!" he yelled triumphantly at Holland. "Now, try to give us a hard time, you rat!"

By now, Molly and Sidney Holland had, of course, stopped running. She glared hysterically at the aged little PR man. "You bastard!" she shouted. "I knew I couldn't trust you. You never told me you were going to do that!"

But Holland didn't just stand there in simple confusion. He was a doer, a man of action. Quickly, he turned on Nat and grabbed the camera out of his hands and hurled it against the wall. "There goes your goddam picture," he told Nat. And then, gesturing angrily at the two of them, Holland added, nailing it all down, "You're both through! Fired! Discharged! Finished! And you, Battganovich, get that damned naked broad out of here before some stockholder sees us!"

Of course, no one ever got fired at Oval's, Al Miller saw to that, and Sidney Holland should have known it. In fact, he did know it, but in the midst of his anger and confusion it had slipped his mind.

The morning after the stabbing incident, Molly indignantly sought out Al, contacting him through Zelda, who put out a distress call to all Eastern stores. But Molly caught up with him in a coffee shop a few blocks from the Oval offices. She explained what had happened, starting with the meeting with the boys weeks ago and their plan and ending with the late-night chase in the corporate offices. "That was quite a nip that sadist gave me," she said, starting to raise her dress to show him. "It took me an hour to find a doctor last night."

"Don't show me," Al pleaded, restraining her. "I can't stand the sight of blood. That Holland, what a vicious bastard!"

"The doctor wanted to know how it happened. I think he wanted to report it to the police, but I told him it was an accident."

"It was a crazy idea in the first place, the scheme, I mean," Al said. "Those *meshuggeners*, you never know what they'll do next. Especially that Nat Batt." He began to smile, but as he saw the hurt in her eyes he stopped. "On account of them, on account of me, you get yourself a sore *tushe*. I am sorry, baby."

He was embarrassed at the melting softness in her eyes. She had never wavered in her feelings toward him, despite the ways she took to show it, despite the things he had done to her. Something in her, under those still luscious curves and smooth, hard shell of hers, was innately soft, deeply loving and wanting to be loved. She was not really an immoral dame, but a big-hearted, soft-hearted, maybe soft-headed dame who thought as deeply with her body as with her head.

But even with that sweeping realization, his emotions cooled. He had given her up years ago, and he was not about to start again. That part of his life was over, and complicated as things were now, they were that less complicated.

He arose. "I'm gonna go up and see Holland. There's a coupla things I gotta settle with him and now is as good a time as any."

"Watch out for that letter opener."

He barged in on Holland, walking past Mrs. May, threw open the door and stood angrily before him. Holland was still dictating into his little machine and his expression at seeing Al Miller was one of near shock.

"Nobody gets fired around here," Al said tightly. "D'you understand that? If they don't measure up, they leave—and that's all. And we don't get rid of anybody by stabbing them, either, you sadistic bastard."

Holland got up from his desk, his eyes almost closed with fury. "You instigated the whole thing," he said.

"I did? All right, so I did, if that's what you want to believe. But I don't want you abusing any of the people, especially those that built up this company from scratch. And, by the way, stick to what you were brought in here to do—supervise the daily operation. That's a big enough job right there without trying to take over everything."

Holland laughed bitterly. "How can I do my job when everywhere I turn there's the mess and the debris of what you allowed to accumulate and even created yourself. Do you actually think I can do a job without making changes? That's impossible. You're the big obstacle. You don't want anything changed."

"I can't see making changes just for the sake of change. Let's change only if it's an improvement."

But Holland didn't respond. He stood behind his desk, his manner growing increasingly contemptuous, and he seemed close to losing his temper.

" 'The Fluke,' " he said slowly. "Do you know that that's what a lot of people call you? You're probably the most inept businessman in the country today. You're really cashing in on an accident—but you're also directly responsible for all of our troubles, because of your long-entrenched poor habits. I never heard of a chief executive officer who never comes into the office. Who makes the decisions around here? No one. Well, I intend to—all of them!"

"All of them, huh?"

Holland nodded solemnly. "Someone's got to—and that'll be me." He reached over and removed a reel of tape from his recorder. "It's all here," he said, raising it to eye level. "I've got a full report on you here. It's enough to run you out of town."

Al smiled vaguely at the wonder of it and at the grim reality. "I get the feeling that you've been getting it ready," he said, nodding at the tape, "from the day you came."

Holland smiled oddly. "Now what do you think? It doesn't matter. Wait until the director's meeting. You'll be lucky to get out of there in one piece."

The annual stockholders' meeting, Holland's second at Oval's, was much like the first one at which he had presided the year before, controlled, tactful and with an aura of greater refinement than any the company had previously known. As the large audience observed him, it saw a totally collected, suave but no-nonsense president who knew what he was about every minute. If their hearts had gone out to tiny, handsome Ben Baron two years earlier for his boyish sincerity, his innate goodness and even his obvious human inadequacy, their reaction to the tall, distinguished, austere figure who commanded the podium was one of respect, confidence and even pride.

And, if that reaction also lacked warmth, the lack was filled by the presence of the ever-silent redheaded man at the end of the long table behind Holland. He never said a word; his expression never wavered at any extreme in the management-shareholder dialogue. But to many in the audience, which consisted not merely of outside investors both large and small but of many of Oval's employees and even executives of other retail firms who had bought Oval stock, the lean, rather hungry-looking redheaded millionaire had become a symbol of one of the most exciting success stories in America. As he sat there in his non-communicative, bemused way, he embodied the hope of any man that he, too, could catapult from nothingness into something-thingness, and this appealed to them more than if he were a loud, extroverted type. He was a son, a brother, a grandson, a nephew and a genius in the bargain.

Few in the audience, except for a handful of Oval employees sitting nervously in the room, suspected what was really going on between Al Miller and Sidney Holland. And they didn't get even a glimmer when Holland, in the course of the meeting, reported: "I regret to tell you that we still have not yet achieved an earnings level that a company such as ours with eight hundred million dollars in sales and its new-store leverage should have. But it is not because we have not been working at it day and night, with all the resources at our command. We are hopeful that we will succeed soon, but, as you can imagine, it is difficult to affect the controls of a vast business that has grown so rapidly."

Although Al Miller remained for the directors' meeting, a fact that surprised almost everyone on the board, he asked Walter Solomon, the vice-chairman, to preside. But even those who didn't know what was coming got an inkling of why he had come when they saw the hard glow in Sidney Holland's eyes.

After they had dispensed with some routine matters, Solomon threw the discussion open. "I'm doing this at the request of General Boatwright," said Solomon. "General, you wanted some discussion of future business before we voted to reelect the officers of the corporation. The floor is yours."

The insurance company chief rose to his full five feet, four inches, put his swagger stick on the table in front of him and cleared his throat. Glancing around the oblong table at all twelve directors, he said, "Gentlemen, if I may borrow a phrase from an illustrious military figure in our country's past, 'Now that we have studied the terrain, let's do something about what we've seen—and damned fast!' Yes, gentlemen, now that we've seen the terrain, let's do something about what we've seen—and goddam fast! One thing that I learned over more than three decades in our country's armed forces is that defeat is often the price of delay. Not quite two years ago we elected a new president of this corporation and we've seen in the clearest terms what can be accomplished. The corporate structure has been reshaped and responsibilities have been reassigned where they belong. Corporate overhead has been slashed—slashed, gentlemen!—and inefficiency has been thrown into the garbage can along with waste, where both belong. Command has been established and staff and line authority have been clearly defined. For the first time in what would seem to have been a long-overdue move in a company not quite twenty years old, each of the five regions of our operations has been put on its own, charged with the responsibility of producing its own profit, keeping its own expenses in line and increasing its sales—or else!"

He paused, looking around angrily, and picked up his swagger stick. As he resumed, he emphasized almost each word with a rap of his stick on the mahogany table. "Gentlemen"—rap—"what we've seen"—rap—"is nothing"—rap—"less"—rap—"than"—rap—"a goddam"—rap—"miracle!"—rap. "A miracle!" he repeated—rap, rap, rap.

Everyone's head was bobbing with each rap. Boatwright lowered his stick to the table. "Before I go on," he said, "I would ask Mr. Sidney Holland to give us a report on the year's operations from his standpoint, not the report to which the normal riffraff of stockholders are entitled but one with the truth, the depth and the scrutiny of our company to which we on the board are entitled."

The little general was out of order, Walter Solomon decided, and he was about to say so when he realized that it was too late.

Sidney Holland had already risen, an imposing figure of authority, prepared to speak. With an expression of gratitude at Boatwright that he could hardly conceal, Holland said, "I'll be happy
to do that. The year just past has been one of great fulfillment
and of great frustration for me. Much has been accomplished, as
the general pointed out, but much remains to be done. Many of
the new policies have been at work only a short time and they
will need refinement as the results begin coming in. . . . May I be
candid, gentlemen? I mean it not at all as a criticism of anyone
present, but after almost two years in the job I have come to the
conclusion that this company has been the most fouled-up, worst-
run business I have ever seen. Wherever I turned there was
laxity, waste, inattention, overlapping and just plain inefficiency.
At times it galled me to think that I sold my own company and
invested more than ten million dollars in a business that was so
badly mismanaged. But I've made a bargain and I mean to stick
to it. . . . If I've made some progress, it's only like sticking all of
my fingers in some leaky holes when inefficiency is spurting out
in all directions. Yes, much remains to be done—but I find myself
thwarted at every turn, gentlemen—thwarted at every turn."

He sat down abruptly, and, as on cue, Boatwright was on his
feet again. "I don't know about the rest of you, but I for one
think we owe our president a rising vote of thanks for his great
accomplishments in the face of overwhelming odds. Congratulations—and thank you, sir!" Everyone rose, everyone but Al Miller. His face growing red, he was already looking anxiously for
the nearest door.

Then, when everyone else had sat down again, Boatwright
remained standing. "Having come to this point," he said, "I believe that it is both opportune and logical for me to make a
nomination as we approach the moment when we will elect
officers of the corporation for the year ahead. I nominate Sidney
Holland for the post of chairman and chief executive officer!"

As Boatwright plopped back into his chair, Walter Solomon
tried to conceal his shock. He had gotten a hint from Boatwright
that this might come up at the meeting, but he had not taken it
seriously. He glanced over at Al Miller. The man was a stoic.
Calm and collected, he had apparently gotten over his embar-

rassment of a few minutes ago and sat drawing circles with a pencil on a pad.

Walter glanced around at the others. The other outside directors—Gordon Leon Jones, "Tex" Stringer and Professor Harrison Winters—seemed surprised, although he was certain that they, too, had been fed hints by Boatwright. The inside directors, Al's boys, were something else entirely. They seemed shocked, angry, offended, ready to explode.

"Well, I think we're a bit out of order," said Walter. "But since the election of officers is the only important item left on our agenda, we might as well take that up now. Any objections?"

There were no objections. Pursuing, Walter said, "All right, then, we have one nomination for chairman and chief executive. Any seconds?"

Stringer, the head of the Panhandle Fund who had replaced Ben Baron on the board, raised his hand. "Second," he said.

Walter nodded nervously. "Of course, technically, the nomination is out of order. We have the recommendations of the committee on elections, which I have right here attached to my agenda. It calls for reelection of the same officers as last year. That means that we have two candidates, Mr. Holland and Mr. Miller. Suppose, then, that we have a closed ballot on the election of a chairman and chief executive, both candidates abstaining from voting."

Ten ballots were completed, folded and turned in to Walter Solomon. The process was not brief, evidently some of the directors having to make a difficult decision. After tallying them, Walter smiled and announced, "I'm afraid that we have a tie. Five for Miller, five for Holland."

It was obvious to them all what had happened. With both Al Miller and Sidney Holland having abstained, the voting had gone strictly along loyalty lines. The five inside directors had voted for Al Miller and the five outside directors had voted for Sidney Holland.

"Well, what do you suggest we do?" asked Walter.

Gordon Jones stirred uncomfortably. He was depressed that the situation on the board had come to this state. But there was no way of avoiding a firm decision at this juncture. He said,

"Perhaps we should have a discussion on the merits of each candidate. Of course, both of them will have to leave the meeting. A discussion would be worthwhile, since it might cause someone to alter his vote, in which case we could then proceed."

Several heads nodded in agreement. Walter glanced at Holland. "Would you mind leaving for a few moments, Sidney?"

Holland got up, but he noticed that Al remained in his chair. "Mr. Chairman, what about my opponent? Shouldn't he be required to leave, too?"

"Al?" said Walter.

There was a strange look on Al's face as he glanced up. He had a faraway expression. He shook his head. "No, I'll stay," Al said. "Personally, I don't give a shit what anyone says about me. I guess I can stand up to it no matter what it is. And no recriminations, either."

Holland sat down in surprise. He should have known. How else would you expect the Fluke to behave?

"I'm willing to stay, too, if he is," said Holland. "It shouldn't be much of a contest anyway."

Walter Solomon stared at Holland in surprise. The man certainly had more than a modicum of self-confidence. Al, on the other hand, he saw, seemed resigned to whatever would happen. "All right," Walter said to all of them, "this is a strange proceeding. But let's have it. Who wants to start?"

Both Boatwright and Stringer raised their hands. "Horace," Walter said, "I think you've already made yourself quite clear on how you stand. Let's hear from Tex."

"In Texas, we rightly believe in giving any man a chance," said Stringer. "I believe that Sidney has demonstrated some real ability. Let's give him full rein and see if he brings the whole herd in. It shouldn't matter too much to Al. Outside of his pride being hurt, as long as he's the biggest shareholder in the company, I expect that Al'd like to see his bundle get the best possible treatment."

All eyes turned to Al. But he said nothing, not a word.

Wallenstein's and Nat Batt's hands went up. Walter nodded at Willie and the shifty-eyed, cadaverous real-estate expert said,

"No recriminations, Sidney?" When Holland shook his head, Willie said, "Personally, I see nothing wrong in continuing just as we are. The public is used to Al as chairman and they seem satisfied to have Sidney running the daily show. I don't exactly know what you mean by being hampered at every turn. It seems to me that Al has let you alone to run things and you've gotten a hell of a lot done. If Al steps down, it's going to have worse repercussions than we realize. So why take a chance on it?"

Walter thought that Willie made sense, but he didn't want to state his position just yet. "Professor Winters, how do you see this situation?" he asked.

The professor hated to get off the fence publicly. In many ways, as an academician, he felt that he was on the board by its sufferance. But he knew notwithstanding that he had to declare himself. "I'm in favor of a change in the chairmanship," he said softly. "I have a strong feeling that, unlike what Mr. Wallenstein believes, appointing Mr. Holland chairman will have a salutary effect on the public and on the investor. It will strengthen the conviction that the board wants an improvement in the affairs of the company. Confidence in our stock will increase and it will free Mr. Holland's hands. As, let's say, chairman of the executive committee, Mr. Miller will continue in a policy-making position and the public will also accept that."

In Walter's view, that, too, made sense. He was becoming a bit confused. He was glad when Waldteufel's hand went up. "Irving, what's your opinion?"

"I, too, like Willie, hope that you'll have no recriminations, Sidney," Waldteufel began. He waited until Holland shook his head and resumed. "I've known Al Miller a long time and I personally think that putting him on a shelf will hurt in a lot of ways. First, the employees of the company will be all shook up. Second, our suppliers will be upset. Many of them feel that though they deal with buyers and merchandisers, they're really dealing with Al Miller like they did for years. Kick him upstairs and they'll lose confidence in Oval's. Third, I'm against it on general principles."

"Gordon, what do you think?" Walter asked.

The lanky, grizzled attorney had been perhaps the most introspective of the whole board during the discussion. As he had closely observed both Sidney Holland and Al Miller, it had occurred to him that it was odd that the opponents were men who each had had traumatic relationships with their fathers. Somewhere deeply buried within that similarity, he thought, lay a strong reason for their personal animosity. Why is it—or is it? he wondered—that so many of the second-generation of immigrants couldn't seem to have a normal relationship with their fathers? Why did so few WASPS seem to have problems of that kind? Was it that no sort of gap existed between them and their forebears that smoothed their relationship or the fact that there was a gap? The whole matter was way beyond him, but he was intrigued and rather irritated by it. Why couldn't everything in life be like the law—explicit, hard-and-fast, and be conceded purely by what the hell was on the record?

But he was dallying and he knew it. So he said, "It seems to me that the decision rests primarily on how restricted Sidney is in his ability to carry on what he has started. I wouldn't suggest it in a court of law, perhaps, but I think it might be worthwhile to ask him to elaborate on that one point."

Walter Solomon nodded gratefully. "It takes a legal mind, I guess. Unless Al minds—"

Once more Al said not a word.

"Well, then, let's hear you on that point, Sidney," said Walter. "How restricted are you?"

During the discussion, Sidney Holland had sat with growing dismay. Instead of enjoying the overwhelming feeling of triumph that he had felt when the even vote had been announced, he had seen that feeling slowly whittle away under the reasonable arguments everyone had advanced. He had not counted on a continuous flow of rationale or logic but on a tide of emotion sweeping him to victory once he had managed to capture half the votes on the board. But the discussion had evolved into almost an academic debate on the merits of the situation, rather than on the merits of the individuals involved. His head had grown warm and then hot. The blackness of despair that occasionally seized him, particularly when some incident reincarnated some of his most bitter moments with Isaac, was beginning to return. And the deep feeling of frustration and resentment that he had felt years ago at his old man was never very far from him in periods of aggravation, and he began to feel its claws on him.

He got to his feet slowly, towering over them. "You want to know how restricted I am, gentlemen? I'll tell you—it's just goddam near unbearable. From the minute I walked into that office, I felt I was an outsider. For over seventeen years this company has operated out of one man's hat and the bigger it got the worse it became. I may be president of the company today, but in the eyes of all the executives and the close to thirty-seven thousand employees there's only one boss and it's not me. All right, that's the emotional environment of the place. But what about the actual administration of the company that is my specific assignment? I'm hampered at every turn. No matter what I tell the executives and the middle management, I always have the feeling that they're laughing at me privately, knowing that their jobs are secure because Al Miller doesn't ever fire anyone. Give them enough rope, he says, and they'll either hang themselves or do a good job. But it doesn't happen that way, gentlemen! It just doesn't happen that way in this world of ours. People have to be disciplined. They have to fear you, they have to be goddam afraid of what you can do to them if they don't perform, if they don't produce the results that you demand! Can there be anything that makes more sense than that? I can't imagine it. But then let's talk about the interference, the chicanery, the conspiratorial things that are done behind my back. Do you know that an attempt was made by two executives of the company to blackmail me? Yes, goddamit, blackmail me! And do you know who was behind it all? Just look over there—at your present chairman—and you'll see who it was! He used seduction, a secret camera and a set-up situation to pull it off—but, let me tell you, it didn't succeed. It didn't succeed for a moment, because he didn't know and didn't take the trouble to find out with whom he was dealing! I can outwit, outthink and outcheat that sonofabitch any day in the year and don't you forget it! I'll tell you men something—I'm just plain sick to death of having to deal with a nitwit, a tricky, non-working, scheming, two-bit coward who runs out on everything. If I had known two years ago what I know now about that goddam bastard Al Miller and this shitty company that he runs, I tell you I wouldn't have come within miles of this insidious combination!" He paused, within a hairsbreadth of completely losing control, and then resumed with a yell: "I'll tell you guys one thing more! You can take this crappy job you're thinking of offering me and shove it right up your old anus, that's what! If I've got to be in the same company with that stupid sonofabitch, I don't want any part of it, you hear?"

Suddenly he bent and retched, throwing up all over the mahogany board-room table. He heaved and heaved, only barely conscious of the burly little general rising indignantly across from him and shouting, "You rotten, sniveling bastard! I'm ashamed of you—yes, downright ashamed!"

Relieved of his burden for the moment, Sidney Holland turned toward the source of his venom and spleen. Al Miller, sitting there with neither a smile nor a frown, still said nothing, not a word. Suddenly Holland could take it no more. He thrust his chair back, grabbed his briefcase and dashed out.

For a few moments everyone sat in silent shock, allowing their emotions to calm. With a faint smile, Walter Solomon gestured warmly at Al. "Congratulations, Mr. Chairman, you've been re-elected," he told him.

Al stared back at him and, possibly for the first time in his life, registered contempt. Finally he spoke. "You're wrong, Walter. I can't accept your congratulations. I withdraw."

Then, Al Miller got up too and left.

Punching Irving Waldteufel in the ribs, Nat Batt whispered, "It's a good thing Holland fouled himself up. But I was ready for him. In case it got down to fine points, I had the goods on him." From a large envelope he withdrew Holland's tape and typed war plan. "I had him by the short hairs, but I didn't even need it, dammit."

After they had all talked it over, Walter told the attorney, "Of course, we can't let Al withdraw, Gordon. See him tonight and tell him that the board has refused to accept his resignation. But tell him also that we expect him to find a new president as soon as possible so that everything can get back to normal."

He looked around the table for a moment and blinked. "Normal? Did I say normal? What's that?"

15

Back to Sam

THE BOTTLE OF SHERRY and the bottle of milk confronted each other not unlike the way the two men did across the table in the lavish kitchen. The dark, dour man fondly tippling from the sherry bottle seemed happy with the world, content with his lot, which was not inconsiderable. But the thin, worried redhead bearing the troubles of the world on his bony shoulders kept drinking the milk and burping with an alkaline bitterness.

"I wonder what the hell keeps me coming back here," Al complained. "Twice we used that goddam elephant toilet paper of yours. Twice I got burned."

"You called me," said Sam. "I didn't call you."

"I know, I know. So why didn't it work?"

Sam Schulte shrugged his heavy shoulders. "Somewhere in my system there must have been an error of calculation," he said. "Or maybe—and this is not intended in the way of criticism—maybe the environment of your company, the climate you built there, defies my system. Maybe it defies any normal system of integrating new executives into its top management. Frankly, Al, I'm mystified—maybe you should go elsewhere. You're certainly free to, Al. I don't want you to depend on me to solve your personnel problems. Believe me, my feelings won't be hurt."

"All right," Al said with a sigh. "Let's cut out the bull. I'm here because I wanta be. I'd rather deal with a friend, some guy I can trust on something this important. Look, the last thing I'd ever deny is that I'm such a bargain to work with and live with. But I agreed to take both guys in good faith. It just didn't work out and I'm not sure I wasn't as wrong as they were."

Sam tippled. Refreshed, he observed, "You talk about bull. Now that's real bull. We just extrapolated wrong, period. You and your so-called faults and qualities actually had little to do with it. When we considered those men, we charted all their qualifications and personnel traits against the needs of the particular job and we came out wrong." He grinned paternally, a stocky, dark man with beetle brows and haunting dark pupils. This gave him the capacity to look paternal one moment and threatening the next simply by raising or lowering his heavy eyebrows and opening or veiling his pupils. "Let me put it this way. Ben Baron never had the experience of being wrong before, so when he ran into opposition he crumpled."

"We gave him the big-ball award," said Al with a smile.

Sam nodded. "I heard. You and your kooks would do something like that. I would have given him the yellow-streak award instead. But it was a nice, a very nice gesture. As for Sidney Holland, he was an authoritarian with a brittle spine. He, too, crumpled, and so while they were entirely different personalities, they were alike that way. Personally, I think you're best rid of both of them."

"Even though I personally didn't like Holland," Al said, "I feel sorry for him. He's always gonna have to prove himself, like his old man is keeping a scorecard on him."

"That," said Sam, "calls for another tipple." He accomplished this with ease.

"Somehow," Al went on, "I got half a feeling that that 'f.q.' business has something to do with it. I never did understand that flexibility-quotient stuff. They were both extremes on the scale, but it didn't seem to mean a damn thing."

"Well, let's stop rehashing what happened. Let me get my sheets and we'll see who else I can stick you with," Sam said. He was back in a few moments with a thick sheaf and, with a gleam in his eye, a new bottle of sherry. He dumped the sheets on the table, took the empty sherry bottle and pitched it through an open window. It shattered musically on the pavement below and its pieces tinkled there for a few moments. Opening the new bottle, Sam observed with a chuckle, "That's what I call making it exciting for the dog. He'll have to watch his step as he pounces around, but it will keep him light on his paws. Maybe that's why we haven't had any robberies around here."

Sam bent to his sheets. "Let's see what we have here." He read down the page, flipped. Then he read down again and flipped over. And again. Every so often he said, "Hmm," or arched his prominent eyebrows, or looked over at Al, then shook his head and went back to the personnel register. After about ten minutes he said, "I'll tell you the truth, Al. I'm so cautious now after the first two times around that nobody looks good to me."

Al sipped the milk and nodded solemnly, burping again. "Yeah, Sam, me too. It's gotta be somebody exceptional this time."

Schulte bent to his sheets again. After a while he straightened up a bit wearily and apparently having given up. "Al, I see nothing on my list that I can suggest to you," he said. "And with that, I've almost run out of ideas for you, except maybe one." He stared at Al a moment and then muttered flatly, "No," as though thinking out loud.

Al set his glass down, trying to figure out what Sam had on his mind. Suddenly it hit like an arrow shot unerringly to the center of his brain. He half rose in his chair, his head pounding, pounding. "Why not, Sam, why the hell not?" he demanded.

"Why not what?" Sam asked, his eyes opening wide.

"You. Why not you!" Al blurted.

Sam stood at the window, looking down where he had hurled the bottle only a short time before. Craning his neck, he told Al, "Look at that hound, walking around the glass on the tips of his paws. The hair is stiff on the back of his neck. He's growling. I pity any stranger that tries to come near the place. Proves something, doesn't it, Al? Nothing sharpens you like a challenge. And that's what you're giving me, a challenge."

He came back and faced Al across the table. "I'm not so damned sure that I need any more challenges," Sam said. "I've made more money than I can possibly use in ten lifetimes and I've given away as much as any man I know. I've come a long, long way in life, as you have, but I'm almost twelve years older than you, so why should I look for a new challenge? Can you give me any good reasons, Al?"

Al shrugged. "I wasn't thinking about it that way. It's just that I think you and I could work well together. We got mutual respect, the chemistry is right. I think we'd make a hell of a team."

Sam nodded carefully at Al's points. "I agree with all of that," he said. "But what's missing is the urgency of making a move of that kind. Why should I do it? I'm fifty-eight, I'm worth more money that I will ever admit to owning and my own business is thriving. Why should I change my life style? It would be a complete change in my life, wouldn't it?"

"It sure would," Al admitted. "There's nothing like the retail business."

"Yes, a big change in my life, a big change," Sam mused. He added, "But there is one reason why I might be willing to undertake it."

Al brightened. "What's that?"

Sam hesitated for a moment. "I've always wanted to be head of a billion-dollar company." A touch of shyness appeared on the dark, dour face and then vanished. "It's the one distinction that I've always aspired to, but it seemed out of reach for my own company."

"I don't get it, Sam," Al said, surprised. "Oval's is crowding the eight-hundred-million-a-year mark, but we won't reach the billion level for at least a coupla years."

"You don't understand," Sam said patiently. "I'm talking about a merger. A merger between Communities, Unlimited and Oval Stores. We're over three hundred fifty million and you're running at about eight hundred million. Combined, that gives us sales of one point fifteen billion a year. There's your billion-dollar company." Sam smiled at Al with satisfaction.

"A merger?" Al said. "That's a new wrinkle, Sam."

"Why not? There's a natural affinity between the two companies. We're builders—you operate stores. We could build your stores and, what's more, we could make sure that Oval's gets into every big regional shopping center in the country. Sears, Roebuck, Penney's, Macy's, A and S, the blue-chip stores, wouldn't try to keep you out any longer because we'd be the builders, the developers and the landlords of new centers, just as we are of quite a few right now. But there's one thing that's even more important. As builders, we get tax shelters for our new and old properties that would become part of the combined companies' cash flow. Do you know what that means, Al? We'd have an immense amount of cash to build as many stores as you could possibly want and we could diversify into any area of building and home supply that we would want. It would be a natural for both of us, and in the bargain, with all due modesty, you would get me."

The door chime sounded. It was the opening three chords of Beethoven's *Coriolanus* overture, the bell version of it anyhow, and, if anything, it added a fateful emphasis to Sam's words. "Sam?" Barbara Schulte called, and when he responded she came into the kitchen. She nodded coolly at Al. She looked wonderful, resilient, well groomed, her figure somewhat less fullbodied than when Al had last seen her. But her eyes were clear, sensitive and aware. She leaned against the gleaming sideboard and listened.

"It makes a lot of sense," Al conceded.

"It sure as hell does," Sam said. "It makes more than sense, Al, the more I think about it. It's pure wisdom. And we haven't even scratched the surface of the synergism this deal would create."

"Why not?" Al said, wondering aloud. "Why not?"

"Let's drink to that," Sam said with a big grin. "And this time you're going to have sherry." He poured a glassful for Al. They looked for Barbara, but she had quietly left. "Here's luck on a deal that's going to be the most important thing that's ever happened to both of us." Sam raised his glass and Al said, "*L'chaim,*" and they both drank.

Sam poured again and took his drink to the window, where he stood exultantly looking out. Al could see that Sam was very excited. With his back turned to Al, Sam said, "There are a few other things involved in a merger of this kind. It all boils down to this, Al. Since Communities, Unlimited is the smaller partner to this deal, we'll have to do a few things so that it doesn't present a bad image to the investor, the Government and the press. Oval's will just have to acquire CU. That means that you'll have to come up with the financing and stock necessary to give us the right multiple. Our lawyers will work out the details, but my guess would be that the cost ought to be close to two hundred million dollars in cash and securities, mostly stock. The point is that rather than have a smaller company take over a larger one, which wouldn't sit well with the Government, the investors or the press, you and Oval's would seem to be taking the initiative. Then, after an exchange of stock we could later convert it to a new one which would probably have a higher value per share than either of our separate stocks. You could easily swing this deal with what you've got, and the banks would go along on the rest. There's no question on that. You've got twenty-six million dollars in cash and treasury stock worth maybe another twenty-five million dollars. That's more than twenty-five percent of the whole deal right there."

"You know a hell of a lot about Oval's," Al observed. "That's a good start."

"Al, I know a lot about a lot of companies," Sam said. "I make it my business. I'm not altogether an altruist. Why do you think I get myself involved in executive placements? Not only to help people but because it helps my business to have such people beholden to me. In the process, it gives me a lot of inside information about other companies, and that helps my business too."

He turned at the window and studied Al over the top of his glass. "You want this deal, Al? It's the only way I'll come along. But I don't want you to get involved unless you're really hot about it—excited and ready to go."

"I am," Al said simply. "It sounds great to me—but I hope the board goes along with it."

"They'll go along with it," Sam assured him. "Believe me, Al, they'll go along with it. But there is one more condition I've got to twist out of you and it's important to me. I don't want to come in as president. I want to be chairman of the board, chief executive officer and president. I'll be most effective that way. What difference should that make to you, I ask you, *boychik*? You'll have what you want, the board will have their man and you're off the hook. You'll become chairman of the executive committee, an important post with the greatest prestige. Under the right circumstances, you can even outvote me when you want to. Okay?"

Al nodded slowly. Perhaps too slowly because Sam Schulte said sharply from the window, "Do you want this deal, Al—or what?"

"I want it! I want it!" Al snapped. "How many goddam times do I have to tell you I want it?" He was pale and a bit weak-kneed. The scope of it all was staggering. "Just give me a little time to get used to the idea."

The board, as Sam had accurately predicted, quickly accepted the deal. In fact, Al was surprised at the eager reaction with which the outside directors greeted the offer. They immediately found the terms agreeable, subject to further exploration, and asked for a full-scale meeting of both boards, after which stockholders of both companies would have to approve the merger.

Walter Solomon, pleased and surprised by the turn of events, seemed to epitomize the viewpoint of the five outside directors.

"I'm impressed with the willingness of Sam Schulte to enter into a merger with our company, Al," he said. "You must have given him quite a sales talk. Everyone knows him. He has an impeccable reputation. Although his company is less than half the size of ours, the marriage will have immense benefits to both concerns. But, aside from that—and that's plenty, I grant you—having a man of the skill and stature of Sam Schulte, a man who revolutionized the building business, to come here and run things under Al Miller's direction, of course, is a stroke of fortune for us." Then, gazing up at the ceiling, he mused, "You know, gentlemen, in a way it's a marriage of the elite." He turned toward Al sitting at the end of the table and added, with enthusiasm, "Al, my hat's off to you. I think it's a brilliant coup on your part to have come up with this solution to all our problems. Gentlemen, frankly now, don't you agree?"

Al's stomach took a queasy lurch as the outside directors' side of the board erupted spontaneously into a spattering of applause. Even General Boatwright applauded. But it was evident to all that his heart wasn't in it. Ever since Sidney Holland's abrupt, embarrassing departure a few weeks ago, Boatwright seemed to have aged and sagged. He had even disposed of his swagger stick. And he nodded dully, as Gordon Jones, Tex Stringer and Professor Winters expressed their approval of it all.

That was the reaction of the outsiders on the board, but the attitude of the insiders, Al's boys, was something else entirely. The five had sat with frozen, distressed faces, and when the others had approved the deal, they had hesitated and reluctantly agreed.

Later, when the outsiders had left and the boys remained in Oval's attractive board room, Al studied them. There was the same hurt, almost stunned look on the faces of Harry, Willie, Irving, Nat and Solly. Although Al had followed his usual practice of leaking the rumor, they had refused to believe it, and being unable to contact him until the board meeting, they finally realized that rumor was fact. Their surprise had given way to consternation and that to fear and hurt.

No one said a word until Solly observed, "Geez, you know what I'm thinking? How long ago it was that we didn't even have a place to hold a meeting and we had to have it in the john. Now, look at this room. Gosh, I guess we really made it."

"You *shmuck!*" Nat exploded. "What's that got to do with anything?"

"Nothing," Solly said, shrugging. "Just thought I'd mention it."

"Hey, Al," said Harry, "remember the time you chased Irving down the hall and you wanted to nail him to the wall with your fists?"

Nat yelled, "You're another *shmuck!* That wasn't Irving. That was me!"

But the nostalgia strain had taken hold of them.

"Remember the time that fat Mottel had a nighttime bargain

sale on the hot tables in the cafeteria?" Willie asked. "We sold hot panties."

"How about the one time Harry put up tents overnight next to Macy's and A and S?" recalled Irving. "Next morning, they didn't know if it was the Indians, the Arabs or the circus."

"Boy, I'll never forget how Nat used to sneak out by taking some bricks out of his wall," said Solly, his eyes warm with recollection. "Hey, Nat, I think one of your guys is missing—did you cement him up in the wall?"

"Talking about remembering things," said Nat in an uncharacteristic soft voice, "remember in the beginning, Al, when you used to give out tickets to the races and to the burlesque to the guys who made the best sales quota? That was one of the best ideas you ever had."

Al stared at them in disbelief, his eyes moistening. "All right, all right, you bastards," he said, his voice quavering.

After a heavy silence, Harry asked, "So why do we need this merger, Al?"

"It's the only way Sam Schulte will come in," Al said.

"Sounds like he's calling all the shots," said Irving. "Why do we let him?"

"I know Schulte from the real-estate business," Wallenstein said. "He's a big man in all departments and a real takeover guy."

"Maybe we need that kind of drive right now," Al said. "If we're all working in the same direction, how can it hurt?"

"How can it hurt?" Nat said. "It can't just hurt—it can kill us. I got a feeling about him. He's gonna be a worse prick than Holland."

"Nobody can be worse than Holland," said Harry flatly.

"I just don't know," said Willie, his voice worried. "Schulte knows my field too goddam well. I got a feeling he's gonna cramp my style."

"Mine, too," said Nat.

"I hope his memory's not too good," Harry said.

"If he finds out what I'm doing," added Irving, "I'm finished. No self-respecting chief executive would let me go on. If he comes in, Al, I go out."

"If he's a takeover guy," Solly put in, "the first thing he'll do is take over operations. I don't know why but they always do."

"Al, honest, weren't we better off in the good old bad days?" asked Harry plaintively.

Suddenly Nat spat out, "I vote against this frigging merger!"

"Now who's the *shmuck?*" said Solly with vicious satisfaction. "You already voted for it, you little bastard."

"So did you, goombah," Nat said.

Heavy silence again. If fate was knocking loudly on their doors, they were behaving as though they didn't want to hear it.

"Maybe—maybe we all oughta get started cleaning up what we're doing before Schulte takes over." It was Wallenstein thinking out loud. "Beat him to the punch. Clean out the desk, burn the stuff in the files, remove the fingerprints from the safe—"

They stared at Willie with but one thought. Trust Wallenstein to figure out the best way to con a tough guy! They shot up from their chairs, a small, well-dressed mob gone rampant, and rushed to the door, bumping into one another and cursing. They were gone before Al could stop them and he was left to sit alone to worry and wonder.

In due course, the proxy statement for the merger came out. Intended to acquaint Oval's shareholders with the terms of the proposed merger, the 122-page document was impressive by its comprehensiveness, its welter of confusing facts and bland terminology and by its skillful avoidance of certain other facts that would have caused the Securities and Exchange Commission to become suspicious. As it was, the SEC after a suitable delay accepted it and its terms without any reservations.

Few saw more in it than they were intended to. Those few, however, tried to find out more by asking questions. But Sam, justifiably suspicious, became incommunicado by flying unobserved to Paradise Island, where he holed up in the penthouse of a high hotel overlooking a deserted lagoon.

Al, too, made himself unavailable and incommunicado, a state that was as natural to him as breathing. But one stockholder, who identified herself as the owner of a sizable block of Communities, Unlimited common, would not give up. She kept trying to get him first through Zelda at the office, then through Sam's office, then through Ruthie at home. She left messages almost every day. After five weeks she warned Zelda that if Al wouldn't arrange for a meeting with her she would go to the Justice Department in Washington.

Now concerned, Al told Zelda that he would meet the woman one afternoon in the rear of a movie house on West 42nd Street. He hoped in this way to avoid a scene or, failing that, to duck out on her by running down the front of the theater and out an exit to the alleyway.

At the appointed time, he waited nervously inside the dark theater. A triple feature presentation of old Alfred Hitchcock movies was under way on the screen. Stealing glances at the flickering horror that unreeled up front, he already regretted having made the date. A woman with a veil on her face slowly approached. She hesitated, then came closer. Al's heart began thundering because as she faced him he realized how foolish he had been. He should have known. It was Barbara Schulte.

"Hello, Al," she said, smiling. "Surprised?"

He nodded sullenly.

"Don't be angry. I didn't know if you would see me if you knew that it was I. I know that you and Sam are trying to avoid seeing anyone before the stockholders' meeting. I don't even know where Sam is, do you? But I do want to talk to you—there are a few things that I must tell you."

He took her upstairs to the ratty lounge that was covered in moth-eaten fuchsia velvet, a pathetic reminder of better days when the structure had housed a legitimate theater. The lighting was better and they were alone on a sofa in the corner, except for one or two frail, rather odd-looking types loitering nearby.

As they sat down, Barbara put a hand on his arm. "Al, please listen to me for a few minutes and don't say anything until I'm finished." She seemed rational enough to him, but he would have liked a less determined frown than she wore.

"So go ahead," he said with a small smile of reassurance. "Shoot the works."

"Don't interrupt now," she reminded, "and hear me out. Al, you just can't go through with this merger. Do you know why?

Do you even have the faintest idea? I didn't think so. You're so naïve and he's so calculating." She paused and he actually saw a spark in her eyes light up into a cool fire. "Do you think this merger and everything just happened accidentally, that it evolved from a sort of trial-and-error process? I can see that you do—oh, Al, how honest and unassuming and simple can you be? He planned everything, he arranged everything. Don't I know him? He never makes any mistakes and he manipulates people as though they were puppets. He has a God complex—no one knows it better than I. He married me for my family's money and he told me so many times. He was on the way up but decided to skip a few steps when he met me. He's promiscuous and he likes to flaunt it to me. Where's his Miss Terry? She's not in his office—and I'll bet she's away with him on one of those interminable shackups of his. Before her, there were others, many others. I've lost count, but every so often he tells me. He likes to tally up his affairs to show me what a man I married— no, bought. . . . Al, Al, when you first came to him for help, he manipulated you into accepting a failure. Then, when you came back, don't you see? He gave you an even bigger failure as the solution to your problem. Don't you know how he did it? Didn't you ever wonder why two people failed in a row? Don't you know what that little legend on the edge of his executive search sheets means? That 'f.q.' indicator? Did he tell you it meant 'flexibility quotient'? It means 'failure quotient'! Yes, failure quotient! Are you beginning to understand? Didn't you even start suspecting that it had all been planned when both Ben Baron and Sidney Holland proved to be totally inadequate?"

The flash that had turned into fire in her eyes had expanded the whites of her eyes so that she seemed to be staring, staring in extreme awareness. A chill had spread through him at what she had been saying and he began involuntarily to recoil from her. He wanted to get away from her. She's off her goddam rocker, unbalanced, a loony, he told himself. But he had to listen. Otherwise, who knew what she might do?

"Even that wasn't enough. Just in case you or anyone else might suspect what 'f.q.' was, he changed the numbers. Oh, he didn't reverse the values. High doesn't mean low and low high.

Oh, no, his mind is too diabolical for that! He devised a code that only he knows. Each digit means something else, not the reverse or the sum to be divided or multiplied or whatever but something altogether different. Al, he carefully manipulated you to a point where he would be your only alternative. After supplying you with two failures that he had carefully built up in advance as top-drawer, he knew they would fail. The 'f.q.' showed it, based on the help of a psychologist he employs. But when those would fail, who else would he have for you? No one—no one, of course, but he himself, Samuel A. Schulte, the only possible solution in all the world for your problem. But then, after all, why should you complain? You got God Himself —how could you do much better, you damned fool!"

She glared at him, shaking, beginning to sob, murmuring, "Fool, fool, fool . . ." Shivering himself from the chill inside him, he got up and gently took her arm. He guided her downstairs and out the theater. On the street, he hailed a cab and sent her on her way home. As the cab pulled away, he saw her turn and look back at him. Her wild, pleading stare was something that he couldn't forget for weeks. And for weeks he pondered on the matters of sanity, insanity, honesty, duplicity. If only the insides of people's heads weren't so secure from examination, he told himself, such dark caverns, life could be so good, so simple, so right, life could have such joy, such *tam*, such a good taste. Instead . . .

The final weeks before the special stockholders' meeting were so full of introspection, confusion and doubt that he seemed to walk on the edges of sanity himself. He decided many times to telephone Sam in his Caribbean lair, but what did he expect Schulte to do? Confirm the accusations? And who would Al say had made them so that an answer was vital? Sam's own wife? No, that was impossible. It was not acceptable, not proper. How could Sam respond to what he would surely call Barbara's ravings? Al was himself at least as certain that she had been irrational as he was that she hadn't been. But, beyond that, assuming that there was some truth to what she had said, did it in any way alter the fact that he and Sam had arrived at what was probably the best solution to Al's and Oval's problems?

There was, however, an overriding consideration, a pair of them, in fact. Having accepted the role of head of a public company—had the move really been so necessary, so urgent? —he had to act in the best interests of stockholders. He didn't really want to, he really didn't think in such terms, he really didn't believe in the concept. Why, after all, should a stockholder rate more attention than a customer? But, of course, he had to accept the responsibility because he had agreed to be the steward of a public company. Why didn't anyone, he wondered, also remind him of his obligations to customers? But the bald, raw fact was that the shareholders needed a company administrator, a doer, a dynamo—whereas the customers already had him—but if this was not to be his role too, one that he both despised and could not handle, he was morally obligated as Oval's founder and chairman to make sure that it would be someone with all the right qualities and especially the dominant personality. Was there by any chance another alternative? Any? No, not one.

The other consideration, of course, was the boys. Obviously, if they disliked the merger and Sam's taking over, what else could they do? Harry, Irving and Willie were in their mid-fifties. Solly was crowding fifty. Nat was seventyish, long past retirement. Mottel was thirty and therefore retrievable. Ernest von Rossem was almost sixty. Molly Bradley was—what? In her late forties— more? Someone had to take care of them in the face of the inexorable, time, public pressure, the earnings game, and if it had to be Sam, at least it would be someone decisive, not of the ilk of Al Miller.

And so the day of the meeting arrived and he blundered, stumbled and shambled his way into a decision. He sat mutely, so mutely, pale and drawn as Walter Solomon convened the meeting, heard the shareholders overwhelmingly approve the merger and watched with mixed emotions and hot, moist eyes as Sam Schulte dramatically appeared at a side door, marched in and warmly accepted the congratulations of the throng of stockholders who flung themselves forward to shake his hand, pound him on the back and gaze with admiration and affection on their new corporate savior and new hero. The board, with the exception of Al Miller, also rose to a man to hail the new chairman. But Al, quite unnoticed, slipped out through the very same door that Sam had triumphantly entered.

Literally from that moment, things changed. A new force had taken over Oval's, a force friendly and beatific but hard and compelling. Behind Sam's warm smile, one could almost make out the iron grimace. Instead of closing his door as Sidney Holland had or of melting away from any decision in the manner of Al Miller, Sam pursued an open-door policy at least in the first few months and tried to be in on everything. He eventually summoned every major and mid-management executive to his office, welcoming them with a firm man-to-man handclasp and a smile. But everyone, with no exceptions, left with pressed lips, an irregular functioning of the left or right ventricle and a sag in their long-entrenched sense of security.

Sam took three immediate steps to bring everyone under his control, both in actuality and in spirit. First, he expropriated Al Miller's office, a lavish chamber which remained as spotlessly clean as when it had first been set up, and added it to his own office. This, as well as the fact that Al didn't come into the office for six months, effectively removed any remaining vestige of Al's presence in the business, except for the fact that he was still chairman of the executive committee.

Then, Sam gained control of the finances of the company by assuming both the posts of treasurer and of chairman of the finance committee. Since he now considered, approved, rejected, watched and spent much of the company's funds, he was, as he cheerfully told everyone, "both the payer and the spender. You know anyone who's got a better deal?" But the fact was that he was fully scrupulous in the handling of the company's money. He also enforced budgeting rules that were at least as stringent as Sidney Holland's—in fact, he adopted both Holland's checks-and-balances and expense-reduction systems—but without the threat of severe disciplinary action if the rules were violated. In

Sam's case, the threat was not expressed but implied with a smile, a pat on the back and the reassurance, "Don't let it worry you, fellow. I know you can handle it." But if Sam permitted his smile to linger a bit too long, allowing a slight hint of doubt to creep in, it could, of course, only be the observer's fear that caused him to make that interpretation.

Finally, Sam took complete charge of the company's store-expansion program away from Wallenstein and handled it personally. He used Oval's great image as a lure to obtain other merchants and service stores to his new shopping centers. But, to be fair and objective about it, it must be said that he also used Communities, Unlimited's clout as a highly successful builder to push new Oval stores into new centers where the traditional, big-store tenant would ordinarily have refused to allow a discounter to enter.

Thus, within the first six months of his tenure, Oval's sixty stores were on the road to becoming seventy and the chain's potential suddenly took on an even brighter aura.

But, here and there, some complaints, some expressions of dissatisfaction rumbled. Had Oval's become subservient to Communities, Unlimited? Was CU getting the major attention, planning and push? If not, why, after only about six months, had Sam Schulte engineered another corporate reorganization in which CU effectively became the parent company and the much larger Oval's became a subsidiary? Could Oval's then thrive? And why was Harry Abner, the general merchandise manager, taken off the board of directors? And, speaking of merchandising, why was that traditional lifeline of retailing being given less consideration by the new management than expansion and operations? And, speaking of expansion, why, unlike the past when every new Oval's store looked different from its predecessors, did the blueprint for the ten new stores show an identical, boxlike structure, windowless except for the entrances, quite indistinguishable from other big suburban discount stores?

Al had heard of some of these things, but it was not because of them that he phoned Sam Schulte one afternoon from an out-of-town store for the first time since the change in management.

"Sam? Al. What the hell's going on back there?"

"Al, *boychik*, how are you? What do you mean?"

"A coupla weeks ago," Al said, "I asked for some major changes in the merchandise assortments out here in the Pittsburgh store. Now I'm back at the store to see how the changes are working out, but the store manager says they were never put through. He says you countermanded them."

"Al, I don't think we can have you functioning out there as a kind of field marshal. We've got to maintain lines of authority and make sure that orders aren't coming from all directions. You see that, don't you?"

"Goddammit, no! Whaddya mean, field marshal? All I asked for were some new fashion lines that we can use out here. Hell, that's why I go out to all stores. I've been doing this kind of thing for eighteen years."

After a momentary silence, Sam suggested, "Maybe it's time for a change. Why don't you come into the office, Al? It's been a long time."

The next morning, still seething, Al came into the Oval's building. Without looking around or greeting anyone, he strode to Sam's office and sternly confronted the beauteous Priscilla Terry at her desk. She ushered him into Sam's office. He stopped short, overcome for the moment by the sumptuousness and the vastness that surrounded Sam Schulte. Sam, in expanding his office to include Al's, now had a luxurious hall of more than seventy feet in which he did his work at a twelve-foot mahogany desk, inlaid on the working surface with sparkling miniature jade. Large tapestries covered each wall, except for one which had a twenty-foot map of the United States, showing each CU property and each Oval's store, existing and to come. There was also a soft gray velvet sofa on which perhaps ten people could have sat more or less comfortably and easily the largest breakfront Al had ever seen, perhaps eighteen feet long. A deep, deep Oriental rug in authentic Indian colors stretched virtually from wall to wall. And standing in the foreground of the breathtaking expanse, with a pleased smile and hairy hand outstretched, was Sam Schulte. Somehow, he did not seem at all puny in the giant room.

"What is all this?" Al asked tightly. "Your throne room?"

Sam smiled, just a bit humbly. "Isn't," he asked, "the head of a billion-dollar company entitled to have an office befitting his role?" His smile expanded and the humility went. "If you're concerned by what stockholders would say, Al, let me assure you that they would love it. There may be a malcontent here or there, but the average stockholder is awed by the chief executive officer of his company and he also expects to be awed by his surroundings."

Certain of himself but gracious, Sam added, "It's just wonderful to see you, Al. Come and sit down here."

They sat and immediately Al blazed out with "What's all this crap about maintaining lines of authority? Hell, one of the successes of this business is that ideas have counted a hell of a lot more than titles. Ideas are what please, haven't you ever heard that? For crying out loud, what do I have, another Sidney Holland on my hands?"

An expression of intense pain passed over Sam's face. "That is unkind, Al. Saying that to me hurts more than I can tell you. Now, look, let's be calm about it and discuss it like—"

"Listen, Sam, lemme lay it on the line. I didn't mind agreeing to a merger if it meant the only way you would come into the company. I didn't mind putting up the stock, the financing to make the merger, even though Oval's wouldn't be the surviving company but part of a smaller company. I didn't even mind too much giving up my titles to you if that would please your ego. But I'll be goddamned if I'm gonna let you stop me from going around to the stores and using my knowledge and instincts to help us get more business."

"Maybe," Sam said softly, "it's time that you considered changing that habit of yours, Al. Remember this is a billion-dollar business. We've not only got to be big-time—we've got to act big-time."

"Maybe this, maybe that," Al said disgustedly. "It's all a lot of baloney. As executive committee chairman, if that means anything, and as still the company's largest stockholder, I think I still stand for something. But, if I don't, there's only one goddam thing to do."

Sam got up from his desk, came around and faced Al. "Calm

down, Al, will you, please?" he said. "You still have a big role around here, a major role indeed. You're executive committee chairman and, well, let me say it, a living symbol of a great business accomplishment. No one, least of all myself, wants to change that." He put a hand on Al's stiff shoulder. "Do you think I can ever forget," Sam said emotionally, "that you were on the cover of *Time*?"

It was another six months before they saw each other again. In that time, many things happened. Apparently either believing that he had cleared the air with Al during their confrontation or that they had reached some sort of an understanding, however hard, Sam Schulte confidently proceeded to carry out the remainder of his program.

An important part of it involved the boys. When it was completed, it could reasonably be said that they had become men.

Harry Abner was downgraded.

He was demoted to the post of merchandising assistant to the chairman of the board. His titles of vice-president and general merchandise manager were bestowed upon a young merchandise man who idolized Sam Schulte and who had a better memory than Harry. Disappointed and rather bitter, Harry nonetheless stayed on, occupying a desk outside Sam's office and functioning as his liaison with the merchandising departments. He was locked into stock options and one million dollars in Oval's stock that he had accumulated, but he might have left and lived on it. However, a strange thing happened. Relieved of the pressures of the top executive job, he found his memory gradually returning after many years. So he continued to sit outside Sam's office, a bald, graying man, a half-smile hovering on his face as he reminded himself of how much money he was worth. But when he wasn't smiling, he frowned, nostalgically recalling with his improved memory greater, more exciting days. The simple fact was that Harry would have been much happier if his memory had just remained bad.

Irving Waldteufel was transferred.

From corporate purchasing agent, he became assistant head of security, working under a former FBI man. The move was an inspiration of Sam Schulte's, who correctly assumed that any man who had stolen so much goods from the company and then returned it because he couldn't steal from Al Miller should be both carefully watched and also be made to utilize his skills against other, less remorseful thieves. So who then could watch him better than an FBI man and who could better beat professional crooks at their own game than Irving Waldteufel?

Solly Patracelli was persecuted.

He had become really quite skilled as operations vice-president, but this didn't help him. His swarthy, determined face and the fact that he seemed to worship Al Miller worried Sam Schulte, who immediately wrote him off. Solly was humiliated by being placed under a sadistic young executive whose first command was that Solly should train him in everything he knew, whereupon he told Solly that he didn't know anything. As a result, Solly became another one who yearned deeply for the good old days when everyone was racking his brains and breaking his back to build up Oval's and secretly trying to help Al Miller without telling him.

Wallenstein was fired.

Since the merger had been made with a real-estate company, who needs to inherit a real-estate vice-president? Try as hard as he could, Willie could never convince Schulte that perhaps he knew a few wrinkles that Sam didn't, and so Willie left, drawing a handsome settlement. When last heard of, he was said to be seeking to regain ownership of Wallenstein, Pennsylvania, a city that had emerged full-grown from his naturally conniving brain.

Matthew Smiles left.

When he first met the obese young, happy sales-promotion man, Schulte's dark face wrinkled with displeasure. "Do you really have to be that fat, young man?" he asked. "It seems to me that from the standpoint of your own interest in the company, you should reduce down to human proportions. Now, I don't want to see you again until you reach that state, do we understand each other? Nothing personal, of course." But since Matthew found this objective impossible to fulfill, he departed and went into the advertising business, a calling where looks and bodily size blend well into the odd practices that prevail in it.

But he did well in advertising, where he should have been in the first place. Yet he, too, missed the old days.

Ernest von Rossem was shanghaied.

That is, the skinny, nervous financial man with the bobbing Adam's apple happened to be within view one afternoon when Sam was told that a statistician in one of CU's more remote offices had been drafted to fight in Vietnam. Sam's roving eye, quite by coincidence, caught Ernest's fearful glance. The next morning the controller, after finally learning in his latter years to master the slide rule, was dispatched to replace a man one third his age and to spend the rest of his career exercising what Schulte referred to as his "slide-rule mentality."

When all these six moves were completed, there was a unanimous, spontaneous urge on the part of the boys to present the big-ball award to both Wallenstein and Matthew Smiles. When the first presentation had been made to Ben Baron several years ago, it was decided that only those who walked out or were canned or who displayed conspicuous gallantry under fire should receive the two-foot by three-foot bronze plaque. So Willie and Mottel got it while serious thought was also given by the boys to presenting it to Nat Batt for his personal altercation with Sidney Holland.

The nasty little PR man had made an indelible impression on all of them when he had stepped from behind the pillar to photograph Holland chasing after a naked woman with what appeared to be a knife in his hand. So they gave him serious consideration for the award, but somehow never quite trusting him, they hesitated. But, based on subsequent events, they would only have had to take it back. He was definitely not of award caliber. Why?

The only one of the boys who did well in the new state of things was Nat Batt. He was promoted.

Although he was rapidly deteriorating physically, Nat remained the lying, omnivorous PR man he had always been and perhaps more so. However, Sam Schulte was drawing considerable pleasure from his new role and began to show it publicly. He took full-page institutional advertisements in *The New York Times*, the New York *Post* and even out-of-town newspapers where Oval's had stores to tell the public some of his key business concepts, or to express his sentiments over the public holidays and even one in which he attempted to explain humbly how it feels to be chairman of the board of a billion-dollar company. Each ad was signed in his own handwriting, "Samuel A. Schulte."

In this effort he soon found Nat a great help. It was Nat who came up with the idea of graphically dramatizing each ad. On Valentine's day the ad was in the form of a swelling heart; on Mother's Day it was a giant greeting card; on Flag Day it was, of course, a flag, with Sam Schulte's face appearing as one of the stars; and on New Year's Day the ad was a larger-than-life-size drawing of Sam Schulte wearing a party hat, looking bleary-eyed and hung over but happy and hopeful.

Nat also came up with the idea of reprinting each ad in advance and of attaching miniatures to the dunning notices sent to charge customers. This served two purposes. It softened the bite of the payment reminders and also began to alter the shape of Oval's symbol in the public's mind. In other words, an oval gradually became a circle, Sam Schulte's face.

As a result of these and other efforts, Nat, at seventy-two, was promoted from the post of vice-president to that of executive vice-president. It was an unprecedented accolade at such an advanced age. From that day on, Nat Batt never thought of Al Miller again.

Of course, there was one more of the "boys" to be accounted for—Molly Bradley. Although she had remained a consultant from Sidney Holland's days, she was as much involved with the company as ever under the new management. She was also distressed at the turn of events. To her, Al Miller was Oval's and always would be and she had stayed as far away from Sam Schulte as she could in order not to betray her feelings. She had also tried to contact Al many times, but as Sam had entrenched himself more and more, Al had receded further and further from public view. She had also tried to forget Al, but she found it wasn't easy, although she told herself that she hated him.

Surprisingly, one day Schulte sent for her. As she came into his office, she was nervous, expecting the worst. One by one, step by step, he had taken care of all the boys, having left her for the last. Sam asked her to sit on his immense sofa and smilingly studied her. She was still a striking woman, all six feet of her. Maturity had robbed her of little but had instead added some feminine features and nuances that many younger women seemed to lack. Sam kissed her hand with appreciation. He had done it once before during his first week when he had met all the executives.

"My dear," he said, "I have been up to my ears in work for almost a year in this new role of mine. But I have heard it said that you are a very creative woman and that, usually, you have something important to show each new president or chief executive officer. Now I, too, would like to have the same opportunity. Can we do that here—or shall we go to your apartment?"

As her eyes had widened in surprise, she thought, delightedly, This old bastard, he's the smartest and the worst one of the whole bunch. And, what was more, he had come after her, an important change in the procedure, while that damned Al Miller had eluded her for years. This was *her* kind of man.

"Of course, Sam," she said, arising and immediately getting herself ready, "but I don't see why we have to go to my place. What's wrong here? This room is fit for a king—and queen."

And she was right. The vast Renaissance chamber that Sam Schulte had made of his office and Al Miller's became reminiscent of many of the days of the Medicis. Debauchery on an enviable scale filled it when she would come several times a week for her consultations with Sam. She was, after all, a consultant. Pert Priscilla Terry resigned in protest after several weeks, and the crowning insult was the calm detachment with which Sam wished her the best.

Molly was in her element. Gratefully, Sam now gave her considerable latitude in the business and even the hot glances of resentment thrown at her by all the boys except for Nat Batt didn't disturb her much. Once having deserted to the enemy, she decided to enjoy it fully and did. Except for one thing. She missed Al Miller all the more, often twisting away from Sam's hungry, hunting hands on the immense sofa in his office with a groan of desire for Al's cool, lean body, his close-cropped red hair and hot, sensuous eyes. At least, this was how she chose to remember him. Sam thought the groans were the early stages of orgasm and they were, only Molly could have told him, they were not because of him.

Several months later on a late afternoon, Al came to his Cord parked in the center of town and found Molly sitting in the front seat.

Surprised, he slid in silently behind the wheel. She moved to him, putting a warm hand on his knee, but he reached over to turn on the ignition and the big car purred out onto the street. "Does Sam know you're here?" he asked.

"No."

"So?"

"I wanted to see you, baby. I've missed you like all hell."

"You finally got what you wanted. You're test-marketing the top man himself. Why should you miss anybody?"

"Bitter, baby?"

"Not me," Al said. "I got no claims on you, so I can't be bitter. What we had was great while it lasted, but it ended a long time ago."

"Did it?" Her hand was still on his knee and it began to press. "Did it?" she persisted. "Are you sure you're not just saying it because of my relationship with Sam? Aren't you just the tiniest bit uptight about that, you reserved bastard?"

"No," he said, uncomfortably aware that he was. "You don't owe me a damn thing and maybe I owe you a lot. I used you, Molly, when I wanted to use you. But one of the few smart things I ever did was to break it off."

He felt her cool breath on his face, her still devastating sexuality pouring toward him like a sea of hot lava, her knees and exposed thighs turning their aim in his direction. "I want you to use me again," she said flatly. He stared in surprise at her, his pulse thickening sickly in his throat. In that moment a vivid recall of many of their nights together, afternoons, sometimes even mornings brought a sweeping ache that ran from his head to his genitals in seconds.

"What the hell do you mean?" he asked hoarsely.

"I mean that I can do a lot for you, baby. Sam has gone all the way with me—he never had what I'm giving him. In all his years of playing around with dames, cheating on that sick wife of his, he never got the kicks he's getting from me. He told me so himself, Al. And he's grateful, so goddam grateful. I can have anything I want. And I want you to use me, baby. If we can just start all over, I can twist Sam around my little finger for you. I can give you the power again, Al. I can even get you control of the business again, if that's what you want."

The magnitude of what she was offering him, and the certainty that she could deliver, flooded him with dismay—and hope. Say the word, he thought, and I'm back in the saddle in more ways than one. But he pulled over to the curb and spoke slowly. "Look, Molly, believe me, I hate to ask you to get out, but I gotta get home. Ruthie and the kids are waiting to have dinner with me. I'm making up for lost time."

She got out. "Once a *shmuck* . . ." Then she recovered. "Don't make up your mind right now. Think it over. You can't have changed all that much. Don't throw it away. You'd be just plain crazy to do that."

The Cord pulled away.

When he came home, he couldn't quite cover up the soft confusion in his eyes. He could never fool Ruthie and he didn't that evening, either. Her instinct was deadly accurate and she quickly surmised the situation. That night, she asked him directly, and while he replied only indirectly, she had all the answer she would need.

The next morning she drove to the city and sought out Molly's office. Molly, looking up from her desk, saw the short, angry brunette advancing on her. She barely got out a greeting when Ruthie stood before her and shrilly demanded, fish-wife style, "You leave my husband alone—or I'll break your neck into two pieces!"

"What?"

Ruthie reached for her and Molly reached for Ruthie and they pulled each other across the desk. Their hands lunged for each other's hair and yanked. They fell to the floor, thrashing, kicking, screeching. Shorter but more muscular and athletic, energized by her anger, Ruthie took the big blonde's measure. She slapped Molly's face hard, saw tears jump into her eyes, dismay pull at her features, and she suddenly let go of the taller woman.

As they sat on the floor, Ruthie saw that Molly's face had a growing red welt, her eyes were filled and her hair was pulled into matted clumps. Staring into her eyes, where a strange expression was gathering, Ruthie saw in the other woman something that surprised her. Taut and pale, Molly's face had hardened with a harassment and despair that had to be more deeply rooted than merely because her hair had been pulled and her face slapped. Why, she's really an unhappy woman, thought Ruthie, miserable, lonely and beginning to worry about her looks and scared at the thought. She's got nothing really of her own, Ruthie realized, and I've got so much, so much.

She got up and helped the surprised Molly to her feet. "I am sorry," Ruthie said. "I lost my temper and I'm terribly embarrassed. I hope you'll forgive me."

After she left, Molly turned to her adjacent powder room, bitter and impatient. She had to get ready for Sam and she was in terrible shape. And as far as Al Miller was concerned, she decided, she would just write him off permanently, the rotten, selfish, wife-loving bastard.

A week before the annual stockholders' and directors' meetings, Al Miller phoned Sam Schulte and was invited to the house in Kings Point. As the first time, he was greeted with skepticism by Ito, the Japanese butler. Al was dressed a little better; he had shed his unpressed jacket and baggy slacks and white sneakers a year ago and wore suits, but it was evident that either he still didn't pass Ito's muster or that the butler remembered him as he had been.

As he was ushered in, to the kitchen of course, Al's ears rung with the resounding overtones of the four-note introduction from Beethoven's Fifth that the chime bell had selected. Sam was sitting at the kitchen table, his inevitable bottle of sherry before him, dressed in a silken smoking jacket. He seemed to accept Al's visit as a matter of course. "Milk or sherry?" he asked.

Al shook his head. "Not a damn thing. Just a little talk."

Sam tippled. Over the bottle he could see that the last half year had been difficult for the lean redhead and he could understand why. Al seemed thinner, more intense than ever and yet more lackadaisical. Always vulnerable, he seemed especially so at the moment. His cheekbones hung out of his face, which had some chalky patches under the bronze, and he kept pursing his thin lips as though a pressure was boiling up inside him.

"Haven't seen you in a hell of a while," Sam said, lowering the bottle. "What have you been doing with yourself?"

"I've been traveling some. And I've been home a lot. Ruthie has seen more of me, the kids, too, than they've seen in the past fifteen years."

"That's good. They're catching up."

Al nodded solemnly.

"Why haven't you dropped around the office?" Sam asked. "It wouldn't kill you. People have been asking. After all, you're still the chairman of the executive committee, not that you've attended any meetings. I know you're making an adjustment, and we all understand that, but just for cosmetic purposes, you could have made an occasional appearance."

Al waited, his lips tightening and untightening. "Maybe," he said. "But you know as well as I do that I haven't been happy about the way things are going."

"Is that so? What in particular?"

"What you did with the boys, for one thing. You didn't even consult me on that."

Sam shrugged. "What was the point? You would have resisted me on each move."

"What about the design of the new stores? They look like laundries."

Sam shrugged again. "That's how you save money," he replied. "Big store or little, if you have an economical prototype, you can just stamp them out and reduce pre-opening expenses. People don't come to Oval's because they're the most beautiful stores, do they? They come for the values and we still give them values, right, *boychik*? You couldn't deny that."

"No, I can't deny that," Al said. "But the way you're doing it, you're cheapening the product. We always gave the public good values and the best quality we could find. But I still shop the stores and I see a lot of fringe lines made for the basement operations and a hell of a lot of imports from the real low-wage countries. What the hell is going on? And another thing—I don't like the thin stocks. Either you're in the store business or you're just a showroom. In a lot of key departments, you've got no depth at all. Why is it every time a non-merchant comes into the business, the first thing he does is cut the stocks? How the hell do you expect the customer to keep coming back?"

For the third time Sam shrugged, but the smile on his face was not at all apologetic. "Our sales and profits are up—they're showing the kinds of gains we haven't had in years," he told Al. "That's the real evidence that customers are coming back, not just the gut count that you use. That bottom line, *boychik*, that tells you everything."

"Not in my book it don't," Al said heatedly. "Tell me that in five years, let's see how the customers like Oval's then, and maybe I'll agree with you. A quick change doesn't always stick— and I've been through too much in the last few years to start cheering about an instant success." He glared at Sam. "I didn't come here for a bull session. I'm here for something else."

Sam tippled again. "What?"

Al hesitated only briefly. "I'm resigning from the company," he said.

Sam dropped the bottle to the table with a bang. "You can't mean that, Al. That would be a tremendous blow to our standing. Wall Street, the banks, our investors, the customers— they'll all be shaken up. Oval's founder quitting at, what, forty-seven? It will rock the company to its foundations. No, I just won't let you do it."

Al laughed, his derisiveness revealing an edge of hysteria. "You won't let me do it? What the hell are you talking about? Are you God or something? You can't stop me. I've just quit."

Sam studied him carefully and saw the determination glaring out of Al's face like a hot bulb. "What brought you to that precipitous decision?" Sam asked, fighting for time. "It has an awful ring of finality."

"Let's just say I don't believe any more in the things you're doing," Al said simply. "I recognize that what we did, what I did, had to be done. But it's not the same company. The push is different, the merchandise is different, maybe even the customers will change. If I can't believe in it, why should I be part of it?"

Sam saw that Al was beyond arguing the point. He had not counted on Al's resigning. He had, in fact, miscalculated on what really lurked under Al's hide. Priding himself on his perception, it made him angry at himself and even more angry at Al. "All right, all right, you do what the hell you want," he said roughly. "You always do anyway. I guess I can't stop you—but it will take a hell of a lot of explaining."

Al suddenly grinned. "Sam, I'm sure you're gonna be able to do that and make it convincing. Nobody I know has got your gift of gab. You can sell anybody on anything and make everything sound right. You should have been on the stage." He paused, then added, "You did a hell of a job on me. But I'm not blaming you one hundred percent. I guess I was ripe for it."

Sam took it as a compliment. "What the hell, Al, you've got your role in life and I've got mine. There are two types of guys in this world who mean anything, the way I see it. The guys who can start something and make it go all the way. And the guys who can just start something. I'm the first, *boychik*, and you're the second."

Al thought he knew a third type, but he didn't spell it out. He had something more important to do. He had to find out something, something that had been irking and yet intriguing him for a year. "There's something else, Sam, that I gotta ask you. That 'f.q.' column, the last one on your personnel charts. You told me it stood for 'flexibility quotient.' But I gotta different idea. I think it stands for 'failure quotient.' "

"Where did you hear that?" Sam said, grinning.

"Never mind. Does it?"

"Where in the hell did you get that idea?" Sam persisted. He glared and then the smile reappeared as if the matter could hardly worry him. "Only one person would know anything about that besides me. Barbara. I told her once in an unwise moment. Poor woman, we haven't gotten along in years. She always thought I married her for her money, but then, as you know, she's got all kinds of hallucinations. That's why she's in a mental home right now but actually getting the best possible care." A smile, almost of little-boy quality in its sheer mischief, broke out on Sam's face. "All right, Al, I might as well confess it," he said. " 'F.q.' refers to failure, not flexibility. Do you think you can forgive me, Al?"

"You sonofabitch."

Sam shrugged. "I'll buy that," he said, the smile growing.

As he accompanied Al to the outside door, Sam made a final attempt to keep him on the string. "Of course, Al, it goes without saying that you'll have to support us in everything we do. Your investment in the company is too great. You may no longer be an officer, but you still own a hell of a lot of shares."

Al glanced at him in surprise and his lips worked into a tiny smile. "Sam, I'm damned glad you brought that up. I almost forgot to tell you. Tomorrow morning, when the news comes out that I quit, I'm selling every share of the stock I own in the company. That's well over a million shares. I thought you understood that when I said I was resigning. What's the point of keeping my money in something I don't believe in any more? I learned a few things, Sam, that you and a few other guys taught me. I'm different—but I guess I haven't changed that much. I still gotta believe in something."

Sam was shocked to his roots. "You can't do that!" he yelled. "You're calling *me* a sonofabitch: Unloading one million shares of stock in a company in one day will rock the whole market. All of our shares will be hit. Al, Wall Street will lose confidence in us, can't you see that?" Then, as he saw Al's smile turn into an ironical grin, another thought struck Sam. "Every share of our stock will drop like a rock. I've got to sell a bunch of mine before you do—or I'll have to take whatever price I can get! I've got to get Walter Solomon on the phone right away and tell him to sell as soon as the market opens. And then I've got to convene the board and tell them what's happened!" He dashed back into the kitchen to get at the phone.

Outside, Al stared up at the kitchen window. Its bright light illuminated the driveway and the pavements below it and he heard some of Sam Schulte's heated recital. Then he remembered the dog. He would have to be careful or the hound might come after him. He turned away, but his foot ground on something hard. He glanced down and saw that it was a sherry bottle that Schulte had apparently thrown through the window. It hadn't shattered because it had landed on the grass rather than on the pavement. Grinning, Al picked it up, raised it high and deftly pitched it up into the kitchen window. He heard it shatter inside, heard Sam's surprised outcry, heard the butler come running and jabbering away excitedly, heard his own heart happily pounding as he ran a furious mile to where he had left the car.

16

The Running Legend

TIME DANCED for Al Miller. Money talked to him. Success pasted itself to him like a fat, sucking barnacle. Fame plucked him from the ranks and held him aloft. Customers whispered in his ears, then gently kissed his lobes. Children shyly confided what even their parents wouldn't. Throwing open their vaults, banks pleaded, "Take." His greatest rivals just couldn't do enough to show how warmly they regarded him. Lawyers and accountants competed with one another to attract such a client. The Government smiled and winked at him. Life, in plain words, had just hopped into bed with Al Miller.

So who cared if he wasn't thirty-four any more but forty-seven?

All that and more everyone was certain of in those days even though in actuality he was no longer officially connected with Oval's. Oval's was Al Miller and Al Miller was Oval's. A legend, don't forget, dies slowly.

Of course, as was his fashion, in those first few weeks after his final break with the company, disaster stared into his eyeballs.

His throwing over one million shares of stock on the open market produced one of the most chaotic days on Wall Street in years. Combined with the disposition of securities by others who tried to anticipate him, his sale caused a widespread break in the price of the stock. Tumbling, it also caused other stocks to tumble. Frightened, big institutional portfolio holders dumped many of their doubtful holdings. The result was a day of not-to-be forgotten fear trading.

The Securities and Exchange Commission announced an investigation. It cited suspicions of illegal insider trading and expressed fears that the market in certain stocks had been rigged.

The New York Stock Exchange issued a statement deploring both insider trading and stock rigging. The American Stock Exchange followed suit.

The Business Advisory Council of the U.S. Department of Commerce, then holding one of its regular meetings, took the occasion to state that the fluctuations in the Dow Jones level of industrial stocks did not and could not portend any similar shifts in the national economy.

The professors who had named Al Miller to the Retailing Hall of Fame were shocked. They expressed revulsion that a man who had founded and led such an important company had suddenly turned his back on it, resigned and pulled out all his holdings. They acted quickly to delist him from the Hall.

In the furor that all this created, Sam Schulte, the directors and the executives tried grimly to carry on. Sam cooperated fully with the authorities and the critics, demonstrating an eager concern to get to the bottom of things. "Whoever is responsible for this, I hope they find him. And when they do, I hope they pin his ears back," he said in an interview with the *Wall Street Journal*. General Boatwright hung up on *The New York Times* after sputtering at some of the questions he was asked, but Tex Stringer spoke profusely on the situation to the Houston *Chronicle*.

Al Miller was unavailable to the press. He had never read the financial pages or cooperated with them and he didn't intend to now. So he stayed at home, refusing to answer the phone or to admit any strangers. He even hired a tough security man who efficiently dispersed any curious visitors.

Within two weeks, it all blew over. The SEC investigation found little if anything with which to make formal charges. The stock exchanges turned to other, newer emergencies. The Advisory Council made plans to explore more cogent reasons for the erratic state of the economy. And the newspapers and wire services tired of endlessly interviewing Sam Schulte and gave up their fruitless efforts to get through to Al Miller.

So, within weeks, he was back where he had been, a legend in his time, and most people soon forgot that he had left Oval's and no longer had even the slightest ownership there. Letters addressed to Al Miller at Oval's continued to come in for years. And probably still do.

After many weeks, Ruthie tired of having him around the neat, quiet house. He was a disturbing factor. First, he was trying too hard to make up for the lack of attention to his family, to himself, to his leisure, to his reading. But this seemed after a while to drain him of his energy, and so after a while he simply sat around the house in his socks reading, brooding, just staring blankly into space or watching his family. Then, Ruthie and the girls had to tell him not to pay so much attention to them. He was interfering with their normal pursuits. Finally, he insisted on playing cards with the security man and disturbed him, too.

On a morning when he had been particularly irksome to the whole family, Martha, the stringy, old cook, warned him flatly, "If'n you don't calm you'self, sad man, I'm gonna straighten you out like I did my old man, God rest his soul. I'm gonna flatten you with a fryin' pan. You already made peace with you'self, so why you frettin'?" Then she took Al by the shirt collar, pushed him outside and locked the door.

He considered selling the house in Queens and buying a much larger, more lavish one, or selling the Cord and buying a new Cadillac or Continental. Why not? The sale of his stock had, contrarily, not brought a loss but a substantial gain. He was worth more than $50 million, and more than a few people thought he could have been the richest man in town. That sort of talk plus the actual ownership of $50 million created a reputation tantamount to being the richest man in town. But he bought neither the bigger house nor the newer car.

Once the extent of his wealth became known and those who like to make judgments on such things decided that he had pulled off a coup in selling his stock, he began to get offers of jobs, offers to invest in large, budding enterprises and offers to give advice. Sam Schulte, after a suitable period, pleased a number of people by trying to get him to come back and letting everyone know about it, but Al refused to meet with him. Macy's and Abraham & Straus and two of the big Chicago mail-order houses extended feelers, but he never even gave them the courtesy of a reply.

Then, heeding Ruthie's command to get out of the house, he began going out, sometimes leaving in the morning and staying out until the early evening. He was seen entering many movie houses and darting in and out of many store fronts to stare inside at the displays of merchandise.

His expression of preoccupation never waned. Months after the break with Sam and Oval's, he felt that he had been right to do as he had, but the feeling of inadequacy that lay deep in him all his life had been moving closer and closer to the surface all that time. Was Sam right? he kept asking himself. Were there really just two kinds of guys—those who start things and carry them all the way and those who just start things? The application stung. He had built a huge company but its very hugeness had proved too much for him. So who and what, after all, was he? Why had he been able to carry things just so far?

Although he had stayed away these last months from his mother, he went to see her in the small apartment in the Bronx. Pesse was never tinier, more dried up, more succinct or matter-of-fact. But a happy smile flickered across her shrunken face as Al came in. They talked and finally he said, "Mom, to tell you the truth, I'm all mixed up. I just don't know what the hell to do with myself. For seventeen, eighteen years I built a tremendous business that employs thousands of people. And yet after succeeding so well, I feel like I failed. What's success, anyway? For the past six months I've been sitting around the house flat on my *tuches* trying to figure it out."

Pesse seemed unimpressed. "Pop always said you would need help," she observed dryly.

"Chaim was right," Al conceded. "He was always right."

But his mother shook her head. "No, not always. He was

wrong about one thing. Albert, you would have been a bad, a very bad stage performer. A joke on the boards. I would have run away from such an embarrassment. As it is . . . Even when he swallowed his disappointment, Pop was proud of you. When he was almost blind, he bragged to everybody that his son was a *gavir*, a very rich man, and that he did this all by himself."

It was a long speech for her, and she leaned back, tired and irritated with herself. It was, after all, difficult to feel really sorry for a son who was worth millions.

Walking along the streets, or shooting up the roads in the powerful car, he realized that at least in one way some of the recent events had come inevitably from his feelings toward his father, his efforts to live up to Chaim's aspirations for him. Strangely enough, no one had ever asked him, but what did the "C." in his name stand for except for Chaim, a middle name that he had adopted out of sheer pride and perhaps yearning? And what was it but some strong affinity, some paternal similarity to Chaim that Sam Schulte had, with his theatricality, his willingness always to help Al as a father might, that had spurred Al to accept Sam as a great friend, adviser, even benefactor?

In the process, Al told himself dismally, he had lost his business, he had lost the boys and he had lost Molly, not that he had given her any choice. He had, it was ironically clear, lost a good deal while making millions. Was that the price you pay for the net-net way of life? Pain for joy, sacrifice for pleasure, loss of friends, face, position for sake of the warm glow around the heart?

One afternoon shortly after his visit to Pesse, as he sat watching a movie in an almost empty theater, he found himself uncharacteristically shifting with disinterest. Movies, like his life, were changing, and again, like him, they did not seem to know which direction to take. He could easily live on his money, invest here and there, perhaps, and, like many wealthy men who had given up an active, full-day participation in a business, enjoy the idle pleasure of dabbling in someone else's efforts. Or he could spend much of his time in cultural, mind-building activities. But that, he realized, was not what he wanted. That sort of passive life would satisfy him only briefly. As he emerged unhappily into the sunlight, blinking and rubbing at his eyes, his restlessness surged through him like a flash in the blood.

What do you do when you have won the world, boggled it and lost it?

Should he start over? He had a big, personal base and he need not depend on the whims and pressures of Wall Street and the money interests this time. But he had no clear interest in entering the retailing arena again. Certainly the discount industry as the seventies approached was more uncertain than ever. It was undergoing one of its periodic shakeouts. The sleazy ones, the companies that had neither geared for the future nor built a bridge with their customers, were already taking advantage of the bankruptcy statutes, hoping to bail themselves out at the expense of their creditors and stockholders. Oval's would, however, survive. It was one of the super-giants and, he knew, no matter what severities Sam Schulte would put it to, or what alterations in its policies he would make, it had become an institution that was as entrenched in the public consciousness as Macy's, the U.S. Post Office or the New York Yankees. Even Sam, in all his egotistical exercises with its image, its advertising and its fashion-quality mix, would not overdo these things. Walter Solomon, Boatwright, Tex Stringer and the others, Al told himself with a rueful smile, wouldn't let him get away with it.

Ruthie was waiting for him at the door when he came home that evening. "Where were you all day?" she asked. "You took off on the run at six A.M. this morning just like you used to and we didn't hear a word from you all day. Are you all right, Al?"

He grinned at her. She hadn't regretted what had happened, his complete break with Oval's, as he had, because she knew that he had done what he had to do to satisfy his own drives and failings. During all the stresses with Ben Baron, Sidney Holland and especially Sam Schulte, she had been resentful and at a loss with him for his patience, his forebearance and his impossible habit of delaying vital action. But she had abided with his wishes in all that time and for months had been pleased and happy that he was out from under those anxieties. "Are you all right?" she repeated with concern.

"Fine, just great," he said, hugging her hard. She returned his grin, satisfied with his reply and happy with him, even though at this late stage she still didn't quite understand him. Their physical rapport had been righted since the exit of Sidney Holland, while their spiritual and emotional compatibility had never wavered.

"Okay, kook," she told him, "let's have dinner before Martha decides to pour it down the drain."

Although he had stubbornly kept away from appearing in any of the Oval stores for over a year, he stopped into one of the three Manhattan stores on a Saturday afternoon, impelled to take an overdue peek. And, as he browsed on the main floor, he became aware of a stir nearby.

An elderly couple was coming to him with the store manager, their eagerness and surprise at seeing him showing in their lit-up faces. Jim Lynn, the store manager, whom he knew, had apparently been approached by them after they had spotted him. "It is him!" shouted the elderly man. "It's that Al Miller!" Several other shoppers joined the trio and suddenly Al found himself surrounded.

"How are you, Al?" Jim asked excitedly. "This is our founder, ladies and gentlemen, Mr. Albert Miller. You must have read about him in *Time* magazine. He was on their cover."

About ten people clustered around Al now. Nervously he said, "I'm fine, Jim. Hey, your store looks good."

And then he was moving, pushing through the group that was still growing in size, and he was running out of the store. But they followed him and others along the sidewalk followed the throng thinking that they, too, had spotted a movie star, a rock singer or a television celebrity. His car was parked nearby and he started racing toward it. A few followed but, miler that he was, they were no match. However, a bearded young man matched strides with him. "Wait, please, Mr. Miller," he called, his breath coming agonizingly. "I just wrote my master's thesis on you—but I gotta ask you, what made you cop out on Oval's?" But the young man, whose muscles were obviously softened by too much study and not enough running, had to give up as Al pulled away.

Driving home, alternately smiling and frowning, Al was filled

with a hot flood of emotions, thinking, brooding, fearing, wondering, exulting, beginning to plan, to probe his own mind and
test his own emotional reflexes. He had changed, he knew, and
yet had he changed? At forty-seven, he was both a new Al Miller
but still the same old one. Look at me, he told himself, observe
closely this egotistical and emotional cripple. A crowd recognizes
me and suddenly, when I thought I didn't care any more about
faith, I love it, I can feel its heat and I can taste its love. Yet, for
this, didn't they tag me the world's biggest *shmuck?* And then
clearer by far than the haze that hovered over the Queensboro
Bridge and dimmed the upper structure, he knew, he was in all
still himself, still the same yo-yo but older and wiser although—
he had to inflict that punishment on himself—perhaps he was
only older but not wiser, only more scarred, his veins thrust to
the surface, his blood thinned and his mind blurred than he had
been in all the earlier years. "Shit, no!" he yelled at the other
motorists. "Not me!" And then, as he sped over the bridge's last
link at seventy-five miles an hour, he wanted to sing to express
the exultation that he felt.

As he came barreling off the bridge, the exultation exploded in
his head and then he laughed and he howled. Of course, why the
hell not! The restlessness that made him overcompensate for his
failings at home in recent months was the answer. It was the
only answer to his life, the only answer to his kind of life, the
only answer to the weird collection of cells and instincts that he
was and would always be.

He stopped the car in the middle of traffic and hopped out.
Ignoring the growing, angry cacophony of automobile horns
interspersed with curses, he burst into a sidewalk telephone booth
and seized the phone. Fortunately, it worked and furiously he
dialed.

    "Hey, Harry! ..."
    "Irving! ..."
    "Willie! ..."
    "Mottel! ..."
    "Solly! ..."
    "Ernest! ..."
    "Charley! ..."

"Listen, listen to me good!" he told them all. "What happened, it's just a goddam prelude—like my Pop would call it, a curtain-raiser—to what's ahead. I gotta see you! I mean, how the hell can this be the end? I gotta hot idea—and it's busting through my head!" Would they be interested, did they have enough gism left, or did they just want to live on memories? He didn't know but he would soon find out. "So are you listening?" he began again. The words tumbled out of him in a torrent. And, in between them, the blare of the hot, angry motorists blocked by the Cord made him howl with delight. The stalled traffic had now backed up all the way to the bridge. He didn't give a damn. He just kept on babbling. But, never being given to few words when many would do, he suddenly realized that he could have said it all in just two.

THE BEGINNING